Caroline comple...
University of Durham. She has a particular interest in the lives of women in the interwar period and the challenges faced by the returning soldier.

Caroline is originally from Lancashire, but now lives in south-west France.

CAROLINE SCOTT

THE BEST OF INTENTIONS

**SIMON &
SCHUSTER**

London · New York · Amsterdam/Antwerp · Sydney/Melbourne · Toronto · New Delhi

First published in Great Britain by Simon & Schuster UK Ltd, 2025

1 3 5 7 9 10 8 6 4 2

Simon & Schuster UK Ltd, 1st Floor
222 Gray's Inn Road, London WC1X 8HB

Simon & Schuster Australia, Sydney
Simon & Schuster India, New Delhi

www.simonandschuster.co.uk
www.simonandschuster.com.au
www.simonandschuster.co.in

The authorised representative in the EEA is Simon & Schuster Netherlands BV,
Herculesplein 96, 3584 AA Utrecht, Netherlands. info@simonandschuster.nl

A CIP catalogue record for this book is available from the British Library

Paperback ISBN: 978-1-3985-2631-0
eBook ISBN: 978-1-3985-2629-7
Audio ISBN: 978-1-3985-2630-3

Typeset in Bembo by M Rules
Printed and Bound in the UK using 100% Renewable Electricity
at CPI Group (UK) Ltd

MIX
Paper | Supporting
responsible forestry
FSC
www.fsc.org
FSC® C013604

'To look forward, I concluded, and to have courage – the courage of adventure, of challenge, of initiation, as well as the courage of endurance – that was surely part of fidelity. The lover, the brother, the friends whom I had lost, had all in their different ways possessed this courage, and it would not be utterly wasted if only, through those who were left, it could influence the generations still to be, and convince them that, so long as the spirit of man remained undefeatable, life was worth having and worth giving.'

VERA BRITTAIN,
Testament of Youth, 1933

Chapter One

Robert had put on his Sunday-best boots this morning, having polished them with particular care the night before. They were wet from walking through the snow now and he wished he was wearing his old gardening boots with the heavier soles. His suitcase seemed to be gaining weight the further he walked and kept banging against his shin. Mrs Fitzgerald had said the house was only a ten-minute walk from the station, hadn't she? Had he taken the right road out of the village? Why had he put so many books in his suitcase?

Finally, up ahead, Robert saw the old red-brick walls around the estate, as Mrs Fitzgerald's looping green handwriting had described. He followed the wall along the lane until he came to a gate and a sign that announced the entrance to Anderby Hall. A driveway curved around towards the gatehouse and there was an ornamental lake on the eastern side of the house, iced over now, with ducks skidding upon it. Beyond, there was a view out over parkland, with fine spruces and Lebanon cedars, a redwood, an ilex and magnificent old magnolias. Robert recalled that Lady Maxwell, the previous owner of the Hall, had been a renowned collector of plants who had written accounts of her tours of Norway, Canada and North Africa. Might there be journals of those trips in the library of the house? Would he be permitted to read them? The idea of it conjured a howl of wolves, the scent of spices, and made him feel he would be taking on something worthwhile here. But could he yet be sure that his place was secure? He hoped that Mrs Fitzgerald had been satisfied by his letter of reference and hadn't seen fit to pursue it further.

Robert stepped through the arch of the gatehouse. The path ahead was lined with overgrown box hedging and criss-crossed with a cat's paw prints. There was nobody about; his were the only human footprints in the snow, and the sudden cry of a peacock – an eerie, otherworldly sound – made it all the more reminiscent of a scene from a fairy tale. He might have fallen through a hole in time or have been en route for a rendezvous with the Snow Queen. When he'd pictured Mrs Fitzgerald, he'd seen her in Indian shawls and turquoise bracelets, but his image now shifted to white furs, colourless lips and an icicle crown. The red of berries seemed to intensify in the bleached-out scene and the frost was like a chalk line picking out the seed heads of sedums and teasels and spires of sea holly. The scrolls of ferns might be cast in copper, the cardoons bronze sculptures stained with verdigris. Robert followed the path into an inner courtyard and then there was the house ahead.

The roofline of the Hall, with its crenellated parapets, spiked gables and clusters of ornate octagonal chimney stacks, matched the embossed heading of Mrs Fitzgerald's notepaper. Was this architecture Elizabethan? The time-weathered brickwork was the colour of gingerbread in the winter sun. It was what one called a Fine Old House, with a façade built to impress, but Robert couldn't help noticing that some of the windows were boarded over, that the rendering around the door was flaking and how the Virginia creeper was well on the way to smothering the far wing of the property. A string of red, white and blue bunting hung limply over the door portico and there was a mildewed banner printed with the words '*Community. Creativity. Equality. Education.*' Hadn't that been on the heading of her notepaper too?

Mrs Fitzgerald's letter had instructed him to come to the front door. Perhaps this was equality put into practice, but Robert always had to use the kitchen door at Scarcroft Grange and he felt self-conscious as he stepped up to the main entrance. He realized, having come to the end of his journey, that his toes and fingers were quite numb with cold. Might there be hot tea inside and a scullery fireside where he could sit for a while? He stamped the snow from his boots and tried to bring the blood back into his feet.

The front door was of stout oak, studded all over with iron nails, and looked to be ancient and extremely heavy. To the right of it, within the porch, there was a bell pull and a slate with the words '*Now please wipe your feet!!!*' chalked upon it. It was a bossy sign, Robert thought, but perhaps there was some humour in the fulsome punctuation. He wiped his boots, as instructed.

Robert pulled the chain and there was a muffled clanging beyond the door. A grey cat appeared and circled his legs, purring volubly as he scratched its ears, and he took in the garden while he waited. It had been a formal garden, he could see, a place of precise shapes and carefully maintained symmetries, but even with the covering of snow it was clear it had become overgrown. Robert's palms itched for a pair of secateurs – and was that a goat he spied amongst the euphorbias? It surprised him to find this once-famous garden now neglected, but there would be purpose to his work here; it would be rewarding and he might make his mark. He'd spent the length of the journey listing positives so that he might not linger on the thought of everything he was being obliged to leave behind.

'Mother won't really go to the police,' Esther had said. 'She wouldn't want talk. But you need to get away from here.'

Robert had agreed to go, in the end, both for Esther's sake and his own. Nobody would know him here; he had no links to this place, and that was for the best, he supposed. Footsteps were approaching the other side of the door now. Robert told himself he didn't need to feel any shame and wouldn't have to justify himself to anyone here. He would never speak Esther's name and there'd be no reason for them to ever find out. This was where he began again as a better man. He was determined to make it so. Still, anxiety threatened his resolve as the door slowly opened.

Chapter Two

The door scraped across the flagstones revealing the blinking lashes of an exceptionally tall woman with red hair and heavily kohled eyes. Robert had expected the door to be opened by a maid, a girl in modest black and white, but the poise of the figure in front of him indicated this must be the lady of the house.

'Mrs Fitzgerald?' he began, wanting to sound confident, but hearing a note of apprehension in his own voice. 'Good afternoon. I'm Robert Bardsley. You're expecting me? I'm sorry, I'm a little late.'

'Robert, how do you do?' The woman blinked again. She looked as if she might just have awoken from a nap, but then her lipsticked mouth parted and revealed very white, straight teeth. 'I'm Gwendoline Fitzgerald.' She extended a manicured hand. 'But, of course, you already know that. Please, do come in. Have you had an epic struggle through the snow?'

His first sensation was relief – and then surprise at her American accent. He hadn't heard that in Mrs Fitzgerald's handwriting. Her silk blouse was parrot green – almost the same colour as her ink – and there were long strands of coral beads around her neck. Her height was accentuated by the great tumble of auburn hair piled high on her head and she kept her chin raised, as though she'd been taught as a girl to make the best of her profile. She reminded him of portraits of Good Queen Bess ready to repel an armada. She was an extraordinary-looking woman. The word for her was *statuesque*, Robert decided.

Mrs Fitzgerald stepped back from the door and beckoned him into a dimly lit entrance hall. There was a lot of old dark oak in the interior and a Christmas tree that had lost most of its needles. The panelled walls had the patina of treacle toffee and all the furniture was highly carved and emphatically antique.

'Goodness, you've carried your suitcase all the way from the station? You should have let Teddy pick it up later.'

'It was no trouble, madam,' Robert replied, though he was glad to put it down now.

'Madam?' She laughed. 'Oh, good God, not here, Robert! You must call me Gwendoline. I *insist*. I shall feel like a fusty old fossil, and be most insulted, if you call me madam again.'

'I'm sorry. Thank you, Mrs Fitzgerald. Gwendoline.'

Could he really call her Gwendoline? Was this how it was here? It pleased him that she wanted them to be on first-name terms; that felt like a compliment – he'd never once called Mr Underhill George – but he wasn't certain he could actually use her name.

'I apologize for the fact it's so frightfully cold,' she went on. 'This house is impossible to heat.' Her breath whitened the air and Robert could see blue veins on her hands. 'I've had the fire lit in the sitting room, but the rest of it remains like a larder. Perhaps it will help to preserve us?' she mused brightly.

'I don't tend to feel the cold. I'm always outside.'

'How politely English you are.' Mrs Fitzgerald put icy fingers to his arm, but her voice conveyed warmth.

Robert observed her posture as he followed along the passage. He pictured a younger version of her circling around drawing rooms with a book balanced on her head. She left a scent of damask rose perfume in her wake and beneath that there was the building's smell of damp stone, old timbers and possibly mice. He noticed there were watermarks on the plasterwork ceilings and cobwebs caught the light in corners. Mrs Fitzgerald looked as if she dressed with care, but the housekeeping seemed slightly lacking.

'It's a magnificent house – very stately, very imposing,' said Robert, selecting his adjectives with care. He wanted to make a good impression. 'Is it terrifically old?'

'This building was constructed by the de Villiers family in the sixteenth century – you possibly noticed their coat of arms on the gatehouse? But it's thought there might have been an earlier structure on the site, probably a priory. There were phases of modernization in the seventeenth and nineteenth centuries, the wood-panelled walls and the plasterwork, but the great hall is much as it originally was.' Her voice had slipped into a guided-tour mode. 'Until the last war, the house had been in the same family since the sixteenth century. I sometimes wonder if I was a rude shock to it, but I'm passionate about these old buildings.' She turned on her heels and looked convincingly passionate. 'This place eats money, it positively devours it, but if I hadn't bought Anderby it might have been split up into apartments, become a golf club, or even been demolished. Can you imagine?'

'That would have been a great pity.'

'A pity? It would have been an utter tragedy!'

They turned a corner and entered a narrower passageway. This house seemed to be a labyrinth of dark, winding corridors and staircases, and then light coming in at unexpected angles. Robert couldn't help wondering if the place might be haunted. Did spectral women in Elizabethan gowns swish along these corridors at night, the dust lifting and resettling in their wake? Did long-dead babies cry in empty nurseries and once-upon-a-time housemaids mutter at the cobwebs while rubbing their eternally tender knees? The building had that feel about it.

The walls on this passageway were hung with framed photographs. There were images of a ballet troupe lined up by the gatehouse, an orchestra on the lawn, snaps from a fancy-dress ball and the costumed casts of various theatrical productions. Robert couldn't help but pause and look. 'These are all events here?'

'Yes. See, this is the Auerbach ballet company. They were with us for several months. There were abandoned ballet shoes and semi-clad bodies everywhere, and rehearsals going on in the most unexpected places. It was pandemonium – and the queues for the bathrooms! But it was a delightful chaos. They're considering leaving Germany permanently now. Herr Hitler is a very dangerous man, don't you agree?'

There were framed newspaper articles on the wall too, re-porting conferences of philosophers and peace campaigners, a festival of Slavic music and an exhibition of West African art. At Scarcroft Grange it was an event when Mrs Underhill hosted the Women's Institute, Robert recalled. This was life on a different scale.

'We have a lot of musical events here, and dance. I adore

dancing!' Mrs Fitzgerald exclaimed over her shoulder and looked as if she might be about to pirouette. 'Don't you, Robert? It can be such a unifying force.'

This house was perhaps four times the size of Scarcroft Grange, but her manner was much less formal than that of Mr and Mrs Underhill. Was that because she was an American? Because she was some sort of philanthropist and inclined to use words like equality and community? Robert had never met anyone like her before and wasn't sure how he ought to behave in response. It was disconcerting not to know the rules.

'Come through,' she invited, leading him into a sitting room. 'I really ought to have had Teddy pick you up from the station. You must be perished. I'll make us some tea.'

The room had an enormous plasterwork chimneypiece, all clustered with carved saints, and yellowed from centuries of fires. The late-afternoon sun lit the diamond panes of the windows in the colours of barley-sugar sweets and two Siamese cats looked up from a brocade settee which they seemed to be diligently unravelling. A bowl of walnuts was balanced on the arm of a chair, someone had scattered fragments of nutshell all over the hearthrug, and a pot of cyclamens dropped soundless petals.

Mrs Fitzgerald invited Robert to take the armchair closest to the fire while she put a copper kettle on a gas ring. 'The kitchen is a hike away. Oh, for the days of being able to ring a bell and have a butler appear with buttered crumpets!' She smiled regretfully and pulled a paisley shawl around her shoulders. 'The Hall employed twenty people before the war, and that was just the inside staff, but those days are long gone. Alas!'

'There are no staff at all?' He assumed he could ask.

'Not one. But don't worry – my husband has tutored me in the intricacies of making British tea.'

It was an enormous house to run without servants, Robert thought. And did this mean there were no other garden staff? Would he be here on his own, then? He hadn't expected that. Mrs Fitzgerald threw another log onto the fire. Ashes fluttered and circled and a smell of wood smoke filled the room. Robert noticed the scorch marks on the rug and he could see where the springs had come through the bottom of the settee.

As Mrs Fitzgerald tended to the kettle, he looked at the portrait to the side of the chimneybreast. A young man in military uniform was posed against a misty, foreign-looking landscape. He had a white grin, eyes creased with amusement and a healthy, burnished glow about him. Robert would have liked to ask who he was, but had learned that enquiries about men in uniforms could provoke awkward responses.

'Hughie,' Mrs Fitzgerald said, catching the angle of Robert's gaze. 'My brother. He died in France. But he also brought me here. He sent me such beautiful poems from this part of England.'

'I'm sorry for your loss.' It was what you had to say, but the words always felt inadequate.

Though he'd been surprised by the American accent, Mrs Fitzgerald spoke with a refined, moneyed voice, Robert considered, the voice of a woman who'd had governesses and inherited family jewels. He could imagine her rustling in silks and taffetas, gemstones sliding up her slim wrists, and heads turning as she entered ballrooms, surrounded by whispers of her money and marriage prospects. He supposed she'd only lately come to threadbare rugs and damp patches on the walls.

'Your brother was a poet?'

'Only an enthusiastic amateur, but I like to believe he had some talent. At one time I did think about trying to get a volume of his verse published. There's always so much to do on the estate, though, and time speeds by.'

Robert took his chance to look around the room while Mrs Fitzgerald busied herself with the tea things. There were heraldic shields in the stained-glass windows, a collection of seashells under a glass dome, pieces of carved jade and coral, and a gilded crown that might previously have adorned the head of a saint in a church. He noticed large Chinese vases in the corners, lacquered with improbable patterns of foliage, silver candlesticks encrusted with dripped wax, and a vase of dried poppy heads all woven with spider silk.

'I expect your previous employer was sorry to lose you?' Mrs Fitzgerald asked, as she handed him a porcelain teacup.

Robert hesitated as to how to respond for a moment. He'd always got on well with Mr Underhill and it had grieved him when his employer had spoken of his *disappointment*. That word, more than any other, had pained Robert. 'I enjoyed my time at Scarcroft Grange, but I felt ready to take on a bigger project.' The teacup felt too fine and fragile in his hands.

'Oh, we're certainly a project!' Mrs Fitzgerald laughed. 'I should tell you that we haven't employed a gardener since I bought Anderby. The community here liked the idea of managing the gardens themselves, making them into an expression of our values, but I'm afraid none of us are expert and most of us are short on time, so the only thing the gardens are expressing now is neglect.'

'It can be put right, I'm sure.' He didn't let any doubt show in his voice. He needed her to believe that he could do this.

'We made a priority of keeping the kitchen garden going – we earn an income from that, but everything else has become rather chaotic.'

Looking at Mrs Fitzgerald's polished fingernails, Robert couldn't imagine she'd done much work on the garden herself. She ran her strings of beads through her fine, white fingers as she talked and they made a soft clicking sound as they trickled into her palm. She kicked off her shoes and wound her long legs up underneath her on the settee. Her abandoned shoes were red Morocco, with straps and very high heels.

'As I said, I wanted to take on more responsibility and I'm sure this will feel worthwhile.'

'I've always dreamed of restoring the gardens to their former glory and was so pleased when most people agreed to the plan. I should probably explain that all the residents on the estate make an annual contribution to a trust, which supports our estate school and the upkeep of communal areas. Some of them rent and others have bought their own properties, but Anderby belongs to all of us. That's how this community works: we're all custodians and share both the advantages and responsibilities of running the estate. That said, my husband and I personally pay for the maintenance of the Hall, of course – and, as the renovation of the gardens is my initiative, I'll be your employer, rather than the trust.'

Robert noticed the *most people*. Did that mean there were some who had objected? 'I read a magazine article about the Greenfields community.' Mrs Fitzgerald had apparently chosen that collective name for the residents of the estate. In the article, she'd referred to her endeavours here as the 'Greenfields project'.

'Oh, not that ghastly mean thing in the *Tatler*?'

'No,' Robert replied. What could the ghastly thing have been? 'I can't remember where I read it now.' The article had spoken of charitable good work, artistic patronage and an aristocratic attempt to create a socialist paradise. Perhaps, on reflection, there might have been something slightly snide in its tone (had it called them 'Gin-Rickey Bolsheviki'?), but its positive points had lodged in his thoughts and returned to his mind when he'd seen the advertisement for a gardener. 'It's essentially a community of artists?'

'In the widest definition; we have sculptors and potters here, wood workers and textile workers, poets and musicians. We set out to create an environment that encouraged and inspired creativity – we sincerely believe that creative self-expression nourishes the soul – but, more than that, we wanted to experiment with new ways of thinking and living together. Our goal was that people might live as vividly and fully as possible here, working collaboratively, with their hands, heads and hearts engaged, and all of us with an equal say in decision making. These are the values we've tried to instil in the next generation through our school and I'd like to believe we've made some difference. Social atomism is the great challenge of our age, don't you agree?'

Mrs Fitzgerald's eyes widened as she spoke and she gesticulated with her hands. It sounded a little like a political pamphlet, Robert thought, and he wasn't absolutely sure what 'social atomism' meant, but he could see she believed in everything she was saying. Having just been brought down to size at Scarcroft, bluntly reminded of his social inferiority, these ideas about equality and collaboration had an appeal. But could they really put them into practice here?

'And your plan now is to open up the gardens to the public?' he prompted. Dusk was creeping in from the corners of the room. In the gaps in their conversation he could hear a mouse scratching in the walls.

'I'm afraid we do always have to be thinking of means to generate income for the estate. My idea is to charge a shilling for entry and it should bring more trade to the café too. I'd like to be open by midsummer – though, of course, I don't expect the gardens to be in perfect order by that stage. I'm aware of the scale of the task and we will make it clear to visitors that we are a work in progress . . .'

'Which doesn't mean they get a discount!' A man entered the room, kissed Mrs Fitzgerald rather enthusiastically on the cheek, and slid his fingertips along the length of her arm. He helped himself to a cup of tea before he turned to Robert and nodded an acknowledgement. 'Do we get an introduction, Gwendoline?' He said her name slowly, splitting it into its syllables. His Irish lilt seemed to make curlicues and scrolls spring from around the letters.

'This is Robert. Remember? Mr Bardsley, the gardener? I told you he was arriving this afternoon.' She smiled as she chastised. 'Robert, this is Teddy, my somewhat absent-minded husband.'

'Bardsley, of course. How do you do?' He stepped to the fire and rocked on his heels as he warmed his back against it. He had strikingly bright blue eyes and the sort of pencil moustache that is generally only seen on the cinema screen. Though he was wearing a gentleman's country tweeds, he looked like an actor dressed to play the part. His impeccably polished shoes seemed conspicuous against the genteel shabbiness of the room.

'Robert has come to us from a place called Scarcroft Grange, up in the Pennines. Don't you think it sounds deliciously Brontë-ish? I picture it with Gothic gables, smoke-blackened stonework and the wuthering wind flinging rooks all around its chimneypots. Tell me, is that how it is, Robert?'

It was a fanciful image – and Robert found that he didn't want Mrs Fitzgerald to be picturing Scarcroft too closely. Moreover, he felt her husband's eyes readied to judge his response. 'They do say the house was known to Emily Brontë.'

'You see, I knew it!' Mrs Fitzgerald clapped her hands together.

Teddy pushed cushions, blankets and cats aside and made a space for himself on the settee. A scent of expensive hair pomade had entered the room with him and he hummed as he spooned sugar into his tea. Robert had never seen anyone take so much sugar.

'I know,' said Mrs Fitzgerald, catching Robert's eye. 'Isn't it obscene? I tell him his teeth will rot. They'll all fall out and how will he eat his mutton chops then? He'll have to live on bread soaked in milk, like a baby.' She looked at her husband with unguarded tenderness, but it was a little like hearing a mother speaking to a favourite son.

'Nonsense,' said Teddy, lighting a cigarette. 'When my teeth fall out I'll have a shiny set of dentures. They'll be grinning at you from a glass when you step into the bathroom of a morning and I'll chase you all around the house gnashing them.'

'Ridiculous boy!' Mrs Fitzgerald unwound her husband's fingers from around the cigarette and took a long drag from it, before placing it back between his lips.

There was something too intimate in their behaviour,

Robert thought. Had they forgotten he was in the room, or
was this a display for his benefit? Mrs Fitzgerald was a striking
woman, with good bones and bearing, a woman who would
still turn heads, but the age difference was noticeable. She was
perhaps in her mid-forties, while her husband must be at least
ten years her junior. Robert wondered how they might have
met. Which one of them had done the pursuing?

'So that accent is Yorkshire?' Teddy asked.

'Lancashire, actually, sir – but right on the county border.'
Robert considered his accent in turn. Was it Dublin perhaps?

'Hell's bells! Don't call him sir!' Mrs Fitzgerald interjected.
'His head is swelled enough already. We'll never hear the end
of it if you start calling him sir.'

'I could get used to it.' Teddy tilted his chin. 'He can call
me sir if he wants.'

Mrs Fitzgerald rolled her eyes. 'Robert, *please* don't.'

'Isn't Lancashire all cotton mills and cobbles?' Teddy went
on. 'Do they have gardens up there?'

'It's not all factories. There are some grand old houses,
though the money does generally come from textiles. Scarcroft
Grange has an Arts and Crafts garden. Mr Underhill, my previous employer, was a great admirer of Gertrude Jekyll.' Robert
used to be proud to talk of Scarcroft's garden, but now felt he
mustn't let the conversation linger here. 'I was there for five
years. Before that I worked for the Parks Department.'

'The Parks Department, eh?' Was there something mocking
in Teddy's grin? 'So you can arrange begonias in patterns? And
know how to plant up hanging baskets for bandstands? Is that
the look you're aiming for, Gwen?'

'Robert, you mustn't mind my husband.' Mrs Fitzgerald gave

Teddy's shoulder a shove. 'He's a notorious tease. I warn you, he's like this with everyone.'

Teddy smiled as he blew on his tea and balanced his cigarette on the edge of his saucer. Robert's grandmother would have called that bad manners, but Mrs Fitzgerald gave her husband a look that suggested she was remarkably pleased with him.

'If you don't mind me saying, you're a long way from home, Bardsley,' Teddy continued. 'You've not come all this way just for work, have you? What are you running away from?'

He said it jokingly – presumably this was an exhibition of the notorious teasing – but Robert felt himself being measured up. Could Teddy sense something amiss?

'Teddy!' Mrs Fitzgerald protested.

'I'm ambitious,' Robert said. That much wasn't a lie. 'I had a good position at Scarcroft, but I wanted to take on more of a challenge. I'd like to feel I've achieved something. I want to make my mark.'

'Ambitious? Is that so?' Teddy angled an eyebrow at his wife. 'Is ambition permitted amongst your people? Are they allowed to admit that?'

'Of course!' There was passion in her voice. 'We're all ambitious. Perhaps not in the orthodox sense of working for monetary gain and social advancement, but we're all striving to achieve change here. That's what it's all about! Some people would call that wildly ambitious.'

Teddy drained his teacup and wiped his mouth with the back of his hand before he announced he must depart to see a fellow about a dog. 'So we'll be seeing you around the place, Bardsley?' he asked as he stood. 'I'll admit, I'm not convinced this garden plan is the soundest money-making venture, but it's Gwen's project and she believes in it. I'd tarmac it all over myself, it would be far more practical, but then I have no feeling for these things.' He leaned over the back of the settee and wound a curl of his wife's hair around his finger like an amber ring. 'I believe we're putting you in the cottage next to Trudie. She'll be thrilled with you! A bit of fresh meat, what?'

Mrs Fitzgerald shook her head and smiled as Teddy closed the door. 'I'm afraid my husband passes through rooms like a whirlwind.'

Robert turned the teacup in his saucer. Teddy had looked at him with narrowed eyes as he'd departed. Had he picked up that he was being selective with the truth? And what had he meant about fresh meat?

'You said in your letter that your previous employer collected old roses?' Mrs Fitzgerald asked.

Sensibleness and order felt to return to the room with Teddy's departure, and Robert was glad of it, but he wished they didn't have to linger on the subject of Scarcroft. He tried to remember what Esther had written in her reference. To his mind, that letter had been blatantly composed in the handwriting and phrasing of a nineteen-year-old girl. She'd signed it with her father's name, but it didn't sound like Mr Underhill's voice at all. Mercifully, Mrs Fitzgerald didn't seem to have sensed that. 'We put in a rose walk and an arbour trained with climbers.'

'I'm afraid you'll find our roses rather under the weather. They were famous once, though. People travelled to see the topiary and the de Villiers roses.' Mrs Fitzgerald stood and walked towards the window. She turned to Robert and he sensed he was being invited to join her there. 'You know, when I first came here I remember looking out and thinking the view must hardly have changed for four hundred years. Imagine, Robert!' She took a sprig of holly from the window frame and turned it between her fingers. He noticed that the curtain behind her had been eaten away by moths. 'I'd trailed around a dozen properties with an agent, but I felt an immediate attachment to Anderby. It instantly caught my heart and my imagination. Oh, it was a sight when I first came here!' Her voice lifted as she recalled. 'The main public rooms had been occupied during the war, but other parts of the house were in a shocking state. Pigeons were roosting in the oratory, ivy had climbed through the windows and wound around the furniture, and water was dripping from the ceilings. I was probably insane to take it on, but I looked out at the view and knew this was the place I was meant to be; I needed Anderby and it needed me. I could make it sound again, give it a future, and we might begin to address why this dear peaceful old house had become a hospital full of tragically damaged young men. There was an irresistible metaphor in it, I suppose – though, in retrospect, falling for a metaphor might not have been my most sensible financial decision ever.'

She turned to Robert, her expression both fond and wistful. He'd taken the chance to observe his new employer as she'd spoken this soliloquy. The light from the window showed the fine lines on her face, but her skin was the colour of the top of the milk and her turquoise eyes were intelligent. She had the long straight nose of a Grecian statue and a wide, amused mouth. It was a face that could have been haughty, but there was humour in the creases around her eyes.

'I've done what I can with the garden over the years,' Mrs Fitzgerald continued, 'and I've always been keen to thrust pruning shears into the hands of volunteers, but I know it's looking shamefully neglected.' She took a hairpin from between her teeth and pushed a wayward curl back into place. 'I've not left it too late, have I? Could it still be revived? The scale of the work required hasn't put you off?'

Robert looked out. How enchanting the garden was under its cover of snow. In his imagination it melted away, the box hedging sharpened into straighter lines, the bindweed and bramble disentangled, and the formal beds bloomed into harmonious colour. It was enchanting in that vision too. This would be more responsibility than he'd ever taken on before, and a test of his skills and his knowledge, but he would apply himself to it. As the house's romantic ruination had evidently appealed to Mrs Fitzgerald, so he found himself drawn to the idea of saving the gardens from dereliction.

'It will be a push to get it into shape within six months,' he admitted.

'I appreciate that. But not impossible to make it vaguely respectable?'

'It would be a privilege to work here. I will do my utmost for you.'

He would give it all his energy and attention, tire his mind and his muscles, and perhaps he might once again be able to fall into a dreamless sleep at the end of his days? He craved that. This was a peculiar place, and not quite what he'd expected, but he was intrigued by it and he needed this chance. There was no going back now.

Chapter Three

The terrace of cottages was to the rear of the Hall. They had low slate roofs and tall chimneys, and might once have housed estate workers, Robert supposed. As they stepped towards the door, there was a sound of barking dogs from the neighbouring property.

'I'm afraid it's rather simple,' Mrs Fitzgerald said, walking ahead with the key, 'but the previous tenant made herself comfortable here.'

There was a faint whiff of mildew and mouse dirt as they entered, and the walls could do with a fresh coat of paint, but it might have been much worse. Robert put his suitcase down.

'It will do me very well,' he replied.

'I appreciate it might need some refreshing, but it's yours to do with as you see fit.' Mrs Fitzgerald lifted a pugnacious-looking Staffordshire spaniel from the mantelpiece, blew dust off it, sneezed and said, 'What a sweetheart! The girls have left you some things on a tray, I believe, and Mr Ingram has filled the wood store, but if there's anything else you need this evening, just hammer on the door.'

'I'm sure I'll have everything I require here. Thank you.'

Finally left alone, Robert explored his new quarters. The

downstairs room had a black-leaded range with an armchair in front of it and a kitchen corner with a sink, a meat safe, a gas ring and a dresser stacked with blue and white china. A tray had been left on the pine table and he lifted the cloth over it to see a plate pie, a bottle of Bass beer, a large Eccles cake and a note that said 'Don't be a stranger!' Ascending a steep, narrow staircase, he found a room furnished with a brass bedstead, a marble-topped washstand and a bedding chest filled with blankets and the smell of camphor moth balls. The window looked out over a little rear garden that was becoming indistinct in the gathering dusk.

Robert stood and listened, hearing only the wind under the roof tiles and his own breath finally steadying. He'd handed his door key back to his brother that morning, leaving behind a house full of family jokes and arguments and his nephews endlessly thundering up and down the stairs. It was so very quiet here by comparison. As the hours had passed in the ever-colder railway carriage, he'd questioned whether he'd needed to come quite so far. When might he see his family again? Did Esther appreciate just how much she'd asked him to give up? Still, this was a clean start, Robert told himself, and he could choose who he wanted to be here; he'd show these people that he was diligent, capable and reliable, and would prove to himself that he was an honourable man. Catching the reflection of his own eyes in the window, however, he was conscious that this was a new beginning built on lies.

Robert licked his palm and smoothed his hair as he waited on the doorstep. His hands smelled of the paraffin he'd used to get the fire going. He batted a flake of ash from his trousers and thought he probably ought to have scrubbed his fingernails before he came to call on his new neighbour. But the porch in front of him contained a rumpled dog bed and a crate of unrinsed milk bottles. Whoever his neighbour might be (as yet, she was merely a disembodied female voice that knew a lot of swearwords), she was unlikely to be a stickler for well-scrubbed nails.

He'd heard her voice raised to the barking dogs when he'd first arrived and then, as he'd descended the staircase, there'd been a beat of music coming through the wall. If he'd heard her, she'd probably heard him, and so he'd reasoned that he ought to introduce himself. He did want to get off on the right foot. The music was louder as he waited on the doorstep now and the dogs were barking excitedly and leaping against the door. There sounded to be an awful lot of them in there.

The woman who eventually opened the door on the far side of the porch was wearing a black silk dressing gown embroidered with red dragons, had platinum blonde hair cut shorter than his own, and Bakelite bracelets all up her arms. She was perhaps in her mid-thirties, and though the smudged make-up around her eyes gave her a look of disarray, she was striking. She reminded him of the sort of woman who was always being photographed leaving London nightclubs in the magazines that Mrs Underhill used to give him to cut up for compost. The sound of a raucous jazz band was playing behind her, Robert could hear it more clearly now, and a pack of small white dogs seethed around her Turkish slippers. So was this what Mrs Fitzgerald's creative types looked like?

'Push them back,' the woman instructed as she opened the door. 'Don't let them out!' She tried to corral the dogs with her feet and eventually issued another stern growl, which sent them scampering back into the interior of the cottage. Though she addressed the dogs in a commanding voice, she showed a brilliant smile as she made eye contact with Robert and switched to an altogether different tone.

'My new neighbour, I'm presuming – am I right? I heard Gwendoline at the door with you earlier. Is it Mr Bardsley?'

'Robert,' he offered his hand. 'Yes, I've just moved in.' He nodded towards his own door unnecessarily. Why did this woman make him feel nervous? 'I thought I perhaps ought to introduce myself.'

'How sweet of you, darling.' She shook his hand vigorously. 'Gertrude Carr. But do call me Trudie. Everyone does. I say, my beasts haven't disturbed you, have they?'

Her voice was unusually deep for a woman's, warm and faintly husky, and had a sound of old money about it. It wasn't a wireless voice, it was less clipped and bouncy than that, but it was a voice that spoke of perfect self-assurance and a pleasure in the finest things.

'They haven't disturbed me at all. I've barely noticed and I love dogs.'

'Do you?' she replied. Her stare was penetrating. 'I think you can tell an awful lot about a person by how they react to dogs. They immediately sort out the wimps and the bullies. Don't you agree?'

'I couldn't agree more.' He found himself wanting to be relaxed and friendly with this woman's dogs.

'Anyway, come in! Do you drink Dubonnet? Do you like Latin jazz?'

Robert stepped into a remarkably untidy room. With the excitement of the dogs, the blaring of the trumpets, and Trudie swinging her shoulders as if she might break into a samba at any moment, the atmosphere teetered on the precipice of chaos. The place smelled of a heavy, spicy perfume, dog beds and Turkish cigarettes.

'Goodness! Forgive my directness, but you are a great improvement.' Trudie shut the door behind Robert and gave him an unabashed up-and-down examination. Her eyes scrutinized his face with an enquiring attention to detail that he found slightly embarrassing. 'I had Miss Bentridge next door until last Easter. She was stiff as an old herring and spent her days muttering Middle English poetry and weaving on a hand-loom. She had absolutely no sense of humour. None at all. And she never stopped complaining about the dogs. I say, things are looking up!'

Robert heard himself laughing in a self-conscious way. 'Thank you. I shall do my best.' He was accustomed to being invisible to this class of woman, a background figure only attributed a name if the lawns were looking neglected, but he felt thoroughly *seen* in Trudie's presence.

'Let me switch this off. It's easier not to have to lip read, isn't it? Though you have a very attractive mouth, if you don't mind me saying. Show me your smile. There. Yes. Oh, you darling boy!' Trudie went to still the gramophone needle. 'Do you like Arlo Marvell? Have you seen him with his band? We were together for a while some years ago, but he's gone back to New York now. God of a man! How did I ever let him slip through my hands? Of course, it horrified my mother. She's an appalling old reactionary. I took him home on the same day she was hosting the church ladies' coffee morning. I didn't intend to – it just happened that way, as these things do. Well, the pince-nez fell off Mrs Sinclair's nose when we walked in – quite literally! – and Lily Dixon choked on a coconut macaroon. Ha!' It was a forcible laugh. 'I abhor colour prejudice. It makes my blood boil. I'm passionately against it. Aren't you? But then the hoo-ha over Arlo was nothing compared with the hysterics over Guy. Dear Lord, the wailing and gnashing!' She rolled her eyes theatrically. 'Mother is such an old cow. She cut me off. Don't you think it's outrageously Victorian?'

She was like a juggernaut. Esther had friends who wore make-up and went out dancing, confident young women who spoke in loud voices, but Trudie was from a whole other world. The rush and forcefulness of her words made Robert want to take a step backwards. 'Will she get over it?'

'No one holds grudges like Mother. She told me I won't get a penny more. Well, to hell with her! I'll get by. Shrivelled old witch. We haven't spoken for eight years and really it's for the best.'

The shoal of small white dogs was rippling around Robert's ankles. He bent down to them, taking the excuse to break away from Trudie's examining eyes momentarily, and they whimpered and nuzzled at him. Small pink tongues and tiny teeth rasped at his hands.

'See, they adore you already! You're going to be the best of friends.' Trudie stood with a hand on her hip as she looked down at him. 'We are a bit overcrowded just now, but Queenie's puppies will start to go out to their homes next week.'

'You breed them?' he asked as he straightened.

'It's a relatively new venture. I started with angora rabbits, but there's more money in Sealyham Terriers. And they are sweethearts. Such lovely natures. Would you like one?' She lifted one of the smaller white bundles and pouted her lips as she nuzzled it against her cheek. 'I could do you a special price.'

'Perhaps in time. If you need a walker or a dog sitter, I'd be happy to oblige.'

'Oh, aren't you a treat? Wherever did Gwen find you?' She put the dog down and clapped her hands together. 'We must have a drink. Look at the state of this place! What must you think of me? Here, help yourself.'

She threw a packet of Lucky Strike in Robert's direction and lit her own cigarette from a shagreen-covered table lighter. As Trudie wafted over to a cocktail cabinet (*waft* was the only word for that walk), her dressing gown billowed behind her and Robert was relieved to see she was wearing slacks and a sweater beneath it. After speaking with Mrs Fitzgerald, he'd imagined the residents of the estate might be worthy and earnest, all homemade sandals and wholemeal bread, but Trudie was shaking apart his suppositions. Like Mrs Fitzgerald, she was tall, but she was also broad-shouldered and angular, as if she might have been athletic in her youth. Robert could picture her playing energetic tennis on well-tended lawns and swearing like a docker at the umpire.

With Trudie's back turned, he took his chance to look around the room. There was a great deal of furniture in it, much of it gilded and lacquered in an oriental style, and all of it draped with drying laundry. There were fashion papers everywhere, framed photographs of dogs, rosettes and trophies, and was that a funeral urn sitting on the mantelpiece?

'I don't have any ice. You won't take offence, will you?'

'Not at all.'

The cocktail cabinet was all mirror panels and walnut veneer.

She was throwing measures into glasses with speed, confidence and some ostentation. The bouncing of the dogs made the bottles on the cabinet chime.

'It's a Corpse Reviver,' she said, finally handing Robert a glass. 'It will warm you up.'

'Thank you.' The glass was painted with a design of fighting cockerels and the scent of the drink was combative too. For the first time today, Robert didn't feel as if he needed warming up. The fire was roaring in here and Trudie's company made him feel rather hot and bothered. 'I've never had one before. What's in it?'

'Gin, Curaçao, absinthe, whichever bottle next happened to catch my eye . . .' She waved her hand dismissively. The bracelets stretched from her wrist to her elbow and clattered as she gesticulated. 'Tchin-tchin, old thing.'

Robert took a sip. He wanted to give the impression he was accustomed to strong drink, but it was remarkably potent and he tried not to cough when it hit the back of his throat. Trudie's mouth kinked up at one corner.

'Is it like the Arctic next door? You must take some extra blankets home with you or a hot-water bottle. Perhaps you'd like to borrow a puppy? I have to admit, I do let them come up to bed with me at night. Do you think that's appalling? Will you tell people? They wriggle about a bit, but if you can persuade one of the little chaps to sleep on your feet, it's divine.'

She pursed her lips and sighed as she let out a long ribbon of smoke. Trudie didn't look like the sort of woman who might possess a hot-water bottle, but then she seemed to be a curious mix of contradictions.

'I lit the range before I came out. It should have warmed up by the time I go back.' The drink was very warming. He felt his cheeks beginning to glow.

'Isn't this weather ghastly? I'm normally at a friend's villa in Nice in December, but it wasn't practical this time with the dogs.' She made an exaggeratedly glum face. 'Isn't Gloucestershire vile in the winter?'

Robert could imagine this woman flying down to Nice, but what was she doing living in a one-up-one-down cottage in deepest rusticity? 'I thought it was beautiful today in the snow. I enjoyed walking from the station.'

'Ah, you see, you're a Romantic, Robert. You probably enjoy climbing hills for no good reason too, don't you? I have no imagination, I'm more bodily than cerebral, and I absolutely can't stand to be cold.' She said this with feeling and visibly shivered as she stabbed her cigarette out in the ashtray. She had a way of saying certain words in capital letters. 'Anyway, you must sit down. Let me make some space.'

Trudie addressed her attention to the table. The surface of it was covered with boxes, many of which seemed to contain coloured beads. She pushed them aside and removed some silky garment from a chair, urging Robert to sit.

'They're beautiful colours,' he said, nodding to the boxes and trying to divert his eyes from her laundry. 'Are they oriental?'

'Some of them are old Venetian glass,' she said, dipping her hand into a box of beads that looked like boiled sweets and letting them trickle through her fingers. She reached for a pair of oversized horn-rimmed spectacles and her eyes became larger. Her voice took on a seriousness too. 'Those are Nepalese. I buy some made from yak bones, these are from Afghanistan, and I get a lot from a trader in Morocco. I'm careful who I buy from.

If you source from the right people, you can do some good in the world, but buy from the wrong sorts and you can find yourself funding all manner of heinousness. My business is called Perles du Monde. Don't you like it? Costume jewellery, you see? I'm a whizz with a soldering iron!' Her voice brightened again.

'And you find dog breeding and jewellery compatible?'

'I know, it's an unlikely-sounding combination, isn't it?' She folded her spectacles away and sat back in her chair. 'But my mother is always bedecked like a Christmas tree – not this stuff, all the handed-down rocks – and Daddy spent every hour he could hunting with hounds. Much as we might try, we can never entirely escape our inheritance, can we? What do your people do?'

'Textiles,' he replied. Should he tell Trudie that both his parents had been operatives in cotton mills?

'But you became a gardener?' She leaned towards him, seemingly genuinely interested.

'I enjoy being outdoors.'

'Do you? I can't stand it!' She stamped her glass on the table with emphasis, spilling a little of her drink. 'But I like a man who works with his hands in the earth. I think it's noble. I say, have you read *Lady Chatterley?*' She smiled at him again, a wide, roguish smile, and he recalled what Teddy had said about fresh meat.

'What brought you to Gloucestershire?' He could ask, couldn't he? He felt it best to divert away from D. H. Lawrence. Esther had read passages of *Lady Chatterley* aloud to him and it was all a little too close to home.

'Gwen was a friend of a friend and I heard about what she was doing here. She was putting the word out, wanting to gather like-minded souls together, giving them grants and studios and encouraging them to find ways to work collaboratively. The talk was all healthful and hopeful, and my life in London had become the opposite of that. It came at the right time for me.' She made expansive gestures with her hands and the bracelets rattled all up her arms. 'You'll probably find us an odd lot at first. You might feel you've accidentally stumbled into a madhouse. We're quite an exhibition of alternative beliefs, fervently held political opinions and unorthodox lifestyles, but there's a great deal of freedom here and we do genuinely try to support one another. We might fall out over politics periodically, but there is a common sympathy amongst us. Tell me, Robert, what is your opinion of Mussolini?'

Nobody had ever asked him that before. 'Don't they say he's a vegetarian and a teetotaller? I read that he spends hours every day doing fencing exercises and eats nothing but fruit. Apparently, he never swears and he drinks camomile tea.'

Trudie gave him a look that suggested this wasn't an adequate response. Robert supposed she wasn't wrong.

'Of course, the local society and clergy have us all down as morally degenerate,' Trudie said with some glee, 'but they love to have Gwen on the guest list at parties.'

'Degenerate?'

'I don't mean to shock you, Robert, but certain couples here aren't joined in wedlock.' She made a faux-horrified face. 'We've harboured divorcees, men have been sighted holding hands, women regularly flaunt their legs in trousers, and the sexes officially have equal rights here! Can you feel the earth quaking beneath your feet?'

'What have I got myself in to?' He returned her smile.

'A veritable moral cesspit.' Her eyes glittered.

'So how many residents are there? Do a lot of them live in the Hall?'

'There are just under thirty of us here now, including the children, variously scattered about the estate's cottages. The personnel has changed as time has gone by and we have lost quite a lot of people in recent years. The house was packed at the start, they were crushed in there like sardines in a can – I suppose it was what you might call a commune – but that was in pre-Teddy days. Teddy isn't a sharer. He's not a joiner-in. He has a horror of finding other people's wet towels in the bathroom, apparently, and he does have a way of influencing Gwen. Most of the house is closed up now. They can't afford to heat it. These old piles aren't practical any longer, are they?'

'And there are really no staff?'

'She let the cook go last year, so now they live on toasted teacakes and tinned soup heated up on a gas ring,' Trudie replied. She took a small dog up onto her lap and began brushing it, almost absent-mindedly, with a metal comb. 'They used to have Hettie come up from the village to do the cleaning, but even she's finished now. Between us, I'm not sure Teddy was best pleased about that. We must all make economies in these straightened times, though, and you have to respect Gwen's resilience. She Vims out her own bathtub, you know, and she's extremely energetic with a carpet sweeper.' Trudie pulled dog hair from her comb and dropped it into a Chinese vase at the side of her chair. Returning one dog to the floor, she scooped up another and began again.

'The estate didn't come to her through family?' As Trudie was in a flow, there didn't seem to be any harm in giving her a further nudge.

'Goodness, no! Gwen's father had factories all over America. Something to do with motorcar parts, as I recall.' The comb stilled and Trudie looked up to the ceiling as she made an effort to remember, but the specifics evidently evaded her. 'He was a self-made man. He went out there from Liverpool as a boy, I believe, and pulled himself up by his bootstraps, right up to the top of society.' She held a peppermint between her teeth and let the dog on her lap take it from her mouth. She turned to Robert and grinned as if this delighted her.

'Motorcar parts?' Robert pictured a corpulent man in a brash checked suit and a Homburg hat, a man with a booming voice and big ideas, with the ear of politicians and vast paintings of angry buffaloes on his walls. He would never have guessed that Mrs Fitzgerald's gentility might have been bought with oily valves and sprockets.

'Of course, she was brought up by nannies and governesses. Only the best would do. The newspapers used to speculate about who she might marry. They called her the most marriageable heiress in New York State.' Trudie was doing her capital-letters voice again. 'How excruciating, eh? Is it any wonder she wanted to turn her back on all of that?'

How had she ended up with Teddy, then? The newspapers couldn't have predicted that outcome. And where had all the money gone? Robert's imagination conjured a forbidden romance, a rushed elopement and an angry severing of family ties. But had it been like that?

'And what does Teddy do?'

'*Do*? As in work?' The question seemed to surprise Trudie. 'Heavens, Teddy doesn't work! He's professionally Gwen's husband, I suppose. He claims not to be able to do any physical work because of the gas – the war, you know? – so he polishes his motors and goes to the races.'

'He was gassed in the war?' Robert hadn't expected that. Teddy looked as healthy as a stallion.

'Don't ever mention it. The tales of Teddy's valour are very tiresome – and quite possibly fictional,' she added with a wink. 'To be frank, he is more decorative than functional, but then we all have our whims, don't we?'

'Does Mrs Fitzgerald still own factories?'

'Not any longer. All of that has gone. Her father got into armaments manufacturing during the war, and lined his pockets very nicely, but it felt like dirty money to Gwen. She didn't want any part of it. Well, you can understand that, can't you? And then with her losing her brother too ... She deliberately wanted to break away from the values of her father's generation, to turn her back on all the old hypocrisies and hierarchies and the money hunger, because as far as she was concerned, only loss and heartbreak had come from that. Anyway, when her parents passed away, she decided she could perhaps do some good with her fortune.'

'She gave it away?'

'She donated much of it to charitable causes and the remainder went into this project. She had to have the greatest experts in to restore the pargeting and the wall paintings, to advise on the forestry and farming and setting up the school, and there were all the conferences and lecture series and arts festivals to finance. But then the stock market crashed and now there's nothing left in the coffers to fix the roof. Sometimes great chunks of plaster fall down from the ceilings and they only venture up to the top floor to empty buckets.'

Robert recalled Mrs Fitzgerald speaking so fervently of her attachment to Anderby Hall. Might it also be her folly?

'Anyway, listen to me rattling on! Don't I sound like a wicked old gossip?' Trudie widened her eyes and let out a bark of laughter. It startled the dog on her lap. 'But I do enjoy a cosy chitchat. Don't you, Robert? I feel you and I shall get along very nicely. Do you know you've got heavenly eyes? Like chocolate buttons. Like a faithful dog. Shall I teach you how to make a Corpse Reviver?'

Chapter Four

Robert awoke to the noise of dogs barking distantly, a message being passed down the valley from farm to farm, and finally picked up by the pack next door. He then heard Trudie letting them out into the back garden and singing as she did so. Hell, she had more stamina than he did. He'd ended up drinking several Corpse Revivers with her last night and had passed out as soon as he'd crawled up the stairs to his bed. He wasn't sure that much could revive his corpse this morning. He was in no mood for singing.

Though Robert was warm under the blankets, he could see his own breath whitening the air and there were ferns of frost on the windows. He stared up at a damp patch on the ceiling, debating whether it was closest to the shape of Australia or Africa – and contemplating if he could feel settled here. Mrs Fitzgerald had seemingly been convinced by his reference and there was no reason for there to be any further contact between her and the Underhills, was there? He resolved that he must give her no cause to question her decision to take him on.

He'd slept in his clothes last night, he realized now, with his overcoat thrown over the bed. Just how much had he drunk? He tried to remember, but parts of the evening were a disconcerting blank ... Had he danced with Trudie at some point, or had he dreamed that? There was a sour taste in his mouth and his head hammered dully. He supposed he deserved it. Getting tipsy with Trudie probably hadn't been the most sensible way to begin his career at Anderby.

He could gladly have pulled the blankets over his head and had another hour in bed, but the barking of the dogs was becoming insistent and he could hear a mouse scratching in the walls. No, however delicate he felt, it was time to get up, to light the range and begin the process of making a new life – a sober, focussed life in which he'd make well-considered decisions.

Robert folded his shopping list into his pocket and set out towards the gatehouse. A pack of children, dressed as cowboys and angels, were playing a boisterous game of pursuit. They weren't exactly attired for the weather, but the boys cracked cap guns and the girls made un-angelic ululations, and all of this energetic chasing must be keeping them warm. Robert tried to smile pleasantly – he supposed they must be the children of families who lived on the Anderby estate – but all the shrieking and running around in circles didn't do much for his fragile head.

'Are you the gardener, mister?' one of the older girls asked in a bold voice. Her cheeks were flushed with running. She was perhaps about thirteen, he guessed, and though dressed in chaps and a Stetson, she held herself in a way that was unmistakably coquettish.

'Yes, my name is Robert. And you are?'

'I'm Kitty Carter-McKay. This is Erin and Unity and Ariel

and Tristan.' She wafted a shiny pistol at each of the children in turn. They'd stopped running around and all eyed him un-abashed. 'I live in the gatehouse with Nancy and Phyllis. My bedroom is up in the battlements. Did you like the Eccles cake?'

Kitty dipped her chin and looked at him from under her hat. It was the pose of a starlet on a cigarette card. Had she practised it in front of a mirror? Robert tried not to laugh.

'It was an excellent Eccles cake. Possibly the best I've ever had.' After drinking several Corpse Revivers with Trudie, he'd consumed the pie and the cake ravenously. He couldn't say he'd eaten with any great discernment, but the alcohol-absorbing pastry had been just the ticket. 'Who made it?'

'Phyllis. She's good at pastry. She says it's because she's got cold hands. But she let me sprinkle the sugar on top.' A smile of childish satisfaction briefly replaced the studied pout.

'Will you tell Phyllis thank you for me? I was very grateful.'

The girl nodded, serious-faced now. 'Is it true you won't let us play in the gardens any longer?'

Where had this come from? 'No. Of course you can play in the gardens. Why did you think that?'

'Because that's what Miss Faulkner said. She told us you'd have a cage and would lock us in it if we walk on the lawns. She said you'd growl at us, have big yellow teeth, like a donkey, and would call the police constable if you caught us climbing the trees.'

'I suspect she might have been teasing you.'

Kitty seemed to consider this. She twisted the toe of her boot in the snow and looked down to admire the effect. 'Miss Faulkner doesn't like you much, but you haven't got yellow teeth, or hair coming down your nostrils, and I don't think you're scary.'

Who was Miss Faulkner? How could he be so disliked by someone he hadn't yet met? And what was all of this about donkey teeth and nostril hair? 'Thank you. I'm glad to hear it.'

'She said you're a mistake. That was her word. I wasn't meant to be listening, but I overhead her saying that to Mr Molyneux.'

'Oh dear. She said that? I'd better prove to her that I'm not a mistake, then, hadn't I?' A *mistake*? What did that mean?

'Nancy says Miss Faulkner is sad because Dickie went away to London to do his boring plays. She thinks Miss Faulkner needs a new chap, that's what she told Phyllis, but Phyl says that's outmoded. I wasn't meant to overhear that either.' Kitty grinned and lifted her chin as if she was proud of her information-gathering skills. 'I'm not sure what outmoded means.'

'I'm probably not meant to hear that either!' Robert laughed. Did this child spend her life listening at doors? Evidently, he'd need to be mindful of her ears. 'Anyway, I must get on. Aren't you all cold? Go and get warm somewhere.' He felt chilled in his overcoat – how could these little ones not be perished in their angel costumes? Their legs looked quite blue.

'We're going to hunt for spooks in the attics and Mrs Fitz has promised to make us Ovaltine,' Kitty replied, her film-star face now forgotten.

'Enjoy yourselves. I hope you find some ghosts.'

They ran away towards the Hall, ghoulish moans mixing with the refreshed ululations.

The snow was beginning to thaw on the lane and water was making a chuckling sound as it ran in the ditches. The sun had finally parted the clouds and it illuminated silvered pastures and ploughed fields set hard. He paused to watch a mistle thrush taking the last of the berries from a holly bush and a pheasant flapped away from him, all bronze and purple and a sharp, croaking call. Robert found himself collecting details and descriptions that he wished he might share with Esther, but she'd told him he mustn't send her letters.

The rooftops of the village were mottled with lichen and gauzed with wood smoke, and he imagined rosy-cheeked families at contented firesides. Robert pictured them cutting into fresh cottage loaves for breakfast, shiny brown teapots steaming from their spouts and the old queen looking stern in mantelpiece prints. There was a quaint timelessness to the lace curtains and caged canaries at windows, and these interiors couldn't possibly contain misery or poverty, could they? Apart from the motor lorry delivering barrels of beer to the pub, he might well have stepped back into the last century – but a nice version of it that didn't have scurvy and rickets. The church was large for the size of the village and the graveyard looked densely packed. It seemed to be the sort of place where life revolved around the church, its spire like the fulcrum of a sundial; the sort of village where nothing much ever changed, where the cycles of the sun and the moon and seasons simply carried on turning, and the names and the faces stayed the same. There would be deference to the squire here, respect for the parson, failure to attend church would be noted, and every person's history would be known to their neighbours.

There was an almshouse in the village square, a set of stocks, an ancient stone cross and a flock of sheep was just departing across the cobbles. It might be a Hollywood film set of Olde England, and Robert was slightly surprised that the shepherd wasn't wearing a smock. Turning in the centre of the square, he noted a baker's shop, a butcher's, a general store and a smithy with a petrol pump outside. The shops were just pulling up their blinds, revealing jam tarts and iced buns, sausages and rolled roasts, Bovril, jars of boiled sweets and tinned peaches to tempt the morning trade. He was satisfied that he would be able to tick most of the items off his list as he approached W. J. Egerton & Sons, Grocery and Provisions. The dead blue-bottles in the window made him feel less embarrassed about having to ask for mouse traps.

There had been few people on the streets and it seemed the greater part of the populace of Little Didford was gath-ered behind the door of Egerton's grocers. A couple of the women had baskets on their arms, and were evidently there with purpose, but it appeared to be an establishment where the community passed the time of day. The shop bell rang out over Robert's head and faces turned to examine him.

'Good morning,' he said. He knew his voice would instantly betray him as not being from these parts, but he was mindful to be well-mannered in compensation.

The group at the counter divided, revealing the establish-ment's proprietors, he in a bow tie and apron and she in black bombazine and swinging jet earrings.

'Good day, sir,' said Mr Egerton (Robert assumed), in a voice that had a hint of unctuousness.

'And how may we be of service today?' put in his wife. She had the accent to play a dairy maid on the stage, but polished up at the edges.

Robert felt himself being closely scrutinized as he approached the counter. But the villagers nodded civilly and smiled, so

perhaps they would be a kind audience. He was reminded of
Kitty listening at doors. This, then, was the countryside.

'I need some basic provisions and cleaning products,' he
began, taking the list from his pocket. 'I've just moved into a
cottage and it needs a bit of freshening up.'

'Always good to have a clean start.' A woman in an
Astrakhan-trimmed coat sounded firm in her approval.

'Cleanliness next to godliness.' An elderly man with a nose
like Mr Punch nodded.

'If you'd like to hand over your list, sir, I'm sure we'll be able
to supply everything you require.'

As Mr Egerton took the list from Robert's hand, the onlook-
ers all seemed to bend towards it. 'Soap, washing soda, a good
firm scrubbing brush . . .' Robert found himself saying, as if he
need satisfy the curiosity of the village.

'Mouse traps,' Mr Egerton read aloud. Robert wished he
hadn't.

'Have you taken a cottage in the village?' Mrs Egerton asked.
'Is it old Mr Poulton's place up by the dairy?' Her earrings
glittered as they swung. 'A nice little cottage, ideal for a young
man, but in need of a bit of spit and polish, I imagine?'

'Beetle traps,' Mr Egerton pronounced.

'No, I'm up at Anderby Hall.'

Did he imagine the collective intake of breath? Suddenly the
eyes seemed to be examining him more intensely and shopping
baskets were held to chests.

'The Hall, eh?' said Mrs Egerton. 'We don't get them in
here often.'

'They don't tend to mix these days,' said a woman in a black
straw bonnet.

'Bottle of carbolic,' Mr Egerton read.

'I wouldn't have put you down as one of them,' Mrs Egerton went on. 'You don't look the type, if you don't mind me saying.'

Robert was uncertain as to whether he minded. 'The *type*?'

'Well, you know, they're a funny lot, aren't they? Men in need of a haircut, women in trousers, sandal-wearers, foreign-looking sorts.'

Robert felt his own attire being examined. He remembered Trudie talking about moral cesspits and tried not to smile.

'Ten tins of pilchards and a packet of Cream Crackers. Ten? Are you sure?' Mr Egerton frowned and clicked his tongue at Robert's list. 'Partial to a pilchard, are you?'

'I haven't met many people there yet, but Mr and Mrs Fitzgerald seem perfectly nice.' He'd thought Mrs Fitzgerald thoroughly nice. He was less certain about Teddy, but still . . .

'When we went to the fête there last year, one of 'em was wearing an evening dress and muddy great farmer's boots. Most peculiar, I call it.' Mr Punch shook his head.

'And what about the clothes they *don't* wear!' the old man who'd been chewing on his pipe added. He managed to look both horrified and delighted. 'Nudists, some of 'em are.'

'That's why they all have ten children! They're a loose lot. They all swaps their wives around, I hear.'

'And their children all have three eyes and five legs!'

Robert wondered: at this juncture, ought he to be defending the Greenfielders? Should he be denying these bizarre accusations? The children he'd just met all had the conventional number of eyes and legs. There couldn't be any truth in these stories, could there?

'We all go to that summer fête, because we like a look at 'em, see. The missus offers tours of the house at a shilling a time and it's better than a trip to the circus.'

'Or the zoo!' put in Astrakhan Coat.

'They had Balinese dancers there last year … least I think they was Balinese? All scampering about with their faces painted and barely a scrap on.'

'They've had Russians there too. One of 'em looked like that Lenin chap. There's always foreigners coming and going.'

'They had Germans there last year. And bold as brass, they were. My Percy had a word or two to say about that, I can tell you. It's not right, is it?'

'Aye, they're a rum lot up at the Hall. Didn't you say they was Bolsheviks, Matthew?'

'I hear they're communists,' said Black Bonnet.

'Some of them call themselves socialists, but Mrs Ampney at the post office says they've all got double-barrel names. And some of their parcels smell most peculiar, she reckons.'

'Course, they don't come to church.' Black Bonnet narrowed her eyes. 'Lady Margaret would be in the front pew every week, but Captain and Mrs Fitzgerald only show their faces at Christmas.'

'And the state of the gardens now! I bet Lady Margaret's spinning in her grave.' Astrakhan Coat shook her head. 'There used to be a good family lived up at Anderby before the war. Quality people. Real gentlefolk. Half the village worked in the Hall and on the estate, but she's sold off most of the farmland and the house isn't kept up like it was.'

'They talk about trying to be "self-sufficient".' Mrs Egerton made inverted commas with her fingers and a dubious face. 'It's one of their notions. Well, perhaps you can tell me, young man – do they grow their own tea leaves up there? I know full well they have orders from grocers in town.'

'They're more town types really, aren't they?' The expression on Black Bonnet's face suggested this wasn't a good thing. 'They have town ways.'

'The missus was forever handing pamphlets around in the early days,' Mr Punch put in, 'wanting people to go up there to listen to talks on this and that.'

'But folks hereabouts don't want talks! They want decent housing, secure jobs and trade to support the village.' Mrs Egerton dusted the top of her cash till with a sleeve.

'There's only Captain Fitzgerald spends any money in the village,' Mr Egerton observed, as he piled the groceries into Robert's basket. 'He passes it over the bar quite generously in the Lamb and Flag. Albert says he's civil enough; he sits there quiet with his racing paper, but he's not really one of them, is he?'

'Mind, I suppose it's her money he's spending, isn't it?'

'He's no fool. No flies on him. He knew what he was doing. I'm not sure I'd trust him if I were her.' Astrakhan Coat raised an eyebrow as she caveated: 'He likes the ladies, that one.'

'*Captain* Fitzgerald, indeed!' Mr Punch spluttered a laugh. 'If he was a captain, I'm the Queen of Sheba.'

Robert found himself apologizing as he took the basket of groceries from across the counter ... though he wasn't absolutely certain why he did so. He recalled how Trudie had spoken of Mrs Fitzgerald giving her fortune away to charitable causes and her own talk of fairness and collaboration – all of that was admirable, surely? – but he could also appreciate why the village might think the Greenfielders peculiar. It left him feeling torn between two tribes, not knowing where his allegiances should lie. As the shop bell rang over his head, he wondered what he'd got himself involved with.

He began by brushing the ceilings and the walls of the cottage, bringing down a rain of plaster dust along with the cobwebs. In so doing, he knocked the oil lamp swinging, and the dogs set off barking again next door. Soon the air was thick with lifted dust and it caught in his throat and made his eyes smart. Once it had settled, he could pull a broom across the floor and make a clear, crisp stripe. He wiped down all the furniture and the walls with soapy water, emptying bucket after bucket out in the back garden, and finally he could scrub the floor. Pulling out the bed, he found several dead spiders and a grasshopper, a sock and a silver cufflink by the skirting board. (Really, Miss Bentridge?) The vigorous work warmed him and he looked out at the snow thawing in the rear garden and made plans for lines of leeks, rhubarb and sweet peas.

With the cottage cleaned, Robert opened his suitcase. As he folded his clothes into the drawers and found a place for his books, he told himself that he had to make the best of this. Yes, the residents here might seem crackpot to the villagers, but he'd liked how Mrs Fitzgerald had called him by his first name and spoken to him as if he were her equal. He'd be earning eight shillings more per week than he had at Scarcroft and returning the gardens to order would give him a sense of satisfaction. Perhaps villages always gossiped and, as a member of staff here, he supposed he didn't necessarily have to choose a tribe. He'd just keep his head down and focus on his work, he resolved – and, Lord knows, there was enough of it to be getting on with.

But who was this Miss Faulkner, of whom Kitty had spoken, and why did she believe him to be 'a mistake'? Hadn't Mrs Fitzgerald alluded to some objection to the garden plans? He pictured Miss Faulkner as an elderly eccentric who enjoyed frightening children with silly stories. Well, if he had to charm the old dear, he would. Pushing his emptied suitcase under the bed, Robert decided that he would add winning over Miss Faulkner to his list of tasks. Although, at this present moment, he seemed to have a very long list of tasks ahead of him indeed.

Chapter Five

'Are you intent on persecuting him?' Daniel had asked her yesterday. 'Had we better warn him? Do you have a mission to drive him out?'

'Of course not!' Faye had replied. She'd known Daniel was teasing. 'What sort of monster persecutes gardeners? He's probably a wholesome son of the soil. He'll have earthy fingernails, pockets full of crumpled seed packets and will conduct conversations with robins. I don't bear the man any ill will; it's just the project I object to – as I'll explain to him when I meet him.'

When Faye had imagined meeting the gardener, she'd pictured him with grey hair, a woodbine dangling from his lower lip and a face etched by the weathers of many seasons. The man shovelling snow from her path was young, though, and going about his task with vigour. He'd already cleared Trudie's path, and his own, and was presently working his way towards her front door. Alerted by the rasp of the shovel against stone, she'd been watching him from the window for some minutes. As he glanced up now, she stepped back behind the curtain.

She might have felt more cruel opposing the employment of an elderly man, she mused, but this energetic youth could prove a more tenacious opponent. No, Faye corrected herself – it wasn't that she meant them to be *opponents*. She shouldn't think of it like that. It was considerate of him to clear the paths and she ought to take him a mug of tea out as thanks. She might not support the garden plans, but that didn't mean there had to be a personal enmity between them.

He looked up with an expression of surprise as her door opened. He'd evidently been absorbed in his own thoughts, and she in turn felt oddly wrong-footed as her eyes met his. He was perhaps in his early twenties (maybe a couple of years younger than herself?), tall and broad-shouldered, with dark eyes and hair the colour of Lyle's treacle escaping from under his cap. Faye couldn't help registering a similarity with Richard's physique and colouring, but the gardener was smiling, and Richard was too self-important to be caught with a grin on his face these days. This young man looked to be enjoying some private joke. Faye felt disconcerted by this and his appearance. He wasn't meant to look like this, was he?

'What?' she heard herself saying. 'What were you laughing at?'

'I'm sorry. Please forgive me.' He lowered his long eyelashes and seemed to be trying to suppress the smile. He wasn't succeeding. 'I'm not laughing at you, I promise. I was just recalling something I heard in the village earlier.'

His voice was warm and he had a self-effacing charm. Many a woman would envy him those eyelashes, Faye thought. She was irritated with herself that she was noticing these things and vexed with him for making her feel uncomfortable on her own doorstep.

'Did you get the story that we're all infidels and Marxists?'

'Amongst other things,' he replied. 'I seem to recall that

wife-swapping was mentioned too. Apparently, scandalous activities go on here. Is that true?'

He leaned on the handle of his shovel, pushed a comma of hair off his forehead, and gave her a lopsided grin. It was a handsome grin and Faye wondered if he was in the habit of using it on women.

'The village likes to talk, but sometimes we do give them reason to frown in our direction. Not that we are *those* things, you understand.'

'Really? I'm almost disappointed.'

He'd been sucking on a piece of liquorice. The scent of it was carried on his words, she could almost taste it, and the colour of it was staining his mouth. Faye told herself that she shouldn't look at his mouth. 'Anyway, thank you for this.' She nodded at the path. 'It's kind of you.'

'It's thawing now, but it might freeze again tonight.'

'Aren't your hands frozen? This wind is bitter. I was making tea and wondered if you'd want a cup? You can step inside, if you'd like. I promise you, I'm none of the things you heard in the village.'

With his north-country accent and his dark hair, she momentarily found herself recalling descriptions of Rochester and Heathcliff . . . but Faye chastised herself. What was she thinking?

She was wearing what looked to be an old sailor's duffel coat. It was too large for her and Robert wondered if it might belong to a boyfriend or a brother. She'd evidently slipped it on, intending to bring the tea out to him, and she took it off now. She was wearing slacks and a Guernsey underneath, made feminine with the polka-dot scarf tied at her neck.

It was warm inside her cottage, but Robert didn't feel he could take his own coat off without being asked. She didn't invite him to sit down either, so they stood awkwardly by the door as they drank their tea. Her cottage had the same layout as the one next door, but while Trudie lived in chaos, this room had a homely orderliness. Bookshelves lined two of the walls and there were seashells and fossils placed amongst her volumes. He had an urge to read the titles on the spines of the books and to tell her how he'd been teased at home for liking novels. There was a vase of winter honeysuckle on the table, he could faintly smell its scent, an armchair covered with a tartan blanket and she looked to have been occupied with a pile of papers. Something about this young woman, and being in her territory, made him feel clumsy and self-conscious.

'It's Mr Bardsley, isn't it?' she asked.

'That's right. I'm Robert.'

'Faye Faulkner. I'm pleased to meet you.'

'Ah, so *you're* the famous Miss Faulkner?'

She wasn't at all how he'd pictured her. He'd got it entirely wrong. She must be around his own age, and instead of steel-grey hair and a long-imprinted scowl, her fair hair curled softly around her face – and it was a rather lovely heart-shaped face. Her eyes were blue-grey and a blush was beginning to colour her cheeks. Her mouth was perhaps slightly too wide to be conventionally pretty and when she spoke he saw there was a small gap between her front teeth. It was an intelligent face, a face with character, and Robert realized he was probably staring at her. He felt an odd compulsion to reach out and touch the gap between her teeth.

'And what does that mean?' she asked with a note of caution.

'Kitty mentioned your name.' She had an educated voice, Robert discerned, but perhaps with a faint inflexion of the accent he'd heard in the village?

'Oh, heck!' She put a hand to her mouth. Her nails were cut short and neat, but there were stains of blue ink on her fingers. 'I dread to think what she said. Do be aware that Kitty loves to listen in to other people's conversations, but she doesn't always understand what she hears.'

'I gathered that. Do I need to be careful? Does she listen at everyone's door?'

'She might grow up to be a highly successful blackmailer.'

'Kitty told me about the child cage.'

'Me and my mouth!' She finally laughed, but then pressed her lips together. 'I must be more cautious about what I say in front of her. I am sorry.'

'She also told me you think I'm a mistake.'

Bloody Kitty, Faye thought. Why did she have to repeat that? He'd smiled as he said it – that annoyingly handsome smile – but she'd have to explain it to him now, wouldn't she?

'Did I use the word mistake? I clearly didn't express myself well – that, or Kitty might have edited my words into something more provocative. It wasn't a comment on you personally, of course. I'd not met you then, obviously, and knew nothing about you, but . . .' She was aware she was prevaricating. It really didn't help that he had that amused expression on his face.

'So it was blind prejudice, then? Oh, don't look like that! I'm only teasing. I will try my best not to take it personally.'

'It's the fact that Gwendoline wants to charge people to enter the gardens – that's my objection. In the past, the gates were always open to local people, and she used to make an effort to welcome them in, but we've become increasingly cut off in recent years and with this project we might as well have voted to dig a moat around the estate. I suspect the villagers already think we're a bit snooty and aloof and that opinion is only going to become more entrenched if our gates are locked against them.' Did he understand? She must make him see. 'Yes, I appreciate the gardens are a little run-down, but we all do our bit, we muddle along together, and it's adequate. Moreover, there are other things we ought to be focussing on just now. There's so much hardship in the local community at present, so much worry and real financial need. We should be trying to support our neighbours; we ought to be thinking about work schemes for the unemployed, allotments, pig clubs, food parcels. This isn't the time to be spending money on topiary and roses and charging people to see them. We ought to be building bridges, not putting up barriers. Do you not see?'

Oh dear. She'd made a speech at him, hadn't she? Faye kept telling herself to put the brakes on, but the words went on falling out of her mouth. She hadn't meant to lecture him, only ... He was still standing there with his eyebrows raised and his mouth curling up at the corners. Was he actually listening? She was beginning to feel exasperated by his invincibly charming smile.

Faye used her hands as she talked. She articulated with her ink-stained fingers and her eyes. Robert had found himself observing this and had slightly lost track of her words. She was speaking to him as if she was addressing a council meeting, but he heard the passion, sincerity and a note of apology in her

voice. The initiative might not do anything to improve relations with the village, he could understand her concern; that
said, wasn't it up to Mrs Fitzgerald how she spent her money?
She'd be the one paying his wages, not the Greenfields community. She'd been quite clear about that, hadn't she?

'Is there genuine distress here? I thought the village looked
quite prosperous, to be honest.' It certainly looked more prosperous than Lancashire. He'd left behind dole queues, soup
kitchens and factories going onto short time.

'You might not see it if you don't know the place, but it's
there behind closed doors, I assure you. Yes, we might not have
shipyards and mines closing, it's not headline-making stuff, but
agriculture has been hit hard. Prices were going down all last
year and farms are struggling to keep going. When they lay
men off they have to fall on the mercy of the Public Assistance
Committees and they can only give the bare minimum. Then
there's been foot-and-mouth disease here too. On some farms
they've been digging pits and burying their sheep. Can you
imagine how demoralizing that is?'

Her eyes were the blue of wild violets, he decided. For a
moment, he'd found himself recalling a scene in a novel where
a man fed strawberries to a woman with violet-coloured eyes,
observing her closely as he held them to her lips. He realized
he'd been watching Faye's mouth as she spoke and had to tell
himself to stop.

'It sounds heart-breaking. I pity them, I genuinely do, but
my employment isn't going to further depress agricultural prices
or make foot-and-mouth spread, is it? Forgive me, but I don't
see the connection.'

'It's the impression that charging for entry gives. What signal does it send if we start behaving like a stately home? Greenfields was meant to be all about making links, cooperating and communicating, not closed doors. Your employment is justified by the fact that this is intended to be a money-making scheme, it's a condition of that, so I had to vote against it. I'm sorry – it's not you – but I just can't support this project.'

'You'd have me sacked, then?' he said with teasing seriousness. She couldn't really do that, could she? 'You'd turn me out of the gates? Have me unemployed too? Would it change matters if I said I had a wife and ten children to support?'

He was making an exaggeratedly offended face at her now. Couldn't he be serious for a moment? He seemed determined to laugh at her. He didn't really have a wife and family, did he?

'I wouldn't have cleared your path if I'd known you're of a mind to drive me out,' he went on. 'And you probably shouldn't have made tea for me.' He returned the emptied cup to her hand. 'Ought we to begin again with more ill feeling?'

'Please understand me – I have no ill feeling for you personally—'

' – only in principle. Yes, you've said that. I do understand—'

' – but I believe it's an important point of principle.'

'Does everything go to votes here?' he asked.

'Most things; certainly every decision that impacts our communal life.'

'It must be peculiar to have to defer to a vote every time you want to spend a little of your own money.'

'Democracy is key to how this community works. We all have an equal say in decisions. Mrs Fitzgerald wanted it to be that way from the start and I respect her for that. I have the utmost admiration for what she set out to do here, but this feels like a misguided step. It's distasteful to be launching a project of this sort just now.'

'Distasteful? Crikey. So it's true you think I'm a mistake? You did say it?'

'Frankly, yes,' she conceded.

'Good Lord, I've never been called a mistake before.' He widened his eyes and blinked at her. 'It's rather wounding.'

'I felt it best to be straight with you from the start.'

'You have been. And the donkey teeth?' He covered his mouth with his hand. 'Should I take that to heart?'

She could see from his eyes that he was laughing behind his hand. Oh, damnation – why had she said that? 'I'm sorry. I got carried away.'

His hands looked strong and capable. They were obviously hard-working hands, calloused on the palms and the nails worn down. She found herself wanting to ask how he'd come by the wound on his thumb and the scar on his wrist, but ... why was she noticing these things?

'Didn't you just? Do you enjoy scaring small children?'

'Of course not. I'm a school teacher.' He looked to be ready-ing to leave and she gladly opened the door for him.

'Ah, that explains a lot. It all begins to make sense. Well, I would have liked this to be the start of a friendly acquaintance, but you'd probably prefer it to be short-lived, wouldn't you?' He bowed his head in mock chivalry. 'Hang on, there wasn't arsenic in that tea, was there? You didn't go in for the pre-emptive strike? That would be very unsporting.'

He looked back over his shoulder and grinned at her as he walked down the path. How perfectly exasperating he was!

Faye felt inclined to stamp her foot. She also found herself watching him out of the window again. It would have been so much simpler if he'd been an old man with a weathered face and donkey teeth. At this moment, she couldn't fathom how she was going to deal with Robert Bardsley. He was possibly the most vexing and confusing man she'd ever met.

Chapter Six

Robert walked over to the Hall with Trudie. She'd knocked on his door, offered her arm, and flashed a silver hipflask. She'd advised him he'd be in need of it by the time they'd sat through three hours of poultry sales, café takings and the traditional tussle over who should do what for the summer school.

'Do you have these meetings every week?' he asked. Trudie was wearing a red leather coat and lizard-skin shoes and looked dressed for an evening in a nightclub, not a residents' meeting.

'Without fail. You can choose not to attend, it's not absolutely obligatory, but our names are ticked off in the register and you lose points for lack of commitment.'

'Points? There's a system of points?'

Trudie squeezed his arm. 'I'm only joking, darling. But Gwen does like to have us all around the table if any decisions are being made. We're all expected to voice an opinion.'

Looking in through the windows of the Hall, seeing the richly coloured walls, the swags of the curtains and so many unfamiliar faces, Robert felt ill at ease. Earlier in the day, Mrs Fitzgerald had invited him to attend this meeting and told him that he should think of himself as a member of the community, not as staff. But how was that meant to work? Even approaching the house by the front door felt like a breach of appropriate behaviour – and what was he doing linking arms with Trudie? (Should he try to disentangle himself?) He'd always been taught to be mindful of his place, but what exactly did that mean here? Would he be required to voice opinions tonight?

'Don't take your coat off,' Trudie advised as they stepped into the entrance hall. 'They'll have lit the fire, but it's always like Siberia. Come on, follow me. We're in the dining room tonight.' Trudie led the way along a passageway lined with tall grandfather clocks, each of them telling a different time. 'A lot of these are Geoffrey Cooper and Gerald Wilson,' she said, wafting vaguely at a group of modern paintings. 'Do you know their work? They've both done residencies here. Of course, the house used to have a Canaletto, a pair of Landseers and a Zoffany of Charles James Fox. It's a shame they had to go, visitors like to see that sort of thing, but they paid for the guttering and the septic tank.'

It struck Robert as a curious trade, and not entirely complimentary to the artists – but, no doubt, practical. 'These new paintings are very interesting, though.'

'Ha!' Trudie barked over her shoulder. She had strands of large ebony beads around her neck tonight and they clanked against her décolletage when she was feeling emphatic. '*Interesting*? That invaluably diplomatic word. Dear boy, you must learn not to be so bloody polite!'

He couldn't help but pause at a table topped with a collection of framed photographs. Younger versions of Mr and Mrs Fitzgerald reclined on the decks of yachts, wore fur coats in skiing resorts and raised drinks to the camera on polo grounds. Various women looked serious in pearls, a young boy grinned with a fishing line and there was a rather mannered photograph of Mrs Fitzgerald holding long-stemmed Madonna lilies.

'Cecil,' said Trudie, picking up the frame. 'Beaton,' she added for Robert's benefit. 'He did me too when I was younger. He encouraged me to wear all my jewellery at once and surrounded me with mirrors, so I'm coming at you from all angles. Always that nod to surrealism, you know? I'm wearing black lipstick and white mascara. Daddy refused to pay for it because he said I looked like a ghoul!'

On the wall above, there were more images from amateur theatricals, conferences and recitals. The assembled Greenfielders were dressed as ancient Egyptians, Elizabethans and a Pierrot troupe. Robert recognized Mrs Fitzgerald playing Joan of Arc, in cardboard armour and bearing a pennant, and was that Trudie in the winged helmet?

'You often put on plays here?'

'Gwen adores her Shakespeare. It's compulsory. You'll be given a part, whether you want it or not. She's probably already pencilled you in as a swaggering young duke or an ill-fated lover.'

Robert's eyes travelled along the assembled casts. They all appeared to be having a jolly time. He found himself looking for Faye and then there she was, dressed like Peter Pan. Her face was whitened with heavy stage make-up and her eyes darkened, but her features were unmistakable. She was carefree and amused here, though. Laughter lit her face. Robert found himself wanting to know the sound of Faye's laughter.

'She makes a super principal boy, doesn't she?' Trudie had followed the line of his gaze. 'Good legs for stockings, deft swordplay and really very charismatic on the stage. She was a joy to be around that first year, so full of positivity and energy, but then Richard got itchy feet and she's been prickly since he left.'

Hadn't Kitty mentioned a Richard? Perhaps he'd been the owner of the duffel coat. Had he been and gone then? Was he not coming back? Robert didn't feel he could ask.

'Anyway, come on,' said Trudie. 'I can introduce you to a few faces before the meeting starts.'

The dining room had faded chintz and fine old plasterwork cornicing, moulded with pomegranates and winding vine leaves, but stained with rust and water marks. The walls were panelled in dark oak and there was an elaborate fireplace, carved with stiff Jacobean figures. Bowls of potpourri and orris root were positioned all around the room, giving off a musty scent but failing to mask the smell of damp. Robert really wasn't sure which to look at first – the décor or the equally curious-looking assembly of Greenfielders.

It seemed to be the convention that people kept their overcoats on, but there were many striking hats, scarves, make-up applications and an array of exotic facial hair. He wondered, did they have any sense of how local people viewed them? Did they even care? Robert found himself staring at a man in a green velvet suit and a woman in an elaborate turban, but the Greenfielders examined him too, in turn, and he felt conscious of their assessing eyes.

Two women appeared with trays bearing cups of tea and cocoa and slices of fruitcake, flanked by Mrs Fitzgerald in her sable coat, flourishing the meeting's agenda. She waved and smiled at Robert, but her thoughts were clearly focussed on the evening's business.

'Here, get it while it's hot, duck,' said the woman with the tray in a strong Cockney accent. 'She didn't let the tea brew long enough, she never does, but wrap your hands around the cup and it will warm them up.'

She had a cherry-red woollen hat pulled over bleached blonde hair, was wearing lipstick of a matching colour, and appeared to have khaki dungarees on underneath her squirrel coat. The cups were fine old porcelain, but every one of them was crazed with cracks.

'Nancy, meet Robert.' Trudie made the introduction and the woman's face split into a wide cherry-red grin. 'Nancy and Phyllis work the market garden and run the gatehouse café.'

'For goodness' sake, don't judge us by this fruitcake! It's stale, but Mrs Fitz can't abide waste. So you're the gardener, eh? About time too, I say! You must come over to the café. Phyl will love to talk with you about the garden.'

'I need to thank you for the pie and the Eccles cake,' he said. 'It was very welcome.'

'I plied the boy with booze on his first night!' Trudie laughed and squeezed him around the shoulders. 'He left me muttering about needing pastry.'

'Well, I'm glad if it did the trick.'

Teddy was following the women with the trays, carrying a bottle of brandy and adding measures to cups. As Nancy moved on, Robert saw him put his arm around her waist. He whispered something into her ear and she tilted her chin back as she laughed. Robert recalled a voice in the village shop observing that Teddy liked the ladies.

'And this is Daniel,' Trudie said, taking the elbow of a man in a Homburg hat. 'Dear Daniel has been at Anderby longer than any of us.'

The man turned, smiled and took off his hat. He was greying at the temples, but had a broad, handsome face. The creases around his eyes suggested good humour. It was difficult not to notice the conspicuous burn scar on his right cheek, though. Robert tried to focus on his eyes and not on the scar.

'Ah, you must be our Mr Bardsley, yes?' He offered his hand. 'I'm so pleased to finally meet you.'

'Daniel is a composer, Robert,' Trudie said. 'There was a performance of his *Elizabethan Song Cycle* in Gloucester Cathedral just before Christmas. It was all lit by candlelight and totally enchanting.'

'Composer is a heavy word; it's a lot to live up to. To be truthful, I spend most of my working life listening to the school children making excruciating noises on recorders.'

'Nonsense! You are far too modest,' Trudie chastised. 'He's writing an epic choral piece about the war. Isn't there a plan to have it performed in Ypres?'

'If I ever finish the thing! I've also written some shamefully sentimental drawing-room stuff.' He gritted his teeth. 'But you must forgive me – I can see Gwendoline flapping papers mean-ingfully in my direction. I hope we'll have chance to speak again soon.' He touched his hat as he departed.

Daniel had set poems by Hardy, Yeats and Keats to music, Trudie informed Robert, his *Gloucestershire Rhapsody* had been broadcast on the BBC and a piece called *Mametz Wood* had reduced the audience to tears when it had been performed as part of a music festival the previous autumn. Robert decided Daniel's scar must be a war wound received during some act of great valour.

'Robert, you should meet Maurice,' Trudie was saying now

and a man in a moleskin coat was scrutinizing his face. 'Maurice runs the pottery and is our unofficial resident historian. He knows everything about Anderby. If you have any questions, he's the man to ask.'

'The house was built by the de Villiers,' Maurice said. 'One of our oldest families. They came over with Guillaume le Conquérant, you know.' He glanced at Mrs Fitzgerald with a look that suggested he found her pedigree decidedly inferior.

'How interesting,' said Robert. Trudie winked at him over Maurice's shoulder. 'It was fortunate that Mrs Fitzgerald wanted to save the house, wasn't it? She clearly has a great respect for its history.'

'Would you say so?' Maurice hoisted a whiskery eyebrow. He had a red, weathered face, as if he might be out in all climates, or have a weakness for whisky. 'Personally, I've always thought it a pity it wasn't acquired by a historical trust. Of course, she's never had the funds for a major programme of renovations. Had she the means, it might have been different. We might have witnessed some horrors!' He'd lowered his voice, but not enough. 'Her father was trade, you know. He made his money from engine parts and then, like all of them, it was armaments during the war . . .'

Faye had entered the room, Robert noticed over Maurice's shoulder. She was wearing a jade green coat with an oversized collar and a fetching matching hat. She was talking with Daniel now and her hand was on his shoulder. Robert wished he might be the one talking with Faye and not stuck here listening to Maurice's insinuations.

Mrs Fitzgerald finally tapped a pen to a glass to indicate the meeting underway. Daniel cleared his throat to ensure she'd been heeded and the Greenfielders took chairs at the table. A Mr Ingram, evidently the tenant farmer, took up the first twenty minutes of the meeting with his thoughts on drainage ditches. He had impressive side-whiskers and a thick Gloucestershire accent, seeming to roll his words around his teeth. Nancy gave a report on the weekly takings of the gate-house café and a market stall and apologized, once again, for the cake. Daniel spoke about the egg yields of chickens, royalties earned from the performance of a piano sonata and a plan to teach the school children Esperanto. Trudie informed the group she'd sold five bracelets to a Sylvia Higham-Hughes and Maurice went to great lengths detailing his experiments with a new ceramic glaze, which hadn't been a success.

There were meeting points about a forthcoming textiles exhibition, a spiritual study circle and a concert of Finnish folk music. The group then went on to debate wheat growing in Italy, farming schools in Czechoslovakia, the causes of famine in Russia and the likelihood of an election in Germany in the spring. Mr Underhill had encouraged Robert to borrow books from the library at Scarcroft, and not just to read novels, but to broaden his mind with histories and biographies. Friends had laughed at him for carrying a book in his pocket, had jokingly called him an intellectual, but he felt conspicuously ignorant in this company. There were so many unfamiliar words, foreign names and incomprehensible statistics. Unable to follow the arguments, he found himself contemplating the painted ceiling and how dusty the tabletop was, but then Mrs Fitzgerald was on her feet and saying his name.

'Many of you will have met Robert this evening, but for those of you who haven't, let me introduce the newest member of our community. Please, Robert, do stand.' She gestured to him to rise. 'I'd like to propose that we set aside some time in our next meeting to discuss a budget for the work on the gardens. I would like to allocate a fund for garden sundries, plants, tools, chemicals, etcetera, all such as Robert will require for his work. I assume nobody would object to me putting that on the agenda for next Sunday?'

Mrs Fitzgerald bowed her head towards Robert. He felt very self-conscious standing there with the eyes of the room upon him. All his working life he'd been taught to be unobtrusive and it was thoroughly disconcerting to be the centre of attention like this. It was only as he was sitting down again that he noticed Faye's raised hand. Mrs Fitzgerald invited her to speak.

'It's for next week, I suppose, rather than now,' Faye began, 'but I would like to remind the group of the objections I raised when we last debated the garden restoration plan. I have spoken with Mr Bardsley this week, and outlined my concerns, so I hope he won't feel any embarrassment. I believe my reasons for opposing the project are still valid and I'd like us to make time to discuss this more fully at the next meeting.'

She nodded to him before she resumed her seat. His eyes connected with hers and, while there wasn't hostility in her expression, there was also no warmth. Mrs Fitzgerald was wrapping up the meeting now, but Robert wasn't listening to her words; all he could hear was Faye's voice saying 'opposing', 'objection' and 'a mistake'.

With the meeting concluded, chairs were pulled towards the fire and the bottle of brandy did a second tour. Phyllis (attired similarly to Nancy, but with dark hair, sharper features and a north-eastern accent) asked if Robert would be clipping the topiary teapot back into shape and he was introduced to a Mr Dunstan and his wife, who were making hand-beaten pewter dinnerware somewhere on the estate. He shook the hand of a Mr Phillips, who was presently sleeping in a tent as he wanted to 'be at one with nature' ('In this weather?' 'I spent several years living in a cave in Tibet'), a Miss Parget, who produced hand-printed silk and taught expressive dance to the school children, and a Lionel Massingham, who tried to sell him some of his fruitwood candlesticks. Everyone was perfectly welcoming to him, and Robert listened politely in return, but his eyes were following Faye around the room. He watched her speaking with Mrs Fitzgerald, with Maurice and with Nancy. From time to time she glanced towards him too. Then, when he looked around the room again, she'd gone.

Robert made his exit with Trudie. A number of people had now gathered on the corridor and were passing a bottle of whisky around.

'There'll be another battle in the garden war, then?' The man speaking was wearing a black roll-neck jumper and had a gold hoop earring, like a pirate. 'I hoped we'd heard the end of it, but she's evidently determined not to let the thing die.'

'Robert, meet Cecil and Iris Cardew,' Trudie said, indicating the speaker and the woman at his side. 'You might know Cecil by reputation. Didn't the newspapers like to call you an *enfant terrible* of the art world at one time?'

'How do you do?' After this evening, Robert felt conspicuously lacking in knowledge of the art world, of politics and plays. 'The *garden war*?'

'It's a polite war, all very nicely mannered, but neither of them will back down.' He spoke in an unnecessarily loud voice with a faint East London accent. 'We've had months of these meeting points already. If you ask me, it would be to everyone's benefit if we could lock Gwen and Faye in a room together until they've fought it out. Must we hear it week after week? That said, it was amusing when Faye slipped the knife in. Ouch! Your face was a picture.'

Robert felt himself colouring. He'd tried not to show a reaction to Faye's words, but had evidently failed.

'You know it has to be this way,' Cecil's wife replied. 'It's a matter for the trust, so it has to be brought to the meetings.' While her husband boomed, filling the corridor with his presence, Iris Cardew spoke in a small, precise voice. 'Don't worry about Faye,' she added, turning to Robert. 'She just feels the need to make her point.'

'And keep on making it, week after week, month after month? I never thought I'd say it, but I'm starting to miss her lectures about work schemes for the unemployed.'

'Lectures isn't a nice word, Cecil.'

'Is harangue any nicer? Or how about preach?' He turned away from his wife. 'I pity you, Bardsley. I wouldn't want to be in your shoes. Our worthy schoolmistress can be like a dog with a rat and she's sunk her teeth deep into this one.'

Trudie's electric torch lit the way as they stepped out. Robert could hear children running around in the darkness beyond. Shouldn't they be in bed at this hour? Was someone supervising them? But then the children at Greenfields seemed to live a semi-feral existence. Did that say something about Faye's abilities as a schoolmistress?

'You always do the meeting notes?' he asked. Given the

disarray in her domestic arrangements, it had surprised him to learn that Trudie was the secretary of these gatherings.

'To be quite honest, nobody else wants to do it. It was Teddy's job briefly, but it wasn't his forte. It would take him a week to type the notes up and they were always such a mess. His spelling is appalling! I don't know where he went to school. He does the estate accounts these days. Numbers are more his thing.'

'Teddy does the accounts?' His role at the meeting hadn't seemed to extend beyond the filling of glasses.

'Don't be fooled.' Robert heard a smile in Trudie's voice. 'He's canny when it comes to money. Can I tempt you with vermouth?'

'Thanks, but I'd better keep a clear head for tomorrow.'

'Don't take Faye's objections to heart.' Trudie leaned on her gate. 'The rest of us supported the garden scheme and there's no danger Gwen will have second thoughts. Not that there'll be a large budget, you understand, but I'm sure Gwen has already explained that to you. Sit tight, let Faye say her piece, and it will all blow over soon enough.'

'Will it? I hope you're right. Everyone keeps telling me not to take it personally, but it's difficult not to feel a little touchy.'

'Just ride it out, darling. You have nothing to worry about.'

He felt Trudie's fingers squeezing his hand.

After the noise and crowd of the Hall, it seemed quiet, still and cold inside his cottage. Robert was almost glad to hear the barking of the dogs next door and then Trudie swearing at them. The light flickered against the walls as he lit the oil lamp and he thought about the look Faye had given him after she'd spoken. Was it disappointment he'd felt? Was it rejection?

He'd enjoyed talking with Faye yesterday. It had amused him
to tease her a little and he'd sensed she'd felt the same attraction
that he did. But had he misinterpreted? Could he have offended
her inadvertently? He imagined her in her neat sitting room
two walls away now and wanted to go and bang on her door
and tell her that he needed this job. But, of course, he couldn't
do that. Was she really determined to have him dismissed? Had
he made that worse? She'd said yesterday that there was nothing
personal in her objections, but ... was he wrong to sense that
might have changed?

Chapter Seven

Robert held the photograph of Esther close to his face. She was swinging on a cardboard crescent moon, which ought to have made it a whimsical composition, but she was frowning slightly at the camera. She'd had it taken in a photographer's studio in Southport, he recalled, and looked very young in it, her newly shingled hair falling to her narrow shoulders. He remembered the scent of Esther's hair and how that frown could so quickly become a smile. He didn't expect that he'd ever see her smile again.

Whatever the complications, there'd been an understanding between him and Esther. Robert knew how he should be with her, and how she would respond. They spoke to each other with their eyes and she often seemed to be able to anticipate his next word. Amongst these new people, he felt he constantly had to be considering the impression he was making. He had to work hard to understand them and not have them misunderstand him. It was like learning a new language and he knew he'd already made mistakes. Sensing a spark of mutual attraction with Faye had definitely been a mistake.

Robert was returning Esther's photograph to his wallet as he heard a knock on the door. He turned in his chair, about to call 'One moment!' to his visitor, when the handle rotated and Teddy's face appeared. He was wearing a woollen overcoat and a cloth cap, pulled down rakishly over one eye. The room darkened as he stood in the doorway.

'How are you settling in, Bardsley?'

It was an innocent enough question, but Teddy pronounced his name as if it amused him. He'd stepped inside now, had picked one of Robert's books from the shelf, and was turning it in his hands. This cottage was his property, Robert supposed, but did Teddy have a right to examine his possessions like that?

'I'm finding my feet, thank you, Mr Fitzgerald. Is Mrs Fitzgerald ready to start? I'm not late, am I?' He looked at his watch and saw that he wasn't. 'I'm coming now.'

'Dropped the "sir", have we? Pity. I rather liked that. Yes, Gwen has just gone out to the garden. Did I catch you mooning at a photograph? Let's have a gander. Do you have a sweetheart back at home?'

There was a grin on Teddy's face, but Robert wasn't sure it was a nice grin. A gold tooth glinted towards the back of his mouth and he looked Robert up and down. Had he been watching him through the window?

'It's only a photograph of a friend.' He mustn't talk about Esther here and he certainly didn't mean to do so with Teddy.

'No special girl, then? It surprises me you don't have some pretty little thing. Still, there's plenty to choose from around here. Old Trudes isn't past it, not by any means, and have you met the fair Faye yet? Oh, but, of course, you have!' He laughed. 'Have you had a run-in already? I should have guessed. You'll have to put some work in there, Robbie lad. Yes, she can be sanctimonious and a busybody, but she's very easy on the eye. You've noticed, haven't you? Yes, I see you have.' He adjusted the angle of his cap and smiled with one side of his mouth. 'Faye is like a young filly, all glossy and skittish. Needs a bit of breaking in, you know?'

Teddy shouldn't talk about her like that, should he? His cigarette dangled from his lower lip and there was something both insouciant and challenging in the way he leaned in the doorway.

'Can I help you with something?' Robert asked. 'Is there something you required?' He tried to sound civil, but he didn't want Teddy to linger.

'It was only to tell you that Gwen will meet you in the parterre.' He tossed the book aside.

'I'm coming now.'

'Good lad.' Teddy's eyes toured his face. He held Robert's gaze longer than was polite. 'You don't have to try so hard, you know? I see you going all out to impress Gwen, don't think I haven't noticed, but do remember you're only here to dig the gardens.'

Was Teddy warning him to stay off his territory, meaning to assert his higher rank, or did he simply mean to provoke him? Robert remembered that he'd voiced doubts about whether opening the gardens could be profitable. Like Faye, would he rather this project wasn't going ahead? 'Of course, Mr Fitzgerald. I understand.'

'Just think on, eh?'

'I shouldn't detain you. I'm sure you have a busy day planned, sir.'

'Right so. I have a date at the races, a mare that I've had my eye on for some time. I do like a win and I feel it in my bones that I might get lucky today.' He took a large gold pocket watch from his waistcoat, tapped the glass and rocked on his toes. 'Run along now, Robbie lad.'

Robert stood at the door and watched him walking away. He felt inclined to keep his door locked against Teddy, but that was pointless. If he wanted to come in here, how could he stop him? But he made a mental note to keep Esther's photograph out of range of his prying hands.

Robert had done some exploring of the estate over the past few days, pushing ajar the doors of barns that proved to be stacked with old furniture or rotting hay bales. There were yards full of mangled rabbit hutches, hen houses and farm equipment that didn't appear to have moved for decades. A Nissen hut was crammed with what looked to be old stage sets, jumps for an equestrian event and an Austin Seven with flat tyres. Forcing doors, and putting his eye to grimed windows, he'd eventually found the shed where the garden tools were kept. There were some tools fixed to the walls, but a great many more had been discarded on the ground and everything was rusted. Was that what Faye called muddling along?

'You look lost in reverie,' Mrs Fitzgerald said as he approached. She was wearing a purple velvet frock coat today. It looked as if it might once have been expensive, but it had gone shiny on the elbows and there were tears in the lining fabric, Robert could see.

'Do I? I was lost in my thoughts. I've been making a list of tasks, and trying to assign priorities, and as I look around I keep seeing items I must add.'

'I should imagine it's a long list.' Her smile was slightly apologetic.

'It is. But it will all be ticked off in time.'

'I'm concerned about the roses.' She narrowed her eyes as she looked up at the façade of the Hall. 'They were planted by the de Villiers at the end of the Civil Wars, the red rose of Lancaster and the white rose of York, and the intention was that they should arc together. Like a peace declaration, do you see? Only they've flowered very poorly for the past few years. I would feel ashamed if they expired on my watch. Imagine if they died of neglect after all of those centuries! Could you bring them back to health, do you think?'

Robert's eyes assessed the roses. They were leggy, full of hips and blackspot, and might well already be dying. It would be a significant achievement if he could revive them. In his mind they sprung into glossy leaf and abundant blossom, the red and white flowers mingling together, and shillings rang into a tin as the fee-paying public nodded approval. 'I will try my best for you.'

'I trust your judgement and your skill.' Mrs Fitzgerald put a hand to his arm.

They followed a well-worn stone pathway between a parterre of square beds enclosed by unkempt boxwood. The beds had evidently been planted with designs, but were now overgrown with brambles, rank nettles and creeping thistles. Everything was brown, waterlogged and flattened after the snow.

'There used to be designs of hearts, diamonds, stars and lovers' knots.' Mrs Fitzgerald indicated vague shapes with her hands. 'We have a wealth of plans and sketches and photographs in the archive. Lady Maxwell, who lived here before the war, was a plant hunter of some renown. Perhaps you know her name? There's a variety of wood spurge named after her.

I understand some botanists use the colloquial name "Lady Margaret's Bonnet" because she had to hide it under her hat to smuggle it through customs. Isn't that charming? But I can sometimes sense her presence in the garden and she's muttering and tutting at me – I need you to spare me Lady Margaret's wrath!' Robert glanced at Mrs Fitzgerald and saw she was smiling. 'Faye talks of me making it like the garden of a stately home, but that's not my intention; I'm not requiring you to redesign the gardens, to win horticultural prizes, or to have journalists flocking in to write articles. I just want it to look cared for again and to be able to generate some income.'

'I understand,' Robert said.

'I believe you've spoken with Faye and she's explained why she objects to the plans?'

'She has.'

'I appreciate why she feels the way she does, and I am sensitive to the impression this project gives – I know there's an opinion that we've become too detached from the village and Faye fears that charging for entry will cut us off all the more. But I'm afraid we must always be thinking of ways to bring money in. That isn't a choice – it's a necessity. I hope we'll be able to retain you on a long-term basis, Robert, but I shan't be profligate in what I spend on the garden. I can't be. I have to warn you of that. The budget will be modest, it won't stretch to major replanting, and this project needs to generate a profit. I hope that doesn't disappoint you too much?'

'There's a lot of structure to work with,' he replied, feeling rather disappointed, but wanting to sound constructive. 'The bones of the garden are good and I can build up stock from seed and cuttings. I can work to a budget.'

'I'm relieved you understand.'

Beyond the parterre garden, they passed through a yew hedge into a space that had evidently been planted more recently with informal mixed borders of daphnes, irises and artemisia, a quince tree and lilacs.

'This is the white garden,' Mrs Fitzgerald said.

Robert had noticed there were a lot of salvaged architectural elements within the garden, stone pineapples and finials, lead troughs and a church font. There were statues too; they'd passed a curiously smiling stone unicorn a moment ago and a man in a tricorne hat, his bronze face stained green, but the sculpture at the centre of this garden looked more modern. It was a limestone figure of a naked youth, crouched on a plinth, with his arms clenched tightly around his knees. Robert found himself circling the statue, trying to discern whether it was meant to convey comfort or despair.

'It's one of Cecil's,' Mrs Fitzgerald eventually said. 'Anderby was a military hospital during the war and it's in remembrance of the men who were here at that time. It's also a memorial to my brother. Cecil carved it using photographs of Hugh.'

Robert thought about the portrait he'd seen on the day he first arrived at Anderby, the young American with the shiny hair and the confident smile. He felt he ought to tread carefully here. If this was a representation of the brother who had sent Mrs Fitzgerald poems, what did this statue say about him?

'Your brother was in France?'

'He was and still is. He's in the American cemetery in Romagne-sous-Montfaucon.'

'I'm sorry.'

Mrs Fitzgerald put her hand to the knee of the statue. 'Hugh

did some of his training in Gloucestershire. He loved it here and
wrote to our parents saying he meant to move to England after
the war and become a sheep farmer. My father exploded at that!'
She shook her head, but she was smiling. 'My parents wanted
his body shipped home at the end of the war. They made plans
for him to be interred in the family mausoleum, but I didn't like
the idea of him being dug up again. It didn't seem nice. It didn't
seem right – do you understand? I told my mother we ought
to let him rest in peace. Relations had been strained between
my parents and I for some time and we eventually ended up
not speaking at all. But they've both passed away in the years
since and Hughie is still there in France. I've been to visit him
several times. I filled a jam jar with soil from his grave and it's
in the foundations under the statue here. I feel a connection
through that, as if I've got part of him here with me in this
garden. I often sit on the bench there and have a conversation
with him. You mustn't mind if you see me. He was a dear boy,
my brother.' Her long fingers played with her gloves. 'He was
a sensitive soul. We were close.'

Robert looked at the statue and wondered what sort of a
man this Hugh was. No one in the family would have wanted
to erect a statue to his father after the war, but then he'd never
been the sort of man who might write poems. Nobody would
have called him a sensitive soul.

They walked on and dew glittered on cobwebs and the sun
picked out scrolls of bronzed brackens. Robert could smell moss
and mint and the peppery tobacco scent of the fallen leaves,
undercut with something sweetly rotten. The stone path along
which they progressed was worn by the passage of centuries of
feet. Robert thought of the people who had walked through

this garden before him, who had pruned its roses, breathed these same scents and paused to hear this same birdsong. Long linked chains of lives had passed within these walls and the garden seemed to be full of echoes of them.

Stepping through a stone archway, they entered the topiary garden. The hedges were all stem and stalk and gnarled old wood, their form and contours lost. Robert thought he could perhaps make out birds and spirals and pinnacles, their outlines casting curious shadows in the winter sunlight, but everything had long since grown out of shape.

'They began planting it in 1695,' Mrs Fitzgerald said. 'All that time ago – and look at the state of it now! It was designed by a Monsieur Caron. He'd previously worked for James II at Hampton Court and had been a student of André Le Nôtre, who designed the gardens at Versailles. Imagine, Robert! What a sight it must have been.'

To get this garden back into shape would be an enormous task, on a larger scale than anything he'd taken on before and with the complication of all that once-upon-a-time prestige. Robert asked himself again: was he up to this?

'I feel a sense of responsibility,' he admitted, 'and a weight of history on my shoulders, but it would be an honour to work on this.'

'I know you won't be able to perform instant miracles, Robert, but I hope you'll be here for a while and that you'll find your own rewards in the work.'

Robert surveyed the garden ahead and pictured it in tighter shapes and sharper lines. He'd give this task his energy and commitment and prove to Mrs Fitzgerald that he was the right man for the job. She had put faith in him and he wanted to repay her for that. He understood why Faye and Teddy had their doubts about this project, but he was now determined to prove them wrong.

'I want to make this a success for you,' he replied.

Chapter Eight

'I thought I heard music,' the young man said. 'I'm sorry, I don't mean to disturb you, but is that a cello?'

'I like to play here sometimes. It's probably rather eccentric of me.' Daniel smiled in reply to Robert's observation. 'I'd pretend it encourages the trees to blossom, but for all I know the roots might be screaming for mercy.'

Teddy had been walking the perimeter of the orchard as Daniel had stepped through the gate, and he'd looked at him and his cello with barely concealed contempt. Daniel rarely saw Teddy in the gardens or the orchard, he took a minimal interest in them, and so it had surprised him to happen upon him here. What had he been doing? Why had he seemed to be pacing? He'd departed without speaking, giving Daniel the merest acknowledgement. It struck him, not for the first time, that Teddy could be quite ill-mannered.

'It sounded beautiful.' Robert was speaking and Daniel refocussed. 'If I were an apple tree, I'd push out appreciative blossom.'

'That might be one of the better compliments I've received.' Daniel put the cello aside and invited Robert to join him on the bench. 'Has Gwendoline been giving you the formal tour?'

He'd heard their voices. He knew Gwen would have shown Robert the white garden and wondered how much she'd told him.

'We've been planning the programme of work. There's an enormous amount to do, but I'm excited to be starting it.'

Daniel took the chance to look at Robert as he settled beside him and lit a cigarette. His dark hair was shiny and his skin had the glow of youth. He looked supremely healthy, strong and energetic, like he might live on bread spread with honey and gulp down pints of milk.

'She's shown you where to find the garden tools?'

'Yes, I was on my way around to the back when I heard the music. I'm getting organized today and I'll begin work tomorrow. I'll have to do a lot of clearing and cutting back for a start.'

'If you need any assistance, any heavy lifting or help with ladders, you will say, won't you?'

'I will. I'll remember that. Thank you. They're cider apples, aren't they?'

Daniel watched Robert looking around the orchard. The winter sunlight brought out the gnarled textures of the old tree trunks and the hand-like spans of the top branches seemed to cradle the sky.

'There's a press in one of the barns,' he said. He took his pipe from his pocket and began to fill it. 'We've tried to sell the cider commercially, but there's no market for it locally. All the farms here make their own. We do drink it ourselves, though, and I'm afraid you will get recruited for the harvest in October. It's all hands on deck when we begin gathering up the apples.'

'Good. I'd like that. I think I can smell the cider.'

Daniel breathed with Robert, pulling the spicy, musky scent

of the rotting leaves and mottled piles of fruit deep into his lungs. The branches were thickly encrusted with lichen, all shades of olive and emerald green and silver in the sunlight. The sheep were grazing beneath the trees towards the back of the orchard and the chickens pecked, each bird tilting into its own shadow. The only sound was the working of the sheep's jaws, the occasional bleat of an early lamb and, now and then, the cawing of the crows.

'In previous years we've done a wassailing on Twelfth Night, but it seems to have slipped by this time.' Gwen normally organized it, she delighted in the old folk traditions, but she hadn't mentioned it this year. Daniel knew she had a lot of other things on her mind, and so he hadn't liked to bring it up. 'Some of these trees are very old. They need a little encouragement.'

Some of them were bent over almost entirely, their trunks twisted and split, but their branches still produced green leaves each spring. That always felt to be a minor miracle.

'You've given them your music today.'

'But they enjoy a bit of cidery carousing.'

Robert was polite and well-spoken for a gardener, Daniel thought. He imagined he might have had a mother who was keen on good manners.

'Trudie said you've been here a long time?'

'Nearly fifteen years now. Anderby was a hospital back then.' Should he tell Robert what sort of a hospital it had been?

'You came here as a patient?'

Daniel heard a hesitancy in his question. 'I did.'

'My father ended up in hospital with gas poisoning. It ended his war, but he died of pneumonia two years later. I was very young when he went away, so he was a stranger to me when he came back. I just remember the house being full of the sound of this strange man coughing. It was a horrible cough. It sounded as if he was drowning sometimes.'

'I'm sorry,' Daniel said. In 1918, Anderby had been full of men who were strangers to themselves, who jerked and had fits and tried to drown themselves in the lake, but Robert perhaps didn't need to know that.

'And you decided to stay on here after the war?'

'I never found a good enough reason to leave.'

He could have returned to teaching at the choristers' school, they would have taken him back, but he'd still had the shakes and nightmares from time to time and boys can be merciless. Instead, he'd lingered on at Anderby – no longer a patient, not quite an employee – helping with the dismantling of the wards and the clearing out of the medical staff. Mr Hobson had said he could stay on in the cottage until the sale of the estate had gone through. By the time Gwendoline Hirsch arrived, he had twenty hens, was earning some royalties from his *Five Preludes*, and playing the wheezing organ in All Saints on Sundays. 'Of course, you must stay,' Gwen had said.

'Kestrel, do you see?' Robert pointed. They watched the bird hover and then plunge.

How old was Robert? Perhaps twenty? Maybe slightly older? At his age, Daniel had been full of ambition and had no comprehension that a war would come along and change the direction of his life. He sincerely hoped Robert's generation might escape that. It was obscene to him that vital young men like this might ever be put through that again. He'd begun following the news of the Geneva Disarmament Conference with optimism, but in recent weeks the negotiations had seemed to be getting entangled in complexities. The will was there, though, wasn't it?

'Gwendoline moved to Europe after the war. She wanted a new start, to begin again, to do things better. I suppose you could call her an idealist.' Daniel smiled. 'It's no bad thing, a little idealism.'

He'd spotted one of Gwen's hairpins on the path as he'd walked across the garden and had picked it up. She was always shedding hairpins. They glittered to the ground as she crossed rooms and found their way between floorboards and under cushions. Daniel was inclined to pick them up, so they also turned up in vases and bowls all over his house. He gripped the pin in his pocket now.

In the first few months of Gwen's reign at Anderby (funny, but Daniel always thought of it as a *reign*), she'd taken to calling him her 'trusty lieutenant'. He'd helped her to make a suite of rooms habitable in the house, hefting furniture for her, painting ceilings and repairing window frames. She'd often invited him to stay for dinner – there were still staff and Mrs Forbes managing the kitchen back then (famed for her crab apple jelly and her gooseberry tart) – and, in the evenings, they'd sat by the fire together, Gwen speaking of her plans for the estate. She'd told him how she wanted to make Anderby a model of collaborative communal living, a place where people might enjoy fulfilling lives, and the next generation could be educated to have respect and understanding for their fellow man. Though Daniel had thought her a bit unworldly at first, her earnestness was endearing and he had an empathy for the background that had driven these ambitions. Moreover, Gwen had seemed to assume he would remain here and be her helpmate in this venture.

When Teddy Fitzgerald had come on to the scene, Daniel had felt as if he'd been robbed of that future; a treasure was being taken from him before he'd quite held it firmly in his hands. He'd cautioned Gwen at first, had wanted her to question the story about Teddy serving alongside her brother in France. He'd urged her to verify that he was who he claimed to be and had asked if Hugh had mentioned Teddy's name in his letters. But then he'd recognized the look on her face and knew she'd already made a choice. What could Daniel do then? What could he say? He couldn't compete with Teddy's youth and looks and confidence of manner. Why would a woman like Gwen want a man who stammered and was so obviously marked by the war?

'Is Greenfields a utopia?' Robert asked.

'That's a strong word.' Daniel had to smile at the way Robert frowned as he asked the question. 'Gwendoline felt that we had to learn lessons from the war, that we all needed to adjust our actions and our mind-set to ensure it could never happen again. We couldn't return to the old ways. Anderby was set up as an example of how people might live with consideration for one another and the land. We all had to put in our hours of physical labour back at the start, working to make the properties habitable and on the farm. We cooked and ate together, made our own bread, and insisted on helping with ploughing the fields and milking the cows ... Well, I say "help", but we might actually have been more of a hindrance, I fear. Mr Ingram runs the estate farm, his family have been here for generations, and they obviously thought us highly eccentric when we first arrived. He possibly still does to a degree.' Daniel tapped his pipe out against the bench. 'Everything was shared in those days, the good and the bad, and we told each other there was dignity and enlightenment in muck and sweat. We worked until our hands blistered, we had such energy and conviction, but we were all younger then! We don't pretend that we have all the answers here, we never did, and utopias are probably unattainable, but we have a responsibility to try, don't you agree?'

Robert seemed to consider before he answered. 'Mrs Fitzgerald clearly had good intentions.'

'She did. She still does. I'm glad you feel that. We believed our experiment mattered.'

Robert nodded thoughtfully, then looked at him and smiled. They'd had excellent intentions in the early days, but back then Gwen's wealth had seemed to be a bottomless pot. It was an unfortunate fact that money always had to come into their decision making now and if projects didn't prove to be financially viable, they tended to be short-lived, no matter how worthy their aim. For Robert's sake, Daniel hoped the garden plans might be granted some time.

As Robert left Daniel, he pondered the irony of a fortune made from munitions being used to create a community that was essentially about preserving peace ... or, he thought again, perhaps that wasn't ironic at all? Maybe Mrs Fitzgerald was overly idealistic to imagine that goal might actually be achievable, but as he'd spoken with Daniel, Robert had recalled his father's black moods and blood-stained handkerchiefs, and he could understand something of the impulse that had inspired this venture. If Greenfields was intended to be a model, an example to demonstrate a better life, surely its garden ought to carry a message too? Shouldn't it be a place of beauty and inspiration, where people might contemplate, come together and simply calmly listen to the birdsong? Robert considered what Daniel had said about responsibility, and Greenfields being a cooperative endeavour, and felt that he'd like to play some part in that.

Chapter Nine

'We take it in turns to go,' Iris told Robert. 'There's a rota. There has to be, or certain people would never do it.'

Despite his name appearing on the rota, Cecil hadn't manned the market stall for months, it occurred to her then. He didn't have time for it, he always said; he had better things to be doing – but they all could have said that, couldn't they? In truth, Iris would gladly have wriggled out of the obligation herself today. Ailsa was teething and had cried through most of the night, Erin and Ewan had been fractious, and Cecil had come back from the workshop in a foul mood last night. He was battling with this commission. He couldn't find any energy in the stone, he said. Iris felt she didn't have much energy either this morning, but perhaps it was no bad thing to be out of the house for a few hours. Cecil had reluctantly taken Ailsa with him to the studio. They could spend the morning grizzling together.

'I've never stood behind a market stall before,' Robert said.

Iris glanced across at him. As they'd packed the van together, she'd noticed he had a polite way about him – she couldn't help contrasting his manner with Cecil's – and she'd felt a brief urge to put her fingers through his shiny, brown curls. He had broad shoulders too and high cheekbones that made him look rather Slavic. It was the sort of face she might give to a woodcutter if she were illustrating a folktale – a noble, courageous woodcutter, who would outwit a czar and win the hand of a fair lady. Cecil had Byronic locks when she'd first met him. He'd been so confident and daring, and with his Italian-London accent and the talk of his Romany ancestry there'd been something exotically glamorous about him. But he'd grown a small paunch in recent years and his hairline was receding. He'd taken to combing his hair back with Vaseline, so that it left greasy marks on chairs and pillows and his collars. She didn't like to touch it now. The crates of vegetables rattled on the back of the van and she reached her packet of cigarettes from her pocket.

'Here, light one for me, will you? And help yourself.' She threw the packet over to Robert. 'I can't say any of us have much pedigree as a market-stall holder, but it's regular income for the estate. Even Gwendoline takes her turn on the stall. She always tends to do well, actually – probably because people like to come and have a look at her. She's the only stallholder on the market with Schiaparelli hats and manicured fingernails.'

Iris looked at her hands on the steering wheel. She used to paint her nails too, but she'd started biting them again after Erin was born. Her hands made her look older, she thought, as did the shadows under her eyes. In her rush to leave the house, she'd slipped one of Cecil's jumpers over her head and it smelled faintly of sweat and his French cigarettes, she noticed now. She really ought to have washed her hair last night, but she'd tied a scarf around her head instead. In Robert's presence she felt suddenly conscious that she ought to have made more effort.

'Trudie told me your husband is working on a sculpture for

the cathedral at the moment.' He passed a cigarette across to her. 'You must be proud of him.'

Robert wasn't going to be another of those young people who liked to crowd worshipfully around Cecil, was he? There'd been a succession of young women at Anderby who had blinked their eyelashes at him and young men who nodded intently at his every word. Cecil tended to play up to the expectations of his acolytes and, in the process, turned into a caricature of himself. Iris asked herself whether she did feel proud of him; she might have felt proud if she had a sense that his success had brought him contentment.

'He's doing a lot of cursing about this commission. The bishop would have a turn if he could hear! It's a figure of Saint Michael slaying Lucifer and Cecil is struggling to breathe life into it. He's worried this one might be a dud. He's had to restart it twice, such a lot of sweating and swearing, and they keep writing to him asking for an update on progress. Cecil can't work like that. He can't create under pressure.'

Iris heard herself using her husband's phrases. He'd slammed the kitchen door after they'd quarrelled last night and all the pottery on the dresser had vibrated. Her grandmother's willow-pattern plates had set up a troubled chatter, as if debating whether to leap from the shelf. Iris tried to remember when they'd become so short-tempered with one another. It hadn't always been like this, had it? Did all marriages go through a stage of slammed doors and lack of mutual empathy? Should she be trying harder? The van banged over the ruts in the road.

'And you're a painter?' Robert asked.

'I was. I wanted to be. I trained to be,' she modified, and felt as if she were taking steps backwards. 'Cecil and I were at college together. Only, I don't have the time now. Motherhood has kept me occupied for the past nine years, not that I'm complaining.' She did sound as if she was complaining, didn't she? She must tone it down. 'I love my children dearly, even if they are a bit feral, and I fit my work in where I can. I mostly do illustration work these days – children's books, calendars, diaries, that sort of thing. I draw a lot of anthropomorphic animals.'

Did she have reason to complain, though? When Erin was young, Cecil had helped to feed her and had liked to brush her hair; they'd shared the responsibilities, but these days he looked at the children as if he found them an annoyance. He no longer read them a bedtime story, and when Ewan wanted to kick a ball there'd always be some urgent work he needed to complete. Iris understood he had a commission to deliver, but he often came back across the yard with whisky on his breath, usually just as she'd got the children off to bed. A cynic might suggest he waited with a glass and pair of binoculars in his hands, but . . . Iris told herself not to think that.

'Do you enjoy illustration work? Do you like anthropomorphic animals?'

Iris couldn't recall that anyone had asked her before. She wrinkled her nose as she considered the question. Her head was full of dear little cats in waistcoats and jolly little mice smoking pipes. Sometimes she hated the cheery little animals.

'I'm doing designs to order, so it can feel like working on a factory production line. There's little creativity in what I do now, but it brings in a regular income, and we need that. No sooner do I lace up a pair of Ewan's shoes, but he's grown out of them. I swear my children have growth spurts overnight. Perhaps I'm feeding them too much?'

She guessed Robert was still in his early twenties – perhaps ten years her junior? While her own life was fixed in routines and roles, he was still evolving into the man he might become, still finding his talents, still discovering his tastes. He was unfettered, Iris thought, wholly living for himself, and she envied him for that.

'Anyway, how are you settling in? Has Trudie taken you under her wing?'

'Something like that. She's quite a personality, isn't she?'

Iris smiled. They must all seem rather odd to him. 'She's actually Lady Gertrude, you know, but there was a rift with her family. They haven't spoken for years.'

'She said something about falling out with her mother. And Faye? Am I right in thinking she's from this area?'

'Her family are over Witney way, but she went off to university in Oxford and then worked in London for a couple of years. Faye's committed to her work. She lives for it. And all the more so since Richard left.'

'Richard?'

'He went back to London. Richard writes earnest plays, lots of laid-off coal miners and angry dockers, and wants to make a name for himself. Between you and me, I thought he was a sanctimonious bore.' Cecil had called him a smug, patronizing arse, but Robert didn't need to be told that. 'It was pretty obvious that he cared about his career more than he cared about Faye.'

'Were they married?' he asked.

'No, they just lived together.' She could see from Robert's face that he was trying to decide whether he ought to disapprove. 'As a group, we might be outraged by people's artistic choices, but we're pretty easy-going in other areas. Does that shock you?'

'I'm starting to realize that I come from a very conventional town with lots of rules about how to behave.' He grinned. 'I never imagined I might be conservative or a prude until I came here.'

'Give it six months and we'll have turned you into a flamboyant libertine, Robert. You'll scandalize your former self!' Iris thought of herself as having become rather timid and dowdy in recent years – she saw a dull, tired woman when she looked in the mirror – but it occurred to her that Robert might consider her a wild bohemian. Perhaps she wasn't entirely finished yet? 'Faye says she's renounced men now.'

'Renounced?' he repeated.

Iris heard an interest in his voice. They were about the same age, weren't they? 'Forsook. Forsaken. Disavowed. She's washed her hands of the lot of you, I'm afraid.' She glanced quickly across at him. 'And what about you – do you have a girl at home?'

It took him a moment to answer and she sensed he was deciding whether he could trust her. 'I did, but it's over now. It ended rather messily. Esther and I had been together secretly for months, but then her mother caught us and they had me thrown out at the gate. It wasn't my finest hour, I'll admit. We were finished and I was out of a job.' His voice faltered, as if he'd decided he was saying too much. 'Can I tell you that in confidence?'

'It does sound messy.' Was she correct to assume the girl had been his employers' daughter? 'See, you're not so conservative really, are you? Don't tell me you've renounced women?'

'It might be for the best.'

'Dear me! It's an epidemic of renunciation! Is this the way the human race ends?'

The church bells clanged out as she pulled onto the square and the blind fiddle player was there on the corner again. Had Robert come here running away from a broken heart? How precarious it was to be young, she thought. But then it didn't necessarily get easier with age, did it?

As Iris drove, Robert had looked out at the hills and the passing villages. They'd driven down lanes like green tunnels and he'd seen ploughed fields with soil the colour of cocoa. Though he identified no sign of it, he'd remembered what Faye had said about hardship hiding behind doors. As they'd neared the town, Iris had pointed out a match factory, a dye works and a cloth mill, but it was nothing like the red-black factory walls that had cast their shadows over his childhood. By comparison with his hometown, this looked like the unspoilt green and pleasant land of hymns. Did Faye have any idea what real poverty meant? With her shelves full of books and her Oxford degree, she probably thought poverty was toast without marmalade, didn't she? Or not being able to afford tickets to the theatre. Yes, there were some shabby-looking farms here, and the village cottages must be dark and cramped inside, but this wasn't desperate hardship, was it? He wanted to take Faye by the arm, to drag her onto a train and to show her dying textile towns and failing mining districts, what 'going without' really meant.

He lit one cigarette after another for Iris as she drove, and when she wasn't smoking she bit at her fingernails, Robert noticed. She often only had one hand on the steering wheel, but seemed well accustomed to manoeuvring the vehicle. She spoke with an accent-less, humorous voice, and didn't seem to mind him asking questions about Anderby. In her corduroy trousers and with her shortly cropped hair, she had a look of a girl playing a boy in a play, he thought, but she had an attractive elfin profile and when she turned to him and smiled, it lit her face. He found himself trying to make Iris smile.

The market was setting up along the town's sloping high street. The houses had steeply pitched gables, mullioned windows, prominent chimney stacks and the stone was of a grey-gold colour that seemed soaked with ancient sunlight. The shops' signs offered high-class greengrocery, bespoke tea blends and antiquarian books to the passing trade, there was a florist's with arrangements of spring bulbs in its Georgian bay window, a smart gentlemen's outfitters and a half-timbered inn with barrels of tawny port behind the bar. The brass door-knockers were all polished to a respectable shine, everyone was well dressed, there were no gangs of men leaning against walls and nobody spat in the streets. An inscription over the door of the almshouse said it was built for poor weavers, but the only sign of poverty today was the old soldier selling matches on the street corner.

They set up the trestle table together and began to unload the boxes from the van. Robert wanted to do the lifting, but though Iris was small, she was strong. She knew the routine, and the surrounding stallholders, and talked with them brightly as they set up. Robert's heart hadn't leapt at the prospect of the early start and a morning of standing behind a market stall, but there was a sense of camaraderie here and he enjoyed listening to Iris talking. Pigeons wheeled around the square church tower as the bells struck the quarter hour and they passed a bag of cinder toffee between them.

They set out boxes of leeks and brassicas, parsnips and turnips, and winter salad from the kitchen garden. There were eggs from Daniel's hens, baked goods from the café and jars of jam labelled with Mrs Fitzgerald's distinctive handwriting. The produce from Anderby was good quality, Robert thought, and they evidently had regular customers, but it wasn't abundant. This weekly stall couldn't raise much income for the estate, could it? He understood that a portion of the takings from the café also went into the community's coffers, but, again, that couldn't amount to much. He hadn't yet figured out how the trust's finances worked – how the income of the Fitzgeralds and the Greenfields community were apportioned and who had responsibility for which parts of the estate. Robert would have liked to ask Iris about these things, but wasn't sure he should.

He stamped his feet to keep them warm and Iris poured them both tea from a thermos flask. Around them there were stalls stacked with wheels of cheese, sides of bacon and faggots, lardy cakes, Madeira cakes and baked egg custards. One could buy hair ribbons here, wireless valves, live elvers or a pair of lisle stockings. Robert liked the sharp, savoury smells of the market, the calls of the stall holders and the gaudy colours of the awnings. He enjoyed watching the passing parade of faces, catching fragments of conversations, and the general animation of the morning streets. Women pushed perambulators up the hill, blazered grammar-school boys walked in obedient lines and retired colonels looked at their pocket watches. In their quiet moments, Iris made concise sketches of the street ahead of them. Robert admired the cleverness of her fast-moving pencil.

They packed up the stall as the church bells began to strike twelve. They'd put their takings in a japanned enamel tin and Iris smiled as she finally turned the key in its lock. Robert would have liked to look inside the church, and to have taken Iris for a drink in one of the inns, but he knew she had to get back to her children.

'Perhaps you'll show me some of your paintings one day?' he said as they were dismantling the trestle table.

'Come into the house when we get back. I'd be glad to show you, but don't have great expectations.'

Iris had kept a bag of pastries behind the stall and she gave them to the old soldier on the street corner before they left. Robert noticed how she put her hand to his shoulder.

'Is it a Turner?' Robert stood in front of one of her Venice paintings.

'A Turner? Good God, no!' Iris gasped a laugh. 'But thank you for the compliment. It's an old one of mine. I lived in Italy for a few months when I was younger.'

'It's beautiful. You're very talented.'

'Thank you for saying that. I shared a flat there with three friends from college and we sincerely believed galleries were going to fling their doors open for us. It seems like a different lifetime.'

'The doors didn't open?'

'A couple of the friends I was there with have had some success, but it didn't happen for me. I tell myself I'll get back to it one day.' She shrugged. 'Perhaps when the children are older.'

'It's a pity you can't make time for it.'

'One day. Maybe. Perhaps.'

Iris found herself contemplating the painting after Robert left. She'd caught the scene at dusk with a denim-blue sky, all glimmering suggestion and liquid light. She recalled that summer in bright colours. Everything had seemed possible to her back then.

'Can't you tidy this mess up?' Cecil asked.

He kicked his boots off and sat down heavily at the kitchen table. The children's plates from breakfast were still out, porridge and egg yolk now hardened on them. He'd filled the ashtray and had evidently eaten amongst the dirty dishes at lunchtime. Iris considered asking why he hadn't tidied the mess up, but thought better of it.

'I've only just this minute got back. It took a while to pack up the stall. Are the children with Gwendoline?'

'Yes, she fed them. I said you'd pick them up. How was the gardener? Was he a chore?'

'Robert? No, he's a sweetheart, actually. He asks a lot of questions, but he's all shiny and hopeful. I enjoyed talking with someone who's not old enough to have grown a layer of cynicism yet.' She handed Cecil his bottle of beer and a glass. He took it without thanks. 'He was asking why I gave up painting just now.'

'What business is that of his?'

'He was only being kind. He thought it was a Turner!' She nodded towards the painting and laughed.

'So he imagines he's an expert on art?' Cecil sat back in his chair with the glass held to his chest. 'He does know he's just here to weed the flowerbeds, doesn't he?'

'He told me I ought to keep my hand in.'

'It sounds to me like he should mind his own business.'

'He was being sweet. That was all.' She began to clear the

table, stacking plates on plates, dishes on dishes. She'd need to leave them to soak.

'He's getting his cottage rent-free, you know. Maurice told me,' Cecil said.

'It was part of the terms of his employment, I believe.'

'Gwendoline made Miss Bentridge pay rent.'

'But Miss Bentridge was using the workshop and selling her textiles. She made an income here.'

Cecil looked dissatisfied by this response. He lit another cigarette.

'I like him.' Iris felt defiant in saying it. 'He's considerate and polite and has a nice sense of humour.' She leaned back against the sink. 'I suspect he's come here fleeing a broken heart. Poor boy!'

Cecil rolled his eyes. 'How long do you imagine she'll be able to keep him on, though? I mean, if they can't afford a domestic any longer, where is she finding the money to pay a gardener? I get the impression Teddy isn't best pleased by that order of priorities.'

Iris pulled a chair out and sat down opposite him. 'Do you think their finances really are that precarious? I saw Teddy in town this morning. He was shaking Mr Simpson's hand as he came out of the bank, but the look on his face suggested they hadn't exactly had an amicable meeting.'

'He was in the Royal Oak yesterday and went all shifty when he saw me. He'd been having a very pally conversation with a type in golfing trousers. I overheard them talking about land prices.'

She pulled her headscarf off and ran her hands through her hair. 'Perhaps they mean to sell off more of the farmland?'

'How much is there left to sell? No, I'm not sure your Mr Bardsley ought to be settling in too comfortably. He'll go the way of all the other half-baked money-making schemes.'

'Do you suppose Robert has a sense of that? Should someone tell him?'

Cecil breathed smoke out slowly. 'He'll discover how things are soon enough.'

Chapter Ten

February brought blue skies, new birdsong, and just occasionally a breath of warmth on the wind. Drifts of snowdrops had appeared in the lawns, daffodils were starting to show and green catkins were hanging from the hazels. The buds on the trees looked tight with coiled energy, only waiting for a few degrees more of warmth before they would unwind. The garden seemed to be expectant with spring, on the very brink of release. Robert saw it everywhere, apart from on the prized de Villiers roses. Perhaps a hard pruning would invigorate them?

Daniel had helped him to carry the ladder around to the front of the house and had volunteered to hold it for him, but Robert had insisted he had no fear of heights and would be quite safe. He'd driven an iron stake into the ground at the base so it wouldn't shunt, but the ladder was disconcertingly riddled with woodworm. As Robert climbed it now, he acknowledged to himself that he'd perhaps overdone the bravado.

Setting about this task, Robert recalled the story of these roses being planted to mark the end of the war between Lancaster and York. Wasn't that the fifteenth century, though? Hadn't Maurice said the house was built in the sixteenth century? The main stems were as thick as Robert's arm, but roses only normally lived for a few decades. Was this perhaps a romantic fabrication? He suspected there might be quite a bit of romanticizing in the stories that got told about Anderby Hall. He also remembered what Maurice and Trudie had said about Mrs Fitzgerald's father being an armaments manufacturer during the war. Had guilt been amongst the mix of emotions that propelled her to establish Greenfields? Did she feel she had to make amends in some way? The newspapers were presently full of Franco–German tensions at the Disarmament Conference, and speculation about Herr Hitler's ambitions, but Daniel said that one had to maintain faith in negotiation and at least the delegates were all still around the table. Though Robert now had new worries to keep him awake at night, he felt more aware of the wider world than he ever had been before and had decided that Greenfields was an education.

The old rose stems were gnarled and knotted and too tough for the secateurs. It wasn't especially easy to use the saw while holding onto the ladder, and branches snagged on his clothing as they fell. Why had the de Villiers planted such thorny varieties? The roses had grown over the window of the oratory and must block the light. As he cut them back he imagined the colours of the stained glass brightening.

He'd made good progress for the past hour. He'd cut a lot of dead, diseased and damaged wood away, and as he stood back now, he could see a symmetry returning. He reached his thermos from his bag and made a temporary seat for himself on the overturned wheelbarrow. Now that he sat, he was conscious he'd been tensing the muscles in his legs for a long time.

'Shirking again, eh?' said Teddy's voice.

Why did he never hear Teddy approaching? He could do with a bell around his neck, like a tomcat. 'I was only taking a moment's break,' Robert replied.

'I see. Is that in your contract?'

'No, it's not, but . . .' Mrs Fitzgerald would allow him a five-minute tea break, wouldn't she?

'I'm only winding you up. You are damned easy to wind up, Bardsley.'

Robert poured the remainder of his cup away. 'I'll get back to work.'

'Now see, you didn't need to do that!' Teddy tipped his head to one side as he looked up at the roses. He tossed his cigarette end into the flowerbed. Robert instinctively wanted to retrieve it, but he could imagine the look Teddy would give him. 'Been having a peer in the windows while you were up there?'

'I'm sorry? No, certainly not.' He turned his back on Teddy and began to ascend the ladder again. If he returned to work, would he get bored and go away?

'You've cut a lot back, haven't you? You really have been hacking at them. You do know what you're doing, don't you?'

'I do.' Must he explain what he was doing to Teddy?

'Only, Gwen won't be best pleased if you've butchered the things.'

'I have no intention of killing them. I intend to revive them.'

Teddy sat down on the overturned wheelbarrow and lit another cigarette. Did he have nothing better to do this morning? Aware Teddy was watching him, Robert's legs felt all the more unsteady and he found himself hesitating over cuts.

'I looked inside the potting shed. I see you've claimed it

now, made a nice little den for yourself in there, with your chair and your bench and all the places for your tools chalked up on the walls. You like to have everything tidy, don't you, Bardsley? Does it infuriate you when things aren't put back in their place?'

Was Teddy laughing at him? Robert heard amusement in his voice. He could do with descending the ladder again, and stepping back to assess the shape he was making, but he'd rather remain at a distance from Teddy. 'I like to know where things are. I don't want to waste time having to search for them.'

'A tidy mind, eh? What else is in there, though? I've been watching you, Bardsley, and trying to figure you out.' Teddy got to his feet now and approached the bottom of the ladder. 'You know, there's a story going around about you.'

'About me?' He didn't like Teddy standing at the bottom of the ladder or the direction of this conversation.

'Apparently, so rumour has it, you got a girl into bother.' He said this as if it shocked him, but then laughed.

'Me? That's not true.' Where had this come from? 'I've never got a girl into trouble.' He hadn't spoken about Esther to anyone, had he? He'd been careful about that. But then he remembered Iris asking him a question and telling her just a little of it. He shouldn't have done that. He tried to recall how much he'd said.

'Are you sure? How puzzling. I heard you got turned off the property for leaving your dirty fingerprints where they shouldn't have been. That's right, isn't it?'

Teddy put his boot on the first rung of the ladder. Robert felt the movement transferred upwards. Did he mean to intimidate him?

'It wasn't like that. You make it sound like something shameful.'

'Oh dear. I do apologize. So it was pure, innocent young love, then?' Teddy grinned. 'Am I correct in surmising this young lady might have been the daughter of your previous employer?'

How had he guessed that? He hadn't said as much to Iris, had he? 'I don't feel ashamed of what we did. We didn't do anything wrong.'

'Is that the case? But they dismissed you for it, didn't they?'

What could he say? 'I'll need to move the ladder in a moment. I'll need to come down.'

'Whatever,' Teddy said. 'Underhill, wasn't it? Scarcroft Grange? I do hope you've kept nothing from us, Bardsley?'

'Nothing that has any bearing on my ability to do this job.' Robert felt the ladder move again as Teddy shifted his foot.

'Is that so? Well, we'll see about that.'

Robert took a breath before he began to descend the ladder. Would Teddy tell Mrs Fitzgerald that he suspected he'd lost his previous job? Could there yet be consequences? Teddy didn't move as he came down, so that he was forced to step into close proximity with him. He could smell his eau de cologne and hair oil and the cigarettes on his breath.

'Please, will you step back?'

He could hear Teddy drawing on his cigarette. He neither answered nor moved for a moment. He exhaled smoke into Robert's face.

'Now, you see, Robert wouldn't let me hold the ladder,' said Daniel's voice.

Robert didn't know how much Daniel had heard, but he

was relieved that he'd returned. 'I told Mr Fitzgerald I didn't need any assistance.'

'But I insisted,' Teddy said, and turned a brilliant smile on Daniel. 'We wouldn't want any accidents here, would we?'

'We most certainly wouldn't,' Daniel replied.

Chapter Eleven

Robert was still occupied with the roses. He'd been up the ladder all day yesterday as well. Faye had set out to speak to him three times, getting her thoughts into line, but as she'd approached the house, first Gwendoline, Teddy and then Daniel had appeared, and she'd rather not have this conversation in front of an audience. Finally seeing Robert alone, she quickened her pace.

'You actually jumped then,' she said. 'Did I startle you? Were you concentrating? Sorry, I don't mean to disturb you.'

'Don't worry,' he replied, looking down. 'I'm ready to take a break.'

'I don't want to drag you down your ladder if you're in the middle of something – only Gwendoline suggested to me that I ought to talk to you. She's keen for us to discuss this idea of getting the children to help with the gardens. I suppose we should talk about how it might work?'

'Ah. That. Yes. She mentioned it to me a couple of days ago. Does the prospect of it horrify you?'

'I'm not awkward for awkwardness' sake, you know.' Did he think that?

'Really?' He raised his eyebrows. He didn't look entirely convinced.

Daniel had gritted his teeth when he'd told her of Gwendoline's proposal, clearly expecting she'd object. And, in fairness, she hadn't been able to resist retorting. 'What? Unpaid labour? Perhaps she'd like them to sweep the chimneys too?'

'I think she might be trying to build bridges between you and Robert,' Daniel had said.

'By forcing me to actively participate in a scheme that I believe is fundamentally misguided?'

'The children would enjoy it and it could be educational,' Daniel had gone on. 'We had previously talked about giving them an area of garden to manage, hadn't we?'

'Has Gwendoline recruited you to convince me?'

'Not explicitly!' he'd laughed. 'But I do see some merit in the idea. Give it some consideration.'

'Do I have a choice?'

'You always have a choice.'

Faye wasn't certain that she did. As Daniel had reminded her, last year she'd put forward a motion for the children to be given their own vegetable garden to work, so she couldn't reasonably object to this proposal. She knew it would look hypocritical.

'We did a hunt for signs of spring yesterday,' she said to Robert now, looking away towards the gatehouse and feeling rather awkward, 'the children and I, that is. We ticked off daffodils and primroses and rooks gathering materials for their nests. There used to be lots of crocuses, but there are fewer this year.'

'The mice eat the bulbs,' Robert said, as he came down the ladder. 'I've suggested to Mrs Fitzgerald that we might renew some of the spring planting.' She heard some hesitancy in his voice. Did he expect her to object? 'I'm glad if the children like the flowers – and, yes, we probably ought to talk.'

He seemed preoccupied this morning, Faye detected. He sounded subdued and slightly nervy perhaps? Did he dislike the idea of being obliged to work with her and the children? Could it be that he felt as cornered as she did?

'Would you like to walk?' he asked. 'I can show you where I've found some wild violets.'

'Yes, by all means.' Why did she always feel self-conscious in his presence?

They walked across the lawn, their footsteps leaving prints in the dew, and down towards the lake. The trees were dripping, there was a golden light this morning, and the low sun was casting long shadows. A blackbird plunged across the path ahead and startled her briefly.

'Did you always want to teach?' He cleared his throat. He evidently felt he ought to make conversation. She noticed that the roses had scratched his hands. They were criss-crossed with fine cuts.

'Not always. I went through phases of wanting to be an actress and a doctor and then a veterinarian. But everyone does that, don't they?'

'Do they? I can't recall ever wanting to be an actress.'

She turned to him with a smile, but his eyes were on the path. 'Did you always want to be a gardener?'

'I'm not sure *want* came into it very much. I don't think it does for most people, does it?' He looked at her and she felt slightly judged. 'There was a chance of an apprenticeship and I like working outside. I do enjoy it. I wouldn't want to do anything else. I couldn't work in a factory. I have to admit that I was glad to leave school.'

Mist was still clinging to the lake. In this light the surface of the water was burnished bronze and the willows and the boathouse might have been lifted from a Japanese silk.

'The school here isn't like others that I've worked in,' she said. 'That was part of the attraction for me. Anderby does things differently.'

'I've noticed that.' He squinted his eyes against the light and skimmed a stone across the water. She glanced away and watched the ripples stretch.

'It's not just about arithmetic and grammar and rote learning here,' she went on. 'We want the children to enjoy their time in the classroom, to be hungry for knowledge and to have questioning minds. We're able to adapt our teaching for each child and we don't want them to ever feel compelled or constrained.'

'They certainly don't look constrained,' Robert said. He picked up another stone and turned it in his hand. 'I'm not sure I've ever seen a less constrained-looking group of children.'

Did he mean it as a criticism? She wasn't sure. 'They do dance, drama, woodwork, pottery and they keep chickens,' she continued. 'We favour experience over textbooks and we encourage them to spend time in nature. Our priority is that the children's school lives are full, stimulating and happy, but we also want them to grow up to be rounded and responsible members of society. I'm sorry,' – her flow paused – 'I can see your eyes glazing over, Robert. Am I boring you?'

'Not at all!' There did seem to be genuine amusement in his smile at last. 'My schooling was all reciting multiplication tables, memorizing the dates of wars and remembering which parts of the world map were pink. I might have liked school more if we'd kept chickens and been allowed to ask questions.' He skimmed another stone. It bounced three times. His smile was still there, but it looked as if he was making an effort. 'That was your reason for coming to Anderby, then – because, as a teacher, it would be better to work here?'

She nodded. 'And I'm not far from my family here. I grew up in this area and knew Greenfields by reputation – a different reputation back then,' she qualified. 'It wasn't always like it is now.'

'In what way different?' He turned to her, seeming to be genuinely interested.

'Gwendoline bought Anderby in 1920 and when she arrived here she seemed so exotic – never mind another continent, she might have come from a far-off planet! She was tremendously glamorous in the early days, she wore beautiful clothes, but she also had totally different attitudes to anything we'd known. There wasn't a hint of snobbery about her, she was very keen to support local farmers, tradesmen and craftsmen, and she put a great deal of effort into making connections. There used to be lots of events going on and the doors of the Hall were open to everyone. There were regular concerts and talks, the Easter-egg hunt in the spring and the cider festival in the autumn. My parents brought me to that. It's a shame they stopped it . . . but, then, so many initiatives have come and gone. At the start, Greenfields was all about setting an example and inspiring change in others, but it seems to have become rather inward-looking in recent years. The banner over the door might still say 'Community', but these days that means us and not them.'

'Why has it changed?'

'People, I suppose.' She shrugged. 'There's always been quite a turnover. And, between you and me, I think she's more inclined to be influenced by Teddy now.' She could say that to

Robert, couldn't she? 'He never bought into the Greenfields philosophy. He's never made any pretence of that. He talks about it as if its Gwendoline's little hobby, it might as well be needlepoint or flower pressing, and he doesn't like people coming into the house. He complains about wear and tear on the carpets and goes on about the public's light fingers.'

'They are an odd couple. Don't you think? What do they talk about behind closed doors?' He frowned as he pulled a rose thorn from his thumb and then put his hand to his mouth.

'Teddy can turn on the charm for Gwendoline. It can be very powerful, Teddy's charm.' She reached for a handkerchief, but Robert shook his head. The blood reddened his lips for a moment. 'The changes have had an impact on the school too. We used to have more pupils, and it was a mix of estate families and locals. We offer free places to children of parents with moderate means, but even so we're down to twelve pupils now. I need to bring the numbers up – I'm under some pressure to do that – but there's a certain amount of cynicism and distrust in the village.'

'Understandable, what with you being a community of heathens and wife-swappers.'

'Quite! And doesn't that tell you everything? To me, this idea of charging people to enter the gardens just creates another barrier. I never wanted to put you out of a job, Robert. I honestly didn't. I just worry about the future of Anderby.'

'I understand.'

Did he? 'You look tired this morning.' She couldn't help saying it. She'd noticed he'd been working long hours. But was it just that?

'I didn't sleep well last night.'

'No?'

Knowing that she ought to have this conversation, she hadn't slept well either. She'd got up early and walked around the grounds, the mist still lifting off the garden, trying to think how they might make this scheme work. Returning to the rear gates of the cottages, she'd noticed Robert by his kitchen window. He was shaving at a glass and angling his chin to the light. She'd stood there for a moment, supposing he wouldn't see her, but then his eyes had lifted. Faye had turned and walked away quickly, feeling her face reddening with embarrassment. Could it be that he'd spotted her? Did he think she'd been watching him? That idea made her feel uncomfortable now.

'So could we assist you?' she went on. 'I know you've got an awful lot to do before June. It would be good for the children to see how the garden changes through the seasons, I think, to observe the wildlife and to learn how to care for plants. They're all interested in why you're here and what you're doing. They all have questions. Perhaps, for a start, you might talk to them about that?'

He seemed to consider for a moment before he nodded. 'I could show them clay pipes and ox shoes I've dug up, fossils I've found in split stones and tell them where I've discovered fox earths. Perhaps they'd like to see old pictures of the gardens? And I could speak about what we hope to restore. Would that be worthwhile?'

There was something rather resigned in his manner this morning, Faye thought. She heard a flatness in his voice, and why did he keep looking back towards the Hall? She recalled the first time they'd met, how he'd teased and grinned at her. The light had gone from his voice and his eyes now, and she found that she missed it.

'Perhaps we could sit down together and make a list of tasks that the children might help with?' The wind brought the sound of church bells from the village, a wood pigeon repeatedly declaimed, and then she could hear the children's voices distantly. It was time she got back. 'I wouldn't want them to do anything dangerous, heavy or difficult, I'm sure you wouldn't want that either, but we will try to be more assistance than hindrance.'

'Yes. Of course. Thank you.' There was a lack of conviction there.

He'd picked a tiny posy of violets as they'd walked, and as she departed he'd held them towards her, pinched between his earth-engrained thumb and forefinger. She'd put them in an egg cup on her desk when she got back to her cottage. Faye knew there'd been no meaning in his gesture, his face had been grave, but her eyes kept returning to the flowers and she bent to breathe their sweet scent again now. What accounted for the change in his manner? Had he been offended by her objections to the garden plans? Did he dislike her for that? It disconcerted her to discover how much his good opinion mattered to her.

Chapter Twelve

Robert had dreamed about the de Villiers roses last night. He'd seen them withering, the leaves yellowing and the red and white petals parting. With that, the long-dead Yorkists and Lancastrians had risen up from graves in the village churchyard. Though reduced to bones and tattered rags, they had taken up their arms again. It was a horrifying dream, and somewhere in the background, Teddy's voice was laughing and asking Robert if he knew what he was doing. He awoke before first light, sweating and confused, and couldn't get back to sleep. He'd been an idiot to talk about Esther. What had he been thinking? He knew Anderby did a brisk trade in gossip. He'd instinctively felt he could trust Iris, but did he really know her at all?

He'd spent the whole of the previous day expecting to see Mrs Fitzgerald striding across the lawn towards him, but it hadn't happened. Had Teddy told her yet? If she heard the Underhills' side of the story, she would surely dismiss him. At points in the night he'd resolved that he'd go and speak to her today, get it all out in the open and make his defence ... but then wheels would be in motion. Would Teddy choose to hold this threat over him for a while longer yet? Was there a chance it might have been an empty bluff? He needed to keep this position and the project had begun to matter to him; he wanted to see the garden returning to order and health, for Mrs Fitzgerald to be vindicated for her faith in the scheme, and he'd begun to enjoy the freedom and interest of life here. It would pain him to leave at this stage. Indecision had kept him awake, and the way ahead was no clearer in his mind this morning. As he set off on the winding path through the woods, he tried to force his thoughts into a straight line.

There was a pristine cleanness to the celandines that skirted his steps, freshly washed with dew, and glossy new leaves were beginning to unfurl from the branches above. Last year's bracken fronds were copper and bronze, the sun lit the moss on branches to a brilliant jade green and the frills of fungi and lichen were ochre and gold. After a second sleep-deprived night, Robert felt sensitive to light and scents and every sound this morning. He closed his eyes, breathed deeply, and listened to the wind rocking the trees. The rushing sound overhead came from the wings of a flock of pigeons, rooks and jays made their harsh cries, and every blackbird in Gloucestershire seemed to be singing.

His thoughts also kept returning to Faye. She'd held the posy of violets to her face and her eyes had closed for a moment as she'd breathed in the scent. Robert didn't know what had made him pick them; it was more instinct than considered intention. She'd been speaking of her work with passion and clearly had a great fondness for her pupils. She'd smiled as she'd talked of the school and he'd found himself thinking how lucky the children were to have her as a teacher. As he'd handed her the violets, she'd looked at him directly for the first time, her eyes tilting up to his just for a second, before she spun away again. Up close, he'd seen there were flecks of gold in her blue eyes.

Mist was clinging to the river and in the hollows of the fields ahead. Robert watched it shift, the landscape revealing and resolving itself. The fleeces of sheep glowed gold and steamed where the sun touched them, and the hills receded in declining shades of blue. Some of the fields had been striped by a plough now and he could smell the rich earth. It struck him that this valley might have looked much the same a century earlier and might well be unchanged a century hence. The countryside here felt like scenes from a folk song, its tune in turn both familiar and foreign.

Smoke curled around chimneypots as Robert approached the village, and he breathed the scent of oak and apple wood. He could hear the sound of a blacksmith striking an anvil, the rumble of barrels into the cellar of the pub, cartwheels rolling on the lane and the voices of a group of children playing marbles at the roadside. Then Teddy's red Bentley tore through, the roar of its engine seeming like a discordant note from a different century. There was a woman with blonde hair in the passenger seat, laughing and holding onto her hat. Perhaps Teddy had other matters occupying his thoughts for the moment? The woman was young and pretty and Teddy had grinned as he looked towards her. There'd been various hints that Teddy had a somewhat casual attitude towards marital fidelity. Was that what he'd just witnessed? Did Mrs Fitzgerald know? Surely she deserved better than that?

Robert had spent the previous weekend in the Hall's library, looking through the archive of documents that related to the garden. As he'd turned through plans, correspondence and books of accounts, he'd had a sense of a long line of people watching over her shoulder. Some of them were wearing Georgian frock coats and a few were even sporting doublets and ruffs. The lake had originally been a monastic fish pond, he'd discovered, fed by springs in the hill, but had been turned into a place for pleasure boating in the eighteenth century. He'd found watercolours of the topiary garden which could have been illustrations from *Alice's Adventures in Wonderland*, etchings of the parterre peopled by figures in seventeenth-century dress and Victorian posters advertising the Hall's annual apple festival. He'd had a sense that he was part of this long history, and knew he was repeating the same tasks that generations of previous gardeners would have done in February, the same movements and processes repeated again and again down the centuries. He felt close to his predecessors, and that connection narrowed when he'd dug a rusted trowel from the earth and unwound old wires from the garden walls. He sensed other hands in the places his own fingers now touched. He'd also liked the idea that future gardeners might look back on the marks he had made. But would he ever get the chance now?

The church bells struck midday. Robert felt chilled and melancholy, and needed some company. The public house he'd passed looked as if it might have a warm fireside. Perhaps he could sit for a while with his thoughts and a glass of beer.

The men leaning at the bar had stared at Robert when he entered, but he greeted them civilly, and their conversations resumed as he settled at a table. The clientele all looked to be farm hands or gamekeepers. There was a lot of old green corduroy and a smell of damp dogs and lamp oil. The conversations were the same as they were in pubs back home – the inadequacies of local councillors, football results and the price of coal – but he had to make an effort to untangle the accent and he felt conscious of being the stranger set apart from the crowd. Horse brasses glimmered darkly around the fireplace, Lord Kitchener looked down from the walls in a scarlet coat, and there were lithographs of horses jumping fences and packs of hounds in full cry. The tabletop was sticky under Robert's glass, but the beer was good and tasted like the scent of haymaking. The voices and the sound of shifting dominoes receded as Robert thought about Faye holding the violets to her face. It was only as the landlord addressed him for a second time that he returned to the taproom of the Farrier's Arms.

'I say,' he repeated himself, 'are you the young chap who's staying up at the big house?'

He did mean Anderby, didn't he? 'Yes,' Robert replied. 'I'm working there.'

'Your voice isn't from around here,' the man remarked.

'No.' Naturally, they'd rather the Hall employed local men. 'I'm from further north.'

'Is that right? They have you working as a gardener, don't they?'

He smiled, wanting to be friendly. 'They do. For the present. That's correct.'

'My father used to be a groom there, back in the day, but it's all gone to wrack and ruin, hasn't it?' It was one of the old men who'd been occupied with dominoes who now spoke up. He swivelled in his seat and gave Robert an unabashed stare.

'It's all gone to the dogs up there, hasn't it?' A young man in dirty overalls piped up.

'She has no staff now.' The senior domino player spoke again.

'They say it's all falling down around her, all crumbling over her head.'

'Mind, they're a queer lot up there, aren't they?' The landlord paused from polishing glasses. 'I wouldn't let my daughter work there.'

'Not normal. Not right,' said a woman in a print apron who now appeared behind the bar. 'They used to be respectable folks up at the Hall – gentry, they were – but they're an odd crowd these days.'

'I heard some of them is Bolsheviks.'

'Some of them is anarchists.'

'They're not Christian. They have heathen ways.'

It was happening again, wasn't it? It was the village shop all over again. But this time Robert felt he ought to deflect some of the criticisms.

'I've been treated kindly there.' He had to raise his voice to be heard. 'Everyone I've met has been hospitable, generous and perfectly respectable.' That perhaps didn't apply to Teddy, he hesitated, but still ... 'Really they're all decent people and entirely well intentioned. They believe in fairness and toleration and they want to make a difference. Yes, they're all a little unconventional, but there's nothing improper or sinister going on up there, and I believe the school is excellent ...'

He drained his glass in the silence that followed, feeling self-conscious and also slightly surprised by the words that had tumbled from his own mouth. He'd spoken instinctively, and reflecting again on what he'd said, he realized that he had meant it. He'd been reading about opposition newspapers being closed down in Germany that week, public meetings being banned and mass arrests. It had made him reflect that the reasons for setting up Greenfields were still relevant; democracy mattered, and freedom of speech, and respect for one's fellow man. He hated the thought that there might be another war, that he'd be tested as his father had been, and preventing that reoccurring was essentially what motivated Mrs Fitzgerald, wasn't it? She might have lost some focus along the way, but surely her intentions were to be applauded?

The men at the bar stared at their drinks as he left. He issued a civil 'Good day to you' as he departed, but the response was a reluctant murmur. Robert knew they'd talk about him as he closed the door, but he hadn't been wrong to speak up, had he?

Taking the road back out of the village, Robert realized that he'd developed an allegiance to Anderby. He'd grown to enjoy the place's disregard for social convention, its unabashed idealism and its interest in the wider world. By comparison, his previous life now seemed constrained, blinkered and colourless. It occurred to him that being at Anderby made him feel more fully alive. He looked straight out along the road and smiled as the shape of the Hall's chimney stacks appeared in the distance.

'I'm an anarchist,' he said aloud and laughed. It was a word he'd never applied to himself before and it amused him to say it. 'I'm a crank. I'm an oddball. I'm a Greenfielder.'

But for how much longer? The thought stilled his pace and made his fingers clench onto fists. Did Teddy mean to drive him out? Would Mrs Fitzgerald summon him to the house this afternoon? Was it all over before he'd really begun? He felt angry with Teddy then – bitterly, fiercely angry – but angrier with himself for not keeping his stupid mouth shut. He kicked at a stone in the road and cursed his own idiocy.

Chapter Thirteen

'You're not one for dressing up, then?' Iris looked him up and down. She had to raise her voice above the music. 'That will never do, Robert! Given that it's your party, you could have tried harder.' She and the children had come dressed as sacred Celtic trees, and had clearly gone to some effort with cardboard, papier mâché and bedsheets.

'It's not *my* party,' Robert replied. 'It's Mrs Fitzgerald's. But to be honest, no, dressing up isn't particularly my thing.' He took another mouthful of the punch. It was really quite unpleasant, but he needed the anesthetizing effect of alcohol tonight.

'Are you having an attack of modesty? Is this you being bashful? You should be proud of what you've achieved so far. I think Gwendoline intends to make a speech later.'

'It is kind of her, I'm not ungrateful, but it just feels a bit, well, premature . . .'

It was premature and precarious, Robert privately thought. A month had passed since Teddy had stood at the foot of the ladder making insinuations. Every time Mrs Fitzgerald had approached him since, he'd been readied for her brow to crease and the questions to come. She'd looked a little flustered as she'd

met him at the door this evening, but if Teddy had said anything to her, she surely wouldn't be throwing this party, would
she? The express motive for tonight's event was to celebrate the
work on the gardens beginning in earnest. They'd gathered in
the larger of the Hall's sitting rooms, which had been decorated
with green paper streamers and branches of forsythia, to give
a botanical effect, as Mrs Fitzgerald said. There were pots of
hellebores, muscari and ranunculus, and every vase the Hall
possessed seemed to have been filled with mimosa. She had
gone to a great deal of effort, and Robert was grateful, but he
wouldn't put it past Teddy to make a scene tonight.

'It just makes me conscious that I've not achieved very much
yet,' he went on. Trudie had taken charge of the gramophone
and it was difficult to have a conversation over this rowdy jazz
beat. 'I've spent most of the past three months dragging dead
wood away and doing battle with bramble and ground elder. I
wish I'd made a more significant mark.'

'You *have* made a significant mark. You should look at my
sketchbooks.'

Iris was in the habit of spending an hour with her sketchbook
in the mornings and had taken to making a chronicle of the
garden. She and Robert would often find themselves working
in the same area and they would talk and share a thermos of
coffee. He'd come to enjoy this routine, and their conversations
were increasingly easy and candid. He still wished he hadn't
told her about Esther, but he couldn't blame her for the fact it
had got back to Teddy.

'How are you coping with Faye and the children?' she asked.
She took a sip of her drink and grimaced at the glass. 'What's
in this? Turpentine? Are they any help at all?'

'They're only slightly more help than hindrance, but it's been entertaining. They're boisterous and enthusiastic and ask hundreds of questions, most of which I can't answer.'

Faye had set the children to work raking leaves into piles yesterday, Robert had then shown them a row of old beehives that he'd found and finally they'd taken them to a place in the wood where he'd seen red squirrels. Faye's voice was kind and light when she spoke with the children; she seemed entirely at ease with them and laughed without any self-consciousness. They'd been learning to identify different trees and she'd tasked them with naming them as they'd circled back around the lake. Robert liked that Faye knew these things and how she spoke with her hands, in turn communicating surprise, pleasure and amusement. When he'd noticed a leaf tangled in her hair he'd pulled it away, not pausing to think whether it was appropriate, and as her eyes met his, there had been the briefest moment of awkwardness.

'You and Faye are getting on better?' Iris asked. 'The truce is holding?'

'She doesn't seem to want me to be sacked any longer. Or, at least, not that she's letting on. That's a bonus, isn't it?'

'That's not the reason you've been looking jumpy, then?'

'Jumpy?'

'You've looked a bit tense over the past month. I hope you don't mind me saying that? Is something worrying you?'

He couldn't risk telling Iris more, could he? He wished he could confide in her, but ... 'Only the time pressure – only concern that I've got an awful lot of work to do before June.' Would he still be here in June, though?

'I've told Robert he ought to have gone to more effort,'

Trudie said as she arrived with the punch jug. She'd come dressed as a banyan tree tonight, she'd explained; that meant a green dress, a lot of Indian bangles and leaves drawn on her face in greasepaint. 'He's gone all shy. It'll never do.' She unwound a tendril of ivy from a lampshade and fixed it around his head. 'There, see, you're a woodland sprite now.'

Mrs Fitzgerald had dressed as Botticelli's Primavera for the evening, in a white shift dress and an orange velvet shawl about her shoulders, with little sprigs of pear blossom pinned into her hair. Teddy had come as Pan, in tweed plus fours and papier mâché horns. His costume – or lack thereof – revealed tattoos of roses and anchors on his upper arms. Watching him across the room now, Robert wondered, did army officers have tattoos? Could Teddy have come from the wrong side of the tracks once upon a time? Robert could picture him as a youth in Dublin, leering at women and cheating at cards, that insouciant cigarette always on his lips. But he'd been a captain in the army, hadn't he? He'd winked at Robert as he'd entered the room tonight. Would it all blow up before this evening was over?

All the Greenfielders, young and old, had been invited and the botanical theme had been adopted with varying levels of enthusiasm. There were a number of woodland sprites, green men, Dianas and Demeters in the room, and also a good many who had chosen to ignore the stipulation and seemed to have turned up primarily for the cocktails and canapés. Phyllis was passing around trays of savouries on toast, dainty watercress sandwiches and little rhubarb tarts. Glasses had been filled with various lurid-coloured jellies for the children and Nancy had decorated a cake with crystallized primroses and violets. Trudie's punch was being ladled from an antique Chinese bowl, chipped around the rims, but obviously very old. She claimed to have extracted the recipe from an American bartender at the Savoy, but Robert had watched her making it and it had seemed to involve a haphazard tour around the bottles in her cocktail cabinet. Whatever the authenticity of the recipe, it was highly potent and by nine o'clock the settees had been pushed back against the walls and the rugs were rolled away so there could be dancing. The volume of the music and hilarity increased, and if Mrs Fitzgerald had meant to make a speech, she seemed to have forgotten about it. Might he now hope that Teddy would keep his silence too?

Having been pressed into dancing with Nancy, Miss Parget, Mrs Dunstan and then Iris, Robert stepped outside for a cigarette and a breath of air. He'd overheard Iris and Cecil arguing as the evening began, and had been concerned for her, but Cecil had made his excuses early, and she and the children were now doing an exuberant tango with Trudie. He watched from the terrace and laughed.

'What are you dressed as, then?'

He spun around. It was Faye's voice speaking out of the darkness. She took a step forwards. How long had she been standing there? She looked tired, but was smiling.

'Apparently, I'm a woodland sprite. Or so Trudie informs me. Is it possible to be a half-hearted woodland sprite? There are more committed examples inside.'

'You've got ivy in your hair.' She took another step towards him, extended a finger and touched it. 'You haven't put very much effort in, have you?'

'So everyone keeps telling me! Can I get you a drink? Are you coming in?'

She seemed to think about it for a moment. 'I'll say yes to the drink, but I don't feel like coming inside.'

'Have you been skulking around in the dark? Peeping in through the windows?'

'I wasn't feeling in the mood to be sociable, to be honest. Could you get that drink for me?'

'Of course.'

Robert couldn't see her when he stepped out again. Had she gone? But then he spied the lit end of her cigarette moving and realized she was sitting on the bench. After the brightness of the room, it seemed densely dark outside and he took cautious footsteps towards her.

'It's Trudie's punch,' he said as he handed her the glass. 'God knows what's in it – half of the cocktail cabinet and a can of pineapple chunks, I think. I warn you: it's lethal. One advantage of drinking in the dark is that you can't see the colour.'

'Is it the one that's meant to be a secret recipe from the Savoy?'

'That's it.'

'She always says that. There's no secret recipe. She slings in whatever she has to hand.'

Robert was glad to sense that Faye was smiling. He could hear it in her voice. He sat down next to her on the bench. 'Your good health,' he said, and touched his glass to hers.

'To your garden,' she returned.

'Are you sure? I know you still have reservations.'

'We spent all yesterday afternoon gathering leaves for you, didn't we?'

'And I appreciate it.'

'My God, it's like paint remover!' she exclaimed as she took a sip of her drink.

'Don't think what it's doing to your stomach,' he advised. 'But you chose not to come tonight – you still feel you can't wholly endorse it?'

He heard her take a drag of her cigarette, saw the end of it glow, and the sound of her exhaling. 'Having been so against it at the start, it would have seemed disingenuous if I'd come along tonight with hurrahs and congratulations, don't you think? And there are still aspects that don't sit well with me. You know that.'

'I suspected you might feel like that.'

'I'm glad to know I'm so predictable.'

'Predictable isn't the first word I'd select to describe you. Difficult – yes. Annoying – certainly.' He dared say it because he saw amusement on her face as she lifted her cigarette to her lips. 'You didn't feel like joining in, but couldn't resist spying through the windows?'

'Phyllis told me Teddy was going to be dressed as Pan.'

'Ah, it was titillation that drew you, then? The allure of Teddy without his shirt on? Do you have a thing for the big blue eyes too?'

'Hardly! I just wanted to see if he'd really have horns and hooves.'

'You'd be disappointed. He's wearing brown brogues.'

'I have to admit, I'm not Teddy's greatest fan.' He heard some caution in her voice. 'You won't tell anyone I said that, will you?'

'You're not susceptible to the charisma? I assumed no mortal woman could resist it.'

'He spreads it on thickly, doesn't he? I wouldn't trust him as far as I could throw him, though. I admire Gwendoline in many ways, but Teddy seems to be her weakness. He runs through money, he doesn't respect her as he should, and he exploits her good nature. I suppose I sound cynical to you, don't I?'

'No. Not at all, actually.' He considered telling Faye about the woman in Teddy's car – but could he be certain of what he'd seen? 'I'm glad I'm not the only one who feels that way.'

They sat in silence for a moment, each with their own thoughts, while the sound of the party went on indoors. Someone was singing 'Love is the strangest thing . . .' and he could hear Trudie laughing. There was still a mauve glow of light on the horizon and the land didn't seem to be quite ready for sleep. He could just make out Faye's profile in the moonlight.

'I've liked it,' he finally said, 'working with you and the children. I'll admit that I wasn't convinced at first, but it's been a pleasure.'

'They're not driving you crazy yet, then?' As her cigarette went to her mouth he saw she was giving him a sideways look.

'You drive me a bit crazy, but the children – well, only slightly.'

'I'm pleased for you that it's all going well.' Her hand briefly touched his arm. 'Gwendoline showed me the new designs for the parterre.'

'You don't disapprove?'

'It's only the charging for entry that I don't like. You know that.'

'I'm glad Mrs Fitzgerald is happy with the plans, I was relieved about that, but I'm not confident I'll be here to see them through to completion.'

'What do you mean?' she asked. He felt her turn towards him. 'Are you going somewhere?'

'I don't want to, I'd like to stay here, but it all feels a bit insecure – the financing of it, I mean, and the commitment.' Dare he say more? 'I have a feeling this won't be a long-term position. It wouldn't come as a shock if they let me go.'

'You're not sounding your bullish self, Robert Bardsley. Not sickening for something, are you?'

Is that who she thought he was? 'I've probably had too much punch.'

'Is that what it does to you? You're going to have an almighty hangover in the morning.'

'If I may be so bold, you're not sounding your combative, prickly self, Faye Faulkner. You're actually being fairly nice to me. I mean, not *wildly* nice,' he moderated, 'but quite nice.'

'Prickly? Really?' There was both surprise and amusement in her voice.

'I did speculate what costume you might arrive in tonight and decided that a thorny rose outfit might suit you.'

'Bloody cheek!' she laughed.

'You sound tired. Are you working very hard?' Trudie had mentioned that she'd seen light in Faye's windows late at night.

'Yes, and not sleeping especially well.'

She rolled her head onto the back of the bench. He heard her sigh and then her steady breath was just inches from his ear. Moths fluttered out of the darkness and a fox yowled distantly. The night was warm and sweet with the scents of spring and he caught a faint hint of perfume on her neck. Was it the smell of violets? He wanted this moment to continue exactly as it was, he didn't want to break it, but also . . .

'Would you like another drink? It might help you to sleep. Why don't you come inside?'

'I'm not sure I could take another one of those.' She finished her glass and handed it to him. For a second her fingertips touched his and then pulled away. 'Is there paraffin in it?'

'Quite possibly.'

'I should turn in. Go back to your party, Robert. And have confidence – Gwendoline is entirely committed to your project. She'd be loath to let you go. Enjoy your night.' She stood and readied to leave.

'Won't you let me walk you back?'

'I'm fine, I have a flashlight, but thank you. Goodnight.'

Robert watched the beam of her torch tracking over the garden. He remained sitting on the bench until he could see her light no longer. He breathed in deeply, wanting to find the scent of her perfume again, but it had gone too. When she'd rolled her head back and they'd sat in silence for a minute just now, he had thought he'd like to kiss her. He'd very nearly done it. That was Trudie's damned punch though, wasn't it? He rubbed his eyes. He knew he'd had too much to drink.

'What are you doing out there on your own?' It was Phyllis's voice from the terrace now.

Robert turned on the bench. The light from the room spilled out onto the garden and the dancers inside were strange silhouettes, at one instant macabre and the next comic. 'Minnie the Moocher' was playing on the gramophone.

'I was just having a moment.'

'Well, you must have it another time, pet. Mrs Fitz has been looking for you. She wants to make a speech.'

'Of course. I'm coming. I'll be right with you.' He followed Phyllis inside.

What would Faye have done if he'd tried to kiss her? Would she have pushed him away? Could he have endangered all the fragile connections they'd been making? But would he ever get the chance again?

Chapter Fourteen

Faye poured herself a glass of water, swilled it around her mouth to get rid of the taste of the punch, and reached the bottle of whisky from the shelf. She stirred the fire back into life, pulled her shawl around her shoulders, and tried to re-find her place in the book she'd been reading. It was coming up to midnight, but she felt too wide awake to go to bed. Instead, she resolved that she'd read until her eyes felt tired – and, Lord knows, this book was dry enough. Perhaps it was too dry, though, because she couldn't keep her attention on the page. She kept losing her place in the paragraph and having to track back. She took another mouthful of whisky, willing it to slow her racing thoughts, and looked again at the clock. She hadn't turned a single page, but somehow an hour had gone by.

When she'd first met Robert she'd thought he was a little too pleased with himself, but she'd begun to adjust that assessment over the past few weeks. She'd watched him being patient with the children, listening to their questions and answering seriously and thoughtfully. He'd been accommodating to her too – after everything, she'd have understood if he resented her – and she'd come to admire the care and attention he put into his work. He laboured tirelessly, had clever hands, and she liked that he recognized the songs of birds and knew the names of moths. She was well aware that Gwendoline valued his efforts and ability too, so why did he have little confidence in his being retained? Faye had barely been able to see his face in the dark, but could tell from his voice that his concern was sincere. And there'd been a quality to his voice tonight that had struck her anew; a warmth to it, a generosity, and she'd found herself leaning towards him. They'd ended up sitting so close that she could feel his breath on her ear. Yes, he was drunk – he'd clearly had far too much of that godawful punch – but, forgetting herself, Faye had almost rolled her head onto his shoulder at one point.

She rubbed her eyes and sat up straighter. Where was she going with this chain of thought? It was just that she was over-tired, Faye told herself, and it had been a long, difficult day. Kitty had decided to be disruptive this afternoon, showing off for the rest of the class, testing the boundaries of what she might get away with, and pushing Faye's patience in the process. As she'd felt increasingly irritated with Kitty, her thoughts had returned to the conversation she'd had at the weekend. She'd run into Miss Carmichael, the headmistress of the girls' grammar school, in town. They'd known one another for years and the older woman had asked Faye if she'd join her for a morning coffee in the Black Swan. When they'd run through all their polite enquiries, Miss Carmichael had come to the point and told Faye there was a vacancy coming up on her staff. An English mistress was retiring and she indicated she'd be happy if Faye were to apply for the role. Miss Carmichael was aware of the declining number of pupils at Anderby and she'd advised Faye that she'd be wise to start considering other options.

She'd have more focussed and motivated pupils at the grammar school, Miss Carmichael had suggested, and in the long term wouldn't it be better for her career? Faye had felt flattered, and couldn't deny she'd been tempted, but she'd found herself defending the estate and its school. Should she consider it, though? Did she have a future here?

She'd also had a letter from Ruth that morning. She and Ruth had started at the high school together as newly qualified teachers, and Ruth had always talked of her hunger to travel. Over the past three years, she'd done stints in India and Burma, working for educational charities, and was now teaching in South Africa. She told Faye how rewarding her work was, how she felt she was making a contribution, and of the exceptional people she was meeting. Ruth hadn't understood Faye's decision to go back to Gloucestershire, to her this was a backward step, but Faye had tried to articulate why it mattered to her. She'd told Ruth how she believed it was important that children from rural families should have educational opportunities, how she wanted to pass on the benefits she'd enjoyed, and had explained the progressive ethos of Anderby's school. Children were at the centre of the Greenfields community, the school had always been an essential part of the plan, and Faye had arrived here feeling excited about what she might achieve, but the number of pupils was dwindling and the budget shrunk every year. Was it sustainable? Was it time to think again?

Ruth's letter had asked after Richard too. Faye was certain she'd already told her that Richard had gone back to London. Had she not? Had it not been clear to Ruth that their relationship was finished? But, then, at first, Faye hadn't been certain their separation was actually an ending. It was now, though;

Richard was seeing Virginia Warner. Faye hadn't heard it directly from him yet, but more than one mutual acquaintance had told her. She didn't miss Richard; she'd actually found him tiresome over the final few months, with his all-too-vocal disappointment and questioning the decisions Faye had made for them as a couple. Virginia was welcome to Richard, but she missed having someone to talk to at the end of the day, a person to drink a glass of whisky with and a shoulder to rest her head upon.

Faye closed the book, having failed to turn a single page. Her eyes were finally tired. Had Robert really called her 'prickly' earlier? Is that how he saw her? It wasn't a nice word, she considered; it was the scratch of brambles and jumpers that left you with an itchy rash. And what was all that about a thorny rose? Yes, she and Robert had had their disagreements, and she'd probably been sharp with him on occasions, but hadn't he given her cause to be? If she was prickly, he was damned annoying. Then again ...

She'd enjoyed their drowsy candidness earlier, the sound of his voice in the dark and his breath on her ear – but if she'd felt a softening towards Robert, it was only because she'd been feeling low and unsettled and he'd just happened to be there. She might equally have put her head on Daniel's shoulder, she told herself, if he'd been the person she'd stumbled upon in the garden. That said, there was the briefest moment when she'd thought Robert might try to kiss her. Of course, he was drunk, but would she have pushed him away? Faye pondered the possible iterations of how she might have responded and alarmed herself. Gathering up her book, she blew the candle out. It was for the best that it hadn't happened. Wasn't it?

Chapter Fifteen

Robert was woken by a knocking on the door downstairs. Parting his eyelids painfully, and squinting at the bedside clock, he saw it was still only six o'clock. He'd been in bed for three hours, and as he stepped down the narrow staircase, he was all too aware he'd had too much to drink. He felt slightly dizzy, had to take the stairs carefully, and the persistent knocking at the door seemed to pound in his head. Whatever was going on? Who could need him at this time?

Faye was standing on the doorstep. She was wearing unflattering dungarees and her faintly vexed expression suggested she hadn't had an especially restful night either.

'I'm sorry to drag you out of bed,' she began. 'You've probably not been in there for long, have you? It's only that Trudie was meant to be with me on the market stall this morning, but I'd have more chance of waking the dead. I couldn't possibly bribe you into helping me, could I? I have coffee and headache powders.'

Robert vaguely recalled that Trudie had still been dancing as he left the party. 'I think I last saw her demonstrating the steps of the rhumba on a table. You really need someone to come with you?' Faye nodded. 'Give me five minutes. I feel as if something has died inside my mouth.'

It wasn't the day Robert would have chosen. He probably would have slept in, made himself a late breakfast and then have done some gentle pottering in the greenhouse. He dreaded today might be the occasion Faye would choose to give him a lecture on the future role of the League of Nations or the implications of the conflict in Manchuria. Couldn't she have chosen another victim this morning? But, then, the entire Greenfields community was probably feeling delicate right now. He gave himself a perfunctory wash and gulped down two glasses of water. When he stepped out of the cottage, she was waiting with the van already loaded.

'I would have helped you with that,' he said.

'I wouldn't have pushed my luck. There's a thermos of coffee under the seat and I'll buy you some breakfast when we get there. I do appreciate this is probably the last thing you want to be doing this morning.'

The springy suspension of the van did nothing for the state of his head or his stomach. He thought he might be sick for a moment, but opened the window and took deep breaths.

'Tell me if you want me to pull over,' she said. 'You do look a bit green. I'd rather you didn't throw up on the upholstery.'

'Thank you for your sympathy.'

'Sympathy? He expects sympathy?' She grinned. 'Is it so bad?'

'Why did I drink that filthy stuff? Please never let me drink Trudie's punch again.'

'That's what everyone says, but we always do. What time did you leave?'

'Around three, I think. It's all a little hazy, to be honest, but the party was very much still going.' After Mrs Fitzgerald had spoken, and Teddy hadn't taken the opportunity to make a scene, he'd felt a sense of relief – and then let Trudie keep on refilling his glass.

Faye whistled. 'Ouch! Don't worry, once we've set up you can crawl under the stall and have a sleep.'

'I might well do that. I hope you're not joking.' He couldn't always tell when Faye was being serious.

He was glad she was sensitive enough not to feel the need to talk all the way into town. As he glanced across at her, he thought she looked pale and tired too. He wanted to close his burning eyes, but that made him feel more nauseous. How he wished he was still in bed. His mind tracked over the previous evening and found blank and blurred expanses of time, but he remembered he'd sat on a bench with Faye for a while and had felt restless after she'd left.

'What did you do with your evening?' He ought to make some effort towards sociability. 'What was so engrossing that you couldn't tear yourself away?'

'I was reading essays on new approaches to teaching English as a foreign language.'

'My God! I'd rather have this hangover.'

She looked across at him with a smile. 'Actually, it might be more fun.'

'As a foreign language? Are you going overseas?'

'Not imminently, but I would like to teach abroad at some point in my life.'

He nodded. 'I'd like to travel. I want to see the gardens of Versailles and Villandry, the Isola Bella and the Alhambra.'

'I've spotted the theme. Do you hanker to see anything other than gardens?'

'Of course . . .' His head felt too foggy to provide an itiner-ary at this moment. '. . . Paris, Rome, the Mediterranean coast, Pompeii . . .' It was as much as he could presently manage. 'One day. Maybe. Between you and me, I've never been anywhere more exotic than Blackpool.'

She talked for a while then of friends who had travelled, and Robert heard a slight wistfulness in her tone. She spoke of Indian tea gardens and temples, of bustling ports and transcon-tinental railway journeys, and of ancient palaces now inhabited only by monkeys and parrots. It washed over him; he was aware he wasn't being a good conversationalist, but he saw the colours of the places she described, the jade-green jungles and the indigo seas, felt the warmth of the sun that she conjured with her words and breathed a scent of jasmine and spices. Her voice might have lulled him to sleep, these foreign scenes had the exoticism of a fairy tale, but he opened his eyes and saw the match factory, the profile of the church at the top of the town, the advertising hoardings with posters for Mazawattee Tea and Sanatogen, and the down-on-their-luck men tramping the roads with their tattered bundles, bent shoulders and billy cans. Then Teddy's Bentley swerved around them as Faye changed gear on the hill, his engine revving and accelerating away far too fast for the narrow street.

'Bloody maniac!' Faye shouted it with feeling and Robert laughed.

They left the van in the usual place and he helped her to set up the stall. There were new spring greens and a few early broad beans this week, and Faye arranged the display as if she were planning to make it the subject of a still-life painting. The hangover was making Robert feel shivery now. The church bells struck seven o'clock and once again he wished he was still curled up in the warmth of his bed.

When they'd finished setting up, she handed him the thermos flask. 'I put sugar in for you. I thought you might need it. You know, my father swears by brandy and a raw egg . . .'

'Do you want me to be sick?'

She let him sit quietly while she dealt with the customers. Everyone knew her name and many of them asked after her parents and sisters. He heard more of the Gloucestershire accent in her voice this morning, and it struck him that he knew very little about her background. If he had to leave Anderby – if she chose to leave – would they ever have the chance to talk about these things? An older woman who came to the stall teased her, asking her why she hadn't got a new chap yet. 'A pretty, clever girl like you! You ought to be fighting them off.'

'I've renounced men. I've taken a vow against them. Do I not radiate confirmed spinster?'

'What rubbish! You want to get yourself out there. You won't have your looks forever and we're dead for an awfully long time.'

As the woman left, Faye turned to Robert with an expression on her face that was at once exasperated and amused. 'I honestly think they'd be more satisfied if I said I'd set myself up in a bordello. When I was at Oxford it was perfectly acceptable that I called myself a career-minded woman, but thirty miles away I'm considered unnatural. What century are we in here?'

Robert grinned. It had entertained him to watch the older woman quizzing Faye. 'Do you wish you'd stayed in Oxford?' He put a hand to her shoulder – and then realized he possibly shouldn't.

'When I'm obliged to have conversations like that, I do, yes.'

He imagined what she might have been like in her university days. Would she have been a bluestocking? He guessed she probably would have been very focussed and determined and a keen member of several debating societies. Hadn't Iris told him that she'd got a scholarship of some kind? He pictured a slightly younger version of Faye on a bicycle, wobbling with a basketful of books, her mouth pursed in concentration and utterly oblivious to the infatuations of all the men around her. He recalled then that he'd wanted to kiss her last night. Hell, he must have been sozzled. Would she have slapped him if he'd tried?

'You look like you're having a serious conversation with yourself. Are you chewing your way through some meaty moral dilemma? Or perhaps you're having some really hard thoughts about compost?'

Robert looked up and realized she'd been watching him. Her head was tilted to one side and she smiled.

'Just recalling follies done in drink.'

'Oh dear! Can we expect consequences later? Will Anderby be awash with scandal?'

A strand of hair blew across her face and kept catching in her eyelashes. He wanted to reach out and tuck it behind her ear. 'It's all a bit blurry, but I feel I might have had more near-misses than collisions.'

'Well, that's a mercy then,' she said.

He noticed a slight straightening in her smile.

He went off to buy them both a bacon sandwich. When he returned, he found her handing a basket over to a young woman and refusing to accept any payment. The woman looked rather downtrodden, her hair was thin and her boots were worn, but should Faye be doing that?

'It's kind,' the young woman said. There was some qualification in her voice. 'I appreciate it, but what we need is for Sam to find work. Still, with these building plans, there might be something for him. Do you think?'

'You mean the new houses being built along the road into town? I hope something comes up for him soon,' Faye replied.

'How do you know her?' Robert asked as the woman departed.

'Her name's Laura Bradley. She's the elder sister of one of the children I used to teach. She's only twenty-two, but you wouldn't think it to look at her, would you? Poor girl. Her husband has been out of work for months now, and she has three children to feed. She says he feels society has no use for him any longer. He feels worthless. Isn't that awful?'

'It's terribly sad. But should you be giving things away?' He'd seen Iris passing on unsold produce at the end of the day, but the morning trade was barely beginning now.

Faye's face hardened. 'You mean I should have asked her to wait until I managed to get a motion approved at a meeting?' Robert heard irritation in her tone. 'Shall I call her back and ask if she'd mind returning in a fortnight – subject to the vote going in my favour, of course, and them deeming her "deserving poor"?'

'I'm sorry. I understand. And I'm sure Mrs Fitzgerald would approve of what you did.'

'She'd approve? Do you think? Oh well, that's good, then. Robert, what a loyal boy you are!'

He had no objection to what Faye had done, he sympathized, but he didn't appreciate her talking to him like that. He felt if he were to say anything in response, they would end up spi-ralling into warring words again, and he didn't have the head for it today. Robert made himself step back, held his tongue and watched the crowds pass by. The silence between them stretched from tension into awkwardness. He felt some relief then as Faye stood to serve a customer, once more speaking in her bright, businesslike voice.

Robert had come to recognize the faces of many of their regular customers and now he touched his cap to Mrs Peterson. Faye had her weekly order set aside. She was here earlier than usual this morning, though, and there was an eager expression on her face.

'I've just heard your news!' she said to Faye. 'Mr Cole told me. He got word of it from someone on the Planning Committee. Will you continue doing the market garden or will that go too?'

'I'm sorry?' Faye paused from counting out Mrs Peterson's change.

'I have to say, it did surprise me. I didn't think she'd ever split up the estate.'

Faye put down the bag. 'Split up the estate? I'm sorry, Mrs Peterson, but I have no idea what you're talking about.'

Mrs Peterson's eyes widened at that. She looked like she had something delicious in her mouth. 'Surely you know? Mr Cole heard it in the council offices. Your Mrs Fitzgerald is selling off the grounds of the house.'

Faye glanced at Robert with a frown on her face. 'That can't be right. She wouldn't do that. I'm afraid you've heard Chinese whispers, Mrs Peterson.'

Mrs Peterson hoisted an eyebrow. 'Perhaps you need to have

a talk with your Mrs Fitzgerald. Happen she hasn't been keeping you in the picture? Word has it, she's sold the old orchard
to a builder and there are plans for a housing estate. Captain
Fitzgerald was at the council offices yesterday, apparently.
They've given permission for an access road.'

'A housing estate? At Anderby? No. That can't possibly be
true.'

Mrs Peterson took her change and snapped her purse shut.
'Twenty Tudorbethan bungalows,' she said.

'A housing estate?' Faye repeated as they watched Mrs
Peterson disappearing between the stalls. Her eyes stared directly into Robert's, but he wasn't certain she was seeing him.
'She's got it wrong. What nonsense! Gwendoline would never
do that.'

Robert thought of the mist curling between the old apple
trees and the melancholy sound of the cello playing in the orchard. It couldn't be possible, could it? But hadn't that young
woman also been saying something about building plans?

They packed up the stall early. Mr Thornton had mentioned
the housing estate too and Mrs Barker-Finch had spoken of
a builder from Swindon whose signature was half-timbered
semis with Tudor gables. With each telling, the project seemed
to become larger and stranger; it gained in whimsies, bay windows and inglenooks, and they planted the fields all around
Anderby with black and white crosses. Robert saw alarm and
confusion on Faye's face and suddenly felt as sober as he'd ever
been. Before the church bells struck midday, they needed to
know the truth.

Chapter Sixteen

'There's some strange talk in town,' Faye said to Mrs Fitzgerald. They'd gone straight to the door of the Hall. 'Mrs Peterson came to us on the stall. She'd heard a rumour and couldn't wait to see our reaction. She told us you've sold the orchard to a builder.' Faye shook her head and smiled, but the question was in her narrowed eyes. 'It is nonsense, isn't it?'

'Will you excuse me one moment? I was just in the middle of ...' Mrs Fitzgerald visibly blanched before she closed the door.

It was Maurice who called the emergency meeting. Within an hour of them returning from the market, the story had circulated all around Anderby. While the majority response had been shaken heads and a dismissal of groundless gossip – after all, it was hardly the first time that the community had been the subject of speculation – Robert thought of the expression on Mrs Fitzgerald's face as she'd closed the door. If it wasn't true, wouldn't she have immediately outright denied it? Could there be something in it?

She and Teddy were conspicuous in their absence as the group entered the house and filed through to the dining room.

There was no sign of them. Mrs Fitzgerald always insisted the Hall's reception rooms belonged to the community, but it felt impolite to Robert that they now openly speculated about the couple's finances as they took places at their table.

'It's absolute rot. It's tittle-tattle,' Iris said. 'Gwendoline would never do such a thing. She wouldn't dream of it. She certainly wouldn't do it without consulting us first.'

'Are you absolutely sure?' Cecil asked.

Robert took a chair at the table next to Faye. They'd talked as she drove home, she speculating at speed and taking the bends a little too fast. All the way back to Anderby, she'd thrown unanswerable questions at him. Would Mrs Fitzgerald really do that? Why might she do it? Why had there been no discussion about it? Robert had thought of the cowslips and lambs in the orchard, of Daniel and his cider press, and of what else Mrs Fitzgerald might have sold off. In her speech last night she'd talked of change and growth and the importance of facing challenges with courage and adaptability. He'd applied her words to the context of the garden and been reassured by them – but had other plans been in her mind as she'd spoken? How would this impact the garden restoration? Was it now in jeopardy? Could she already have decided to give it up?

When Mrs Fitzgerald finally entered the room, Teddy had a hand on her shoulder. They seemed to have decided to present a united front. It was the first time Robert had seen her without her red lipstick, her face looked different without it, and had she been crying? The room was perfectly silent as Teddy pulled out his wife's customary seat at the table.

'Tell me it isn't true,' said Iris.

No one spoke as Teddy went around with the whisky bottle. Most people shook their heads. Robert could feel a tension in the silence.

'Well?' Nancy finally said.

Mrs Fitzgerald, at the head of the table, visibly took a deep breath.

'It *can't* be true!' Phyllis protested. 'The cider orchard? You wouldn't!'

Mrs Fitzgerald accepted a glass of whisky from her husband. She drank it down before she spoke. 'We needed the money,' she said, her normally strong voice now barely more than a whisper.

Lionel Massingham's chair scraped back. 'You sold it to a bloody builder? Our land?'

'We wouldn't have done it if we had other options. I need you to understand that. We're at our wits' end. We've tried to get loans, but we've been refused. We can't get credit. We can't pay our rates or our tax bill. We didn't have any other choice.'

'You didn't think to consult us?' There was anger in Daniel's voice and his face had reddened. 'You didn't feel it ought to be a community decision?'

'I should have spoken to you sooner, Daniel. I realize that. I wanted to, but ... You're absolutely right. I am ashamed of my conduct. You shouldn't have found out this way. I truly am sorry.'

It was the first time Robert had heard Daniel raise his voice, and the fact he was now doing so to Mrs Fitzgerald shocked him. He'd assumed Daniel was her closest ally and confidante. The look on his face suggested this was a personal blow as much as a betrayal of the community's principles.

'But this hasn't been mentioned in the meetings,' Miss Parget said. 'You didn't give us any indication that money was so tight. Why haven't we talked about this?'

'We should have been more open with you. I just hoped we might be able to work something out without it impacting the community.'

It was only then that Robert noticed Mrs Fitzgerald's bare fingers. Hadn't she worn emerald rings when he first met her? There was only the plain gold band of her wedding ring now. Was that what 'working something out' meant?

'Without impacting the community?' Maurice repeated. 'Well, that plan failed, didn't it? This is going to have an enormous impact on us all!'

'We've been struggling enough with the day-to-day running costs and our tax bills are horrific,' Mrs Fitzgerald went on. 'But there's also the issue of the roof now.' Robert heard the emotion in her voice as she spoke. 'When the snow thawed, the water was pouring in. We're tripping over buckets upstairs. There's only so much we can do with tarpaulins. We've put it off for as long as we could, but it's reached the stage where we have to employ a builder. It's a necessity, not a choice. If we don't, the house might fall down around us next winter. Teddy's had a couple of quotations for the work; it's going to cost a small fortune.'

'But it should have been a community decision,' Daniel said again. 'This isn't how we work. I don't understand how you could have done this.'

'We could have found a solution together,' Phyllis said, her voice more pleading than angry. 'We've coped with crises before. We could have worked as a group and found a way.'

'You mean you could have organized a whip-round for us? Perhaps we could have had a jumble sale? Or sold raffle tickets?' Teddy's tone was derisive. 'There was no other way.'

This seemed to rile Maurice. 'If you were half a man, you'd go up there and get on with the repairs yourself,' he said.

'You know Teddy can't!' Mrs Fitzgerald objected.

'What can Teddy do apart from fritter away money on racetracks? Is that where it's all gone? Is that why you can't pay your bills? I don't suppose it's ever occurred to you to go out and get a job, has it?'

'Do you want to take this outside?' Teddy stepped towards Maurice. There was a snarl on his face. He might not be up to fixing roofs, but he looked ready to punch Maurice.

'Please, can we discuss this calmly?' Mrs Fitzgerald appealed. She appeared to be on the verge of tears.

'No, we bloody can't!' said Maurice.

'Is it true that the land's been bought by a builder and they're intending to construct a housing estate?' It was Trudie who spoke up now. She was wearing dark glasses and a pained expression.

'And are they really going to be Tudoresque bungalows?' Maurice asked. He said the words as if they tasted unpleasant in his mouth. 'Surely that's a macabre joke?'

Mrs Fitzgerald shook her head. 'A mix of bungalow cottages and semi-detached villas,' she said quietly.

'But we have sixteenth-century plasterwork! We have wattle and daub! We have pargeting and authentic Tudor roses!'

'You can give backword, can't you?' Nancy asked. 'You can change your mind. We can find another way. You can tell them there's opposition to the plans.'

'It's too late. All the paperwork has gone through. It's already in motion,' Teddy said.

There was a moment of silence and then everyone was talking at once.

'Bungalow people!' Maurice exclaimed.

'Who will they be?'

'Will they share our values?'

'We haven't had our say. We ought to have been consulted. So much for equality!'

'And so much for turning our backs on materialism!'

'Haven't we always talked about respecting the history of the site? Trying to work in harmony with the landscape? This blatantly goes against our principles!'

'This makes a mockery of the values we've tried to live by!'

'Do you not realize what you've done?'

Robert watched the room, the angry faces and ugly gesticulations and the increasingly bitter words. Everyone was shouting. No one was listening. At the centre of the maelstrom sat Mrs Fitzgerald. She stared silently at her empty glass and dashed a tear away with the back of her hand.

Finally, Teddy's voice was raised above the clamour of the crowd. 'That's enough,' he said. 'Will you listen to yourselves? She's bankrolled this project for the best part of fifteen years and this is the thanks you give her? You should be ashamed of yourselves.' He put an arm around his wife and ushered her from the room.

'Why must it be the orchard?' Daniel asked.

'It's treachery,' said Maurice.

'It's the end of us,' Lionel said.

While the room had been full of accusatory words, neither

Robert nor Faye had spoken. At the end of the day, he was an employee here, and shouldn't Mrs Fitzgerald be given the space to explain? It wasn't like Faye not to voice her thoughts, though. Robert had seen the tension in her hands on the table and heard it in the sound of her breath. He found himself wanting to take her hand now and ask her how she was feeling. Why did she think they'd done it? What would happen next? But she didn't seem to want to meet his eye as she rose from the table and crossed her arms across her chest.

Chapter Seventeen

'Faye! Please wait for me!' Robert had followed her out of the house and down through the walled garden. She was now leaning against the gate of the orchard. When she finally turned back towards him, he saw that she'd been crying.

'Here.' He reached for his handkerchief, not certain quite what else to do or say. 'Everyone got so angry in there. I thought people were going to come to blows.'

'Thank you.' She dried her eyes. 'Of course they're all angry, Robert. They feel betrayed. She's done this behind our backs.'

She suddenly looked younger, wounded and vulnerable. He wanted to put his arms around her to comfort her, but there was also anger in her voice.

'Maybe she felt too ashamed to tell anyone? They've clearly got themselves into financial difficulties. She's obviously not proud of what she's done.'

Trudie had spoken of Mrs Fitzgerald losing money in the market crash, but he hadn't realized quite how precarious their finances were. On reflection, there seemed to be so many signs that he'd missed seeing. She'd been late with paying his wages twice and as his eyes had travelled around the dining room just now, their problems were evident in the absences of particular clocks and bronzes and cabinets. Imagining Mrs Fitzgerald having to take her personal possessions to dealers and salesrooms, he pitied her. This situation must be painful and humiliating. She must have been frightened for the future. Was his salary in danger, though?

'But the whole point of this community is that we share our problems and find solutions together.' Faye's eyes shifted, focussing on nothing in particular as she struggled to centre her thoughts. 'We're meant to be open and honest with each other. We don't hide things. We don't deceive each other. We certainly don't sneak around and make major decisions without considering how they'll impact other people. That's now how it works.'

'Desperate measures?' he suggested. 'Maybe she didn't feel the community could help with this? Maybe she felt it was her responsibility to put it right?'

'But she must have known full well that if she brought the idea of this sale to the meetings, not one person would vote for it.' Faye's tears had finally stopped falling, but she blinked at him with red-rimmed eyes. 'There used to be a statement of aims up on the wall of the dining room – a sort of charter that Gwendoline and Daniel had drafted back at the start. It talked about how there must be no hierarchy here, I remember, and no decisions without discussion and consensus. Everyone's views would be heard and valued equally, everything must be considered and fair.' She counted points out on her fingers as she recalled the wording. 'It spoke of how we must try to live in harmony with one another and respect the landscape and the nature around us. We should strive to put back more than we took out of the land and we must preserve the historic buildings, being mindful that we were only their current custodians. We were meant to be turning our backs on a commercial, material life and striving for something better. That's what it said. That's what this community was meant to be about. But she's gone against all of that.'

Over Faye's shoulder, Robert could see the sheep grazing in the orchard. The new lambs were testing their legs, all ponderous and comical, and the buds were just starting to break on the trees. It was difficult to imagine how this place might become a housing estate. He tried to picture it. It was horrible and shocking to think that the trees might be felled and the grass covered over with concrete. It was a sickening thought and he could also appreciate how this decision went against the community's rules and spirit. How could Mrs Fitzgerald do such a thing? 'I knew this was the place I was meant to be,' she'd said on the day he'd first met her. 'I needed Anderby and it needed me.' She'd spoken those words with sincerity, he was certain of it. He'd heard the emotion in her voice and seen it on her face. But was she, even then, contemplating having to sell paintings and furniture and the orchard? Surely those must have been agonizing decisions?

'She's not done this lightly. You could see how upset she was.'

'But she's gone against *everything*!' There was a note of frustration in Faye's voice now. 'They took that charter down when they were having the wall panelling repaired and it never got put back up again. That must have been four or five years ago. I hadn't thought about it until today. Maybe we ought to have noticed sooner and asked why they did that.'

'I can't imagine it was deliberate.'

Faye's eyes flashed. 'Must you make excuses for her, Robert?'

'I'm not making excuses. I'm trying to understand why she's done this. Everything you say just reinforces my sense that she can't have wanted to do it.'

'But she did! And it's done!' Faye held her hands up towards him, her stretched fingers like exclamation marks. 'All these things she set out to achieve don't seem to matter to her any longer – clearly! – so why are we here, then? What is this community for? How are we meant to carry on? As Lionel said, this feels like an ending for Greenfields.'

Robert understood why she was upset and angry, but surely this wasn't an ending? It was just the shock, the emotion of the moment that was making her talk like this, wasn't it? Or was everyone now feeling this way? With all the sincere endeavour of this community, all the hope and belief that had been invested in it over the years, they couldn't seriously walk away, could they? But he looked at Faye's face and saw such a depth of sadness and disappointment there. Had their belief in this venture just died?

Chapter Eighteen

Spring had arrived and each day dawned as clean and bright as a newly minted coin. There was a scent of wild garlic in the woods, clouds of white blossom had burst from the roadside blackthorns and new lines of wheat were showing in the fields. The spring felt transformative this year. Robert was more aware of it than ever before. Every morning he made new discoveries in the garden, and as the hillsides greened, the valley had the appearance of an entirely different country. It was a revelatory spring, but all everyone talked of now was the land sale.

It had taken him a while to get the motor-mower going. The task had required some patience and effort with spanners and an oil can. Like many of the garden tools at Anderby, it was distinctly antique and not inclined to be cooperative. He hadn't wanted to stop the motor once he'd finally got it started, but as Trudie had strode across the lawn towards him he could tell from her walk that something was amiss. The motor had spluttered to a halt with a belch of black smoke and he'd obediently followed her around to the front of the house. They'd stood looking up at the defaced banner together.

'Who do you suppose did it?' she'd asked.

'I haven't the first clue,' he'd replied. It might have been one of many people, Robert had thought. 'But it's mean-spirited, don't you think?'

'It's nasty. There's something threatening about it, isn't there? But then people do feel strongly.'

As Robert sat in the café now, and looked around the gathered faces, he couldn't help wondering who might have felt *that* strongly. Since he'd arrived at Anderby, the banner had hung over the door of the Hall, proclaiming Greenfields' core values (*'Community. Creativity. Equality. Education'*) in slightly mildewed Gothic lettering. But this morning someone had put a thick line of blood-red paint through the word *'Community'*. It looked like a grisly knife wound and had dripped down the fabric and pooled onto the flagstones below. One of the cats had trodden through it and so there were also red paw prints all over the steps. Robert's immediate response had been that he ought to get a bucket of hot soapy water and a stiff brush, but Trudie had led him away.

'They must have used a tall ladder,' Nancy said as she put the replenished teapot on the table. They'd drank a lot of tea over their speculations this morning. 'Where did they find one?'

'Any of us might have access to a ladder,' Trudie reasoned.

'They must have done it early this morning before anyone else was about. Nobody seems to have seen anything.'

'I was out by seven,' Robert said. 'I was busy in the workshop. I didn't walk around to the front of the Hall, but I might have seen if someone had taken a ladder from the barns.'

'It will have been a man. No disrespect to you, Robert,' Nancy put her hand to his arm, 'but a woman wouldn't do a thing like that, would she?'

'I'm not so sure,' Trudie replied. 'When I was younger I had a darling friend who was a militant suffragist and she delighted in breaking glass and starting fires. Her pretty little Kensington sitting room became a regular factory for incendiary devices. Defacing a banner would have seemed a feeble gesture to Olivia. She'd have scoffed at it.' Amusement and fondness showed on Trudie's face. 'Dear Livie! She'd have gone straight for the petrol bomb.'

'Who would have red paint? Who might use it in their work?' Phyllis asked. 'Whoever did it, they might have paint down their fingernails.'

'You mean they might literally be caught red-handed?' said Iris, smiling faintly for the first time that morning. 'Are you going to want to inspect our fingernails? Isn't this all getting a bit Agatha Christie?'

'It makes me think about when we did *Macbeth* last year and Maurice wringing his red hands on stage. Do you remember? You don't think . . .' Phyllis left the question hanging in the air.

'You wouldn't get it past a jury,' Trudie advised.

Robert was aware that they were each of them looking around the table and examining fingernails on cups and slices of fruitcake. Were they all mentally rifling through the names of the community? Weighing up opportunity and motive? This wasn't healthy, was it?

'Maurice was furious, though, wasn't he?' Phyllis went on. 'Did you see his face? Did you hear the name he called Mrs Fitz? He said this housing estate would be a scar.'

'Maurice calls the Methodist chapel in the village a scar,' Iris cautioned. 'Anything less than three hundred years old is a scar to Maurice.'

'She must have desperately needed the money,' Robert

suggested. He felt he ought to move the conversation on. He wasn't comfortable with these speculations. 'They must have been at their wits' end. She said that, didn't she?'

'They can't be penniless, surely?' Nancy looked doubtful. 'They have income from rents, tenancies and the farm.'

'The estate has generally run at a small annual loss in recent years,' Trudie said, 'which was tolerable while Gwen still had investments and money in the bank, I suppose. I guess they've got to the point where all of that has gone and the banks are now shaking their heads. The day-to-day upkeep of the building is hideously expensive, I know that, and everyone is utterly crippled with tax now. My father liked to pronounce that the English landed class would be taxed out of existence – though, in many cases, that would be no bad thing. About bloody time too!' She gave one of her barked laughs. 'Even my mother is obliged to let the public in at the weekends these days. Apparently, Mrs Billington won't let them out again unless they've bought a slice of cake and a lavender cutting. I believe she's merciless! But even if Gwen was on her knees, they shouldn't have done this without discussion.'

'If they were so desperate, why has Teddy not sold his motors?' Phyllis frowned as she lit a cigarette. She smoked with an elegantly angled wrist and elongated fingers, like they did on the films. 'Surely he doesn't need three cars? It shows their priorities, don't you think?'

Nancy took the packet from Phyllis. 'He'll go himself before he parts with his Bentleys.'

'There must have been other things they could have done? It seems madness that just two people are living in that huge house. Couldn't they let rooms out? She used to do that, didn't she?'

'Teddy doesn't like having people in the house.' Trudie rolled her eyes.

'And Teddy must always have his own way?'

'Could she not have sold off more farmland? Why the orchard?'

'She's already let the best of the land go,' Iris said, 'and this would be more lucrative, I suppose.'

'It's in the contract that the builders have to preserve the walls around the orchard,' Trudie said. 'It'll be partially screened by the walls, Gwen told me, and it's convenient for them to put in an access road there. Not screened enough, though, I'd say.'

'Hiding it away?' Iris topped up her teacup. 'Gwendoline said she felt ashamed. She looked it too, didn't she? I couldn't help but feel a bit sorry for her. She must have dreaded the news breaking.'

'Not easy to hide twenty bungalows, is it? How long was she going to wait before she told us? Until the builders arrived on site? I can't feel sorry for her,' Nancy said.

'What do you suppose these houses will be like?' Phyllis asked. 'Will they try to make them nice? My cousin lives in a bungalow in Lytham St Annes. She says it's very comfortable and she doesn't miss stairs.'

'No disrespect to your cousin's bungalow,' Trudie said, 'I'm sure it is nice, darling, but they will look out of place here, won't they?'

'At least they're going to make them look old.'

'But they won't really look old, will they?' Trudie's bracelets jangled emphasis as she gesticulated. 'Not against the Hall. I hate to sound like Maurice, but they'll look pastiche and cheap.'

'Imagine felling all those trees!' Nancy held her hands to her chest. 'I can't bear to think about that!'

'Did you see poor Daniel's face?' Iris said. 'It will break his heart.'

'She might have done that already when she decided not to tell him. I thought they told each other everything. I imagined they were as thick as thieves.'

'I've always had the greatest respect for her,' Phyllis reflected. She put her cigarette out and immediately lit another. 'I'm sorry if they're short of money, but I also feel let down. We came here because we wanted to be part of a community where people cared about one another's interests, didn't we, Nance? I thought we'd found that here, I believed that was what Greenfields was all about, but I feel like I've been cheated now. We should have been consulted. Our interests should have been taken into account. I can't understand how she could have behaved like that. It goes against everything she's always said.'

'Teddy's influence is all over this.' Trudie's brow creased as she looked up from her teacup. 'He probably told her to keep it hush-hush. It's just not like her. It's entirely out of character.'

'Quite possibly. But she should have known better. It's underhand the way they've behaved.'

'The whole thing is horrid, isn't it?' said Iris.

'And I fear it will get worse yet.' Trudie looked uncharacteristically solemn as she sat back in her seat.

Chapter Nineteen

Daniel left the motor in the builder's yard. This felt a little like an act of subterfuge, but he needed to know the truth. There was a large wooden hut to the far side of the yard, which the signage indicated to be the Estate Office. As he approached, he noticed there were pictures in the windows of various models of houses. They were artists' impressions, he saw as he stepped closer. Smiling couples stood arm in arm on thresholds, rosy-cheeked children played in improbably green gardens and even the dogs had jauntily wagging tails. They reminded him of some of the illustrations Iris had done for children's books. *'Just the House You've Always Wanted!'* insisted a sign.

Daniel's eyes refocussed and a young man in a loudly striped suit appeared at the side of his own reflection. He flashed a professional smile, raised a hand and beckoned Daniel towards the door.

'Can I help you, sir? Are you interested in one of our developments?'

'Are these your houses?' Daniel asked.

'Yes, this is the signature Houghton & Halford style – a traditionally English aspect, but incorporating the latest advances in construction and complete with all modern conveniences. Please, sir – would you like to step inside?'

Daniel looked around the office. It smelled of linoleum and new pine. There was a model on a table at the centre of the room and he found himself drawn towards it. An arrangement of toy houses stood on an undulating expanse of green plastic turf. Tin foil had been used to simulate a duck pond and the trees appeared to have been made from pieces of sponge and pipe-cleaners. It could have been a model village, or something a train set ought to circle, but there was nothing charming about it. The houses might have been fashioned from match-boxes, each with a lino roof and its own particular arrangement of black and white lines.

'We go for a naturalistic feel,' the young salesman went on, pushing against the evidence of Daniel's eyes. 'Some of our competitors build to a standard model, but we like to vary the exterior aspect, so the properties look as if they've evolved, like an old town. Characterful, quaint, picturesque, do you see?'

'Yes,' Daniel replied, though he felt far from convinced. The matchbox houses looked like something that could have been stamped out on a factory production line. They might be ingots.

'The timber cladding is purely decorative, of course. No wattle and daub here!' The salesman grinned. He had remark-ably white teeth. 'No, they're modern brick underneath and a steel framework. These houses are built to last. But the look is important to us – quintessentially English, wouldn't you say? The England of Shakespeare, what? Some people use the term "mock-Tudor", but we prefer "neo-Tudor"; it sums up that ideal blend of olde-worlde charm and up-to-the-minute efficiency. Of course, they all come with modern sanitary con-veniences and kitchens with built-in cupboards, electric light and gas and a constant hot-water supply. Isn't that the perfect combination?'

'I have an outside privy,' said Daniel distractedly.

'And so, naturally, you want to upgrade to modern comforts! Our bathrooms and kitchens have chromium-plate fittings – wonderfully labour-saving for the lady – and we do synthetic wood panelling in a variety of finishes. We have six different models: from the Woolsey, a luxurious three-bedroom with two reception rooms, to the Boleyn, a cosy one-bedroom, perfect for newlyweds.'

'Isn't that a bit ironic?' Daniel asked.

'I'm sorry, sir?'

'Never mind.'

'Is there a particular development you're interested in, sir? Mister – I'm sorry, I didn't catch your name?'

'Molyneux. Daniel Molyneux. Is it true you're building at Anderby Hall?'

'Here, let me give you my business card, and do call me Gus. Everyone calls me Gus. Has word got out about Anderby already, then? Marvellous! It's going to be a smashing project. We're expecting a great deal of interest from Mr and Mrs Homeseeker. It's in the grounds of a stately home, you know. Very prestigious. A stunning prospect. Just ripe for development. We've bought the orchard and have initial plans for twenty houses there but, if we can acquire additional land, it might be more.' He touched a finger to the side of his nose, indicating he was privileging Daniel with hush-hush information. 'We intend to retain some of the old walls and perhaps a few of the mature trees to give it character, you see? It will all be sympathetically done, extremely tasteful, a mix of our Woolsey,

Raleigh and Howard models, each with garden front and rear, and parking for a motor. Very desirable. We expect this one to sell well. Are you familiar with the location, sir?'

'I am,' Daniel replied.

He remembered Anderby in the autumn of 1918, the mist clinging to the lake in the mornings, the caw of the crows and the call of the collared doves. The medical men had done what they could, they'd patched him up and sent him on, but after a three-year stint in France his spirits had been utterly sapped. Released from the General Hospital, he'd been transferred to Anderby. Dr Lowe had wanted him to try hypnosis and had encouraged him to talk about his experiences, to face up to them, to address them, as he said. Daniel had found that difficult — why would he want to look back? — and it wasn't as if there'd been a single triggering incident that had caused his nerves to unravel. His injury might have been the result of a shell blast, but what he'd been suffering from wasn't shock. What afflicted him was total exhaustion and the mental attrition of three years of responsibility and anxiety. Ultimately, it had been the place more than the therapy that had helped him. Anderby, with its perfect peace and sense of long history, had engaged his senses, slowed his breathing, and made him look beyond the turmoil in his head. He'd possibly be dead now if he hadn't been sent there. Anderby had probably saved his life. He couldn't let this happen, could he?

'When will it begin?' he asked.

'The Anderby Hall development? Oh, quite soon. We're hoping to be on site within the next six weeks. The intention is that the first residents will be able to move in by Christmas. Lovely to have Christmas in a new home, isn't it?'

'So it's definitely happening?'

'Oh, yes. We're already taking deposits. If you're keen, it would do no harm to think about making a commitment toot sweet. Fortune favours the brave, what?'

'Is that so?' Daniel replied.

'They're mean little matchbox houses,' Daniel told the group. They'd gathered in Iris's kitchen. There were bottles on the table and children underneath it. Daniel had needed a stiff drink when he'd got back. 'They're going to squeeze twenty of them into the orchard and they're keen to buy more land. I don't know whether Gwendoline is already negotiating with them to sell more. They'll be on site within weeks.'

'So fast? Surely not? It can't happen that quickly, can it?' Trudie asked.

'Seemingly it can.'

'But the orchard is ancient.' Iris filled glasses again. 'It's part of the history of the house. It must have been there for centuries. Didn't they used to have a cider festival here every autumn? Aren't there rules to stop them doing things like this?'

'Unfortunately not.'

'We could organize a petition,' Nancy said. 'We could take it into town. If we could get a few hundred signatures they'd have to pay attention to that, wouldn't they?'

'Do you think?' Daniel doubted it.

'We could chain ourselves to the trees. That would halt them in their tracks. You tied yourself to a railing for suffrage once, didn't you, Phyllis?'

'We might hinder them, but I'm afraid we wouldn't be able to stop them.' Daniel hadn't struggled with his stammer for years, he barely even thought about it these days, but he consciously had to resist it now.

'What if we raised money and could offer the building company more than they paid for the land?' This was Trudie's proposal.

'But how could we do that?'

'Cecil could sell some of the sculptures that are in the garden,' Iris suggested. 'Technically, they're still his property.'

'They wouldn't raise that much and I'm not sure I want to part with them,' Cecil countered. He didn't look best pleased by the suggestion. 'Besides, I have a family to feed – had you forgotten?'

'And we do eat a lot,' a voice said from under the table.

'It will have an impact on the value of our properties,' Cecil went on. He sat back with his glass of whisky. 'That's inevitable. No wonder she didn't want to consult us.'

'We bought on the understanding that we would be consulted on any major changes to the estate,' Lionel said. 'We might not have signed any contract to that effect, but it was explicit in our conversations. We bought in good faith. Is there any legal recourse we might take?'

'I very much doubt it,' Daniel replied. 'It's her land to sell and she's not breaking any written agreements.'

'Are you certain? I'd like to discuss it with my solicitor.'

'Do as you see fit.'

'It's why we pay the annual residents' contribution too,' Phyllis spoke up. 'We pay so that we get a say. That's how it's meant to work, isn't it? That must exist in writing somewhere?'

'I regret to say it, but I'm not certain it does. Gwendoline and I wrote up a statement of aims at the start, but there was never anything prescriptive or binding. We never went in for drafting rules and regulations, procedures and contracts. We just weren't of that mind-set. The community was meant to be about sharing and trust, mutual support and collective decision making. We wanted this to be about people, not dictates on paper. I don't think we ever considered what might happen if a dispute arose. We never envisaged that.' Looking back, Daniel wondered if they'd been naïve.

'Well, you've certainly got a dispute on your hands now, haven't you?' Cecil downed his whisky and refilled his glass. 'Sorry if it offends your sensibilities, Daniel, but collective decision making seems to have been thrown out of the window, hasn't it? And the word *trust* sounds pretty hollow now, wouldn't you say?' His tone was a little snide. 'Personally, I think we ought to consult a property agent and get some good legal advice.'

'We could contact the newspapers too,' Nancy offered. 'We could all write letters.'

'Do you suppose anyone would care? It's not really newsworthy, is it? Landed estates are being sold off, split up and demolished all over the country. It's the times, isn't it? Why are we special here?'

'Oh, Daniel – don't sound so resigned!' Phyllis threw up her hands. 'To hear you speaking like that makes me despair. We have to *try*. We have to do something.'

'We mustn't give up hope,' said Iris. She leaned across and squeezed Daniel's arm.

'I'm afraid it may already be too late,' he said. He hated to say it, but it was true – wasn't it?

Chapter Twenty

'*Tudor homes of distinction*,' Robert read the strapline of the advertisement aloud. The hoarding had appeared overnight, fixed to the old perimeter wall. The image upon it was a curious mix of contemporary motifs and the cosily quaint; a sunset split the sky into segments of acid yellow and tangerine, while the property in the foreground had a look of Anne Hathaway's cottage. '*A unique high-class housing estate*,' he read on, '*splendidly situated in unspoilt countryside, with every house constructed in the modern Tudor style.*'

An advertisement for petrol had been erected next to it. '*Chose BP for a smoother journey*,' Trudie pronounced in a faux-chirpy voice. '*It's our tetra-ethyl-lead that lets you go that extra mile!*' She turned to Robert and wrinkled her nose. 'Why does everybody want a house that wears Tudor fancy-dress now? The family pile is genuinely fifteenth century and it's a terribly dark, gloomy, cold house. Half-timbering just says woodworm, rot and draughts to me. It evokes the smell of mildew and the need to wear a vest until June.'

'Nostalgia?' Robert ventured. 'Perhaps a desire for something that looks solid and permanent?'

'Maybe. Though the promise of permanency might

disappoint and I struggle to make the mental link between the Tudors and happy family homes.' She shrugged. There were shadows under her eyes this morning. She'd been starting to tell him about a letter from her mother as they'd come across the advertising hoarding. He'd got the impression that the old family pile had been far from a happy family home. 'Daniel says they're going to call it "Orchard Close",' she went on. 'Apparently, the builders intend to plant an apple tree in every garden.'

'Isn't that a good thing? Isn't that a nice gesture?'

'Do you suppose? Daniel shook his head as he told me.'

'I understand why people are angry about not having been consulted, but these houses don't look so very objectionable, do they?'

Whatever Trudie's doubts about Tudor timbers, the house on the poster had a comfortable and trim appearance. The lawn had been mowed into stripes, the gravel paths were perfectly weeded and its privet hedges were tidily squared. A shiny Baby Austin was parked on the driveway, a smiling housewife was carrying groceries from it, and two well-dressed children were petting a Fox Terrier. They looked like the sort of children who might be in the Boy Scouts and Brownies and listen to *Toytown* on the wireless. Didn't Faye want more children for the school? The father had a pipe in his mouth and was standing with his arms folded across his chest in a posture suggestive of the squire surveying his ancestral acres. All in all, it communicated respectability, pride and security.

'That's just advertising, isn't it?' Trudie narrowed her eyes at the hoarding. 'It's an image that's specifically designed to sell. I suspect the houses will be smaller and humbler in reality, and that "modern Tudor style" will look all wrong in this setting, won't it?' She made inverted commas with her fingers and then swore at the dogs who were tangling their leads around her legs.

'All wrong?' Robert took half of the dog leads from Trudie and they walked on. 'Aren't we getting ahead of ourselves? Do we know that yet?'

'It's the same builder who's bought up land along the main road into town. You must have seen the new houses as you're driving in? Those boxy little places right by the road? They don't exactly enhance the view and it will be even worse here. They'll look cheap and unconvincing against the backdrop of the Hall and it will be irreparably disfigured by them. Yes, I know I sound like Maurice, but . . .' She lit a cigarette, cupping her hands against the breeze, and offered him the packet. 'I'm not one of those people who believe everything must stand still, I don't think buildings must be preserved just because they're old, but there's something particular and special about this place. Don't you sense that? It has an atmosphere, a spirit, a personality – and that could so easily be damaged. Anderby is a serene, wise old lady and we ought to respect her. I always believed that Gwen felt that way too.' She breathed smoke out with a sigh. 'I'm not averse to change, don't misunderstand me, Robert. I'm all for shaking things up, and welcoming new people into the community, but we need to be careful that we don't destroy it in the process.'

Robert could hear her trying to make diplomatic word choices. Not everyone had been so restrained. Maurice had called the houses bourgeois, jerry-built, sham-Tudor shacks; Lionel kept talking about blots on the landscape; and Cecil said the development was positively blasphemous. There'd been

much discussion about artistic good taste and aesthetic awareness – and a general consensus that these houses exemplified
the reverse of that. Weren't people being a bit narrow-minded,
though? Wasn't this all terribly snobbish? While the word
'Equality' was plastered all over Anderby, Robert had recently
been struck that there was an elitism of taste here, of culture and
manners. By no means everyone had those attitudes, but those
who did presently seemed to have the loudest voices.

'We could plant trees that will screen it to a degree,' he said.

'How long would they take to grow? Alternatively, we could
build a really high wall and perhaps some of that camouflage
netting they used during the war?'

Robert glanced at her. She was joking, wasn't she? 'We'll get
used to it in time. Won't we? Yes, it's a shock, but I'm sure it
can't be as bad as everyone is suggesting.'

'We probably all sound rather self-interested to you, don't
we?' A black cat was sitting on the wall, flicking its tail, and
the dogs leapt at the ends of their leads. The cat looked down
with something like disdain and carried on with its toilette. 'It's
just that some of us have been here for a long time and we feel
a strong emotional connection to Anderby and the Greenfields
project. We want what's best for it and are concerned that this
is short-term, back-to-the-wall decision making. I'm convinced
Gwen wouldn't have considered it for a moment if she wasn't
under pressure. You know they're planning to put in an access
road that will cut across the parkland?'

'Is that true?' To get to the site, the road would have to curve
around the back of the walled garden. Robert thought about
the old cedar trees and the bank of rhododendrons that might
stand in its route. 'Is that definitely going to happen?'

'I believe so. The plans had to be approved by the council. All the heavy machinery will come in that way and then the houses are likely to all have motors. The fact they have parking seems to be one of the selling points. It's not as if we have access to public transport here, is it?'

'I hadn't thought of that. I'd assumed they'd use the main drive.' He wished Mrs Fitzgerald had shown him the plans.

'This will have consequences for all of us.' Trudie looked at him, widening her eyes and pressing her lips together. It was a meaningful look. 'We'll all be impacted by it. We have a right to voice our objections and doing so isn't being selfish. Wouldn't you say?'

Robert considered how the gardens might be impacted. He pictured heavy wheels churning up the lawns and then lines of traffic passing through on a daily basis. Even after the construction work was complete, there would be noise and exhaust fumes and it would irretrievably change the atmosphere of the gardens.

'I'm sorry it's happening, I'm sorry she needed the money that badly, but what can we do? It's already signed and sealed and we'll just have to learn to live with it. There's no alternative, is there?'

'Argh! We *can't* just let it happen!' Trudie splayed her fingers and Robert heard her frustration.

'Anyway, you were beginning to tell me that you'd had a letter from your mother?' he prompted. He'd be glad to talk about something other than the land sale. It was all anyone had spoken of for the past week and the conversation seemed to be going around in circles.

'Yes. Astonishingly.' Trudie's voice changed key. 'It's the

first time I've heard from the old witch for nearly nine years. I guess it's an olive branch, but it wasn't worded in the warmest language. I've been summoned back to Dorset – a command, that is, not an invitation. It's a three-line whip.'

'And will you go?'

It took her a moment to answer. 'To be quite honest with you, I haven't decided yet.'

They rounded the corner, heading back towards the gatehouse. Swifts were wheeling around the battlements, dipping, soaring and whistling piercing cries. He'd been glad to see their arrival. It always seemed like a landmark in the year. A window opened and Nancy leaned out shaking a rug.

'Why did you fall out with your mother?' He'd heard various hints of stories over the past months, but had learned that Anderby gossip often embellished and sometimes blatantly invented.

'Oh, the usual thing – you lousy men!' Trudie nudged her shoulder against his. Her smile lacked its accustomed wattage. 'Guy was complicated. Certainly too complicated for my parents' liking. I think my mother genuinely hated him. On reflection, yes, we did run a bit wild together, but all his crowd were like that after the war. Everyone needed to let off steam, to let go, to live a little. That was just how it was in those days.'

'What happened to him? Can I ask?' Robert looked up at the blueing sky. The high clouds were like the faintest chalk marks and a buzzard was riding the air currents, circling higher and higher. He remembered how his father would sometimes drink all his wages on a Friday night, the shouting when he came home and how his brother would try to hide the bruises.

Was that letting off steam too? He heard Trudie taking a breath before she replied.

'Guy died. Ignominiously. It was all over the newspapers. They said the most vile things – lurid speculation and outright lies. I suppose I could have tried to reach out to my parents at that point, but Mother had been ghastly through it all and I couldn't face the "I told you so" speeches.'

'I'm sorry.' Robert wondered if Guy might be inside the urn on Trudie's mantelpiece. He'd seen her having conversations with the pot, raising a glass in its direction and had once caught her dancing with it in her arms. 'That's when you came here?'

'I arrived here in a bit of a state, I'll admit. My life in London had been all high-speed and top-volume; it left me not knowing which way was up, but Anderby enveloped me with its calm and kindness. Everything slowed down and it all began to make sense once more. There was space to breathe again, I was able to start to put things in perspective, and the best of it was Gwen. She was extremely kind to me. She's always been generous and considerate and patient. She's really the best of people. All of this business over the land sale is entirely out of character. It's not at all like her to behave this way, to show so little consideration for other people's feelings. I suspect it might be more Teddy's initiative than hers.'

'You may be right.' Robert had thought that too. Every time he'd seen Mrs Fitzgerald recently, Teddy was gripping her hand or had an arm around her shoulder. It looked more like steering than emotional support. Could he have steered her into the sale too? 'Perhaps everyone ought to be angry at him instead of her?'

'She's always been inclined to let him take advantage, but even if he pressured her to do this, she shouldn't have let it happen, should she? I thought she was stronger than that. She used to have a backbone.'

They walked on in silence, each occupied with their own thoughts. 'You should make your peace with your mother,' Robert finally said. They might be estranged, but he'd noticed how often Trudie spoke of her.

'Possibly.' She sighed. 'But it's difficult to forget all the horrid words that were said. When my father died, she actually told me it was my behaviour that had killed him. Can you imagine being told that? I adored Daddy. She even tried to stop me attending his funeral.'

'But you're strong, Trudie. You're made of stern stuff. You've got an excellent backbone.'

'Do you sincerely think so? Is that how you see me? Stern stuff?' She said it in her capital-letters voice and smiled at him, but something different had flickered across her face momentarily. There'd been a vulnerability there for a second. She linked her arm though his. 'Thank you, dear man. We'll see.'

Chapter Twenty-One

May brought the sound of nightingales and the scent of elder and the orchard was full of blossom. It sparkled with it under the blue sky this morning. Robert would have liked to sit with his back to the trunk of a tree for an hour, just breathing in the freshness of the new day and the hum of the bees, but the surveyors had been in the previous afternoon and mysterious pegs and lines of tape had appeared on the ground. He'd seen men with plans in their hands and measuring instruments, talking of drainage and access; for a while they'd seemed to be everywhere on the estate, pointing their fingers and nodding their heads as they looked all around. When they'd gone, they'd left cigarette ends behind in the grass and their footsteps had flattened the columbines and cowslips.

'I think there are more bees than ever this spring,' Daniel said. 'Does nature have a sense of irony? We might have had a bumper crop of apples this year.'

'Perhaps it might be good for our sobriety?' Iris suggested. 'I've had some stinking hangovers from the cider over the years.'

'I don't know about that. Personally, I seem to have made a dint in quite a few bottles of whisky over the past couple of weeks,' Daniel admitted.

'Have you thought about asking Mrs Fitzgerald if you might plant another orchard?' Robert had to squint his eyes against the sun and the white shimmer of the blossom.

'I have given it some thought,' Daniel replied. 'I've considered taking grafts. Some of these varieties are ancient stock and rare now. I'm not sure we could easily replace them.'

'I could help you with that,' Robert volunteered. 'I gladly would.'

'I probably ought to do it, but I'm struggling to find the heart for it, to be absolutely honest. If we were to plant a new orchard this year, it would perhaps be viable in another ten years. That seems like an awfully long time to wait, doesn't it?'

'All gardens are investments for the future,' Robert said. 'They're all a statement of faith.'

'But some gardens are important because of their history and I'm not sure I have much faith at present.'

Daniel seemed to have aged over the past month. Robert saw it when he looked at his face in the bright sun now. New lines bracketed his mouth, his eyes were bloodshot, he hadn't shaved this morning, which was most unlike him, and there was a weariness to his voice. Robert wondered whether it was the impending felling of the apple trees that had brought on his despondent mood, or the fact that Mrs Fitzgerald had kept him in the dark about her plans. As he filled his pipe Robert noticed a slight tremor in his hands. Was that last night's whisky, or something more?

According to Faye, he hadn't put much time in at the school recently. Last week she'd knocked on his door and found him still not dressed at lunchtime. He was in a dark, introspective mood, Faye said, and she didn't know what to do to lift him out of it. Robert wasn't sure if Daniel had actually had a conversation with Mrs Fitzgerald since the news had broken. He wished she might make some reconciling gesture and that they could find a way to talk again.

He and Faye weren't presently on the best of terms either. She said that while the village desperately needed decent, moderately priced housing for working people, this estate was being built purely for profit. It would offer no benefits to the local community, she said; it would only take something precious and ancient away. In recent weeks, Robert had felt they'd begun to understand one another; he'd found himself looking forward to the days when she and the children were in the garden, but now they'd fallen back into the pattern of irritably misconstruing one another's words. Faye had been short-tempered when their paths had crossed yesterday; she seemed to have no interest in anything apart from the land sale, and she'd stopped bringing the children to the garden.

'I'd intended to take some more photographs,' Daniel said. 'I've taken hundreds of pictures of the orchard over the years. It's irresistibly lovely as the blossom starts to break, isn't it? These few perfect days before it begins to fade ... I've kept meaning to walk over with my camera, but now I see all these pegs in the ground, I realize I've already left it too late.'

'You haven't,' said Iris. She put a hand to his shoulder. 'You should do that, Daniel.'

'We could always take these out?' Robert tested one of the pegs with his boot.

'That might be criminal damage.' Iris smiled. 'Though it is tempting.' Her wellington finished the work Robert's boot had begun.

Iris agreed with Robert that the loss of the orchard was tragic, but people were going too far with their criticisms of Mrs Fitzgerald. Iris had spoken with her and told her she understood why she had to do it. Angry and incredulous voices still dominated, though, and Mrs Fitzgerald had been noticeable in her absence for the past fortnight. Robert missed happening upon her as he worked and having her there to validate his decisions. As far was he was aware, she hadn't even visited the white garden. He imagined she must miss speaking with her brother. How sad it was if she felt she must hide inside the house.

Robert shut the gate to the orchard and they followed the path through the vegetable garden. The espaliered quinces and medlars were flowering against the old walls and he could hear a cuckoo calling. Nancy was tying broad beans to stakes and looked up as they approached.

'I can't bear to go in there now,' she said. 'It's too sad. Some of the men came into the café yesterday and Phyl refused to serve them. I know it's not their fault, they're only doing their jobs, but we don't have to have our noses rubbed in it, do we?'

'You'll probably find you have more trade from the new houses,' Iris said. 'It might be good for business.'

'Perhaps, but I'd rather keep the orchard.'

At that moment Phyllis appeared in the doorway of the walled garden. 'Something horrible has happened,' she said, and Robert could see it on her face. 'Someone has smashed a window in the house.'

As they rounded the corner, there was a group standing in front of the Hall. Robert saw the sunlight glittering on the shards of broken glass and Trudie turned towards him. 'Someone threw a brick through the window.'

'A brick? Who would do that?'

Teddy was standing with an arm around his wife. Mrs Fitzgerald hadn't pinned her hair up today and it hung limply around her face. She had no make-up on, her eyes looked vulnerable without their habitual rings of kohl, and there were dark circles beneath them.

'Whoever did it, I'll knock his bloody block off,' Teddy said.

'Darling!' Mrs Fitzgerald put a pacifying hand to her husband's cheek. 'People are angry. They have a right to be.'

'They have no right to launch bricks through the windows.'

'You said "his",' Iris remarked. 'It might have been a woman.'

'Well, did any of you do it?' Teddy looked around the group. Under his scrutiny, they all found themselves regarding the flowerbeds. There was a hardness in his blue eyes today.

'Did you see anything?' Miss Parget asked.

'I was in the armchair by the fire,' Mrs Fitzgerald said. 'I jumped out of my skin! I went straight to the window, but there was nobody there. It's a new, red brick, which is meant to be a message, I suppose.' She took a breath. 'I understand the message.'

'It might have injured you,' said Teddy. 'And how much is it going to cost to fix the window? I'll give them a ruddy message when I find out who did this.'

'Did you genuinely not realize how upset people would be?' Trudie asked. She was looking at Teddy. 'Or did you simply not take anyone else's feelings into account? Yes, this isn't right, no one should be launching bricks through your windows, but if you treat people with contempt you can't expect them to respect you in return. Of course everyone is angry.'

'So you're the voice of morality now, Trudie?' Teddy raised his eyebrows and laughed. 'That's a bit rich!'

'Teddy . . .' Mrs Fitzgerald put a hand to his arm.

'You're lucky it was only a brick.'

'Is that a threat?' The laughter had gone from Teddy's face. He took a step towards Trudie.

'Please, can we stop this?' Mrs Fitzgerald appealed. She put herself between the pair of them. 'Please, can we all calm down?'

As he looked on, Robert was struck by the change in her appearance. Her shoulders were rounded, her characteristic poise forgotten, and her hands seemed restless this morning. She looked smaller somehow and suddenly strikingly thinner. Even the brightness of her hair seemed to have faded.

'I agree with Trudie, but we should stop this,' Daniel said. 'This is too much. This is going too far.'

'It is,' Iris agreed.

'She's being terrorized,' Teddy said. 'First that red paint and now this. You're all so morally superior, but this is intimidation.'

'It's not intimidation. Nobody would want to hurt Gwendoline. It's just an expression of outrage and frustration,' Phyllis said. 'Do you not realize how betrayed everyone feels? How upset? How let down?'

'Dear God, you bloody people and your righteousness!' Teddy widened his eyes. 'It's our land. It's our house. Why should we have sought your permission to sell? Now get over it!'

'It's not your land – it's *her* land,' Phyllis corrected. She turned to Mrs Fitzgerald, clearly hoping for an acknowledgement.

'Get over it?' Trudie repeated. She looked as if she wanted to strike Teddy, but then there was an exchange between her eyes and Mrs Fitzgerald's. Something flashed between them and Trudie took a step back.

'Come on. Come away,' said Iris, her hand on Trudie's shoulder. 'Let's leave this. We're all going to say things that we'll regret.'

Trudie finally consented and turned to walk away with Iris, but her gaze hardened as she looked back at Teddy. 'There are things that I sincerely regret not saying sooner.'

Chapter Twenty-Two

There were voices inside the barn. Robert had heard them as he passed with his wheelbarrow and curiosity had stilled his steps. His mind being occupied with Teddy's intentions, and how the land sale might now impact the garden plans, he'd quite forgotten that the first read-through of the play had been scheduled for this afternoon. But they didn't still intend to go ahead with this performance, did they? Maurice, who very possibly had put the brick through the window, had been cast as King Lear. Mrs Fitzgerald was meant to play Cordelia. The Greenfielders were unconventional and surprising in many ways, but surely they couldn't have a temporary ceasefire just for the sake of a theatrical performance?

He found Trudie, Maurice and Iris inside the barn. The sunlight through the tiled roof cast lozenges of light onto the packed-earth floor. Someone had dragged in a large wicker trunk full of stage clothes and the children were variously trying on ruff collars, clown hats and a bear costume. The air was dry and dusty and the bear sneezed. This high-raftered barn was sometimes used as an exhibition space and the arrangements of pikes and muskets on the walls were purely there for decorative purposes. Robert hoped they might remain that way.

'I didn't know if this was still happening,' he said. He'd been given a mercifully minor part as a servant in the play, but in the circumstances he hadn't even looked at his lines.

'None of us know what to do.' Iris flopped onto a bale of hay. 'We were having a dither and wondering if anyone else might turn up.'

'I haven't thought about costumes, or stage sets or selling tickets yet,' Trudie said. She smiled at Ewan, who was now blundering around in a donkey's head. 'Should we start? Is there any point?'

'Life has to go on, I suppose,' Robert said, though he wasn't entirely sure what that meant.

'Does it, Robert?' Maurice asked. Was that sarcasm in his tone? He was wearing a lopsided cardboard crown and looked ready to rant and rave.

'We normally have a fête at midsummer,' Trudie said, as she arranged a feather boa around Robert's shoulders. 'Anderby has always hosted a summer fayre, it's an institution, but nothing has been organized this time. We haven't advertised the summer-school courses yet and have barely begun to discuss the timetables and accommodation.'

'It won't happen this summer, will it?' Maurice tossed his cigarette away.

Robert had to wonder why Maurice had turned up here if he suspected the play wouldn't go ahead. Had he been hoping for a showdown with Mrs Fitzgerald? He seemed primed for a confrontation.

'Summer is cancelled, then?' Trudie's eyebrows lifted above her oversized sunglasses.

'Shouldn't we try?' Iris asked. 'Isn't it time we made some effort to get back to normal?'

'And what is normal?' Maurice replied petulantly. He tended to spit slightly when he was moved. 'Normal no longer exists. Normal is extinct. She ended normal.'

The light shifted in the barn as Mrs Fitzgerald's silhouette appeared in the doorway. Seeing her, Maurice turned his back and crossed his arms over his chest. It was brave of her to have come here, Robert thought, but was it wise? She couldn't have made a more dramatic entrance onto a stage.

'I didn't know what to do,' she said. 'I felt I ought to show my face, but ...'

'We felt the same,' Trudie admitted.

'That's not like you, Gwendoline. Indecision? You're normally so decisive.' Maurice didn't turn to face her.

'I'm sorry,' she said. 'I know you're angry, Maurice, and I understand why. All I can tell you is that I regret my actions. I can't emphasize enough how much. If I could wind back the clock, I sincerely would.'

'You betrayed us,' Maurice said. He did turn then. 'You betrayed Greenfields. You went against the principles we've all adhered to for so long and I'm afraid you showed your true colours, Gwendoline. When it came down to money, you could soon enough sidestep your avowed ethics. Why should we abide by rules that you can so casually lay aside? It makes me wonder what all of this has been for. Why have I given this place ten years of my life? I imagined we had an oasis of beauty, honesty and harmony here, that we had higher ideals, but it seems I've been swindled. What a terrible waste of time and hope this has been. You're not fit to be the custodian of Anderby.'

'You sound like it's the end. It's not the end, is it?' Mrs Fitzgerald appealed. She looked at each of them in turn. 'This doesn't nullify everything we've achieved, does it? Surely we can find a way to carry on? Please, there was nothing remotely casual in what I did.'

'Some villain hath done me wrong,' spat Maurice.

Mrs Fitzgerald turned and silently walked away.

'He went too far,' said Iris. They'd regrouped in Trudie's sitting room and she'd unleashed the emergency bottle of Dubonnet. 'Yes, we're all upset, but what's done is done, and we have to find a way to live together again.'

'Is Maurice going to leave?' Robert asked. 'He was talking as if he might.' Privately, he felt Maurice had enjoyed the drama of the moment a little too much. Had he practised delivering that line? If he'd been wearing a cape, he might have swished it.

'Not that he's said.'

'I'm sorely disappointed in her, I wish I had a better understanding of her motivations, but I suspect this isn't entirely her fault.' Trudie took a dog up onto her lap and rested her chin on its head. 'I don't want this to be the end of our community. That would be tragic, wouldn't it?'

'It would be awful,' Iris said, 'but it's not just Maurice who wants to go for her jugular. Cecil is calling Gwendoline "The Traitor" now. Yes, it's slightly in jest, but that's how he refers to her all the time. He won't say her name. I feel I want to bash heads together. How long can this go on for?'

'I'd quite like to bash Maurice's head against something,' Robert admitted. 'I think he expected applause after he delivered that line.'

'But how do we start to put it right?' Trudie asked.

Iris's sigh was audible. 'At this moment I haven't a clue.'

Chapter Twenty-Three

The orchard was poignantly beautiful. The white blossom was veined with pink and drifting on a gentle breeze today. The sheep and hens had already been moved out, and the grass was trampled now, but the thought of saw teeth tearing into trunks and of ancient roots being wrenched up was almost unthinkably horrible to Faye. It would be an outrageous act of vandalism. It would be abominable. Of course, they had to do something.

Most of the trees had been planted towards the end of the last century, but Daniel said some of them might be considerably older. These venerable trees, with their knotted and twisted boughs, had lived through wars, floods, droughts and the age of the ox-drawn plough. They were the elders of their community and ought to be revered. Surely? The prospect of felling them seemed flagrantly disrespectful. Apple trees had potent symbolism in the history of England, she'd studied that with the children in school, and they were an integral part of the story of Anderby too. The walls of the orchard were marked on the very earliest plans of the estate. It might even pre-date the Hall. It was visited by greenfinches, fieldfares and redwings in the winter, little owls and lesser-spotted woodpeckers nested in the hollow in the trees, and on summer evenings bats streaked the sky. They couldn't lightly let all of that be destroyed, could they? The Hall, the landscape and its wildlife needed to be protected and preserved for future generations to enjoy. How would posterity judge them if they didn't act? She'd put all these arguments in her letters to the newspapers and conservation societies.

Faye's footsteps made a circle around a tree. In the first years she'd been at Anderby they'd done a wassailing ceremony on Twelfth Night, encircling the trees with raucous carolling and clashing pans to drive the evil spirits out, reverently pouring mulled cider onto the roots and hanging soaked bread from the branches to encourage the attention of robins, the trees' guardian spirits. Gwendoline had been the one who organized these festivities every year; she loved the old Gloucestershire folklore and had spent years studying Anderby's history. What could have made her turn her back on that? Because that's what this amounted to, wasn't it?

Well, they wouldn't let it happen. These chains would resist the teeth of saws and axe blades. They would stop them in their path. It was just frustrating that the chains were so tangled and the padlocks had rusted. This was going to take her some time. Mr Ingram had produced them from one of his barns and they had a ferrous smell about them that set Faye's teeth on edge. She settled herself with her back to a tree trunk as she began the slow process of disentangling them. There seemed to be a metaphor in these knotted chains, but she wasn't of a mood to ponder it at present.

She'd left Trudie and Iris painting placards and Nancy and Phyllis were turning a bedsheet into a banner which they planned to unfurl from the gatehouse as the builders arrived on site. It was to be emblazoned with the legend '*Nature not Neo-Tudor!*' Phyllis had come up with that and was rather pleased with it. Iris had expressed concern that their protest might upset Gwendoline – but, well, she hadn't exactly given much consideration to their feelings, had she? What mattered now was to stop the trees being felled. It was imperative that they do that. They had every right to oppose this and Gwendoline should have anticipated that.

It wasn't by design that this would be an all-female protest, but Cecil was concerned it might sully his reputation (ha!), Lionel said it sounded unseemly, and Maurice claimed to be heartsick with the whole thing. Every man had an excuse ready. Only Daniel, with his camera, would be helping them. Faye hadn't even approached Robert, who was talking about planting new trees to hide the view, seemingly having already accepted that the orchard was lost. He might call that pragmatism, but to her it sounded like defeatism. Why had he taken that attitude? Was it that he feared to offend the hand that fed him? Because he felt his position here wasn't secure? But didn't a person some-times need to take a risk? When Faye saw him at the gate to the orchard now, she knew he wasn't here to offer his assistance.

'I thought you were joking when you said you were going to chain yourselves to the trees.' He smiled as he approached and twirled a stick between his hands.

'Joking?' Faye paused from her task and looked up at him. 'Why might that be a joke?'

'Well, it's just a bit silly,' he replied, still smiling. 'What will it achieve? Yes, you might delay them for a few hours, and succeed in irritating them, but they'll come along with bolt cutters or call the police.'

'And then we'll do it all again the next day. Or something else. And, in the meantime, I'm writing to all the newspapers and Daniel is going to take photographs. People need to be told this is happening. We need to draw attention to it. There are lots of right-minded people who will feel outraged when they know, and together we can exert pressure.'

'So you're prepared for the police to come and arrest you?' He switched at the grass with the stick.

'Yes, if necessary.' She had to shade her eyes with her hand when she looked up at him. Did he have to stand over her like that?

'Aren't you meant to be the responsible schoolmistress, setting an example for the children, and all of that?'

'And?' She wasn't sure she liked his tone. 'You think this is irresponsible?'

'Frankly, yes.'

'Personally, I'd say passivity is irresponsible. You don't think children should be taught to stand up for what they believe in?'

'I don't think they should be taught to chain themselves to trees.'

He crouched down on his haunches, picked a daisy and twiddled it between his fingers. Faye was glad he wasn't looming over her any longer, but sorry if he meant to stay. There didn't seem to be much point in having this conversation.

'I thought you loved trees, though? Isn't that meant to be what you care about? Why aren't you outraged? I have to admit that I don't understand you, Robert.'

'I do love trees.' He furrowed his brow. 'And, of course, I'm not happy this is happening, not remotely, but it's too late to stop it and it would be tragic if the community was to split apart over this. We've just got to try to make the best of it now, haven't we? You told me yourself that much of the local housing stock is antiquated and insanitary. The building of this estate will provide work for local men, who definitely need it, and it might bring more pupils into the school. Haven't you been worrying about that?'

'But these won't be houses that local people can afford. What we're short of is decent housing to rent to low-paid workers. That's not what this is. You can't pretend there's anything remotely altruistic about this development; it's simply about profit for the building company and a quick way of raising money for the Fitzgeralds. It's ugly, rapacious, short-sighted capitalism.'

'Crikey. You do talk like a political pamphlet sometimes, you know.'

She shook her head. She wasn't in a mood for his teasing words. 'These are the wrong houses in the wrong place.'

'And lived in by the wrong people?' He raised an eyebrow. 'That's what certain people here are saying, isn't it? God forbid they'll be middle class! Heaven forfend they'll have offensive accents and work in shops! It's so elitist – all this talk of the houses being philistine, bourgeois, base, vulgar . . . I heard Cecil calling them horrible perky little houses for horrible perky little people!'

'You know those aren't my opinions.' He did, didn't he?

'Whether we like it or not, sometimes we can't resist change. There used to be a priory here and a medieval village, but it all got scraped away when the house was built and the gardens landscaped. I've seen old plans in the archive. I'm sure there were people who hated those changes, but sometimes it's just not possible to stand in the way of progress. Nothing stays the same forever, does it?'

The daisy in his gesticulating hands somehow seemed to undermine his gravity. He could be rather patronizing, she thought. 'Do you genuinely believe this is progress? I'm more inclined to think it's destruction in the name of progress.' Could he not see that?

'But don't you think it might do Greenfields good to have new people coming in? You're the one who talks about it being too clannish, about the walls being too high – well, this will blast our gates open, won't it?'

'Has Gwendoline fed you these arguments?'

'No. I can think for myself, you know.' He frowned and threw the daisy away. 'Anyway, you're certainly not going to stop this development by tying yourself to a tree. No one will take this protest seriously. You'll just look like hysterical women.'

'Hysterical?' A laugh escaped from Faye's mouth. Was he seriously telling her she was a hysterical woman? 'Because that's what woman are, isn't it? Silly females ruled by their emotions and their bodies and not by their intellect?'

'I'm not saying that. Of course, I'm not! But I don't think this is an especially intelligent thing to do.'

Did he mean to anger her? If he did, he was succeeding. 'God, Robert, you're so passive. You're so apathetic. I want to shake you by the shoulders! Do you feel passionately about anything?'

'Apathetic? I've never been called that before. There are lots of things I care about.'

'Like what?' she asked. 'Do tell me. I'm genuinely interested.'

'Making a success of the gardens here, proving to Mrs Fitzgerald that I was the right man for the job . . .'

She might have predicted that. 'Are your horizons really so narrow, Robert? Do you ever open a newspaper? Do you ever read a book – I mean, one that's not about gardening? Do you have any awareness that there's famine, racial hatred and religious persecution going on in the world right now? That books are being burned in Berlin, that Jewish children are being segregated in schools and they're permitting enforced sterilization? There's so much that's vile and frightening happening in the world beyond our walls, but, well . . . our lawns are nice and tidy, aren't they?'

'I'm not ignorant and illiterate just because I work with my hands, you know. I do read a newspaper.' He looked slightly offended. 'And I suppose you believe you can stop those things happening as well?'

'We have to try, surely? If we don't act on our consciences, if we all look away, unwilling to face up to conflict and unpleasantness, there are no limits to the cruelties and injustices that might be done.'

'Fine words, Faye, but there's a limit to what you might change. No matter how outraged you feel, there are things you can't make right. It's naïve to suppose otherwise.'

The fact he smiled and shook his head as he said it irritated her all the more. 'I assume you believe this whole venture is naïve, then?' She found him so frustrating. She'd tangled her fingers into the chains until they hurt. 'By your terms, I guess we're all wasting our time here, aren't we? Oh well, thank you, Robert. How enlightening. I'm sure everyone will be very grateful to you for setting us straight on that score.'

'You like to think you're so compassionate, Faye, so sensitive to other people's problems, but you never once try to see things from my side, do you?' He got to his feet again, took a packet of cigarettes from his waistcoat pocket, and frowned as he looked down at her. 'I'm an employee here. I need this job. It's fine for you people to go around expressing your affronted feelings all the time, but do you not see why I can't behave that way?'

'Is that what it is? Is that how you feel?' She threw the chains to the ground. How he maddened her. 'Dear God, have some courage, man! I'm employed by the trust. I'm a tenant here. But sometimes we have to speak out.'

'Yes, nothing ever stops you speaking out, does it?' He lit his cigarette and shook out the match. 'You're so utterly convinced of your moral rightness, Faye, and for some reason I always have to be in the wrong, don't I? Why is that? What did I do to offend you so badly? You know, life here would be considerably more pleasant if you weren't forever ambushing me with your lectures and rages and disapproving scowls.'

He turned to go and she was glad. If he'd stayed another minute she might have thrown the chains at him. He had the capacity to irritate her more than anyone she'd ever met. Why had he come here? He had no understanding of what this community was meant to be about and he would contribute nothing to it. Faye despised him for his self-centredness, for his compliance, for his complacency, just because . . .

Chapter Twenty-Four

'I think she might be the most annoying woman I've ever met,' he told Iris. 'I swear she willingly misunderstands me. It's like she constantly wants to catch me out. I try to be nice, I try to understand her, but every conversation we have seems to be full of tripwires.'

'Oh dear. I thought the two of you were getting on better?'

'Not any longer. Not now. I feel we've just crossed a boundary.'

Robert came to stand in the shade with her. She'd been sitting with her sketchbook under the pear tree. He hadn't seen her at first in the dappled light.

'Faye's angry at the moment. She's upset.' Iris closed her sketchbook. 'You probably just caught her at the wrong time.'

'When is Faye not angry about something? When is the right time?'

'She's passionate. She's principled. She feels strongly about the things that matter to her and I admire her that she speaks out.'

'She can be damned hard work.'

'She might think the same about you!' Iris lifted her eyebrows at him.

'I don't doubt it.' He knew he was probably sounding petulant, but . . . he kicked at the long grass.

'Do you need a strong coffee and a sympathetic ear? I was just about to go home and put the kettle on.' Iris gathered her pencils together and brushed her trousers down as she stood. 'Or perhaps you need something calming? I might have some camomile tea at the back of the cupboard.'

'I'm sorry, Iris. Forgive me. I'm disturbing you, aren't I? You don't need to listen to me ranting on.'

She tilted her head to one side as she smiled. 'It's not a problem, Robert. It makes a refreshing change from listening to Cecil's ranting.'

He took one of the rush-seated chairs at her kitchen table. She'd been making chutney the previous evening; there was a sharp lingering smell of vinegar, and a cluster of sticky-looking bottles by the sink. She apologized for the washing draped around the range and the crumbs from the children's breakfast. Robert knew she worked at this table, moving her papers back and forth between mealtimes. It seemed rather unfair that Cecil had his own studio, but she didn't even have her own desk. He could hear the baby grizzling in the next room.

'Is Ailsa alright? Do you need to go to her?'

'She just likes grumbling to herself.'

'She takes after her father, then?' he suggested, knowing he possibly shouldn't.

'Robert!' Iris made an outraged face, but then laughed. 'Have you simmered down yet?'

'Sorry. I apologize for blowing steam at you.' He took the coffee cup from Iris gratefully. 'Faye's planning to tie herself to a tree. Has she told you? She's sitting in the orchard surrounded by all these chains and padlocks.'

'I know. Trudie's going to do it too. They were trying to persuade me to join them earlier.'

'Will you?'

'Possibly.' Iris pulled out a chair and sat down opposite him. 'If I can persuade Cecil to look after Ailsa for a few hours, I might. The thought of them felling the trees is just so horrible. I was in there sketching yesterday and the idea of it made me feel quite tearful.'

'I think she'd have liked me to volunteer too.'

'You didn't, I take it?' She passed him the milk jug.

'How could I do it?' He sat back in his chair. 'Yes, I'm unhappy about the land sale. I hate it, in truth. I think it's awful that the orchard is going to be felled, I sincerely do, but I work for Mrs Fitzgerald. I take her orders. I need her to pay my wages. And, God knows, my position here is precarious enough as it is. Teddy only needs the slightest excuse to get rid of me. I'm already on thin ice.'

'Thin ice? What do you mean?' Iris was frowning at him. 'Gwendoline endlessly sings your praises. She believes in your project and wouldn't be able to manage without you. It wouldn't cross her mind to let you go. I'm certain of that.'

'No? You don't know how it is, Iris. It would only take one word from Teddy.'

'Why? What are you talking about, Robert? Why do you imagine that Teddy would want to get rid of you?'

He hesitated. Dare he trust that she would keep this to herself? 'If I tell you something secret, will you promise – I mean absolutely swear – not to share it with anyone else? Not even Cecil?'

*

Esther's mother had used words like degenerate and defilement when she'd found them together, dreadful words that made it sound as if he'd taken something from Esther without asking and tainted her in the process. Those words had cast an ugly light over his memories. Robert had found himself going back to the start, trying to recall Esther's words and his, her actions and his, and feeling he must justify himself – but there had been nothing ugly about it. Not at all. On several occasions he'd almost told Esther that he loved her, but he knew that their relationship could never go anywhere and so he'd kept it to himself. Looking back now, he was glad he hadn't said it.

'She wasn't an innocent,' he told Iris. 'Not like her mother wanted to believe. We both went into it with our eyes open.'

'Mothers generally always want to believe their daughters are innocent, even if there's overwhelming evidence to the contrary. You said Esther was engaged to be married? I guess that made you all the more an unwelcome surprise! She does want to marry this man?'

'I think Mrs Underhill's greatest fear was that we might jeopardize Esther's engagement. Lawrence is a wealthy man, he owns two cotton mills, so he was a good catch. It was all arranged before Esther's eighteenth birthday – and she wanted it too. He might be older than her, but he's got a big house and moves in smart circles. For months, all she could talk about was her trousseau and her wedding dress and the hotel in Torquay that they'd chosen for their honeymoon. She'll have a comfortable life.'

'She never thought of breaking it off?'

He shook his head. 'Not that I'm aware of. No, I can't imagine that she did. What we had – well, it was just a fling.'

'And now it's well and truly flung? When will the wedding be?'

'This coming September.'

'Do you feel an urge to stand at the back of the church and shout about impediments?'

He smiled. The sunlight cut through the kitchen window, illuminating the milk bottle and slanting a shadow from the coffee pot. He turned his hand in the light experimentally. 'No. I just hope she'll be happy.'

'That's magnanimous of you.'

'Is it? I couldn't have offered her anything. I know full well that she would never have wanted to be a gardener's wife. She'd have been horrified if I'd suggested it! She'd have laughed in my face.'

'Do you honestly think so?' Iris reached across the table and quickly squeezed his hand. 'You poor boy!'

'Oh, not really. I can't feel sorry for myself. We drank stolen bottles of champagne in her room, she liked to read risqué passages of novels aloud to me and she fed me on Battenberg cake. It was highly educational in its way.' He grimaced and then grinned. 'And I wouldn't have got this job without her. She wrote my letter of reference.'

'Ah. Hang on . . .' Iris bit her lip. 'I take it Gwendoline doesn't know that your former employer's daughter wrote your reference?'

'I didn't mean for her to ever find out, but that's my problem now; Teddy somehow seems to have worked it out. He suspects I've been dishonest and, unfortunately, I can't deny that.'

'But how has Teddy found out?'

'Anderby talks, doesn't it? How it loves to talk! I should

have kept my mouth shut. It was stupid of me. I never meant to mention her name.'

'Oh God!' Iris's hand went to her mouth and her eyes widened. 'You said it to *me*, didn't you? I only told Cecil. I barely said anything to him, but . . . I'm so sorry. This is my fault.'

'It's not your fault, it's mine.'

'Oh, Robert! I feel awful now. Can I speak to Teddy for you? Could I have a talk with Gwendoline?'

'What would be the point? What could you say? When she knows, she'll have to dismiss me.'

'Not necessarily – if you make your case, if you tell her what you've just told me . . .'

'She will. I've lied to her. I got this job under false pretences.'

Iris pushed her coffee cup away and sat back in her seat. 'I feel so bad. I'm responsible for this.'

'No, you're not. Please don't think that. I can't blame anyone but myself.'

'I hope you haven't done too much self-flagellation? It seems to me that you've been rather ill-used.' She put her hand towards his again. 'I imagine Teddy is thoroughly enjoying dangling the noose?'

'I suspect so. I've been waiting for it to tighten for a few weeks now.'

'No wonder you've looked out of sorts. Could we not—'

At that moment Robert heard the door opening and then Cecil's voice was there in the hallway. Iris flinched with the sound, she quickly withdrew her hand, and her coffee spilled onto the table.

'Who are you dissecting now?' Cecil asked, entering the

kitchen. 'You know, it's womanly to gossip, Bardsley. You should buy yourself a bonnet.'

'We weren't gossiping,' Iris replied. 'We were talking about the orchard.'

Robert exchanged a glance with her. He knew he could trust her now.

'They're going to chain themselves to trees, you know. I think Faye expected me to join in. For God's sake, I'm a member of the Royal Academy!'

Iris laughed. 'Cecil used to have lots of opinions on politics, Robert. When we first met he was forever making impassioned speeches in pubs and writing irate pamphlets. Can you believe that he was once a very angry young man?'

'That was a long time ago.' Cecil didn't look amused. 'You might have noticed that I now have three children to feed and clothe.'

Iris reached another cup and passed the coffee pot down the table to her husband. Cecil had tied a red spotted neckerchief around his throat today. Its polka dots seemed rather too jolly for his personality, Robert thought, and it looked as if it could do with laundering. Perhaps he mopped his brow with it while he wrestled with Saint Michael and Lucifer? As Cecil sat down at the table, Robert could smell sweat and last night's whisky on his breath.

'It still stinks of vinegar in here. It's making my eyes smart,' he said. 'Can I eat? Is it ready? I want to get back to work.'

Iris produced an enamel dish from the stove. She slid a slice of pie and potatoes onto a plate and placed a loaf and a knife down on the table.

'Robert, would you like anything?' she asked.

'No, it's quite alright. Thank you.'

Cecil ate in a hungry way, hunched over his food, his cigarette smouldering on the side of the plate. His hands were creased with dust from the workshop and left fingerprints in the bread. Robert felt he ought to go – it was impossible to continue their conversation while Cecil wolfed down gravy and potatoes and was so obviously listening and judging – but he was reluctant to leave Iris. The baby began to cry next door, adding to the tension in the room.

'Can you not shut her up?' Cecil drained his cup and wiped his mouth with his neckerchief.

'She needs feeding.'

'She permanently wants feeding. She'll grow up to be a fat child.'

Robert saw the reaction on Iris's face. She rose from the table and brought Ailsa in, gently rocking and cooing to soothe her. As Robert watched her, he thought Iris looked pale, tired and nervy today, but was it any wonder?

'I'll need the van on Saturday,' Cecil said, dipping bread into gravy. 'I'm meeting Peter O'Leary in Oxford.'

'But it's my turn to do the market. I've already told you.'

'Well, you'll have to swap, won't you?' He ground his cigarette out. 'Or perhaps Robert can drive?'

'But Robert doesn't have a vehicle.'

'Well, Trudie then. I don't care. One of you will just have to do it.'

'Couldn't you have arranged to meet Peter a different day?' There was an edge to her voice now.

'He's coming up from London especially. It's important. It's for work.'

'So it's not the usual session around the pubs, then?'

Robert found himself staring at his coffee cup. He shouldn't be here, he knew. Cecil was making it obvious he wasn't welcome. He ought to go, but ... If Cecil treated Iris like this in front of people, how did he speak to her when the door was closed?

'I should get back to work and let you both get on.' He rose to leave, feeling unsettled and uncertain.

'Yes, you do that,' Cecil said.

Iris followed him to the door. 'I apologize for Cecil,' she mouthed on the doorstep. 'He's short-tempered because he's under pressure.'

Is that what it was? Robert shook his head, smiled and squeezed Iris's hand. 'I hope you're alright? You know you can always talk to me, don't you?'

She nodded, but her smile looked as if it had taken an effort. 'I do. Thank you for confiding in me earlier. It means a lot that you still trust me and I won't say a word to anyone, I swear. I really am so very sorry.'

Chapter Twenty-Five

They'd moved in with heavy vehicles now and were pulling up the roots. Daniel watched through the gate. The women had been ready to chain themselves to the trees, but the work had begun at first light, they'd caught them unawares, and before they could get down to the orchard, the men with the axes and saws were already well into their work.

There'd been an ugly tussle then, the women had tried to get into the orchard, but the builder's men seemed to have come readied for a fight. Faye had kicked and screamed when they'd dragged her away. She was wild with fury and tears streaked the mud on her face. Daniel had taken photographs at first, as she'd requested, but he'd had to put his camera down and intervene. As the orchard was surrounded by walls, it was easy enough for the men to stand guard at the two entrances. There had been a gloomy couple of hours then as the women had shouted protests and waved placards, but they'd had to look on powerless as tree after tree fell. In the end, it was too agonizing to watch any longer and they'd all drifted away.

The earth tremored and groaned as the roots rose and it was tempting to imagine the trees were resisting. What fragments of history had surfaced with the roots? How long was it since this earth was last disturbed and saw the light? These old trees would have witnessed the heyday of Anderby Hall, Daniel supposed, when its owners still hosted hunt balls and shooting parties, had money in the bank and ambitions. There were already miniature apples forming behind the faded blossoms, blushed with pink and swelling day by day. There was something grotesque in the act of curtailing their formation. Fires had been lit and men were breaking up the branches and pushing them into the flames. The green wood hissed and crackled as it caught. They'd poured petrol onto the fires to get them going and its smell cut through that of the churned earth and wood smoke. Looking into the orchard now took Daniel to France in the March of 1917, the sight of the burnt-out villages and all the freshly felled trees weeping sap at the roadsides.

He remembered when he'd first seen the orchard in bloom in the spring of 1919. There'd been something revelatory in the blaze of white blossom; even after everything – after all the destruction and anguish and ugliness he'd witnessed – pure, sweet, good things could still dependably return. He'd sat with his back to one of the trunks, lit a cigarette and breathed deeply as he looked up at the swaying boughs, silhouetted then against the brightening sky. He'd closed his eyes, his breath steadying, and that image had seared itself onto his retina and into his memory. He closed his eyes and tried to see it again now, to take himself back to the serenity of that moment, but the noise of the saws and the smell of petrol intruded and all he could see behind his closed eyelids was angry explosions of red and yellow. He felt sick to his stomach. They'd sent them to war to defend English landscapes, history and culture, hadn't they? Wasn't that what they were meant to be fighting for?

'We failed,' said Faye, there at his side then. 'How could it all have happened so fast?'

Daniel hadn't heard her approach. He put his arm around her. Sudden tears wet her cheeks and he reached for his hand-kerchief. 'Here.'

'We should have been ready sooner. If we'd been prepared, we could have held them back.' She had a nasty scratch on her forehead and a bruise was starting to shadow her cheek. 'Why did they come so early?'

'Perhaps they guessed they wouldn't get a welcome reception?'

'Look at it,' she said. 'I hate it. I don't know that I've ever seen a sadder sight.'

'It hardly seems real. It was all over so soon.' The twitch was there again. He felt it. He had to rub his eye to stop it.

'I hope Gwendoline has seen it and feels shame for what she's done.'

There was anger in Faye's voice and he understood why. 'I imagine she'll be upset when she sees it.' That had to be true, didn't it?

He remembered how Gwen had often talked to him of her brother's letters from Gloucestershire. She'd bought Anderby because of the pleasure that had radiated from her brother's words and the feeling, as she stood at his graveside in France, that she'd needed to do something to make a difference. Daniel recalled, in the early days of them being here together, how she'd spoken with such imperative and urgency. Gwen couldn't really want this – this violation of nature, this callous disregard for history, this fracturing of the community – could she?

'I can't stand to watch any more of it,' said Faye. 'Don't stay here, Daniel. You shouldn't watch it either. There's nothing more we can do today.' He felt her pull at his arm.

They walked back through the walled garden. Butterfly wings flickered between the rows of cabbages and bees busied themselves in the medlar blossom, but the insistent rhythm of the saws took away the hum of the insects and the birdsong. The smoke from the fires made the light in the garden hazy.

They walked in silence, unable to find words to make it any better, but the late-afternoon sun lit the Virginia creeper on the end wall of the Hall and the windows were all mirrors full of sky. A movement took Daniel's eyes higher and there, for a moment, was Gwen's face behind the reflected clouds. She was looking out from one of the upper windows towards the orchard. Had Daniel seen her lift a handkerchief to her eyes, or was it just the shift of a mirrored cloud?

Chapter Twenty-Six

The word *violation* came into Robert's head; it was a pitiful and shocking sight. It reminded him of photographs of battlefields he'd seen printed in the newspapers as a child and he could now understand the look he'd seen in Daniel's eyes yesterday. The builder's men had finished for the weekend, leaving behind a mess of churned mud, shattered branches and piles of smoking ashes. One of the pleasures of working at Anderby was the sense of being part of a long history; there was a feeling of inheritance and eternally revolving cycles that had appealed to Robert's imagination, but this act seemed like a rude, crude fracturing of the line of continuity. Robert turned his back on the too-sorry sight and walked away.

He'd heard the women shouting their protests yesterday, Faye's impassioned voice occasionally distinguishable in the mix, and he'd felt a pressing indecision. He'd been potting on seedlings in the glasshouse and couldn't concentrate on his work, particularly when the shouts had conveyed distress. For hours, the women had chanted and sung and there'd been screams of outrage at one stage. As he'd worked, he'd contemplated what Faye had said about owls and bats, about ancient apple varieties and short-term thinking, about old plans of

Anderby and quick profits, and, in truth, he couldn't disagree with any of her arguments. Part of his brain told him that he needed to rush to join the women, adding his voice to their demonstration of resistance – but, at the end of the day, he was an employee here. He was staff and didn't need to give Teddy any more ammunition to dismiss him. It wasn't the same for him as it was for the others. If he could have joined the women's protest, he would – and he truly hated the sight of the felled orchard – but he wasn't at liberty to express his opinions.

He didn't especially wish to talk to anyone today (after all, what might he say?) and so he walked into the village. The low sun made a long shadow of the church spire, stretching it over the graveyard, and angling out into the ploughed field beyond. He recalled what Daniel had said about there being wartime gravestones in the churchyard and put his hand to the lychgate.

There was a bookcase full of photograph albums in the Hall's library, all pre-war family gatherings and jolly seaside excursions, but he'd also found a box of loose prints that Daniel had taken with his Kodak. Robert had begun leafing through them, hoping to be able to study the planting of the parterre garden back in 1918, but had found himself distracted. Daniel's photographs showed the great hall and the library of the house filled with rows of narrow iron beds. The dining room was set up with an array of mysterious medical equipment and doctors consulted behind desks in the sitting rooms. Robert had initially assumed that Anderby had been a convalescent hospital, but Iris had told him it specialized in neurasthenia cases towards the end of the war. Daniel had photographed men in invalid uniforms milling around the grounds, sitting on benches and at tables set for tea on the lawns. They stood in pairs by the lake, which was netted over then, and looked lost in the topiary garden, staring at the camera with faraway eyes. Robert had found a couple of images of Daniel himself: one standing by the main door with a man in a tweed suit and wire-rimmed spectacles (perhaps a doctor?) and another of him holding a Jack Russell Terrier whose back legs were blurred in movement. The scar on Daniel's face was more noticeable in these images and he appeared curiously older rather than younger.

Robert looked up at the church now and saw that Saint George was dependably slaying dragons in the stained-glass windows. He recognized a coat of arms in the glass too; it was the same one that was carved over the arch of the gatehouse at Anderby. He supposed the de Villiers family would have sat in the front pew here every Sunday for centuries. As he'd been looking through the photographs in the library, Robert had noticed a portrait of a couple, a Lord Frederick and Lady Catherine de Villiers, perhaps painted in the eighteenth century. They looked self-satisfied in silks and brocades and, in the background, the house and garden were immaculate. What would the de Villiers think of how the gardens had deteriorated? And of the flaking plasterwork inside the Hall? What would they say if they'd witnessed their orchard being levelled in preparation for the construction of twenty mock-Tudor bungalows?

Robert stepped between headstones with Georgian lettering, the last resting places of sheep farmers and wool merchants, blacksmiths, wheelwrights and vicars formerly of this parish. The headstones proclaimed these men to be sleeping peacefully after a lifetime's labours done. The tombs of local squires were carved with cherubs and urns, chiselled by the hands of more expensive masons, but all mossed and lichened now, like the rest. A path had been scythed through the nettles, and daisies nodded between the stones. A thrush was singing in the elms and the weathercock on the church porch creaked as it revolved.

It wasn't difficult to find the soldiers' graves. Compared to the old headstones, they were starkly white and angular at the edges. There were five of them, seemingly all soldiers who'd died at Anderby Hall. Had they succumbed to wounds sustained overseas, or was there something darker here? Some of the men in Daniel's photographs had terribly anguished faces. Robert imagined the rows of iron beds being disturbed as terrors split the silence of the night. He remembered, as a boy, being woken by his father's nightmares.

Robert had been a schoolchild in 1918, but he had a vague memory of flags being moved on maps, the names of soldiers read out in assemblies, and being instructed to pray to God to bring his father home. He had come home, those prayers had been answered, but that man was a stranger and frightening sometimes. He spat glistening red globs of his lungs up into a blue spittoon and would take his belt off and use it on his brother, Joseph. There'd been a kinder, more patient version of their father before the war, Joseph had said; he remembered a father who would hike to the tops of hills, who'd build dens with him and swim out to the horizon on holidays – but Robert had no memory of that man. There had been occasions when he'd prayed that his father might go away again, and within two years he had done, the cotton dust he'd breathed on the factory floor completing what the chlorine gas had begun. If he'd been able to come to somewhere like Anderby, would it have been different? Might his mind and body have recovered?

Anderby's passageways may once have echoed with the cries of nightmares, but none of that feeling lingered now, and Daniel must have found peace of mind there. As well as the day-to-day life of the hospital, his photographs showed smiling men gathered around gramophones, playing billiards and cricket, and being taught how to embroider tablecloths. They faced one another across chess boards, frowned at knitting needles, and sat on reclining chairs in the sunshine, shading themselves with painted Japanese parasols. Robert recognized the shapes of the cedar trees behind posing groups, the texture of the walls of the kitchen garden, and Daniel had photographed the cider orchard through every season. His lens focussed on piles of fallen fruit, on swelling buds and on sunlight through blossom. He returned to the latter subject again and again.

The light through the trees made shadows shift over the gravestones now and Robert thought about Mrs Fitzgerald and the long shadow of her brother's death. The existence of Greenfields ultimately came down to that, he considered; he was only standing in this particular churchyard, at this moment, because a young American had died before his time in France. He could understand how she'd felt a need to make some amends after the shock and sorrow of her loss, how she had to try to do something to stop all of that happening again. Did she still feel like that, or did her recent actions indicate a change of direction?

Daniel had photographed the empty rooms of the Hall after the medical staff had moved out, the bedframes stripped bare, rows of abandoned bath chairs and wheelchairs, and his new experiments with chicken farming. Then, in 1920, a young woman called Gwendoline Hirsch had appeared in front of his camera lens. Suddenly there were dozens of photographs of her – repairing window frames in the Hall, laughing with a milking pail and ladling soup for a queue of helpers – and what had struck Robert was the candidness and intimacy of these images. There was an obvious empathy between the subject and the photographer. In one snapshot she and Daniel were sitting on a wall together sharing a plate of sandwiches and Robert had been touched by how thoroughly contented and natural they looked in one another's company. Their eyes were connected and they seemed oblivious to the presence of the person behind the camera. This version of Daniel was an entirely different man from the anxious-looking figure standing beside a doctor a couple of years earlier. No wonder he seemed so unhappy that Mrs Fitzgerald hadn't consulted him about the sale of the orchard. But it was about much more than the orchard, wasn't it? Robert watched the wind stirring the tops of the yew trees and felt sadness and pity for Daniel.

Chapter Twenty-Seven

The stall had sold quickly that morning, but there'd been no satisfaction in the brisk trade. All their customers had been keen to talk about the housing estate. They'd queued up to ask questions. Everyone wanted to know – was it true the work had started already? Was it really the case that Mrs Fitzgerald had sold the land without consulting any of the tenants? Had they heard correctly that there'd been a falling out, a rift, and the Greenfields community would break up now? At first, Iris had felt irritated by the questions, but as the morning had gone on, and she'd had to repeat the same responses over and again, she'd felt less angry and more sad. As they sold the last of the produce, and loaded the emptied baskets back onto the van, she felt weary. Would the community split up now? Was that the inevitable conclusion? When Trudie had suggested they cheer themselves up with a drink in the Black Swan, she'd nodded.

'It's put Cecil in a foul mood,' she admitted as they carried their glasses of beer to a table. 'Though, in fairness, that's not unusual these days.' The lounge bar was always busy on market day and there was some privacy amongst the hubbub of voices. Around them people were talking about their lumbago, their neighbours and the price of fish. 'He says it's upsetting his work, that he can't concentrate with all the noise and the comings and goings. We had an awful row last night. We do nothing but argue now. We really are wretched with one another. I tell him to keep his voice down, I don't want the children to hear, but this morning Erin asked me why Daddy is always shouting.'

Trudie reached across the table and squeezed her hand. 'I don't think any of us are at our best at the moment. I'm not sleeping well and I could smell the whisky on Daniel's breath from six feet away yesterday.'

'Between you and me, Cecil has friends in a collective in East Sussex.' Dare she share this with Trudie? 'Martin Cooper has been telling him for ages that he ought to join them there and they've spoken on the telephone a couple of times this week. I think Cecil wants to go over and have a look at it.'

'He'd actually consider moving away?' There was a note of surprise in Trudie's voice. Her fingertips had been making stars and hearts in the spilled beer on the copper tabletop, but she looked up now.

'I don't know. I'm not sure. I can't tell how serious he is.' Iris thought of how Cecil called Gwendoline 'The Traitor' and how Maurice had spoken of betrayal – would they have to face those words too if they decided to sell? 'He's become obsessed by how it's going to impact the value of our house. He's talking about it endlessly; I find calculations on the backs of envelopes, and he seems to be of the opinion that it would be best to act fast. It slightly surprises me just how much he cares about that. I didn't realize he was so motivated by money. It didn't used to be his priority.'

'Had you been thinking about moving before all this trouble started?' Trudie sat back with her glass.

'Not at all! Not once. But when he's not holding forth on the likely decline in house prices, Cecil's argument is that we bought into a creative community and that's not what it will be any longer. He says he expected to be amongst people who shared our ideas and principles.' Iris found herself imitating her husband's voice. He could sound terribly pompous sometimes these days. 'He seems to have a horror that he'll find himself living next door to a commercial traveller who has a suitcase full of cleaning product samples or a retired shoe-shop manager.'

'How horrendous!' Trudie rolled her eyes.

'Cecil has always been a bit of a snob. When he was at college he looked down on anyone who wasn't in his set, but it's shocking these days. I'm embarrassed to be associated with him sometimes. I want the earth to swallow me up. I dread to think how outspoken he'll be as an old man.'

'Didn't Cecil grow up in Clerkenwell? I'm sure I've heard him telling stories about a barefoot boyhood and stealing cabbage leaves from under vegetable stalls. I distinctly remember the sound of the violins.'

'His father had a fried fish shop, but his mother brought him up to believe he was something special. Elsie Cardew has a lot to answer for.'

'Fried fish is nobler than cleaning products, then?'

'God knows! I ceased to understand my husband's logic years ago.'

'And how would you feel about moving away?' Trudie asked. 'Would you want to go?'

For all the recent tensions, Iris had good friends at Anderby, and the children were settled there. She'd painted every wall in their house herself, sewn every curtain and cushion, and had made it into a home for her family. She'd invested care and thought and her inheritance from her parents in it, and had supposed that they'd live there at least until the children left home. Besides, she wasn't especially fond of Martin's crowd. There was too much bullish masculinity in that group; they brought out the worst in Cecil, and Leonora O'Connell had a workshop there. Iris had accepted Cecil's apologies when his fling with Leonora had come out, she'd believed him when he'd swore it was over, but she wasn't sure she could stomach having her as a neighbour. Would Cecil expect them to become friends?

'No, of course not!' she replied. 'I want things to go back to how they were. But can they now?'

'I don't know, darling. We have to try, though, don't we?' Trudie rested her chin on her shoulder and her eyes swivelled to the passing crowds on the street. 'There's Lionel. Wherever did he buy that suit? And those shoes! He's not often in town, is he?'

'Wasn't he talking about seeing a solicitor? I think he wanted an opinion on whether they might take any legal action against Gwendoline.'

'That's right, yes, but ... Hang on, it looks as if he's with someone. I say, that's no solicitor – that's the builder chap, isn't it?'

Iris turned in her seat. 'It is, you know. That's the man I saw skulking about in the orchard a few weeks ago. Are they together?' Her question was answered as the men turned towards one another, tipped their hats and shook hands before parting. 'That looks a bit suspect, doesn't it? What do you suppose he's up to?'

'I haven't the vaguest notion, but I don't like the look of it,' Trudie replied.

Chapter Twenty-Eight

Robert had spent the morning working in the topiary garden, trying to bring to mind the photographs of how this part of the garden had looked before the war. Spiders scuttled away from the blades of his shears and their cutting revealed an abandoned nest, as perfectly cupped and feather-woven as a nest in a nursery-rhyme illustration. He stepped through a litter of leaves and branches, and thorns pushed into the soles of his boots. His palms wept with blisters and he resolved that he must wear gloves tomorrow.

He was cutting back the topiary clouds, trying to achieve a well-curved cumulus, when Trudie appeared behind them.

'You're like the sun emerging,' he said.

'I'm afraid I might be more of a thunderbolt, darling.'

She was wearing striped lounge pyjamas, but her face was serious. He put down the secateurs. 'What do you mean? What's happened?'

'Daniel has called an emergency meeting. Can you come now? Maurice has been shouting and Nancy says there's been a fight.'

Most of the Greenfielders were already assembled around the table as they stepped into the dining room. There were violet

shadows under Mrs Fitzgerald's eyes and there was no sign of
Teddy. Daniel was pacing a circle of the table and Faye was hugging her knees and frowning. Her eyes briefly connected with
Robert's as he took a seat, but she immediately looked away.
He noticed that Maurice was sitting with a tea towel pressed to
his face. When he lowered it, an ice cube slid across the table
and Robert saw that his right eye was swollen.

'Good Lord, Maurice!' Trudie whistled. 'Bit long in the
tooth for fisticuffs, aren't we? Whatever has happened? You're
going to have a shiner there.'

Maurice put the towel down and lit a cigarette, wincing as he
exhaled smoke. 'I'm not proud of myself, but I'd like to think
he came out of it worse.'

'Who did? Out of what?'

Trudie's questions were answered as Lionel entered. Phyllis
was leading him by the elbow and he was holding a piece of
steak over his face. Phyllis rolled her eyes at the group as she led
him to a chair. 'Scrapping like schoolboys,' she said.

'You look a fright,' said Iris.

'It's no less than the wretch deserves,' Maurice observed.
'Well, aren't you going to share your news with everyone,
Lionel?'

'I've barely sold anything for the past couple of months,' Lionel
said, 'and it certainly doesn't help that we've had no events here.
I have three children to feed. I have a wife who wants parquet
flooring and a washing machine. She says I'm not appreciated
here, that my voice doesn't carry any weight, and she might
be right.'

'I wasn't aware that you were struggling financially,' Mrs

Fitzgerald said. 'We could have had a conversation. I didn't know you felt like this.'

'You being so sensitive to people's feelings?' Maurice put in.

'Is it true you've agreed to sell your property?' she went on. 'I possibly have no right to ask, but have you already signed a contract?'

'I can't imagine they'll knock it down and build on the land,' Lionel replied. 'It's not a big enough plot. I suspect they're buying speculatively.'

'Speculatively?' Daniel queried.

'They were asking me who else had bought their own properties here.'

'And, of course, you supplied that information?' Maurice stabbed his cigarette out with unnecessary force and pushed the ashtray away. 'We're going to be surrounded. It will be like living in a stockade. Like being under siege.'

'Don't be so bloody melodramatic, Maurice,' Lionel replied. He turned back to address the table. 'Had they not offered me an advantageous price, I wouldn't have considered it. You know I've always been loyal.' He looked to Mrs Fitzgerald, seeking assent. 'We've put a deposit down on a three-bedroom property in Stow. Julia gets her parquet flooring and I'll have a sales premises right on the street. It really is worth considering the price they're offering. After all, values are guaranteed to go down here once the housing estate is built.'

'Loyalty, my foot!' said Maurice.

'Thank you for your financial advice, Lionel,' said Daniel, with heavy irony in his voice.

'I've seen 'em about the place, that Houghton fellow and his surveyor.' Mr Ingram slid his cap off and scratched at his nicotine-yellowed hair. 'They were walking over my land last week, poking sticks into ditches and pacing about, quite as if they owned the place. I had to see 'em off. I know full well they're talking to some people around this table.' His eyes made a slow tour of the room.

'Go on, tell us,' Maurice prompted. 'So is this where the rats start to desert the sinking ship?'

'We're not sinking,' Phyllis said firmly. She lifted her chin. 'We wouldn't dream of selling and have no intention of sinking.'

Lionel laughed. 'Easy to say when you don't even own your property! I guarantee you'd be giving it some thought if you did.'

'It's just like you to take the dirty money, Lionel, and then to gloat over it. It's absolutely the behaviour I'd expect of you,' Maurice said. 'I wonder who'll be the next traitor to show their colours?'

'Oh, Maurice, how you adore a drama!' Lionel scoffed. 'Who needs *King Lear* when you can strut and glower and menace in your own production?'

'This isn't helpful,' Daniel said.

'Very well,' Mrs Fitzgerald finally spoke then. They all looked towards her. 'I have no right to assume the moral high ground, I'm painfully aware of that, but I'm sorry you felt inclined to sell, Lionel.'

'You have no right to judge at all!' said Maurice. He laughed bitterly. 'You started this. This is your fault. If this community tears apart, as it may well now, it should be on your conscience.'

'How much land does Lionel own?' Robert asked, as they walked back to the cottages.

'Only the house, the garden and the workshop,' Trudie

replied. 'It's not a sizeable garden and I can't imagine they'd demolish the house to build there. It's probably worth more as it is. As he said, it's likely just speculation.'

'Do you suppose the builders are talking to other people?'

'I wouldn't be at all surprised.'

With a noise of scuffling on the gravel, they turned back to see Maurice and Lionel squaring up to one another again. Lionel was jabbing a finger at Maurice's chest and he was raising his fists in a boxer's stance.

'How frightfully embarrassing,' said Trudie.

As they watched them tussling, Robert found himself thinking of his father and how he would quickly resort to using his fists. He'd imagined these people would be different – and wasn't Greenfields meant to be an example of harmonious, peaceable living? They didn't seem to be doing much of that at present. Maurice had Lionel in a headlock now.

'I know he's the last person who would sell, but I can't help wishing Maurice might decide to go,' he admitted. 'Is that awful of me?'

Trudie smiled ruefully. 'Maurice will hold out to the end. He's enjoying the drama far too much to make an early exit from the stage.'

'The end? Do you believe it will come to an end, Trudie?'

She put an arm around him. 'Not if I can help it, darling. I say, Faye, do you want to have a coffee with us? In the circumstances, we might have a shot of Cognac in it.'

She'd approached behind them, heading back towards her cottage.

'Kind of you, Trudie, but I've got a pile of reading to do this afternoon.'

'Don't overdo it! Perhaps see you later?' Trudie lowered her voice as Faye walked on ahead of them. 'Are you two speaking at the moment? Have you had another tiff?'

'Faye and I can't seem to be civil to one another,' he replied. 'We don't seem to be capable of it, so it's for the best if we don't speak.'

They hadn't exchanged a word since they'd argued in the orchard and he had no desire to break the silence. He'd found himself going over the things she'd said and had decided he could do quite well without Faye telling him what he ought to care about and who he ought to be.

'But how ridiculous! How silly!' Trudie said. She held him by the shoulders and looked perplexed. 'Must I knock your heads together? The pair of you are very alike actually – proud, single-minded and terribly stubborn.'

'Alike? Do you honestly think so? Don't say that to Faye. She'd be most offended.'

'Really, darling?' Trudie laughed. 'Oh God – what it is to be young!'

Chapter Twenty-Nine

June brought the smell of new-cut hay, honeysuckle and meadowsweet. The light was golden in the mornings and seemed to linger in the upper branches of the lime trees at the end of the days. The wheat was turning from green to bronze in the fields all around, cattle were swishing their tails at the muddy edges of ponds, and the hedgerows were full of dog roses. With all the noise and dust and rancour on the estate, Robert was glad to walk away from it at times. He missed the peace he'd formerly known in the gardens, the solitude and the birdsong.

He'd spent the past week in the topiary garden, balancing on ladders and stretching out with secateurs. He'd been using the photographs in the archive to work out the original shapes of the hedges. When he'd studied one of these images with a magnifying glass, he'd spotted a man in a convalescent uniform almost hidden in the shadows of the topiary doves. He was standing staring at the camera, and though his face was blurred, there was something challenging and disturbing in his direct gaze. Robert heard the voices and footsteps of soldiers everywhere in the garden now. Their absence had become a presence. There'd always been a feeling of melancholy at

Anderby, of grandeur faded, but it intensified after he'd seen the white graves and imagined those men's sad last days being lived out in this place.

'It's starting to look cared for again,' Mrs Fitzgerald said. Robert looked down to see her standing with a hand on the ladder. She'd approached as silently as a ghost. It was the first time he'd seen her in the garden for weeks.

'It's rewarding to do this. I feel I'm getting a nod of approval from all the people who have cared for the garden before.' She nodded slightly too, but he couldn't quite read the expression on her face. He came down the ladder. 'I've been assuming that we still plan to open up to visitors later this month? I've been working towards that goal. Am I correct in thinking there's normally a fête at midsummer and that you'd hoped to officially open then?' He was glad to have this chance to speak with her. He'd been worrying that the land sale might have changed her plans.

'That had been my intention. We've always hosted the fête – I inherited the tradition from the previous owners – but I don't know that anyone is in the mood for it this time. Perhaps we might skip a year? Teddy thinks we should. To be honest, I didn't realize the builders would move in so quickly and make so much mess.'

She glanced in the direction of the orchard – or what had been the orchard. Smoke from the fires was still drifting and there was a noise of heavy excavation this morning. The vehicles had been chewing up the lawns, trenches had been dug for power lines this week and there were muddy tyre tracks everywhere. Robert saw sadness and tension in Mrs Fitzgerald's expression and she seemed distracted this morning. Without her face powder, there were fine freckles on her skin, he observed, and her unpainted eyelashes were pale blonde. She looked older and more vulnerable than she had done at the start of the year.

'It would be a pity to let it go by if it is a tradition,' he offered. 'And it might be good for us to work together on something.'

'Perhaps you're right,' she said, but there was no conviction in her voice. 'Listen, there's something I have to say to you, Robert. Something serious, I'm afraid. I've been meaning to bring it up for weeks, but what with everything . . .' She waved her hand towards the building work.

'Yes?'

'It's about your previous employer. Teddy heard a story going around, he had some suspicion, and at his insistence I wrote a letter.'

'Ah.' Robert turned the secateurs in his hands. He'd dreaded that Teddy would do that, but time had gone by, and then with all the upset over the land sale, it had ceased to be foremost in his thoughts. Had the lie caught up with him now?

'I had a reply,' Mrs Fitzgerald went on. She frowned at the ground. 'I know what happened. Mr Underhill told me the full story. He explained why you were dismissed.'

After all the work he'd done here, and with everything more he yet hoped to achieve, would he be dismissed again now? Was this where it came to an end? Robert recalled the ugly words that Mrs Underhill had used. Depraved. Deceitful. Dishonourable. Would they have been repeated in that letter? He hated the thought of Mrs Fitzgerald reading those words and thinking him that sort of man.

'I regret it,' he said. 'Sincerely. I wish I could go back and change my actions. Would you permit me to tell you my side of the story?'

'I have to say, it shocked me. I thought better of you, Robert. There were some nasty allegations in that letter.'

'I never took advantage of Esther. I know her parents see it differently, but it wasn't like that.'

'You lied, though,' Mrs Fitzgerald said. 'I believed your letter of reference was written by Mr Underhill, but he was clearly entirely unaware of its existence. I am disappointed in you for that.'

'I hated having to lie. I'm not a dishonest person.' How might he convince her? 'But you would never have taken me on if I'd been entirely honest. I had to be economical with the truth.'

'Teddy thinks I should dismiss you.'

That was what he'd wanted all along, wasn't it? 'I'm not a bad man. I'm not like that at all. I always had a good relationship with Mr Underhill, but they were horrified by the idea that I might have laid a finger on their daughter. Mrs Underhill reminded me, quite explicitly, that I was their social inferior. Suddenly what mattered was my social class and not my character. That's part of why it's been a pleasure to work here – because, from the start, you accepted me for who I am.' Could she understand why that mattered to him? She ought to, shouldn't she? 'I want to do the right thing and I want to stay here and finish the gardens for you.'

She was silent for a moment, her eyes scrutinizing his face. 'As Maurice reminded me recently, I have no right to take the moral high ground at present. I haven't been entirely honest with you either, I'm well aware of that, but I did feel sad and angry when I read that letter.'

'I can understand that, but please believe me – that's not who I am.'

'You have been dishonest, but I can appreciate why you felt you had to lie.' She held his gaze for a long moment before she looked away. 'We all make errors of judgement sometimes.'

'Please, if you'd allow me to stay, I won't let you down again.'

'If I don't let you go, I'll have to justify myself to Teddy. He won't be happy. I know that. He's always been doubtful of the wisdom of this project and would have had me dismiss you weeks ago.' She paused again, as if considering her next words. The hesitation seemed interminable. 'Prior to all of this, I'd had no grounds to question your ability, your commitment or your character. You have worked tirelessly and I've valued your loyalty.'

'If you give me another chance, I promise you won't regret it.'

He could feel her eyes evaluating, see her weighing the arguments. He had a sense that his future was tilting in the balance.

'Very well,' she finally said. 'I would still like to go ahead with the plans to open the gardens and I can't do that without you.'

Robert felt a rush of relief and realized he'd been holding his breath. 'Thank you.' The words weren't adequate. 'Thank you for trusting me. Thank you for giving me another chance.'

She nodded, but her face was still serious. 'You know, I think we will have the fête this year. I've been in two minds about it – but, as you said, it might be good for us to work together on something.' She lifted her chin a little higher as she looked towards the Hall. 'You and I both have regrets, we've both lied, but we can be honest with one another now, can't we?'

'We can. We will be. I swear. Thank you.'

She'd become shockingly thinner over the past month, the bones showed at her wrists, and she pulled her shawl around her shoulders as if she were cold. Robert wanted to say, 'I know you felt you had to sell. I see what it's cost you.' Instead, he said, 'If we're planning to open for midsummer, I'll finish planting up the borders by the gatehouse.'

'I'd appreciate that.'

Robert watched her walking away. Teddy had been conspicuous in his absence over the past weeks and there was something lonely about her figure walking through the garden this morning. Nobody seemed to want to approach her at the moment. No one wanted to be seen talking with her. But he owed her his loyalty – more than ever now.

'I will stand by you,' Robert found himself saying. Though she was far out of earshot, he saw her turn and raise her hand as she looked back.

Chapter Thirty

'Stay where I can see you, please!' Faye shouted towards the children. 'Let's leave the builders alone. They're allowed a lunch hour too.'

Trudie laughed. 'It's the one and only compensation – there are some pleasing specimens of the male physique on show, don't you agree? I know you've officially renounced, but you must have noticed? I understand the children's fascination.'

'I've a job keeping them away from the building site.' Faye sat down on the travelling rug at Trudie's side. Their shared lunch had been lemon curd tarts and slices of shortbread from the café. It perhaps wasn't the most balanced meal, but still – she screwed up the paper bag. 'Seemingly danger, loud noise, mud and strangers have a powerful allure. Kitty is the worst – she'd spend all day staring at them. I guess it's her age and it doesn't help that a couple of the builders have given her sweets and cigarette cards. I'm not sure whether I ought to say something to them.'

'Her age?' Trudie lay back on the tartan rug, her eyes hidden behind large sunglasses. 'You mean one is meant to grow out of that sort of thing?'

As Faye had led the children away from the site just now,

she'd seen that Teddy was with the builders. The men were pausing to eat their packets of sandwiches in the sun. They were sitting on a stack of cut timber, between the piles of rubble and sand, and there was Teddy rolling up his shirtsleeves. Faye and Trudie had looked on as he joshed with a digger driver, shook hands with the site foreman and then laughed with one of the surveyors as he pointed in the direction of the Hall.

'Teddy actually appears to be enjoying it, doesn't he?' she said now. 'Given how thoroughly glum Gwendoline looks, it seems rather callous.'

'I didn't think you had much sympathy for Gwen?'

'I hadn't, but it's impossible not to contrast her mood to his. How can she tolerate him?'

'I know lots of perfectly sensible women who are married to thoroughly ghastly men. They don't always see it, do they? Or maybe we willingly blind ourselves to these things? I'm not entirely blameless myself on that score – and your Richard had his moments too, you have to admit?'

'Yes. Perhaps.'

Faye could think of plenty of moments, but that was all in the past now and she'd never let herself be so naïve again. She checked on the children. They were playing chase, hide-and-seek amongst the flower beds, and gathering rose petals in jam jars which they meant to make into 'perfume'. She'd told them they could do that, but must be careful of bees, mind where they were putting their feet and only take the flower heads that were already going over. Robert wouldn't be best pleased per-haps, but he could be too protective of his garden – and what were a few rose petals compared with the felling of the orchard?

'Can I interest you in some contraband?' Trudie asked.

'I'm sorry?'

'Here. It might amuse you – or make you want to sob.' Trudie sat up, reached into her bag and produced a brochure. She passed it across to Faye before she flopped heavily down onto the rug once more.

Faye turned the booklet in her hands. The cover announced '*The Orchard Estate, Anderby Hall*' in an antiquated font and was printed with a drawing of a half-timbered house, its roof tinted a beefy red and its shrubberies lime green, set against a silhouette of the Hall's roof line.

'Where did you get it?'

'Daniel. Apparently, he's being pursued by a salesman who hasn't yet figured out that he actually already lives at Anderby.'

Faye turned through the pages. Photographs of various houses were reproduced inside, all of them a mishmash of architectural features and with everything a little exaggerated. The builder's signature style appeared to be large chimney stacks, bow windows and outsized door porticos. There was a lot of herringbone brick, asymmetric gables, and half-timbering seemed to be mandatory.

'I'm no expert in architecture, but they somehow look like caricatures of English houses,' Faye observed. 'Don't you think? For some reason they put me in mind of actors giving hammy Shakespeare performances – too much prithee mistress and flourishing of frilly cuffs. Do you know what I mean?'

'Read the foreword,' Trudie said, her voice starting to sound drowsy. 'It's got very frilly cuffs.'

'*The parkland is studded with noble oaks and other trees of large growth and great beauty*,' Faye read aloud. 'Presumably apple trees are insufficiently noble? *The pleasure grounds slope gently to the south-west and are well arranged with attractive planting and extensive views over magnificent country. The open aspect and pure air of the Anderby Hall parklands make it an ideal neighbourhood for home building.* Well, yes, we did once have pure air. I could smell petrol fumes when I stepped out this morning.'

'*Nestled in richly wooded and undulating country*,' Trudie quoted, in a voice full of ripeness. 'Have you got to that bit yet? "Nestled" – why do estate agents and builders love the word nestled? Read on. You get an honourable mention.'

'*The neighbouring village has a range of traditional shops and there are excellent schools within easy reach.* Does that mean us?'

'It surely does.'

'We're a selling point! I feel slightly sullied.'

She reclined back on the rug and shut her eyes against the sun. It was true that the housing estate might well bring her more pupils, which the school very much needed, but ... She thought again about the note from Miss Carmichael. Did she want to be here next year?

'Have you read the paragraph about modern horrors?' Trudie's voice interrupted her thoughts. 'Carry on. That's a juicy bit.'

Faye's leaned up on her elbow. Her eyes scanned down the page.

'*There is nothing in common between this handsome, high-class estate and that modern horror, the housing scheme, with its ugly mass-produced dwellings.*' She couldn't help but laugh. 'Oh God! Maurice could have written that bit.'

'I told you so,' said Trudie. 'Are you feeling reassured now?'

'Not much! *The general design of the houses is pleasing to the eye, with rustic facing bricks of varying colours, leaded light windows*

and traditional timber framing. Houghton & Halford use only the best
English cement (we guarantee – no foreign cement used) and all internal
woodwork has three coats of top-quality lead paint.'

'There's a price list at the back.'

Faye flicked on through the pages. 'They start at £530. I
can't imagine that many people around here could afford that.'

'Exclusive, you see. No riffraff.'

Faye lay back on the rug, shading her eyes with the brochure.
'Do you think Gwendoline will sell more land to them? Is this
just the start? Is all the beauteous parkland potentially on the
table?'

'I really don't know. I've not been brave enough to ask her.
Daniel thinks Houghton is hungry to buy, so I guess it depends
on the price and just how much Gwen needs the money.'

'So much for open aspects and pure air!' Faye watched ants
crawling in the grass. The drone of bees' wings was soporific,
but then the engine of a digger started up again. 'Are you determined that you will stay on, Trudie?'

'I want to believe Anderby has a future. We have to, don't
we? You're determined to stay too, aren't you?'

Was she? What might that future look like? Miss
Carmichael's letter had arrived by post the previous morning,
inviting her to take a tour of the grammar school, to meet some
of the pupils and to discuss potential terms of employment. For
the past twenty-four hours Faye had been imagining an alternative life in which she rented a nice little flat in town, had a
six-week break all to herself through the summer and went to
the pictures at the weekends. She could join the Literary and
Philosophical Society in town, she'd decided, might be able to
afford a foreign holiday and, in time, perhaps she could save up

to buy a motor of her own. Faye felt the warmth of the sun on her face and could hear Trudie's breath at her side becoming slower. She was picturing herself taking weekend hikes over green hills and talking with well-spoken young girls about their ambitions as a loud crash from the building site curtailed her imaginings.

'Jesus!' said Trudie, sitting up. 'What was that?'

'It's the reason why the children mustn't go anywhere near it. I've told them, but will they listen?' They'd stopped their games and were all looking towards her now. 'You see!' she shouted. 'Perhaps I could talk to Gwendoline about erecting some sort of barriers?'

Trudie flopped back onto the rug. She'd smudged her lipstick slightly. 'We just have to keep on reminding ourselves that this won't go on forever. We have to remember why we came here and be confident we can return to that. We must cling onto it, mustn't we?' There was resolution in her voice. She reached out and squeezed Faye's arm with a strong grip.

'I'd better start herding them back to class.' Faye got to her feet and began to dust grass clippings from her skirt.

'Please, Miss.' She turned around to see Maudie Higgs holding a daisy chain in her small hands. 'I made it for you, Miss.'

Faye knelt down and the little girl placed the fragile chain carefully over her head. She looked into the child's large innocent brown eyes and smiled.

'You're my favourite teacher, Miss.'

'I'm your *only* teacher, Maudie!'

'Oh, how sweet!' said Trudie.

There were lots of reasons to make the break now – Faye had spent last night mentally listing them – but . . . could she really?

Chapter Thirty-One

'They've offered him a three-bedroom house and a large studio with north-facing windows,' Iris said. She put the lid on the teapot. 'They clearly want him there. They seem to view him as a prize catch. It was all flattery and enticements, all deference and hearty backslaps. I could almost see his head swelling.'

'So Cecil wants to go?' Robert asked.

'He says it would be a good move for his career. He'd be mixing with influential people – people who win prizes and have the ear of wealthy benefactors. Magazine articles get written about the art community at Biswell. It's always in the newspapers. I can't argue with that. And he says Greenfields is finished now.'

Robert watched Iris's face as she poured the tea. Obviously, this move would be advantageous to Cecil, but he couldn't tell if she wanted it. 'Surely it isn't finished? It will just be different.'

'But different in a way that's not attractive to Cecil.' She took a piece of sewing from the table, holding it up to assess it, then began to move pins. 'He's complaining about all the dust and noise from the building work, there's likely to be months of that ahead, and he says the most awful things about the bungalows. He thinks they'll be bought by the type of people who have nests of occasional tables, miniature windmills on the mantelpiece and prints of *The Hay Wain* on their walls. He says they'll have little wishing wells and gnomes in their gardens, crazy paving and pampas grass.'

'Crikey.' Robert tried not to smile. 'I never expected Greenfields to be as snobbish as it is.'

'Seriously? Certain people here are hideously snobbish – not least my husband! They might criticize the old prejudices of money and class, but they have their own elitism based on culture and education and what they deem to be good taste. They have a horror of any object that a worthy, authentic, horny-handed artisan hasn't sweated over. Woe betide these new people fill their houses with factory-made, mass-produced furniture!'

'And how do you feel about leaving? And the children? Would it be better for them in this other community?'

She'd tidied her sketchbook from the table as Robert had come in, but he'd glimpsed tender pencil drawings of Erin and Ewan. She was always sketching them and he knew they mattered to her more than anything. Iris would do what was right for them.

'We haven't had the conversation with the children yet, but I know they won't be happy.' Her needle made a smooth rhythm, stabbing in and pulling out. 'I'm dreading it, to be honest. They adore the school here, their friends here, the freedom – I mean, who wouldn't?'

'Cecil?' Robert ventured. Iris's needle paused, she lifted her eyebrows, and he saw her unspoken assent. 'And would this move benefit your career?'

'What career?' Iris put down her sewing and stirred another spoonful of sugar into her tea. She looked as if she needed it today. 'I'm only working to keep food on the table and the children in shoes. If Cecil picked up more commissions, I suppose I could be choosier about what I take on. Ultimately, if this move would benefit his career, it must be good for us as a family, mustn't it?'

Robert couldn't help thinking she sounded as if she was trying to convince herself. 'Cecil is going to talk to the builders?'

'He already has done. He went into town yesterday. He says their offer is a good one, it's a fair price, and it's certainly more than we paid for the house.'

'He's already made the decision, then?'

'It would break my heart to go, Robert.' Iris looked up from stirring her cup. She'd been stirring it far longer than necessary. She pushed her sewing away and her shoulders slumped. Her guard fell too and, for the first time since Robert had sat down, her voice sounded candid. 'I'd feel treacherous, like I'm deserting you. Can you imagine what Maurice will say? Cecil has been so beastly about Gwendoline, but we'd be doing the same thing.'

'Who cares what Maurice says? I don't. Everyone else will understand your reasons.'

'I have to think what will be best for us as a family. Plus, a fresh start might be no bad thing for Cecil and I.' There wasn't much optimism in her voice. 'Things haven't been good between us recently. We've been going through a difficult period. All marriages do, I know, but we disagree about so much these days and seem to have little common ground.' She'd been staring into her teacup as she'd spoken and only now looked up. 'I'm sorry. I probably shouldn't have told you that.'

'You know I won't tell anyone else.' Robert wasn't convinced a move would bring them closer. All the advantages of it seemed to be on Cecil's side and he worried how Iris might cope without friends around her. As far as he could see, she was only going along with this to keep her family together. 'Perhaps, if Cecil is happier, it will be easier?'

Iris shrugged. For her sake, Robert wished she looked more certain.

Chapter Thirty-Two

Maurice had pinned posters up at the railway station, in the public houses and in the village shops. Printed in a heavy Gothic font, so that they looked like something that might have been issued by the Witchfinder General, they summoned all to a *'Mass Public Demonstration against the GRIEVOUS OUTRAGE being perpetrated at Anderby Hall'*.

There had been a discussion as to how many chairs should be laid out in the barn. (How many bottoms on seats constituted a mass public demonstration?) In the end, they'd decided to put out a hundred chairs and Maurice said the remainder of the people would just have to crush in at the back. The cobwebs on the barn walls had been attacked with a broom, the cobbled floor had been swept, as best was possible, and a stage had been erected with a lectern upon it. The placards which the women had made for their protest were propped up at the back of the stage and the *'Nature not Neo-Tudor!'* banner was hanging above it. Having been so ineffectual on the day when the builders arrived, there was now something pitiful about the placards' exclamation marks and forbidding words, Robert felt.

Maurice had spoken of the Swing Riots as they'd laid out the chairs, of Ned Ludd and the great Chartist demonstration on Kennington Common, but it looked as if he wasn't going to get the massed ranks he'd anticipated. The widows Renishaw, Cavendish and Lloyd, habitués of the café, had turned up and there were half a dozen women from the village who'd arrived together in the baker's delivery van. They'd brought sandwiches and flasks and had a bright-eyed, amused look about them, as if they might have come out for an afternoon at the circus. Most of the parents whose children attended the school were dutifully showing their faces and there was a gaggle of Maurice's friends – a collection of fellow potters, archaeologists and local historians, replete in beards, tweed knickerbockers and yellow knee socks. Together with the residents of Anderby, there were perhaps forty people in attendance. This would be no Kennington Common.

Most of the Greenfielders had brought their children along and the little ones were having a splendid time, jumping from chair to chair and writing their names on the petition in large, studied letters, some of them with accompanying illustrations. Cecil and Iris sat together looking subdued and Robert wondered how many people were aware they were negotiating a price with the builders. He hadn't told anyone, but he knew Iris had mentioned it to Trudie and discretion wasn't her strongest suit. Given that Maurice was now shaking Cecil's hand, he clearly hadn't heard.

Maurice habitually dressed like a villager from a sixteenth-century Flemish painting; he had a fondness for sheepskin jerkins, woollen gaiters and a cowhide apron, but he looked particularly Brueghelian today in his green tunic and a felt cap. He'd tied his hair back with string and was wearing a flint arrowhead on a leather cord around his neck.

'Does Maurice think he's Robin Hood?' Trudie whispered. 'Or perhaps he imagines he's Wat Tyler? Are we expected to revolt at the end? Is he going to whip us up so that we froth at the mouths and take the Hall by siege?'

Trudie was wearing orange silk harem trousers today, an extravagantly large black straw hat and long ropes of sandalwood beads. She wasn't dressed for a siege.

'For all the talk of the people rising, I suspect he'd love to be lord of the manor,' Robert said.

'Can you imagine? He'd have us all wearing coifs, eating pottage and lit by tallow candles. I can almost smell it! I wouldn't be able to pack up my house fast enough.' Trudie altered her voice and expression as Maurice approached. 'Bit of a disappointing turnout, what? Maybe we should have handed out flyers.'

'I am disappointed, I'll not lie, but I'm also not surprised. People are impassive and short-sighted. They have no feeling for history any longer and no aesthetic sensitivity.'

'Maybe they don't find the look of the houses that offensive?' Robert suggested. 'And I don't suppose it will have much impact on the village. If anything, it will probably be good for the village shops.'

'But, Robert, people *ought* to care. They ought to be offended. These so-called Tudor dwellings are a travesty.' He waved his hand as if he were trying to shoo a cloud of midges. 'And for them to be built here, of all places, where we cherish beauty and authenticity! Nailing half-inch boards onto brick buildings and putting plaster between them is not architecture – it is philistine. They will insult the landscape and the history of this site. It's an abominable scheme.' He looked around the barn. 'But then we live in philistine times.'

'This is fascinating,' said Trudie, unconvincingly. 'But we probably ought to take our seats. There might be a last-minute rush.'

They sat in the row behind Daniel and Faye. 'Was Maurice warming up his rhetoric on you?' Daniel asked over his shoulder.

'I'm sorely regretting not bringing a hip flask,' said Trudie.

'He must be disappointed by the turnout,' Daniel said. 'He's going to be addressing a lot of empty chairs.'

Robert turned and looked at the rows of unoccupied seats behind. The children were playing a boisterous game of tag at the back of the barn and Mr Ingram's three collies were being remarkably tolerant as Kitty and Erin played a game in which they were professional dog groomers. The village women were sitting in the back row, passing a bag of sweets between them as they waited for the spectacle to start.

'Wasn't it meant to begin at three?' Robert looked at his watch. It was already a quarter past.

'If he doesn't start soon, people will drift away.'

Faye hadn't moved while they were speaking. She sat looking forwards with an unreadable expression on her profiled face. She had her hair pinned up today and was wearing fine pearl drop earrings that trembled ever so slightly with her breath. Robert found his eyes drawn to them and the pretty shell of her ear. They'd been avoiding one another – which one couldn't do easily or inconspicuously here – and this was the closest he'd been to her for over a month. He couldn't presently imagine how they might begin to talk again.

Clearing his throat, Maurice drew the attention of all to the lectern and, finally, the meeting was in progress. 'This valley is a green lung,' he began, in full orator voice, 'or it has been until now.'

He spoke of ancient landscapes, of the druids, the Romans and Saxons passing through, of woods loud with the song of nightingales, of green nooks and blossomy knolls. He made it sound like a folk tale, or something from the bible, Robert thought; it was a veritable land of milk and honey. But then he brought on the fire and brimstone.

'It will all change now,' he said. 'This corruption will fester and disease will spread out from it.' Change would accelerate into the valley, he predicted; industry would inevitably follow, the river would clog with chemicals and motorcars would race though the village day and night. Electricity pylons and telephone lines would slice across the horizons and their peaceful, winding lanes would become straightened tarmacadam roads lined with ugly villas, petrol stations and advertising hoardings. 'It has begun here at Anderby,' he said, 'and now it will roll outwards, until all the woods are felled and the fields are concreted over. In another twenty years' time there will be no definition between town and country; our green and pleasant land will have become a grey, despoiled, sprawling suburb.' Maurice spread his arms and narrowed his eyes as he looked into the middle distance, like a prophet witnessing a vision. Could he really see that? Robert felt he was going a little too far.

'Where will the rabbits go?' Maurice asked. His top lip was starting to sweat. 'What about the habitats of the badgers, the hedgehogs and the otters? Where will our children play if we lose the woods and the fields? Do you want your sons and daughters to be loitering on street corners and joining criminal gangs? Must we accept our valley being filled with the noxious fumes of factories and motor engines? Are we prepared to hear our children coughing and see their eyes streaming? Some might call this progress, the irresistible advance of the modern world, but it isn't – it's robbery. We're about to witness the destruction of a landscape which all of us, our ancestors and our descendants, had a common right to enjoy. Moreover,' he raised an index finger, 'isn't this what we fought to preserve in the war? Didn't recruitment posters urge us to enlist to save England's green fields? Now, in this hard-won peacetime, surely we shouldn't allow our countryside to be ravaged?'

Robert thought of standing up on the moors and looking down at the lines of terraced houses and mill chimneys and the gasometer of his hometown. Had that ever been a milk-and-honey valley? If it had, it must have been a long time ago. But it wouldn't happen here, would it? Surely this was exaggeration? He also thought of the last house he'd called home, the neighbours' voices through the thin walls, the outside lavatory that six families shared and always the smell of damp and coal dust. By comparison, these houses would be modern, clean, airy, each with their own garden, hot running water and an inside bathroom. What was so wrong about people wanting a patch of ground of their own and a house that they might make into a home? Wasn't that what soldiers had been promised when they came back from the war?

'This is how the greedy maw of Mammon works,' Maurice went on. He dabbed at his top lip with a handkerchief. 'On the construction company's part, this is purely a money-making venture. They don't give a damn for the damage they're doing. They have no interest in sympathetic design. They will take their profit and move on. But *we* ought to care and those who established this community certainly ought to have higher standards.' He made a dramatic pause, lowered his brows towards his audience and jabbed a hand towards the Hall. 'She has let us down. She has inflicted his wound. This is a crime against tradition and truth, insulting the architecture, history and ideals of this place, and it is her responsibility. Are you prepared to accept that?'

'Does he want us to go and lynch her?' Trudie whispered.

Daniel shifted in his seat, sitting forwards with his head bowed. He didn't look at all comfortable, Robert thought.

'But perhaps that behaviour should have been expected from someone who is not from here?' Maurice posited. 'Someone who doesn't have a real connection with the land, who doesn't have this place in their blood and in their soul?' He put a hand to his chest and looked to the back of the room with a solemn face. 'Should we possibly have predicted this behaviour from an incomer? From a foreigner? Should an outsider ever have been permitted to become the custodian of our heritage?'

Robert calculated on his fingers that he'd been at Anderby for six months now. People probably still considered him to be an incomer, didn't they? He couldn't help feeling there was an ugly implication in Maurice's words.

'Maurice isn't local to here, is he?' he whispered to Trudie. 'Where is he from?'

'Abergavenny, I think.'

'And these people in the new houses, who will they be?' Maurice asked his audience. He hoisted his eyebrows up. 'Where will they have come from? What will their values be? Will they understand and respect our values? I suspect not. The class of people who aspire to neo-Tudor bungalows will want picture palaces to entertain them, dances at golf clubs, boogie-woogie salons and transport cafés.' He spat these words out with distaste. Trudie sniggered at the boogie-woogie salons. 'They won't appreciate nature. They won't care about history. They certainly won't value authenticity.'

'I wouldn't mind the cinema and boogie-woogie,' Trudie said, *sotto voce*. 'Eh, Robert?'

Faye got to her feet and apologized as she began to make her way along the row of chairs. Some of what Maurice was saying echoed her own arguments, but Robert could see from her expression that she felt the latest direction of his rhetoric to be distasteful. It was making Robert feel uncomfortable too and he found himself wanting to say that to Faye. He would have liked to stand up and walk out with her, but courage failed him.

'I'm not saying people don't have a right to a decent home,' Maurice qualified. 'But. Not. Here.' He spoke in staccato and stabbed his finger at the lectern. 'Housing estates should be built on the edges of towns, where there is access to employment, bus services, shopping parades and the inhabitants will be amongst their own sort. They most certainly shouldn't be built on ancient apple orchards. It's too late for our dear old apple trees now, but we must fight for our green valley and our values. We mustn't let greed and indifference destroy what we have here. It's time to stand up for our rights and our way of life, for our traditions and our children's inheritance, for the greater common good. This is not acceptable. This work must be halted. And those responsible must be held to account.'

He'd built it to a crescendo and the audience duly clapped, but Robert suspected it might be from relief at the meeting's conclusion as much as assent with the sentiments. Maurice stood with his arms spread and eyes closed, clearly expecting a more rapturous and lengthy applause, and it was slightly embarrassing how quickly people vacated their seats. Robert wasn't inclined to linger either.

He didn't dare to go and knock on Faye's door, but found himself walking around the grounds and hoping their paths might cross. He wanted to tell her how he disliked the snobbishness, the insularity and the double standards. Yes, there was something in what Maurice said about preserving the countryside for future generations, but his definition of the 'common good' seemed to have a lot of caveats. He obviously didn't want to live alongside people who were *too* common. These weren't the values this community was founded on, were they? Was this what Faye had meant when she said Greenfields had lost its way? In his haste to leave, he hadn't signed the petition, Robert realized. But he wasn't sorry. He couldn't help wishing the builders might buy the land around Maurice's house and populate it with travelling salesmen from Swindon who enjoyed a round of golf at the weekends and ate off factory-made crockery.

Chapter Thirty-Three

The disappointing attendance at the protest meeting had left Maurice in an irritable mood. Curses and the noise of smashed pots had been issuing from his workshop for the past week and he'd boycotted the last residents' meeting. Relations were strained enough anyway, the meetings had been antagonistic and awkward lately, and his presence hadn't been missed.

Meanwhile, the foundations of the houses had been going in this week; all day long there was a sound of cement mixers working, pipes were being laid out on the ground, and scaffolding and crates of bricks had been delivered onto the site. This was Accrington brick, one of the builders had told Robert. 'They'll last forever. They'll be here long after the big house. Does the American lady know these are the same bricks they used for the Empire State Building?' The modern orange clay looked too bright against the Georgian bricks of the orchard walls. Perhaps, with time, the surfaces would weather and look more like they fitted here, but how long would that take?

Robert had been working on the parterre garden, now gaining form with its drifts of salvias and nepeta, phlox and foxgloves, stachys and santolina, but he laid his tools down as the turret clock struck eleven. The residents had agreed to gather in the café to discuss plans for the summer fête. It would be a low-key affair this year, what with all the work going on, but there would be the usual refreshments, bazaar and tombola, the barrel organ and the book stall, and Mrs Fitzgerald would give her guided tours of the Hall. Some people were refusing to participate, there was still a good deal of bitterness, but others were wearying of the tension and agreed they must make some effort to get back to the normal programme of events.

'Phyllis puts on her big brass earrings and reads people's tea leaves,' said Kitty, leaning on the back of Robert's chair. 'They queue up at her tent. She can do you, if you'd like, Robert.'

'A gypsy who used to come to the Town Moor fair taught me,' said Phyllis, in every seriousness. 'She said I had the gift.' She gestured for Robert to pass her his teacup.

'What does it say?' Kitty asked, hanging over the cup. Her sandy pigtails were tied with tartan bows today, and up close Robert could see she had freckles over her nose. 'Is there a lady? Will he have a romance? Is she pretty?'

'I don't have time for romance; I have two hundred snapdragons to plant out!' Robert thought Kitty had a bit too much interest in romance and, at this moment, he certainly didn't want one thrusting into his own agenda.

'Go on,' prompted Nancy, her painted eyebrows raised. She winked at Robert. Mrs Fitzgerald looked on with a smile. Faye seemed to be applying great concentration to spreading butter on a toasted teacake.

'Turbulence and tribulation,' said Phyllis, pronouncing both words with solemnity.

'Hell's bells! Haven't we had enough of that already?' Nancy rolled her eyes.

'But it will all come right in the end,' Phyllis continued, her voice forcibly brightening in a way that suggested this was a habitual qualification. She patted Robert's hand. 'Don't you worry, pet.'

'Here comes tribulation,' said Trudie as Maurice's face appeared at the café door.

'We're talking over plans for the fayre,' Nancy said as he entered. 'You did get the notes from the last meeting, didn't you? It was on the agenda. Here, let me get you a chair.'

'Don't bother. I'm not stopping,' he said. 'You're guaranteed to have a big turnout this time. I'm sure you'll get a lot of gawkers. People can't resist looking at a car crash, can they?'

'I take it you're not proposing to assist this year?' Daniel sat back in his chair and steepled his fingers.

Maurice normally did a coil pottery session with the children, Nancy had mentioned, and his throwing demonstration usually drew a crowd.

'I shan't be here,' he said, rocking on his heels. 'I've begun packing up my workshop. You might as well know, I've decided to cut my losses.'

The room had silenced. 'By which you mean?' Trudie asked.

'I'm selling my house. All of this is over anyway,' he gestured around the room. 'It will just be a long slide downhill now and I've found a workshop in Radnorshire.'

'But . . .' Phyllis began.

'What?' Trudie demanded.

'You've sold your house to the builders, I take it?' Daniel's question broke through the clamour.

'But after everything you've said!' Nancy protested. 'After that speech and all your talk of treachery! You actually divided us up into Turncoats and Loyals! But now you've decided to switch camp?'

'It's not that long ago that you were talking about rats deserting sinking ships,' Phyllis pointed out. 'Does this make you a rat, then, Maurice?'

'This is just a consequence,' he responded, his voice resolute. 'She put this into motion.' He levelled his eyes at Mrs Fitzgerald, who had thus far remained silent. 'She's the one who took a wrecking ball to what we'd made here. This is no longer a conducive environment in which to work. I am merely responding to a change of circumstances initiated by others.'

'How conveniently your conscience operates,' Daniel observed.

'Do you actually have a conscience?' Trudie asked. 'What a frightful hypocrite you are, Maurice. Was it just amusing to play the rabble-rouser for a few weeks? Were you enjoying the spotlight?'

'After all that bile you spat!' said Faye. 'After all the bad feeling you've stirred up!'

She was angry, Robert could see. She twisted her pen in her hands and had sat forwards in her chair. Iris, at her side, appeared tense and shocked. She'd spoken little over the course of this morning's meeting and Robert assumed she was mindful that she'd soon have to break her own news to the group. Maurice's exit might make that easier.

'I understand your reasoning,' Mrs Fitzgerald finally spoke. 'We will be sorry to lose you from the community, Maurice, and we've appreciated your contribution to it over the years, but I suspect you might be happier elsewhere.'

'I certainly will!' There was a bitter edge to his laughter. 'But

I don't believe you understand anything, Gwendoline. You have no idea how much damage you've done. Perhaps you will in time, though. They'll all desert you, you know.' He indicated the group around the table. 'Even your acolytes and faithful dolts. Even your useless cad of a husband. They'll all scurry off over the next few months and then we'll see how you cope here on your own. You'll have plenty of time to contemplate your errors then. I hope you look out of your windows, see black-and-white cladding all around, and know what a fool you've been. You've let us down and you've let Anderby down. You might have been born into money, but you've shown yourself to have no class.'

'That's enough!' said Daniel. His chair scraped back and fell to the floor. He looked like he wanted to hit Maurice.

'Perhaps we should take a break? Could we adjourn this meeting for five minutes?' Mrs Fitzgerald gathered her papers together and stood. The expression on her face made Robert think of a cornered animal, but then she seemed to steady her nerve. 'If you must know, Maurice, I do thoroughly regret my actions and I'm sure I will repent them. But I still believe in the values this community was founded upon and, going forwards, I mean to uphold them.'

'What – community? Equality? You've made a mockery of those words. Do you even know what they mean? How can you say that after what you've done?'

Daniel took Maurice forcibly by the arm at that and dragged him towards the door. They exited with raised voices and the noise of feet scrabbling on gravel.

Mrs Fitzgerald's composure seemed to collapse as they went out. She sat down again and her shoulders slumped. 'He's not wrong. I have let you down. You deserve better than this. But we had to find a way to keep going. Our backs were to the wall. I really didn't want it to be the orchard, but . . .' she broke off.

'This isn't easy for any of us, but we can all see that it's agony for you.' Phyllis frowned at Mrs Fitzgerald. 'Maurice is so angry. He won't get over it. It will be easier if he goes.'

'We need to find a way to move forwards,' Nancy added. 'And that might be easier without Maurice.'

'Will we go forwards? Can we?' Mrs Fitzgerald looked up.

'We shall give it a bloody good try,' said Trudie.

'And maybe something positive will come out of this,' Faye suggested. 'Perhaps it's an opportunity for us to rethink what matters to us, to regain some focus and make plans for what we want to do next? It could be a new beginning for us.'

'Faye's right,' Robert said. 'Let's be optimistic and ambitious and remember why you started this.'

'I don't deserve your forgiveness,' said Mrs Fitzgerald. 'But if you'll give me the chance, I would like to make this right.'

Chapter Thirty-Four

They'd spent the week getting ready: cleaning windows and beating carpets, stringing up lengths of bunting and setting up the tents and stalls. Nancy and Phyllis had been baking day and night, Daniel had sorted all the second-hand books into alphabetical order, the brightly painted donkey carts had been rolled out and a Mr Buckland had arrived with his monkey and barrel organ. Iris was going to oversee the punting on the lake, Cecil had agreed to give a stone-carving demonstration, Trudie would judge the dog show and Mr Ingram had erected a pen full of freshly shampooed piglets. Daniel and Mrs Fitzgerald would give a recital of cello and piano in the afternoon, Miss Parget was organizing the jigs and reels, later on Nancy would sing and there'd be Chinese paper lanterns and a dance floor for the evening. Robert looked at the stripes of his new-mown lawns and blossoming borders and felt some sense of pride at the prospect of the gardens being opened up to the public for the first time.

As Maurice had predicted, there was a queue at the gates by ten o'clock – and then a regular trail of people down through the kitchen garden towards the building site. Robert recognized faces from the village, many of their regular customers from the market were there, and some of the builders who'd been working on the site too, scrubbed up today with clean fingernails and pressed shirts. The men were keen to have a first look inside the Hall and they were polite and deferential to Mrs Fitzgerald. As Robert listened to their good manners and intelligent questions, he wondered whether they'd been unfair in having first met them with placards and words of abuse.

Faye had organized a treasure hunt for the children, with clues secreted around the house and grounds. A pack of little ones was running about excitedly and intermittently returning to her with questions and answers. The girls had arrived in their best white pinafore dresses and the boys in starched collars, but faces were now flushed and grass stains greened knees.

'I'm afraid we're scuffing up your lawns,' she said to Robert as their paths crossed. 'You look calm on the surface, but are you having paroxysms inside?'

It was the first time she'd spoken to him directly since their row in the orchard. She was wearing a sprig-print dress, sandals and a straw hat. He couldn't see her eyes beneath its wide brim.

'Actually, it's nice to see the gardens full of people enjoying themselves. My paroxysms are on hold for the moment.'

'Well, I never. You do surprise me, Robert Bardsley.' The light through her sunhat made a pattern on her face and there was the faintest smile on her lips. 'Do I risk telling you that some of the children have been picking little posies of flowers?'

'You wouldn't have encouraged them to do that, of course?' She seemed more at ease, more playful today, and he felt reluctant to let her go.

'Would I?' There was definitely a smile then. For all the harsh words they'd exchanged, receiving Faye's smile still felt like the warmth of the sun on his skin.

He had been assigned to fetch and carry for the day, and spent much of the morning lugging crates of cider and tea urns, sprinting between stalls and replenishing supplies of scones and small change. He collected discarded glasses and couldn't help picking up sweet papers and apple cores too. But he'd meant what he said to Faye; it gave him pleasure to overhear comments about the changes in the gardens, to see the de Villiers roses blooming and to notice people pausing to breathe the scent of the jasmine.

Families were sitting on rugs on the grass, passing babies and bags of toffee around. There were iced buns to be eaten, siblings to chase and a lot of cider to be drunk. Trudie was giving out the raffle results, her voice sounding haughty through a megaphone, and the barrel organ sent up its strange swirling melodies. Girls made hopscotch circles in the gravel on the drive and boys had brought cricket bats and peashooters to fire at their sisters. People were throwing sticks into the lake for dogs to retrieve and there was laughter and cries of horror as the wet dogs shook them- selves, impressive showers of water extending out in the sunlight. Overexcited dogs and children seemed to be running every- where, and then the piglets escaped from their pen. There was a smell of trampled grass, toffee apples, warm cider and punnets of strawberries gone too ripe in the sun. All was light-hearted and boisterous, as it might have gone on in past decades. Dandelion seed blew in the gauzy gold light, necks reddened with sunburn and the house cast a long, lordly shadow over the garden.

Robert tagged along with one of Mrs Fitzgerald's tours of the Hall in the afternoon. She was a natural tour guide, warm and friendly, bringing drama to the house's stories and evidently full of pride that she called these rooms her home. She looked more like herself today, her hair pinned up with tortoiseshell combs, her lips painted and strings of pearls at her throat. She was strikingly thin now, though, and Robert noticed how her wedding ring slipped up and down her finger as she gesticulated. The tour completed, the visitors began to disperse back out into the milling garden.

'I say, have you seen Teddy?' Mrs Fitzgerald asked as she approached him. 'He went into the village to pick up some crates of beer, but he should have been back a while ago.'

'Not for some time.' He'd last seen Teddy that morning with his arm around a giggling brunette, but didn't feel he ought to share that detail with her. 'You carry on here. I'll go and see if he's come back.'

Robert looked everywhere for Teddy – in all the tents and booths, in the café, on the donkey field and in every corner of the garden. He searched the faces of the crowds, walking between the young women in their best summer frocks, the men in their Sunday waistcoats and the children giddy on ginger beer and liberty. He asked Iris if she'd seen him down at the lake, Ingram if he'd been near the agricultural pens and Faye if he'd surfaced anywhere around the circuit of her treasure hunt. They all shook their heads.

'Have you seen Teddy recently?' he finally asked Trudie, who was doing a stint manning the refreshment stall.

'I wish I had. He was meant to be bringing crates of beer up from the Lamb, but that was hours ago. Daniel's just gone down in the van now. We've run out of cider and chaps are giving me murderous looks when I try to persuade them a glass of lemonade might be just as refreshing.'

When Daniel came back from the pub, he told them that Teddy had never arrived to pick up the order.

'Wherever has he got to?' Nancy asked.

'Is there a race meeting on today?' Phyllis lifted an eyebrow.

It was in the evening, as the crowds were thinning, that Mrs Fitzgerald went up to her wardrobe for a shawl and saw that his clothes had gone. Teddy hadn't taken everything, but he'd taken enough. It wouldn't be until the next morning that she'd notice the door of the safe ajar.

Chapter Thirty-Five

With the shock of Teddy's disappearance, they'd none of them had the heart to begin clearing up last night. This morning the garden was a mess of sagging bunting, discarded cigarette ends and abandoned glasses. The music and dancing had become rather raucous after midnight and the Hall was wearing a morning-after face now. But Nancy brought out plates of bacon sandwiches, the sun was gathering warmth, the sparrows were twittering in the hedges, and they would attack this task together.

'He never turned up at the Lamb, but the landlord's daughter has disappeared too,' Daniel told them as they began to dismantle the refreshment stall. 'From what I overheard last night, people were putting two and two together.'

'How could he?' said Nancy. 'Yes, he's a flirt, but I always believed it was only teasing.'

They looked from one to another. Robert didn't share Nancy's faith in Teddy.

'Mrs Harrison told me her husband saw him filling up his motor at the petrol pump,' Miss Parget said.

'Perhaps he's just gone away on business?'

'Without telling Gwendoline? There was a young redhead with him in the car.'

'Ah,' said Trudie.

'He's not coming back, is he?'

'If she were to take him back after this, she'd be a fool,' Iris said.

Nobody had seen Mrs Fitzgerald since she'd come out onto the steps last night and told Phyllis about the empty wardrobe. She'd gone back into the house and Phyllis had heard her turning the key in the lock of the front door.

'The sound of it made me feel quite odd,' she said now as she scraped plates and piled dirty cake forks. 'I dithered for a moment, I didn't know what to do for the best, but she obviously wanted to be on her own.'

There'd been a debate as to whether they ought to go and knock at the door this morning, but the curtains were still drawn at Mrs Fitzgerald's bedroom window and they'd finally agreed they should give her a little time to herself. She would come out and speak with them when she felt ready.

Robert busied himself picking streamers out of the topiary. There were beer bottles, pie crusts and half-eaten plates of cake in the parterre. He'd found a woman's shoe, a child's toy dog and a trampled straw hat. There was a smell like urinals behind the potting shed and he wasn't best pleased to find that someone had thrown up amongst the shrub roses.

'The savages! All over the Duchess of Portland!' he said to Trudie. 'They were doing staid country dancing when I went to bed.'

'Don't believe there's anything staid about country dancing! These things are all fertility rites really, aren't they?'

'It's always a bit of a bacchanalia,' Daniel said as he folded a tent canopy with Robert, 'but it boosts the coffers and gives local people a sense of connection with the Hall.'

'Relieving themselves behind the potting shed is rather too much sense of connection, if you ask me,' Phyllis put in.

They were taking a breather as Mrs Fitzgerald unlocked the door and stepped out. 'I'm sorry. You've been working so hard! Would you like to come in? I've laid out lunch for you all as a thank you,' she said.

They followed her through the passageways and down to the kitchen. After the brightness of the garden, it seemed very dark inside the Hall. They glanced at one another, but no one dared speak Teddy's name.

Robert had never had cause to go into the kitchen before. It was a large room with a flagstone floor and a high ceiling. There were bacon hooks in the blackened chimney recess, lines of pewter tankards, rows of charger plates, fish kettles and copper pans in need of polishing. A grandfather clock in the corner ticked with a rhythm that seemed ponderously melancholy.

Mrs Fitzgerald had laid out a spread on the table. There was a raised ham pie and a cold joint of roast beef, pickles, salad and hard-boiled eggs. Robert thought, had Mrs and Mr Fitzgerald eaten their meals at either end of this long table? Had Teddy quaffed from a pewter tankard like a gentleman farmer? Would she now eat down here on her own? The oriental-pattern dinner plates were chipped at the rims and had browned from having gone into the oven too many times.

A round-bellied jug of cider was passed from hand to hand. It was incised with the motto '*Long life to the jolly ploughboy*', and the ease and volume of their conversation increased as it made its repeated circumnavigations. They were all ravenous, and it would have been a companionable lunch had the unspoken questions not tingled on their lips. It was left to Mrs Fitzgerald to bring the subject up. Pushing her plate away, she finally took her glass of cider in both hands and leaned back in her chair.

'He won't come back,' she said. She'd put her make-up on this morning, but had applied her powder and rouge rather heavily, so that she looked like a mask of herself. Robert saw pain, but also stoicism in her kohl-ringed eyes. 'As I told Phyllis last night, a suitcase and a lot of his clothes have gone. Then when I went to my jewellery box this morning, I found that empty too. I'll admit that shocked me. There's a touch of melodrama about it, don't you think? Like something out of a farce. The thing is, I'd already sold off anything that had any value. I sent my mother's amethysts to auction last year and my emeralds are all long since gone. Teddy saw how much those decisions pained me, but I had to do it to keep us afloat. All that remained was bits of trinkets, cocktail rings and paste. Most of it was jewellery that Teddy had bought me himself and I wouldn't have parted with it for sentimental reasons. More fool me, eh?'

The slow, solemn ticking of the clock went on, seeming slower still against Mrs Fitzgerald's uncharacteristically rushed voice.

'I can't believe it of him.' Nancy held a napkin to her face. 'I'm so disappointed in him.'

'I don't understand how he could have done this to you,' Daniel said, reaching for his pipe and filling it distractedly. 'Why has he done it? Why now?'

Faye's gaze met Robert's across the table. She widened her eyes ever so slightly in a mutually comprehended gesture that communicated this wasn't such a surprise.

'That isn't the worst of it, though,' Mrs Fitzgerald continued. She put her glass down and laid her hands flat on the table. 'I noticed the door of the safe was open this morning.' She pressed her lips together and looked as if she was gathering her resolve. 'The money from the land sale had been in there, or everything that was left of it after we'd paid the most pressing of the bills. It was there in an envelope. I saw it just days ago. But it's gone now. So all of this upset has been for nothing.'

'The utter shit!' said Phyllis with feeling, and then put a hand over her mouth.

'Like a common burglar?' said Trudie. 'What an absolute toad.'

'Have you telephoned the police?' Daniel asked. He rose from his chair. 'You need to go to the police.'

'What might that achieve?' Mrs Fitzgerald's face was pale as alabaster, but colour was rising from her throat. 'If a husband decides to leave his wife, and takes his money with him, that's not a crime, is it? That's how the police would view it, isn't it?'

'But it's not *his* money – it's *your* money,' Faye said. 'Everyone knows that. It was your land. Please tell me the house is still in your name?'

'It is. We did have conversations about changing that. Teddy felt we ought to, he spoke to his solicitor about it, but I never got around to completing the paperwork.'

'Thank Christ for that!' Trudie said. She downed the last of her glass of cider. 'He can't be allowed to get away with this. Have you any idea where he might have gone? I'm of a mind to get in my motor and go after him. I've got one of my father's old shotguns somewhere.'

'He might be anywhere!' Mrs Fitzgerald threw up her hands. 'I've absolutely no idea where he'd go. And what good would confronting him do?'

'I'd like to do more than confront him,' Daniel said. He was pacing a circle of the table.

A grey cat appeared, stretching and yawning widely. It leapt onto Mrs Fitzgerald's lap and she stroked it absent-mindedly. Robert could hear it purring and a low growl came from the grandfather clock as it readied to strike the quarter hour.

'The no-good wretch,' said Trudie.

'I'm so angry with him – and with myself.' Mrs Fitzgerald's hands balled into fists. 'I didn't see it coming. Not at all. I trusted him. I feel such an idiot.'

'None of us saw this coming.' Nancy smiled sadly at Mrs Fitzgerald.

'Things haven't been good between us recently; we've had a lot of arguments about money – that's partly why I agreed to sell the orchard, but I never imagined he'd leave me. That never crossed my mind. What a stupid, gullible, vain old woman I've been. I feel thoroughly ashamed.'

'You're not stupid,' Iris said. 'You wanted to see the best side of him, to believe in him. That's not gullibility – that's love.'

'Iris is quite right,' Faye said. 'You mustn't blame yourself. You shouldn't feel ashamed.'

'We were together for twelve years and I thought we were happy. Yes, we've had our ups and downs, as all couples do, but I believed he cared about me. I'm sure he did. I have precious memories ... or was that all a charade?' Her eyes were full of questions and brimming with tears now. 'Have I been blind? Have I been hugely naïve? Was he planning this all along?'

Nancy rose from her chair and went to put an arm around Mrs Fitzgerald. She frowned as she looked back down the table. 'I can't imagine this was a long-term plan.'

'I've got nothing left. There's nothing in the bank. Yes, of course, I've got this house, but in financial terms it's more of a liability than an asset. What am I going to do about the roof now? We needed that money.' A tear slid down Mrs Fitzgerald's cheek, leaving a trail in her face powder. She quickly wiped it away. 'I sincerely wouldn't have sold the land if we hadn't been in dire straits. You do understand that, don't you? And now, what has it all been for?'

Chapter Thirty-Six

'Is she up to company today?' Robert asked. He looked towards the Hall.

'I called in earlier,' Faye replied. 'She was sorting through piles of paperwork. She seems to want to keep herself busy. I can understand that.'

'Is she still upset?'

'She's put her stoic face on, but she doesn't look like she's had much sleep. It's obviously been a genuine shock to her and she's clearly very concerned about her finances now.'

'She must be.'

'Are they for her?' Faye nodded to the bucket of flowers that he was holding to his chest. 'They're pretty.' He'd picked peonies, sweet peas and sweet Williams, all in tones of pink and purple.

'I thought they might cheer her up. I chose the frilliest, brightest, most scented flowers I could find. I know Mrs Fitzgerald loves sweet peas.' His eyes squinted against the sun. 'Though, in the scheme of things, it seems a pretty pitiful gesture. Why should flowers cheer her up?'

'She'll appreciate the gesture. It shows you care,' she replied and smiled at him. She could smell the scent of the sweet peas and the earth on his hands.

He put the bucket down and straightened, stretching his neck as if it was aching. 'I imagine she must be feeling hurt and confused right now – anyone would – but she's better off without Teddy. She's always seemed so forgiving of his behaviour. I've never really understood how she could be.'

'I suspect he swept her off her feet at first, it was probably all wine and roses, and I think he must have been a rather talented manipulator.'

'But she's an intelligent, educated, principled woman. She doesn't suffer fools. Why didn't she see through him sooner?'

'I guess emotional decisions aren't necessarily always rational, are they? Lots of people fall in love with the wrong person and then spend years trying to justify the consequences to themselves. Thousands of women spend the whole of their married lives trying to turn Mr Wrong into Mr Right. It's tragic really, isn't it? What a waste of life!'

'Perhaps.' He shrugged, seemed to contemplate for a moment, then cocked his head to one side with a smile. 'You're not a sentimentalist, are you, Miss Faulkner? Is that what you teach the children?'

'Sorry. Do I sound like a cynic?'

'No, I'm only teasing. I happen to completely agree with you. But is that experience talking?'

Faye thought of Richard and could no longer remember why she'd loved him, or even especially liked him. 'To some degree.'

'Hence the famous renunciation of the male of the species?'

'You never met Richard, did you?' She wrinkled her nose.

She'd spoken with Robert on few occasions since their argument in the orchard and had begun to feel that she ought to make some gesture of reconciliation. Looking back, she knew she'd gone too far in the heat of the moment, said things she shouldn't have done, and she hoped he might feel the same way. She'd meant to speak to him as she'd seen him leaving his cottage the previous evening, but he hadn't looked in her direction. For some reason that she couldn't explain to herself, she'd ended up following him at a distance and had seen as he'd gone down to the lake. He'd dived off the jetty of the boathouse and she'd watched as he took long strokes out into the water and then floated on his back. It was a warm evening and she'd envied him the coolness and his evident lack of self-consciousness. She would have liked to walk down to the lake's edge and step out into the water, feeling that coolness too, but found herself hiding behind the trunk of the holly tree instead. Afterwards, back in her cottage, she'd shaken her head at her own behaviour. If anyone had seen her, what would it have looked like? What would he have thought if he'd seen? The idea of it made her blush now.

'I feel there are times when I should perhaps have said something to Gwendoline about Teddy,' she admitted, 'when he did certain things, when he made certain remarks. But I always wondered if I was being oversensitive or overcritical. I told myself to mind my own business.'

'I feel much the same. There are things I saw too. But would she have listened if you'd said anything? She must have had doubts and suspicions, she had to have, and decided to ignore them.'

'I'm so very angry with him. I'm disgusted with him. The way he's behaved – well, it's cruel. She deserves better than that.'

'If I could track him down, I'd quite like to wallop him.'

She smiled. 'We might have to form a queue. Daniel said he'd like to take a horsewhip to him and I'm not sure it was in jest.'

He laughed briefly, but then his face was serious again. 'Faye, I've been thinking that I might owe you an apology. I've kept meaning to say something, but it's never been quite the right time.' There was a note of hesitancy in his voice now. He looked down at his boots, evidently feeling a little awkward. 'I'm sorry if I spoke out of turn that day in the orchard. I said some stupid things, I know, and words I didn't mean. But I felt to be in an impossible position. Mrs Fitzgerald pays my wages, Teddy was always obviously opposed to her employing me, and I didn't feel I could risk speaking out.'

Faye could hear an appeal in his voice. He clearly wanted her to accept his justification. 'Everyone here has ties and conflicts of interest. It was complicated for all of us. We all spoke up at a risk, but . . .' She told herself to adjust the tone. She was glad he'd brought the subject up first and she ought to accept his apology. 'I'm sorry – I probably went too far as well.'

'You called me narrow-minded and apathetic.' He bit his lip and raised his eyebrows at her.

'You told me that I harangue, rant and scowl at you!'

'Well, what can I say? You do have your moments . . .' He grinned and looked away. 'Can we please have a truce? Can we put this behind us?'

His brown eyes were bronze in this light and the sun had streaked copper strands through his hair. She thought how much she liked his eyes, his smile, his voice – even, grudgingly, his company – and accepted his handshake.

'Let's give it a try.'

Chapter Thirty-Seven

The builders were putting the window frames in now. 'The glass looks like old leaded lattice, doesn't it?' one of the bricklayers was explaining to Daniel. 'But it's actually an aluminium frame fused onto a single pane of glass. You'd never know from a distance, would you? Clever, don't you think?'

Daniel nodded. He supposed it was clever, and might look convincing from some feet away, with a squinted eye, but so much here was shortcuts, fake and heavy-handedly antiqued. All the beams for the half-timbering had to be whimsically crooked, patches of herringbone brickwork and pebbledash were being applied, and stained-glass panels now adorned doors, showing citrus-coloured sunrises and galleons tilting on high seas. He disliked Cecil's description of them as nasty, perky little houses (that choice of words said so much about Cecil), but there was something slightly kitsch in their design.

'The frames are steam-dried pine and they've been treated to be rot-resistant. The gaffer likes to use all the new technologies. If they'd known about these things in the old days, your Mrs F wouldn't have so many problems now, would she?' The man whistled as he looked towards the roofline of the Hall.

Daniel couldn't deny that. 'She's spent a fortune replacing

timbers and repairing the plasterwork, but it's still rotting all around her.'

'A terrible worry for the lady.' The builder touched his cap, as if he might be reflecting on a bereavement.

'Yes,' Daniel agreed – though, at the moment, the wet rot seemed to be the least of Gwen's worries.

He walked back through the kitchen garden. Nancy and Phyllis had been digging up potatoes and had left a fork planted in the overturned earth. Daniel remembered, back in the spring, happening upon Teddy helping them to put in the seed potatoes. It was one of the few occasions when he could recall Teddy dirtying his hands. He'd been making much of his Mayo ancestry that day and jokingly drawing hard on the violin for the women. Daniel considered: could he have been thinking about leaving, even then? Could he already have been negotiating with the building company and planning to make his exit after the sale? Daniel wasn't a violent man, but socking Teddy in the jaw would give him some satisfaction right now.

Gwen was walking between the bean rows with a basket over her arm. Her hair was red gold in the sunlight and she was so slender and angular now that she might have stepped out of a Klimt canvas. Daniel didn't understand how any man could have chosen to leave her.

'I've just been talking with the builders,' he said as he approached. 'These houses are full of modern wizardry.'

'Ever the diplomat, Daniel! Have you spent a long time trying to come up with something positive to say?' She raised her red eyebrows and gritted her teeth together, as if braced for it all to go downhill from here.

'The black and white might look a bit stark at first, but it will soften and weather with time, won't it?'

'What a nice man you are.' She reached out and squeezed his hand. Despite the warmth of the morning, her fingers were cold and quickly withdrawn.

'I take it there's been no news? No word from Teddy?' He wasn't absolutely sure he ought to ask. Up close, he could see that her eyes were bloodshot. She'd admitted to him that she hadn't been sleeping.

'I can't see him sitting down and writing a letter. Much as I'd like an explanation, I know he won't send me one.' As she squinted into the sun, the light showed new lines on her face.

'Have you thought any more about speaking to the police? You really should. I'd go with you, if you'd like.'

'What would be the point? Anyway, I wouldn't want him to be arrested. I don't want vengeance. It wouldn't make me feel better if he were punished.'

'I'd like him to be punished,' Daniel admitted. 'It would make me feel better. Sorry, it's possibly not my place to say that.'

She smiled at him. 'I appreciate your righteous indignation.'

They walked on together through the garden. The colours were intense this morning. A malachite-green lizard skittered away on the wall and sparrows were having dust baths on the path. There was a low drone of bees and a more distant humming of saws working. Daniel could smell the sweet scent of the bean flowers – he thought, hadn't the Elizabethans worn them in their buttonholes? – and occasional wafts of bitumen from the building site. He'd started doing his breathing exercises again recently and the doctor had prescribed him sleeping tablets, but if anything was making him feel better it was probably

Teddy's departure. He hated how his leaving had hurt Gwen, but personally he wasn't sorry he'd gone.

'I was trying to remember how you first met Teddy. He'd served with your brother, hadn't he?' Daniel knew all of this, he remembered it well enough, but he wanted to hear it from her again. He couldn't help feeling he ought to have been more alert to the warning signs.

'He was a junior officer in Hugh's battalion. He was so terribly young. Poor boy!' She glanced at Daniel and he was surprised to see there was still fondness on her face. 'He wrote me the most charming letter afterwards, about Hughie's kindness to the men and how they all adored him.'

'And that's how you came to meet?' He said it as casually as he could, bending to break dead flower heads from a dahlia. He didn't want her to feel he was prying.

'We agreed to meet up and have tea in a dear old-fashioned place in Stow. He was very considerate and had such beautiful manners. I looked across the table and felt myself drowning in his eyes – isn't that what they say in romantic novels? I fell in love with him there and then. But you probably remember me mooning around?'

'Had Hugh mentioned him in his letters?'

'Teddy?' She turned to Daniel and narrowed her eyes. 'What are you suggesting? Where's this going?'

Daniel considered. He'd read newspaper stories about chancers seeking out wealthy grieving women after the war. There'd been a time when the papers loved that sort of story. 'I'm sorry. I didn't mean to imply anything.'

'Are you certain you didn't, Daniel?' She frowned at him. 'I don't want to have that thought in my head. Yes, it might have gone terribly wrong at the end, but Teddy and I were together for twelve years – twelve mostly happy years. That's a long time. Are you suggesting that my husband was some sort of villainous extortionist who explicitly set out to bleed me dry? I'd like to think I'm not quite that stupid.'

'I know you're not. I apologize.' Daniel looked down at the dust on his boots. But the thought nagged at him. Gwen had been an affluent young woman when she first came to Anderby. Yes, the house had soaked up funds, and she'd lost a lot of money when the market crashed, but how much more had Teddy squandered on cars and racehorses and potentially siphoned away? For Gwen's sake, Daniel hoped it hadn't been such a cynical exploitation, but he couldn't help asking himself: had Teddy's decision to leave been prompted by the money drying up?

Chapter Thirty-Eight

It had been Teddy's job to wind the mechanism of the turret clock and a month ago it had ceased to strike the hour. On the first day, Robert hadn't noticed that the hands of the clock had frozen in their motion, but now he'd become aware of the absence of its sound and his former reliance upon it. Was it the case that Mrs Fitzgerald couldn't wind the mechanism herself, or did she not want to hear it striking? Did she feel it appropriate to have the clocks stopped? He'd volunteer to wind it himself, but didn't want to impose upon her.

'You've probably realized that my coffers are pretty empty now,' she said as they walked down the path together.

Robert had realized this and was all too aware of the implications it might have for his employment. 'Do you need to suspend the garden plans?'

He'd put in long days to get the topiary garden back into shape and was often still working in the greenhouse after dark, the moths circling around his hurricane lamp. He worked every day until his muscles ached, and when not physically labouring, he was reading, so that he was always contemplating challenges and solutions for the garden. He fell into bed exhausted at the end of every day, but it gratified him to see the garden reviving. He'd hate to leave it at this stage – might he have to, though?

'I know I'll have to make some difficult choices over the months ahead,' Mrs Fitzgerald went on, 'but I'm determined not to let the gardens go back and I do want to keep you on. We've had a good number of visitors through the gates over the past month, we've broken even, and I still have faith that the gardens will generate a profit in the long term. Meanwhile, I've consulted an auctioneer this week and plan to do a sale of furnishings, and I've been talking with Mr Ingram about how we might improve revenues from the farm. I can't guarantee anything, Robert, but I want you to know that paying your wages is one of my priorities.'

'Thank you,' he said. 'I appreciate you being so candid.'

'I appreciate all your hard work. I used to look out at the gardens and feel a sense of guilt, but now, noticing the daily changes, seeing it all coming back to life, I feel wonder and optimism. I'm grateful to you for that.'

They walked on between areas of dense shade and bright colour and, passing under the archway, came into the white garden. He'd maintained the colour scheme she'd established, but had added drifts of cosmos, larkspur and delphiniums which he'd brought on from seed. Night-scented stocks gave off their sweet perfume in the evenings and at twilight this garden was opalescent.

Their footsteps circled the sculpture. This afternoon's bright sunlight made the limestone appear to glow, so that Robert had to squint his eyes when he looked at it directly. He'd seen Mrs Fitzgerald sitting on the bench here on several occasions over the past fortnight. He hoped she found some solace in this space.

'Iris came to see me last week,' she said, her footsteps finally stilling. 'You know they're going, don't you?'

'Yes, she told me. I was sorry to hear it.' He paused to pick a peacock feather from the path and handed it to Mrs Fitzgerald.

'They're moulting.' Holding the feather between her hands, she looked like a figure from a Pre-Raphaelite painting. 'I'm not convinced Iris wants to leave; I sense the drive is from Cecil, but she seems to feel she must go along with it. I hope she's making the right decision.'

Robert nodded. He'd spoken with Iris after Cecil had signed the contract for the sale and he could tell how torn she was. It was strange to think of her house, which was so much an expression of her personality, being emptied out and locked up; even more disconcerting to imagine it might be levelled and built over now.

'I'm sad that our ranks are becoming so depleted,' Mrs Fitzgerald went on. 'I sincerely regret that. But I take heart from what you and Faye said at our meeting in the café – that perhaps this is an opportunity to review our priorities and go forwards with new determination.'

Robert hardly remembered what he'd said now, but recalled he'd unexpectedly found himself agreeing with Faye. 'She'd like us to be more outward-looking, to have more connection with the local community, and I think that's right.'

'We have become too insular, I do see that,' Mrs Fitzgerald said, 'and it's the absolute opposite of what we intended when we first established the community. This project wasn't about escapism; on the contrary, we wanted to build something that would inspire imitation. It mattered so much to us at the start and we really believed we could make a difference. It still matters.' She looked up at her brother's statue as she spoke and Robert saw both sadness and resolution in her expression. But then her eyes shifted to his face and he saw a question there. 'Can I ask your opinion, Robert – do you think there genuinely is the will amongst the group to carry on? I know that people have felt betrayed and unsettled and everyone must have considered whether they do want to stay here.'

'I think most people will stay on,' he replied. A month ago he might have answered differently, but the mood had changed since Teddy's departure.

'Good. Thank you. It's probably more than I deserve, but I am glad to hear that.'

She nodded her head as she departed, but as she turned on the path Robert saw her dash a tear away from her eyes.

Chapter Thirty-Nine

They'd been up since dawn, carrying boxes out and trying to corral the children into compliance. By midday Iris's head was pounding. Her dress stuck to her back with the heat and, with every journey from the house to the van, she felt less certainty. She now heard something sad in the echo of their voices in the emptied rooms.

She cupped her palm to drink from the kitchen tap, then pressed her cool, wet hand against her forehead and her neck. Looking out of the window, she saw Cecil trying to separate Erin and Kitty again. They'd wrapped their arms around one another and Cecil was pulling them apart with a little too much force. It had surprised Iris how fiercely the children had opposed the proposed move. She'd expected some resistance to changing school and leaving friends, but hadn't anticipated quite so many tears and tantrums. Erin had bitten Cecil's hand that morning, as he'd had to carry her out of her bedroom. He said this was Kitty's influence, and it would do the children good to get away from that. Iris just felt guilty that she was making them do something which they so obviously didn't want.

Over the past couple of days she'd watched all their possessions being carried out to the furniture van: her dressing

table and the chests of drawers that had come from her grandmother's house, the kitchen table that they'd bought at a house
sale in Chelsea just before they were married and, finally, this
morning, their brass bedstead. These objects were normally
comfortingly familiar to her, but they'd looked strangely
forlorn as they were carried away. She'd reminded herself
that she'd have a larger kitchen in Biswell, there was a sitting
room with French windows on to the garden, and the children could each have their own bedroom. Their books would
settle onto new shelves, their dinner service onto new dressers,
all their inherited teaspoons and napkins and framed family
photographs would find new positions. With time it would all
become as familiar as this house, and she would find her place
too, but . . .

She took one last tour around the empty house. The sitting
room looked larger with the carpets rolled away and the paintings taken down from the walls, and harshly bright without
the curtains at the windows. Her feet sounded strange on the
bare boards, but even though this house was now a shell, it still
reverberated with her memories; she saw Erin's first Christmas
in this room, could picture her parents smiling at the dining
table, could hear the laughter of parties and remembered the
scent of the climbing roses through the open window as she'd
sat nursing Ewan on the first day she'd brought him home.
Would she still be able to hear her parents' voices in the new
house? Would she still be able to see their faces? She wasn't certain that this would be possible, or at least she was sure it would
be diminished – away from their original backdrop, wouldn't
these memories lose some of their clarity and immediacy? That
thought suddenly made tears flood her eyes. She wiped them

away quickly with her fingers, knowing that Cecil would think her idiotically sentimental.

As she entered each room she remembered choosing the colours for the walls, painting the designs on the doors and the window seats, and the murals in the children's bedrooms. She'd invested time, energy and hope in this house – and she would do it all again in Biswell, but at this moment she didn't feel much enthusiasm for the task. She looked out at the rear garden, at the summerhouse she'd had built with the money her parents had left to her, and the weathered bench under the cherry tree where she and Cecil had liked to sit in the evenings in their early days, when they were still full of the excitement of being together. There were peonies that she'd transplanted from her parents' garden – she really ought to have dug them up – and she recalled how she'd chosen the colours of the irises with her mother. It didn't seem right to be leaving these things behind. She'd never imagined that she'd have to do that. Cecil said this move would be a new beginning. Why did it feel like an ending, then?

'Where the hell are you, Iris?' he shouted now. 'We need to get going.'

She stepped out, narrowing her eyes to the over-bright light. Ewan was sitting on the back seat of the van, his face crumpling with tears, and Erin had entangled herself with Kitty again. Cecil was ordering her to get in the vehicle, but the more he raised his voice, the tighter the girls clung together.

'Iris, will you control your bloody children! She's refusing to get in.'

'Come on, darling.' She bent down, put a hand to Erin's back, and tried to coax her. 'It's time to go now. Let's not make Daddy angry.'

'But I don't want to go! I don't want to live in stupid, horrid Biswell. I don't know anybody there.'

'But you'll soon make new friends and you can write to Kitty. You can send each other nice letters, about everything you've been doing, and won't it be lovely to receive them?'

'I don't want letters.' Erin glowered. 'I don't want new friends.'

'You can come back here for visits sometimes, if you'd like. It's not as if we're emigrating to Australia. I'm sure Auntie Nancy would let us stay.'

'I don't want to visit!' Erin stamped her foot. 'I want to stay. Kitty says I can live in her bedroom.'

'Please, Mrs Cardew!' Kitty appealed. 'It's not fair!'

'Will you just get into the bleeding van,' said Cecil, forcibly lifting Erin onto his shoulder.

'Cecil!' Iris couldn't help but protest as tears sprang from Erin's shocked eyes.

He physically pushed her into the vehicle, slammed the door, and stood with his back against it. 'Get in, Iris, for God's sake, before she finds a way out again.' He mopped his face with a handkerchief.

'You need to give me a minute.' She turned and heard herself sigh as she saw the waiting faces.

'I'm tempted to throw a tantrum too,' Trudie said, stepping towards her and putting her arms around her. 'Is Cecil going to blow a gasket?' she whispered into Iris's ear.

'I might not be sorry if he did.' Iris had to take a deep breath to stop herself from crying. 'Oh God, this is horrid! I hate goodbyes.'

'I know, darling. I understand.' Trudie's hand rubbed her back.

Nancy and Robert stepped forwards then, their arms encircling her.

'I will miss you,' Robert said. 'I'll miss our routine in the mornings. Who else will let me steal their coffee?'

'Don't make me cry! I'm struggling as it is.'

'Poor love,' said Nancy, and stroked her hair. 'You will keep in touch with us, won't you?'

'Iris, the baby's woken up and is starting to wail!' Cecil shouted from the van.

'Oh, let him cope with it.' Phyllis rolled her eyes. 'Now, do remember – if you don't like it there, if you're not entirely happy, you can always come back.'

'Phyl's right,' said Faye, taking her hand. 'You're part of our family and you always will be.'

Daniel had stood apart from the group, frowning at his boots and fiddling with his tobacco pouch, but he approached as the others finally broke away. 'You will take care of yourself, won't you? If you need us, we're here. We'll only ever be a telephone call away.'

'Thank you, Daniel. I appreciate that.'

'We need to go!' commanded Cecil. He'd got into the driver's seat and was turning the engine over. 'Will you get in before your children all get out again?'

Iris glanced back at the van. Kitty and Erin were pressing their hands together either side of the window. Erin's face was crimson and furrowed with tears.

'I'm coming,' Iris said, but then Gwendoline was running across the gravel.

'This is awful,' she said as she put her arms around Iris. 'I'm so sorry it's come to this. It's all my fault.'

'Please don't feel like that, Gwen. You've given us so much over the years. I'll never forget your kindness.' The tears she'd been holding back finally broke.

'Iris!' Cecil yelled. 'Are you trying to test my patience?'

'I'd better go.' She wiped her face with her sleeve and gripped Gwendoline's hand one final time. 'Thank you for everything.'

Kitty ran after the van, banging her fist on the rear window. The other children joined her, all of them shouting and waving as they followed behind. Iris could feel Erin's feet beating against the back of her seat.

'Little savages!' spat Cecil, revving the engine. 'Bloody brats! The sooner we're away from here, the better . . .'

Iris looked back as they turned through the arch of the gatehouse. Everyone was still standing there on the drive, arms raised or in embracing groups. When Cecil had begun talking of moving, she'd been certain that something would occur that would stop it from actually happening: the numbers wouldn't add up, circumstances would change or they'd resolve that it was better to stay. Now the day had arrived, she felt angry with herself for having been so passive, for just letting it happen. Why hadn't she spoken her mind? Why hadn't she resisted this more? Was she allowing herself to be steamrollered by Cecil as much as she suspected Gwendoline had been by Teddy? Iris shut her eyes tight shut to stop the tears coming, but they ran unwilled and hot down her cheeks.

Chapter Forty

'Do you think we can keep going?' Faye leaned her chin on the handle of the broom. The blackboard had been wiped clean, leaving only the date in her neat, copperplate hand. Chalk dust dazzled in the light.

'Are you worried?' Daniel asked.

'Should I not be? Can the trust afford to keep paying my wages? Is it financially viable to keep the school open with only eight pupils?'

'No one has spoken of discontinuing, not that I'm aware of, but if you need some reassurance, I'll talk to Gwendoline. Are you happy to carry on teaching such small classes? Are you reconsidering whether you want to be here?'

Faye tidied the books on her desk together and seemed to reflect on how she might respond for a moment. Daniel breathed the classroom's familiar smell of chalk, ink and pencil shavings.

'To be honest, I was approached about a position at the grammar school earlier this summer and have thought seriously about whether I ought to take it.' She sat down on the desk, hugging a book to her chest. 'I was feeling unsettled at that time. I was unsure whether I was in the right place. In some ways, I'm more optimistic now, but I am concerned whether the school will be part of the community's future. How small do we let the classes get before we decide it's uneconomic to continue? Seven pupils? Six? Kitty will only be with us for another few months. I don't feel too much security at present – I can't do. What would happen to the children if we had to close?'

'I'm not sure Mr Edwards at the C of E could cope with Kitty! Can you imagine? Gwendoline would be loath to let the school close, I know that.'

'But does she have the means to support it? Does the trust? I know Gwendoline's sending more furniture to auction and selling off books from the library. I overheard her talking with a dealer yesterday; they were negotiating a price for the books by the yard. But she can't keep on stripping the house, can she? That's got to come to an end.'

'She will do everything she can to keep the school going. It's so important to her – it's at the heart of what we set out to do here and she hasn't stopped believing in that.' Daniel didn't know Gwen was selling off the library, and was sorry if that was the case, but he was certain this was true. 'She still has income from the estate farm and the tenancies and she's determined to do whatever else she can to generate revenue. I understand she's in the process of selling Teddy's cars and I suspect her outgoings must have fallen considerably since he left.'

'She was probably supporting several bookmakers – how they must miss Teddy!'

'The bungalows might bring you more pupils too. I believe several of the families who've bought them have children. We should be proud of the education we provide here and make a case to them. We have bright, happy, inquisitive children. What parent wouldn't want that?'

'You don't think they'll want to send their children to the village school?'

'Not if we make an effort to welcome them and show them what we're able to achieve.'

Faye stood and began tidying the nature table and the remains of the grey-looking bread rolls that the children had baked yesterday. Daniel could hear their voices as they came back up the road. 'We must welcome them,' she agreed. 'Whatever we might have felt about the land sale, it's not their fault, is it?'

'And, who knows, with time they might breed amongst themselves.'

'Daniel!' Faye's hand flew to her mouth. She looked both shocked and amused. 'How awful that sounds! We need to start being nicer about the bungalows, don't we?'

'I'm joking!'

He had said it in jest, but in truth they needed to make an effort to be friendly when the new people moved in. They should try to be good neighbours. It still made his chest ache to think of the old orchard, but it was done now, and they all had to move on.

He found Gwen in the white garden. Amongst the jasmine and roses, in her ochre-coloured dress, she looked like a figure from a Rossetti painting. Dew was jewelling the petals still and cobwebs trembled with wet caught light.

'Are you dead-heading? Does Robert let you do that?'

'I'm his apprentice,' she smiled as she turned towards him. 'He's quite a strict boss, you know. If I miss bits, he makes me do it again.'

There was dirt down her fingernails and scratches on her arms. She'd caught the sun on the back of her neck and Daniel thought how natural and lovely she looked.

'I've been talking with Faye,' he said. 'She's worried about the school.'

'I called in yesterday. It looked rather sad with just the eight little ones at their desks.'

'Can we afford to carry on?'

Gwen put down her secateurs. 'I've been giving some thought to what I might do to raise more revenue for the trust. It seems utterly ludicrous that I'm rattling around in the Hall on my own – I mean, one woman does not need eighteen bedrooms! – and I've been considering how I might make it pay for itself. I'll have to cope with the roof as best I can over the coming winter, I can't pretend I'm not concerned about that, but I'm planning to let some of the rooms out. Given the state of them, and our woeful plumbing arrangements, I know I wouldn't be able to charge much rent, but it could generate some regular income. Don't you think? Teddy always hated the suggestion of having other people in the house, but it's not up to him now, is it?'

'You'd do that? You'd be comfortable having people in the house?' Daniel marvelled at her resilience.

'We did it at the start, didn't we?' She pinned up a stray curl of hair. 'We were packed to the rafters that first summer! Of course, I'd want to let to people who are sympathetic to our principles – people who want to live and work collaboratively, creative people ideally, who'll enjoy contributing to our education and arts projects. It might be good for us, don't you think?'

'Faye would certainly approve. She's always said it was a pity to have so many empty rooms.'

'Do you remember how we were in the early days, Daniel, when people were sleeping on bunk beds in the library and we tried to run a workers' canteen?' Her eyes brightened.

'I remember eating a lot of cabbage soup and waking up with some horrendous hangovers, but we laughed a lot, didn't we? I miss those old times.'

'It would be good to get some of that spirit back, don't you agree?'

Gwen cocked her head to one side as she recalled. The sun had brought out the freckles on her face, Daniel noticed. They made him think about the speckle on a blackbird's egg. There were a lot of things he missed from the early days.

'It would,' he replied. 'I keep meaning to say, I don't have a fortune stashed away, but I do have some savings. If ever there are months that are difficult, if ever you're struggling to pay bills or wages, will you ask me?'

'That's very generous of you. Are you sure?'

He nodded. 'I want to help you keep it going.'

'After everything?' she grimaced. 'I shall do my best not to call on your kindness, but I sincerely appreciate it.'

He looked down, feeling slightly embarrassed, and noticed she'd slipped her sandals off and was standing barefoot in the flowerbed. 'Gwendoline Fitzgerald, you've got filthy feet!'

'Haven't I?' She wiggled her toes and smiled.

'Whatever would the neighbours say?'

'Ha! "When her husband left she really let herself go"?'

'And more fool him! You're looking better. I'm glad to see that,' he dared to say.

'I'm sleeping again. Perhaps it's all this fresh air? I barely slept for weeks after Teddy left, my head was too full of questions, but then I hit the point of exhaustion. I can't wait to get to bed at nights now and I'm learning to accept that some questions have no answers.' She stepped out of the flowerbed and stretched her shoulders. 'You know, I keep dreaming about Hugh. I haven't done that for years.'

Daniel glanced at the statue. Was that why she'd been spending time in this garden? 'Upsetting dreams?'

'No, but it does feel as if he's come back to wag a finger at me. I wake up feeling chastened but determined. Hugh wouldn't have approved of me selling the orchard, I know that, and I find myself trying to justify the decision to him. I tell him I thought it was the only way we could carry on and how unrelenting Teddy was with his arguments. I tell him about all the bills we couldn't pay, how ashamed and frightened I felt, and how Teddy said that doing this would make all of that worry go away.' She looked at Daniel and he could see her eyes appealing for his understanding. 'I know that Hugh would want us to try to carry on here. None of my thinking has changed since the early days of coming here. I still believe that we have a job to do – in fact, when I look at the newspapers these days, it seems more important than ever. I read this week that a young woman can now be imprisoned in Dortmund if she's seen dancing with a Jewish man in public. Apparently, that's an offence to German nationality. The newspapers make depressing reading at the moment and I do feel like I need to be doing something.'

'The world seems to have become rather darker over the past few months, but I'm glad to hear that determination in your voice again. I've missed it.'

'Thank you for standing by me, Daniel.' She put her hand

to his arm. 'You're so good and so loyal. I don't deserve your kindness.'

It took him by surprise. 'You know I'll always stand by you.'

'Even when I make idiot decisions and cut down your beloved apple trees?'

'Yes,' he said. 'Even then.'

Chapter Forty-One

The bright light had seemed to bleach out the colours of the garden that morning, making it look like a painting that had been hung by a window too long. Sweat had run into Robert's eyes as he'd worked and, though he'd gulped down water, his mouth still felt parched. The rasping rhythm of grasshoppers was all around and he'd seen lizards sunning themselves on the walls, but the birds were panting in the hedges and even the cats had taken to the shade. By midday his head had been pounding and he'd needed to escape the sun's unrelenting glare.

He'd met Nancy by Iris's gate and the two of them stood together in the shade of the walnut tree as they observed a man with a measuring stick walking in lines around the Cardews' old house. He'd already trampled through the Welsh poppies and scrambled up the lilac bank. As they watched his oblivious footsteps heading towards the rockery, Robert wanted to intervene, but what might he say? He and Nancy leaned on the gate, the garden ahead of them quivering in the heat, both of them feeling rather gloomy and powerless.

'One of the plasterers told me they'll squeeze three bungalows into the garden,' Nancy said.

'Iris loved her garden. She lifted the dahlias every winter and put blood and bone meal around the roses.'

'They won't notice the roses, will they? They'll just come in with vehicles and scrape it all away.'

'My priorities are possibly wrong, but I think that's awful.'

'You have nice priorities, Robert.' Nancy leaned her shoulder against his. 'But don't forget they're bespoke Tudorbethan abodes.' Her tone was wry. 'Reassuringly high class. It says so on the poster. Even their dog kennels are half-timbered.'

'Daniel reckons the plaster and plywood will have fallen off within ten years.'

'We might not be here to see it.'

'Are you contemplating our mortality or predicting the fall of Greenfields?' He turned towards her as he asked.

'Mostly the latter. Bit by bit, we're all going off in different directions, aren't we? The glue that kept us together seems to be losing its power.'

'Community, creativity, equality and education?' Robert found himself repeating the motto.

'Not much creativity going on at the moment, is there? Everyone's too distracted. And community cooperation seems to have gone into reverse. Last night Phyl asked me if I'd sell up if we could.'

'And you replied?'

'We spent a nice hour theorizing about how we could run a lovely boarding house in Brixham. We even decided upon the pattern of the curtains and the crockery.'

Nancy's eyes looked far away for a moment. Was she hearing seagulls, happy punters and a dinner gong? 'But you wouldn't – not really – would you?'

'If we had a house to sell, we might have been tempted. I understand why people have done it.'

'Oh God – don't watch them hacking up Iris's garden!' said Trudie, arriving with four small dogs tangled together on leads. 'You might as well stick pins in yourselves.'

'Has anyone heard from Iris?' Robert turned to lean his back against the gate.

They both shook their heads. 'She'll be busy,' Nancy said. 'She'll have her hands full with the children and sorting the house out.'

'I worry about her.' It showed on Trudie's face.

'I know. I do too.'

'Is Kitty still upset?' Robert asked.

'If sulking and tantrums were competitive sports, my child could have a chestful of medals, but I do have to feel sorry for her at the moment. She's just lost her best friend.'

'I say, I've just heard something intriguing.' Trudie took a step towards them, shaded her eyes with her hand, and lowered her voice to a conspiratorial whisper. 'I was doing the circuit with the dogs and got chatting with Mr Holland, he's the foreman on the site, and a thoroughly nice chap. Not everyone does, I know, but I like a young man with sandy hair,' she asided. 'Anyway, he started telling me how all of this came about.' She wafted vaguely in the direction of the building site. 'As usual, two men meet in a pub and one says to the other, "I've got a tasty bit of business, fancy coming in on it?" The recipient of this offer was Mr Houghton, who owns the construction company, and the instigator was his old army pal, one Edward Fitzgerald.'

'Teddy?'

'According to Mr Holland, he approached them with the proposition.'

'Presumably Mrs Fitzgerald knew he was going to do that?' Robert said. 'I assume they'd made the decision together to look for a buyer?'

'I've no idea, but I wouldn't put it past him to have cooked it up on his own. I've always suspected this was more Teddy's initiative than hers. I can hardly imagine that she came up with the plan. Can you?'

'Oh Lord!' said Nancy. 'Imagine if she didn't know. Imagine if she only found out after Teddy had put the wheels in motion. Would he do that?'

Robert could well imagine it. 'And then, having done that to her, he bolts with the money?'

'One other flavoursome titbit,' Trudie leaned in closer. 'Messrs Houghton and Fitzgerald weren't strangers, as I say. They knew each other from army days and, apparently, Teddy worked for him as a labourer for a few months after the war.'

'But Teddy never did any physical work. All that business about his lungs?' Robert had always been dubious about the story, but Teddy had styled himself as the debonair but tragically disabled ex-officer. 'He wouldn't even carry his own bag of groceries from the car.'

'And he was a captain, wasn't he?' Nancy narrowed her eyes. 'It must have been a comedown for him to have been working on building sites. I thought he used to do something connected with the financing of racing stables?'

'I've always thought that was a lovely euphemism for liking a bet.' Trudie's eyebrows arched.

'You know, I had a soft spot for him,' Nancy admitted. 'I

thought he was a charming rascal, just a tease, an essentially harmless flirt, but could he actually have been an utter rotter?'

'It all sounds a bit irregular, doesn't it?' The dogs were getting restless and Trudie was struggling to stop the leads winding together. 'I can think of a stronger word than rotter that might suit him.'

'She might have been an innocent party through all of this,' Robert said. Questions were racing through his head now. 'And all of those words that were thrown at her . . .'

'Treachery? Unfit to own Anderby?' Trudie wrinkled her nose. 'We all talked about feeling betrayed, but it starts to look like she's the one who has been thoroughly ill-used.'

'If she is the victim in this – if it was all Teddy's doing – why doesn't she say so now that he's gone? Why doesn't she tell us? Why doesn't she just blame him?'

'Some lingering loyalty? Guilt? A feeling that she should have done more to resist it?'

'Poor woman,' said Nancy.

'Quite.' Trudie frowned. They stood silent, each occupied with their own thoughts for a moment, until a cat leapt from the wall and set the dogs spinning wildly on their leads. 'Anyway, are you absolutely sure you'll be able to cope with the dogs, Robert?' Trudie had to raise her voice above the barking. 'It was terrifically sweet of you to volunteer, but they can be a handful and I know how busy you are.'

'Of course. It will be a pleasure,' he replied. Trudie hadn't responded to her mother's letter in the spring, but now there'd been a telegram summoning her to the maternal sickbed. Robert had advised her that she might regret it if she didn't go.

'A *pleasure*? You may want to revise that choice of word by the time I return. I expect I'll be back by the weekend. She's given to drama. She's probably only got indigestion, but it's almost a decade since we last had a scene and maybe she feels one is overdue. I'll grant her that, but I shan't linger. Even with the assistance of hard liquor, forty-eight hours in the old trout's presence is as much as I can stand.'

Trudie was determinedly making light of the situation, but Robert sensed the telegram had unsettled her. 'Take as long as you need. Let her enjoy her scene.'

'He's a treasure, isn't he, Nancy?' She planted a kiss on his cheek and then scrubbed the lipstick mark away with her fingers. 'We'll have a cocktail evening when I get back, yes?'

'Is that meant to be an incentive or a threat?'

Chapter Forty-Two

'It was somewhere around here before, wasn't it?' Daniel held the picture frame up against the wall.

'That's right. I think that's pretty much exactly where it was,' Gwen replied. 'But are you sure about this, Daniel? I look at the points on that list now and feel conscious that I've reneged on every one of them. I could put a black cross against every line.'

He could hear from her tone of voice that she was uncomfortable, but this was the right thing to do, wasn't it? 'That's not true. I'd give you far more ticks than crosses.'

'Discussion ... consensus ... no decision to be enacted without majority endorsement.' Gwen squinted her eyes as she looked towards the document in his hands. 'Never mind what it says about respecting the land and the history of the site. I understand why people felt betrayed.'

'That was then, but now ... We all understand why you felt you had to do it.'

'Do you? Looking back, I'm not certain I entirely understand my own choices.' She crossed her arms across her chest. 'I certainly can't justify them.'

'Just pass me that nail, will you?'

'Are you doing this to spite me?'

He laughed. 'I'd never do that!'

When Gwen had brought the old document downstairs to show him, Daniel had told her that it ought to be restored to its former place on the wall. It had been taken down five years ago, while they were having the woodworm in the wall panelling treated, and for some reason it hadn't been hung again. She'd found it recently in one of the wardrobes upstairs, where Teddy must have put it all that time ago. Daniel believed her when she said it was just an oversight that it hadn't been reinstated, it wasn't a deliberate act, but why hadn't any of them noticed? Did that say something about their group state of mind? Had they let things lapse?

'It doesn't look like a bossy gesture, does it?' Gwen asked as she watched him hammering the nail in. 'I mean, might people suppose that I want to remind them of the rules and regulations? Dear God, how hypocritical that would be!'

Daniel turned back to her and smiled. 'No! Not at all. And they're not rules and regulations, are they? It's a precious ancient relic of our foundation story,' he romanticized for her amusement. 'I think it's no bad thing to remind ourselves of what we set out to do.'

He stood back with Gwen and looked at the framed document, now back in its place on the wall. It reminded him of a night thirteen years ago when the two of them had sat up late at the kitchen table and worked out what they wanted to achieve here. They'd drunk the last dusty bottle of pre-war Burgundy from the cellar and when they'd finally agreed their wording they'd toasted to the future together. Daniel remembered a feeling of optimism at that moment, an excitement, a determination, and Gwen reaching across the table and squeezing his hand. She'd then copied their draft out in her best handwriting and he'd looked on as she'd formed her elegantly looping letters, the tip of her tongue held between her teeth as she concentrated. In the morning, she'd found a picture frame and they'd hung it up on the wall here. Her green ink had faded slightly now, but the memory remained vivid to Daniel. He could still feel the sensation of her hand slipping through his arm as they stood side by side and hear her voice saying, 'Well, my trusty lieutenant, I suppose we'd better make a start, hadn't we?'

'You might have noticed that our old statement of aims is back.' Gwen was standing to address the residents' meeting. She glanced over her shoulder to where it now hung on the wall once again. 'I really don't want anyone to feel like that's some sort of instruction or correction – hell, if anyone needs the correction it's me! I just happened to find it as I was clearing out a room upstairs and Daniel suggested we ought to put it back up again. I have to admit that I look at it and feel very conscious that I've not lived by these values in recent months – but perhaps, as Daniel said to me, it's no bad thing to be reminded of what we hoped to achieve.' She looked around the room. 'Nobody objects to it being here, do they?'

'Did Teddy hide it very thoroughly?' Phyllis's eyebrows lifted as she asked the question.

'Phyllis McKay!' Nancy's tone was reprimanding, but then she laughed. 'I'm sure he didn't *deliberately* hide it.'

'Quite sure?' Trudie queried.

'Anyway,' Daniel went on, 'Gwendoline and I have been discussing our current situation and what we'd like to do next. We do want to carry on. We're resolved to keep going.

As Gwendoline said to me this week, when one looks at the newspapers now it seems all the more important that values of internationalism and pacifism and respect for one's fellow man are articulated. Do you know that sixty thousand Jewish people have fled Germany since the Nazi regime came to power this spring? They've effectively shut down all political opposition. It's now a crime to be a pacifist, a socialist, a communist or even a liberal. Tens of thousands of people have been arrested and the most awful stories are emerging about conditions in the prison camps.' There had appeared to be a shift towards authoritarian government in so many countries over recent months, it didn't bode well, Daniel felt, but he told himself to maintain a constructive tone. 'We need to be active again, to help in whatever way we can, holding fast to the values that first brought us together. We want to plan a new series of talks for next year, to relaunch the summer school and to reach out to like-minded organizations. It's time to reinvigorate discussion, research and creativity here – or, at least, that's how we feel.' He looked at the faces around the table – were they with him? 'Gwendoline has expressed some concern about whether everyone might be in support of that, whether you might have different ideas about how you want to go forwards, and, well, of course, we'd like to hear your views. Please do feel free to speak. Don't feel you must agree with me. Would anyone like to suggest an alternative course?'

'Well said, Daniel.' Trudie spoke up. 'I couldn't agree more. I had a heart-rending letter from a friend in Germany this week. Life is becoming unbearable there. It made me want to shout and write to politicians and newspapers – and, well, we should do that, shouldn't we? Hear, hear, Daniel.' Trudie began to clap her hands and then everyone followed suit around the table.

'I'm so pleased that we're united over this.' Gwen glanced at Daniel and he nodded. 'Daniel and I have been talking a lot and, on a more local level, we've agreed that we need to make an effort to re-establish good relations with the village as we go forwards, and, if possible, we'd also like to involve the people from the new houses in whatever we do next. I'd hate there to be any tension. It would be horrible if we ended up with a divide between "us" and "them". So, as we plan for the New Year, I'd like to think about how we can include the village and the new residents in events, how we can establish links and dialogue and potentially work together. Our original idea was that Greenfields should be a model of how people can live in harmony and understanding, and as we see so much intolerance, discord and isolationism emerging in the world, that still feels like a relevant ambition. Don't you agree?'

As Daniel watched her speaking, and the motion being carried, he remembered the day he'd first met her. He'd found her trying to force the door of one of the barns – a tall, slim young woman, with cobwebs in her red hair – and he'd been struck by her odd, earnest manner. They'd walked through the gardens together and she'd told him how she'd exchanged letters with leaders of communes in Japan and India, her ideas about collaborative working and spiritual fulfilment, and how it was imperative that there must never be another world war. By the end of that first day, Daniel had admired her; he'd thought her spirited, far-sighted, emotionally perceptive and unusually, exceptionally kind. Gwen might have had her self-doubts earlier, and he could fully understand why, but as he looked at her now, he saw that same exceptional woman, and how brave she was.

Chapter Forty-Three

'So he'd been siphoning off money for years?' Robert asked.

Trudie pushed the pile of ledgers away. With the chaos that always seemed to reign in her house, Robert had assumed her attitude to book-keeping would be casual, but he'd got this entirely wrong. Having taken over management of the estate's accounts, she'd quickly identified anomalies.

'I have to hand it to him – he's played the long game and done it with some subtlety. He never took enough to set off alarm bells and he covered his tracks well. But, bit by bit, he's filtered off significant amounts over the years.'

Trudie had put on a pair of heavy-rimmed tortoiseshell spectacles while she'd been showing him the ledgers. They magnified her red-rimmed eyes. She'd been telling comical anecdotes about the summoning to her mother's sickbed earlier, how unrelentingly imperious she'd been and the cutting personal comments she'd made, but she'd admitted the prognosis wasn't good.

'Do you think Mrs Fitz had any idea?' Phyllis asked. She joined them at the table with the replenished coffee pot.

'Maybe she suspected, but chose not to believe it? She did determinedly see the best side of him.' Trudie took the spectacles off and put a hand through her hair. 'I'm not sure what we ought to do now. Should I say something to her?'

'Would she do anything about it? She didn't want to go to the police when he emptied the safe, did she?' Robert said.

'Perhaps it's best to leave it in the past?' Phyllis suggested. 'What's done is done? I think she feels bad enough already.'

'He took from the trust as well as from Gwen, though. He's effectively stolen from all of us.'

'Maybe, for her sake, we let it go?'

Over Trudie's shoulder, Robert could see Faye leading a croc-odile of children towards the gatehouse. She smiled and pointed, and he could tell she was directing the children's eyes towards the swifts that streaked and screeched around the battlements.

'I really don't like that he's getting away with it.' Trudie poured another cup of coffee. 'I don't like it one bit. It doesn't seem just, does it?'

'Some people manage to go through life getting away with things.' Phyllis shook her head. 'I hope all the horses he backs lose and his cars all rust.'

'I wouldn't call him a confidence trickster exactly,' Trudie mused. 'He was with Gwen too long. I suspect that rather than a cold-blooded exploitation, it was more a way of life to Teddy. Perhaps more of a habitual parasite than a conman?'

'Poor Mrs Fitz,' said Phyllis.

'I think he might have deceived her about the state of their finances too – all that talk about them not being able to pay their rates and settle their bills. Most of her money has gone, that's true, but they weren't absolutely at the bottom of the barrel. He might have exaggerated just how bad things were in order to push her into the land sale.'

'Fully intending to take the money and run? That always being the intention?'

'I think so.'

'It's such a cruel deception. I'm not sure she needs to know any more of it. Her head must be in a spin already.'

'Daniel is doing his best to keep her distracted,' Robert said.

'Aye, they're very pally these days, aren't they? Have you noticed?' There was a hint of mischief in Phyllis's smile. 'Do you suppose they spend their evenings playing duets and discussing how they might turn the tide of international politics?'

'What are you meaning to imply, Phyllis McKay?' Nancy asked as she joined them. 'Daniel isn't like that. He's a gentleman. He holds Mrs Fitz in the highest esteem. He's been a rock to her since Teddy left.'

'Is that what you call it? Even gentlemen have their moments, you know.'

'I think she must be lonely,' Robert said. 'That's why she keeps inviting us into the house.'

'I've had an idea about that.' Trudie tapped her pen against her chin.

'Prime Daniel with Dutch courage? Lock them in a room together? Is it true what they say about oysters?' There was outright devilment in Phyllis's grin.

Trudie had bathed him, brushed him and tied a tartan bow around his neck. He gave off a distinct scent of lavender bath salts and had been given a peppermint to sweeten his breath.

'We could give Daniel a haircut and some new eau de cologne as well,' Phyllis suggested, but Trudie narrowed her eyes at that. The puppy's name was Hubert and he was What Gwen Needed, Trudie pronounced in her capital-letters voice.

They found Mrs Fitzgerald in the library working through a box of old letters. She'd let a cup of tea go cold in front of her and appeared to be absorbed in whatever she was reading.

'The last of Queenie's litter?' she smiled as she looked up. 'Oh, isn't he an absolute darling? This is Hubert, isn't it?'

'His Sunday name is Hubert Burford Bonny Boy,' Trudie said. 'Grandson of Salisbury Sunbeam, best in show for three consecutive years,' she added.

'What a pedigree!' said Phyllis. 'But can he compose a piano sonata?' she asided and winked at Robert.

'He's a poppet,' Trudie went on, resolutely ignoring Phyllis. 'And I've decided he ought to be yours.' She placed the wriggling dog in Mrs Fitzgerald's arms.

'What? But I couldn't!'

'Of course you could. He will give a rhythm to your days and get you out of the house.'

'Do you worry I'm becoming a hermit?' Mrs Fitzgerald frowned, but then smiled as Hubert set about removing her face powder with his tongue.

'A little,' Trudie admitted.

'But this is your livelihood!'

'And you are my friend.'

'Oh, Trudie!' Mrs Fitzgerald's face changed at that moment and the tears she'd been holding in for so long finally broke. They clotted her eyelashes and then ran unchecked down her cheeks. Trudie put her arms around her and then tears overspilled from her eyes too.

'It's the most generous thought,' Mrs Fitzgerald said as

Hubert's wriggling finally broke up their embrace. 'I am touched and obviously I'll adore him. I don't know what to say!'

The dog had taken her handkerchief and was now studiously shredding it on the rug, but Mrs Fitzgerald looked down benignly.

'In the grand scheme of things, it's absolutely nothing,' Trudie replied. 'You gave me kindness and purpose when I was lost. You gave me back my sanity and self-respect. I'll never be able to adequately repay you for that. And I also owe you an apology. I've said some things that I shouldn't have done over recent months.'

'Haven't we all?' Mrs Fitzgerald replied.

The two women wiped one another's tears away and Robert contemplated that this was what Greenfields actually meant; this place wasn't about conferences and exhibitions and lecture series, not really; fundamentally, it was about kindness – and that had to be worth preserving, didn't it?

Chapter Forty-Four

September brought a first breath of autumn in the mornings and Robert felt a pang of sadness as he realized the swallows had departed already. He searched the sky for them, but they'd gone. The Virginia creeper that draped the far wing of the Hall was a glorious red, pears were ripening on the walls of the kitchen garden and he'd come across circles of tiny mushrooms on his walks. He felt a sense that the cycle was turning once again.

Carrying a basket of vegetables over to the Hall, he met Faye by the steps. She was trying to discourage Hubert from drinking the yellowing saucers of milk put out for the cats.

Mrs Fitzgerald looked on laughing. 'It's either the case that I lack all natural authority or he's picked up something of Trudie's personality. Perhaps a bit of both, I fear.'

'But he's very sweet,' said Faye, lifting the small dog and hugging him to her chest.

'And he gets away with murder because of it! Anyway, would you two like to see what Mr Kelly is doing?'

'Mr Kelly?'

'Daniel found him on the building site. He might well be a miracle.'

They ascended the great carved oak staircase, following Mrs

Fitzgerald. The stairs became narrower and the newel posts less ornate as they climbed higher. Mrs Fitzgerald explained how Mr Kelly worked as a carpenter for Houghton & Halford, but his great passion was for old buildings. Daniel had asked him if he'd take a look at the roof and he'd apparently jumped at the chance.

'I assumed we'd need a whole new roof,' she went on. 'Teddy said the timbers were riddled with deathwatch beetle and all the tiles and leadwork would have to be replaced. Every builder he consulted sucked at their teeth, but Mr Kelly is of the opinion that a certain amount of patching and reinforcing might see us through another couple of decades.'

She led them along the top-floor corridor, past the old servants' rooms. Robert looked through the open doors and saw little iron bedframes, drawers full of shredded linen where the mice had nested and a crucifix hanging crookedly on a wall. There were rat holes in the skirting boards, bird feathers and droppings, and Hubert ran around excitedly. Robert could hear the wind in the chimneys, the creak of footsteps on the floor above and a whispering sounds as lengths of peeling wallpaper shifted in the draught. At night this place must be all scuttling and scurrying and the gossiping ghosts of housemaids. He wondered if Mrs Fitzgerald was really comfortable in the house on her own.

'All these empty rooms are rather sad,' he said.

'They are, aren't they?' Mrs Fitzgerald agreed. 'But I have a plan for that.'

The final staircase up to the roof space was made of rough old timbers. The temperature rose as they climbed and there was a smell of ancient dust and damp. Mrs Fitzgerald led with an electric torch and they picked their way between moth-ravaged lampshades, ancient perambulators and stacks of linen stitched with

the initials of long-dead residents of Anderby. Robert watched
the torch beam tearing through the darkness, spotlighting trunks
plastered with Cunard Line labels, piles of mouse-nibbled bibles
and the momentarily horrifying faces of dolls.

'Is this what it was like to enter Tutankhamun's tomb?' Faye
whispered. She turned to him and smiled, her eyelashes casting
shadows in the torchlight.

There were buckets placed around and stretches of tarpaulin
had been strung across the sloping eaves in places, but the roof
wasn't in *such* a dire state as Teddy had indicated. Robert had
expected to see crumbling beams and slices of sky between sagging tiles, something precarious and conspicuously costly to put
right, but . . . Might Teddy have exaggerated this too? The dust
left a peppery smell in Robert's nostrils, he felt himself walking
through cobwebs, and he failed to stifle a sneeze.

'Bless you,' said a man's voice. For a second, it might have
been Teddy's voice and Robert checked himself. He was relieved to see that the man further up the roof space was older
and of a heavier build. He'd taken an area of tiles down and appeared to have begun work reinforcing some unsound timbers
with new wood. The sunlight and chatter of sparrows seemed
amplified through the gap in the roof.

'Look at him! Isn't he a marvel?' Mrs Fitzgerald said.

The man nodded acknowledgement as she made introduc-
tions. He was wearing paint-splattered clothes and there was a
vague whiff of turpentine about him. 'There are a few sections
I'll have to replace, but I'll shore it up where I can. It really isn't
as big a job as you feared, Mrs Fitzgerald.' He addressed her
with deference. His accent was the same as Teddy's, but more
marked, and it lilted like a rocking horse.

'What magic words! I dreaded the house was going to collapse around me next winter. I truly feared that. Teddy was extremely pessimistic. He said another heavy snowfall might bring the whole thing down like a house of cards, and every builder he consulted seemed to be in agreement.'

'There are some awful cowboys around. They'll take terrible advantage of people.' Mr Kelly frowned and shook his head. 'This roof is overdue a little tender loving care, but it's largely sound. Please put your mind at rest, Mrs Fitzgerald.' He extended his hand to touch the rough-hewn beams. 'This old galleon has a few nautical miles left in her yet.'

'What did I say? He's a godsend, isn't he?'

'I've been called many things in my time, but I've never been heaven-sent before.' Mr Kelly smiled broadly, showing nicotine-stained teeth.

'Talking of heaven-sent, is that a bishop's mitre?' Faye asked and pointed.

As the women stepped away to explore the attic's curiosities, Robert found himself alone with Mr Kelly. His smile had been extinguished and he was now giving Robert a hard stare. 'I knew your man before,' he said under his breath.

'I'm sorry?'

'Fitzgerald, I mean. He didn't remember me – well, why should he? – but we laboured on the same site back in Dublin years ago. He was workshy in those days too and always chasing after the skirt. It took me a while to place his face because I never imagined he might end up somewhere like this. Him playing the squire in his suit and his shiny shoes! Sure, what are the odds?' Mr Kelly had greying hair, but prominent dark eyebrows, lifting now. He reached a tin from his shirt pocket and began to roll a cigarette.

'You worked with Teddy?'

'He was always full of talk, always the grand schemes, but we thought he was just a gobshite.' He licked his cigarette paper. 'Houghton knew him too. He had nothing good to say about him back in the day, but then the boot was on the other foot here. I suspect your man got a bit of a thrill out of lording it over his old gaffer.'

'I imagine he did.' Robert could imagine that all too easily.

'It all had to be hush-hush, you understand?' Mr Kelly tapped a finger to the side of his nose. 'We were told that. It mustn't get back to the missus that Captain Fitzgerald had sweated alongside the likes of us. God forbid!' He laughed. 'But I don't suppose it matters now, does it?'

Robert considered. Did it still matter? 'As far as I'm aware, Mrs Fitzgerald doesn't know any of that. I'm not certain she needs to find out.'

'Right so.' Mr Kelly nodded. He stashed the cigarette behind his ear. 'If you think that's for the best, she won't hear it from me. She's a grand woman, your Mrs F, she's a diamond. She was too good for that sly little shite.'

Robert wanted to ask so many questions, but he could hear the women's voices coming closer. 'I entirely agree.'

'And don't you worry, I'll see her right.'

'Hubert has cornered a rat!' said Mrs Fitzgerald, returning to their side. 'Have you two been having a good manly conversation about rot and parasites?'

'Something of that sort.'

'Don't you agree with me that he's a miracle worker, Robert? Perhaps the angels are on my side after all?'

'They may well be.'

They left Mr Kelly, whistling tunelessly as he worked. Robert didn't have cause to doubt what he'd said about Teddy. After all, why should he lie? From their first meeting he'd never felt inclined to trust the man, but he couldn't have guessed the extent of his deception. Should Mrs Fitzgerald know, though? Would there be any advantage to her hearing the truth? But he recalled her saying what a fool she'd felt, how naïve she'd been, and this could only make that worse. He decided she didn't need to know.

'Stand still for a moment, Robert,' Faye commanded. She was coming down the staircase behind him. 'Your hair is full of cobwebs. You look like Miss Havisham.'

'Isn't Miss Havisham a manipulative old woman who wears a wedding dress?'

'Quite. Now turn around.' Robert felt very conscious of standing so close to her. Having pulled the cobwebs from his hair, she took a handkerchief from her pocket and wiped something from his forehead, as she might do with a child. It was an automatic gesture, but then as her eyes met his and held his gaze for a moment, there was something quite different between them. 'There. You'll do,' she said.

'Mr Kelly is moving in.' Mrs Fitzgerald's voice was tailing away down the staircase ahead. Robert turned and they followed. 'He's been renting a house in the village, but it will be more convenient for him to be here. He'll fit work on the roof around his commitments on the building site. He doesn't seem to mind that the room is pretty basic, and he likes to cook. He's promised to make Yorkshire puddings on Sunday. I do have a weakness for the Irish lilt and he has those dancing eyes. Did you see?'

Robert glanced back at Faye over his shoulder and they raised their eyebrows at one another.

'What a find he is!' Faye said.

'I'm intending to smarten up some of the other rooms and make them available for rent,' Mrs Fitzgerald went on, 'but it strikes me that if I can find other artisans who might be willing to trade labour for accommodation, we could be on to something. Don't you think? Perhaps we could develop it as a scheme, and let people learn trades here as well? God knows, there's enough to work on!'

'You wouldn't mind having the house full of plasterers and carpenters?'

'It would be marvellous! I'd enjoy hearing voices in the house and knowing that more repair than decay was in progress.' She turned towards them on the landing. 'I really didn't want to sell the orchard, you know. Teddy and I battled over it, and it hurt all the more since I gained nothing monetary from it in the end, but perhaps some good may come out of it yet?'

'You might have happened upon a way to save Anderby,' Robert said.

'And Greenfields,' Faye added.

She put her hand to Mrs Fitzgerald's arm, smiled towards Robert and he felt a renewed sense of optimism. Five months ago, Faye had predicted that this venture would end, that it was all over, and he had felt her despair. But was the tide now turning? Robert realized that he wanted to have a future here, for Greenfields to go forwards, and for Faye to stay too. He returned her smile and dared to hope.

Chapter Forty-Five

'We plant marigolds in between the tomatoes because the whiteflies hate the smell of them, and nasturtiums next to the Brussel sprouts because they lure the aphids away.' Robert picked a nasturtium flower and handed it to Maudie Higgs with a flourish of chivalry.

'Can I keep it?' the child asked. She twirled it between her small fingers.

'Of course you can, Maudie. You can eat it too, if you want.'

'Eat it?' Maudie looked horrified. Faye laughed.

The children had been planting drills of turnip seed in their area of the garden this morning. Robert had shown them how to dig the soil over, had supervised as they'd sown the seed, and the children were now going back and forth with watering cans. There was an earthy smell as the water soaked into the parched ground.

Back in the spring they'd talked of giving the children their own area of vegetable garden to manage, but with all the up-heaval over the orchard sale, the project had been put on hold. It was Robert who had suggested to her that they ought to revive the idea and, in truth, Faye had been glad to sit at his table making plans once again. She'd enjoyed watching him working with the children this morning and had been struck by his patience. He'd talked to them about planting to encourage bees, had told them a story about how he'd tried to tame a fox when he was a boy, and had suggested that for next spring he might make some bird nesting boxes that the children could observe. He'd answered all their questions, was gentle and considerate with them, and had pulled conkers, acorns and aniseed balls from the pockets of his waistcoat.

'I think they might be trampling on as much as they're planting, but they're all very interested and enthusiastic, aren't they?' He came to lean against the wall at Faye's side now. He'd rolled his shirtsleeves to the elbow while he'd worked and she could see a paler line where the sun hadn't touched his skin. He smelled of fresh air, turned earth and aniseed.

'Who knows, it might distract them from trampling on your flowerbeds for a bit too, eh?'

'Damn it all, she divines my scheme!' He furrowed his brow at her, but then grinned. 'When did I last complain to you about that?'

'Gosh, it must have been at least a week ago. Are you mellowing?'

'I must be, mustn't I? Here, you've got a friend.' A ladybird had landed on her shoulder. He leaned towards her, his eyelashes cast down in concentration. 'Ladybird, ladybird, fly thy way home. Your house is on fire and your children all gone.' He gritted his teeth. 'When you think about it, most nursery rhymes are pretty grim, aren't they?' The ladybird crawled onto his hand and then opened its wings to fly away.

'The little ones were singing "Three Blind Mice" earlier. How very sweet, I thought, but then I remembered it's about

Mary Tudor blinding and executing Protestant bishops!' He'd leaned so close that she could feel his breath as he'd spoken. She felt herself colouring. 'Tilly was reading *The Tale of Peter Rabbit* in class yesterday. She asked me if you were like Mr McGregor and put poor dear bunnies in pies.'

'I have to admit, I am partial to a rabbit pie.'

'I knew it. If you say that to Tilly you'll make her cry.'

Robert turned to her smiling and looked away again quickly. 'You were right when you said we could make the vegetable garden more productive. I've been considering how we might do it. We could probably grow twice as much produce as we do now and we should give some thought to your idea of a food parcel scheme. With some planning, we could still take the same volume to market, and the remainder could be given away. It's just a question of thinking ahead and, of course, you'd have to defer to Nancy and Phyllis. This is really their territory, not mine.'

When Faye had proposed the scheme at the last meeting, Robert hadn't passed any comment. She hadn't been certain he'd support it, but he'd evidently been deliberating how it might be feasible. 'I'm sure Nancy and Phyl wouldn't object.'

'Let's talk it over with them, then. If you work out the practicalities of how we might distribute it, I'd be glad to do whatever I can to help on the growing side.'

'You'd have time? I know how busy you are.'

'I'll make time.'

The old garden wall was warm against Faye's shoulders and it was pleasant to watch the children absorbed in their tasks. They'd painted a new banner for over the door of the Hall last week and Robert had climbed up a ladder to hang it. There were still some faint traces of the red paint on the steps, but everyone presently seemed to be making renewed efforts at cooperation. Clearly that spirit had touched him too. For her part, Faye had arranged to meet Miss Carmichael in town the previous weekend, had thanked her for her support, but had told her that she couldn't take the position at the grammar school. Her future was at Greenfields, she'd said.

'Would you like some flowers for the classroom?' Robert asked. 'I could cut an armful for you to take back.'

'From your precious flowerbeds?' She couldn't help the word escaping from her mouth. The wind stirred his hair and she suppressed an urge to reach out and curl a strand of it around her finger.

'Yes,' he widened his eyes at her, acknowledging the teasing, but not throwing it back. 'We've got so many dahlias and asters still flowering. An armful won't be missed.'

'Thank you. That's kind of you,' she said.

He nodded his head at her and Faye watched him heading out through the door of the walled garden. Had he matured over the past few months, she wondered, or was it that she'd softened? There was a bucolic straightforwardness and solidness about him, she'd thought today as she watched him working with the children, but also a nobility. He made her think of John Clare poems and she wanted to lend him her volumes of Edward Thomas and Robert Frost. Faye reminded herself he was picking flowers for the classroom, not for her, but couldn't quite stop herself from smiling.

Chapter Forty-Six

By October the traffic and noise from the building site was beginning to abate. The roads were less muddy, the overturned earth was starting to green again, and with the roof tiles and external cladding on, the houses were looking nearly completed. Lengths of picture rail and banister were being carried inside this week, along with pieces of bathroom suite and kitchen cupboard. There was a peppery scent as the asphalt pavements were rolled, then creosote as the garden fences were painted, and Mr Kelly told them the build was on track for the first residents to be moving in before Christmas.

As Robert got changed for the evening, he thought back to the previous Christmas, when he'd found himself suddenly out of work and Esther had told him he needed to move on. Joseph had sent him a paragraph about Esther's wedding cut from the local newspaper a few weeks earlier. While it had smarted a little to read of the radiant bride, Robert no longer carried her photograph in his wallet and he hoped she would be genuinely happy. Mrs Fitzgerald was talking of hosting a Christmas Day dinner in the Hall and on Christmas Eve there'd be a party to which they'd invite the builders and their new neighbours. They'd discussed this as a group and decided it was the right thing to do. The meaning of 'community' might have shifted at Anderby, but it was still something they'd strive to achieve.

Tonight Mrs Fitzgerald was hosting a meal, and wanted to debate her idea for how renovation work on the Hall might be combined with a vocational training scheme. She'd invited Mr Kelly and Mr Houghton, keen to know their thoughts, and hopeful they might be able to work together.

'I find myself wanting to ask Houghton about Teddy,' Trudie said as they walked over to the Hall. 'Don't you? But I can hardly mention it in front of Gwen.'

'She cleared out the last of his clothes at the weekend,' Robert replied. He'd debated whether to share what he'd heard from Mr Kelly, but in the end had decided to keep it to himself. 'I sense that she wants to look forward, not back.'

'And I admire her for that.' Trudie linked her arm through his. 'The past tense is where Teddy belongs. For her sake, I hope he remains there.'

'I couldn't agree more.'

Daniel met them at the door, looking smart in a dinner jacket. 'Well, aren't you dapper, Dan!' Trudie said.

She was wearing purple silk and Tibetan silver bangles and Robert felt rather underdressed in his shirtsleeves and waistcoat, but he reminded himself this was Greenfields ... and, well, anything goes.

'We're in the winter sitting room,' Daniel said. 'I've lit the fire. She's plying Houghton with sherry. We've just advanced beyond awkward civilities and are getting down to business.'

Mr Houghton was speaking as they entered, so they made mute greetings to the room and took sherry glasses and places on the settee. Robert found himself sitting next to Faye, who looked elegant in a black dress and red boots. She circled one of her ankles as she listened to the conversation and Robert had to make an effort to focus on the words and not on her movements.

'And I should tell you,' Mr Houghton went on, 'we've decided that we're not going to build on the pottery site or the former Cardew property. After evaluation, we've concluded that neither location is ideal for construction. We'll do some modernization work on both properties, put in wiring, new kitchens and bathrooms, and then it's our intention to sell them on. With the workshops, they might well be taken on by people who want to become part of your community. Don't you think? Perhaps there are contacts you might approach? We'd be happy to cooperate with you in advertising the properties for sale.'

'That's good news,' Daniel said.

Robert thought of the murals that Iris had painted on her walls, her sunny kitchen where they'd so often sat together and her well-stocked garden, and couldn't help feeling glad that the property wouldn't be demolished. He knew that Daniel had met with Mr Houghton on a couple of occasions recently, keen to establish a mutual understanding, and if this might be the outcome of those efforts, perhaps there was some grounds for optimism.

'For the moment, we're not seeking to buy any further building land at Anderby,' Mr Houghton continued. 'That was originally our intention, but all the potential sites we've looked at have been problematic. Moreover, having talked with Mr Molyneux, I think it would be to our mutual advantage to keep this project small scale. I appreciate that you have something special here and we don't mean to spoil that.'

Robert glanced at Mrs Fitzgerald and saw she was smiling. Daniel put his hand to her shoulder and she looked up at him with undisguised pleasure.

'Thank you,' she said. 'I'm sincerely grateful for your consideration.'

Her words were cut short as a vehicle's headlights raked across the room. They all looked towards the windows. A motor had pulled up outside, the noise of its engine stilling now, and being replaced with a sound of footsteps on the gravel. Hubert gave a low, throaty growl.

'Are we expecting anyone else?' Nancy asked.

'I don't think so,' Mrs Fitzgerald replied. The expression on her face had changed. Had her thoughts gone to Teddy too?

Robert could hear a voice outside – and now multiple voices. There was the sound of a car door closing and a torch beam was moving across the drive.

'It appears we've got visitors,' Daniel said. 'Do you want me to go to the door?' He looked at Mrs Fitzgerald.

'No, it's alright. I'll go.'

As it was, they followed her to the door. The headlights had been turned off, but the beam of the torch was flickering on the terrace and the steps. It raked across the garden, showed the door of a van, opening now, and then there were Erin and Ewan climbing down.

'Iris?' Nancy ran out into the dark.

Daniel stepped out with another torch and they all saw the children's pale, tired faces and the van piled with luggage. Iris, looking equally exhausted, was holding the baby in her arms and ushering the children towards the house.

'I'm so sorry,' she said. 'This is an imposition, isn't it? I should have telephoned ahead, I know, but it all happened quickly and I didn't know where else to go. Is there room at the inn for a group of refugees?'

Chapter Forty-Seven

Iris found Robert in the parterre garden. 'It's all come on since we left,' she said. 'Everything has grown and filled the spaces. The difference is remarkable. You must have really been putting in the hours.'

'The weather has been kind and I've brought down several tractor-loads of manure from the farm. I must have made fifteen trips. It's more muck than skill!' He looked up from his work and grinned. 'Is the difference really noticeable? I'm glad to hear that. I'm more inclined to focus on how much I've got left to do.'

She sat down on the wall and took the thermos from the pocket of her coat. 'Coffee?'

'I've missed you, Iris Cardew.'

She laughed. 'I've missed all of this – this routine, this place, all of you. I didn't realize I'd miss it quite so much.'

Nobody had yet directly asked her why she'd come back and what had happened. She'd been glad not to face questions last night. Instead, they'd busied themselves lighting fires and making up beds. The children were shivering with exhaustion and her first priority had been to get them settled. It was coming up to midnight by the time she'd finally sat down with Gwen and they'd drunk a whisky together. Gwen hadn't required any explanations, only told her she was glad to have her back here and that the rooms could be hers permanently if she wanted them. Iris had been so utterly worn out last night, they'd only spoken for half an hour before she'd had to apologize and retire to her bed. She'd been grateful for Gwen's kindness and sensitivity, but she felt she needed to talk with someone today.

'How are the children this morning?' Robert asked as he took the coffee from her.

'They're fast asleep still. I crept out. They had a tough day yesterday. We'll take it slowly and gently today.'

'And how are you?' He sat down on the wall next to her.

She shrugged. 'Do you want the polite answer or the honest one?'

'Can I have the honest one?'

She could see concern on his face. 'Is discombobulated a word? I feel as if I've woken up on a placid sea after a storm, but the horizon tilts again when I think of what I've done and what happens next.'

'Cecil isn't following you, I take it?'

Iris heard a hesitation in his voice. Mirrored clouds moved across the surface of her coffee and she found herself hesitating too for a heartbeat. 'I've left him,' she said. It was the first time she'd spoken those words out loud and they felt odd as they left her mouth. 'I didn't flit in the night – we've been having the conversation for a couple of weeks – but once I'd made up my mind, I wanted to go. Things have been difficult between us for a while. I hoped it might get easier after the move, if he was happier, but it hasn't been.'

'We could all see that on the day you left. We worried about you. Cecil means to stay on in Sussex, then?'

'He does. As far as he's concerned, it was the right move. He's at home in that crowd. It's all very machismo there; they all strut around in leather aprons, talking about steam-powered hammers, and anvils, and the size of their commissions. He's in his element really.'

Robert pressed his lips together, clearly trying not to smile. 'I can picture it, but it wasn't for you?'

'Everyone was keen to welcome Cecil, they all wanted to invite us for supper, but I felt like a hanger-on, like I wasn't really a person in my own right. It's weeks since I've had a conversation about anything other than Cecil's career. And the children were terribly unhappy. Erin hated it.'

'I suspect Nancy and Phyl mustn't have told Kitty yet. When she knows, she'll be like a piece of elastic released! She's been remarkably subdued since Erin left.'

Iris smiled. She'd still had a few doubts as she'd packed up the van last night, but now she knew it was the right thing to have done. 'I feel a sense of relief to be back here, as if I've come home again. Is that awful?'

'No, of course not. The move might have been right for Cecil, but we were all concerned it wasn't right for you.'

'But I'm his wife. I ought to stand by him and support him. That's what I signed up for.'

'At what expense? You also have to consider what's best for you and the children.'

She nodded. She could justify it as being the right decision for the children. 'I went to look at our house just now. I half expected it might have been levelled already. I was braced for the metaphor.'

'They're not going to build on the land. They're going to sell the house. Would you want to live there again?'

Iris considered the question. 'I probably couldn't afford it, and I don't think I'd want to live there now anyway. Too many mixed memories – do you understand? Gwen says we can have rooms in the Hall. I sense she'd like the company and the children would love it. I'm inclined to accept her offer.'

Iris had woken up in a bed carved with Baroque cherubs. As she'd slowly come to, thinking through the events of the previous night, she'd looked up at the unfamiliar ceiling. There was a frieze of painting around the top of the walls, a looping ribbon banner with flaking Latin words inscribed upon it, only faintly visible, but she could make out something about truth and time. It had occurred to her that dozens of people had probably awoken in that room before her; her own story was merely a brief paragraph in a long narrative, and there was some perspective and calm to be derived from that. All she'd been able to hear was the sound of the wind in the trees and a peaceful call and reply of wood pigeons. It seemed such a contrast to the strain and bitter words of the past few weeks. For the foreseeable future, she would be content to wake up in that tranquil room.

'If our house is being sold, I might go and steal some plants from my old garden. Would you care to join me in a raid?'

Robert smiled. 'With pleasure. Just tell me what you want digging up and where you'd like them to be replanted.'

'Thank you. You're a nice man and I've missed your company.'

He fussed with his cigarette and looked slightly embarrassed. 'We've missed you too and we've missed the children. Faye will be delighted to have them back in school.'

'And how are relations between you and Faye? Dare I ask?'

'We've progressed from cool civility to tepid and tentative toleration.'

'You really have made progress! Do I need to start looking for a wedding hat?' she laughed.

'Iris!' He looked genuinely shocked. 'Faye would spit fire if she heard you saying that!'

'Don't worry,' she reassured him. 'I wouldn't dare.'

It was endearing how he blushed. Iris wondered, did Faye realize he had feelings for her? And, come to that, was he admitting it to himself? She didn't like to interfere, but at that moment she felt a pressing compulsion to apply a sharp elbow to the pair of them.

Chapter Forty-Eight

The train needed to be put back on the rails, Mrs Fitzgerald said: Greenfields must return to its programme of cultural and educational events. Setting about this task, she'd organized a music evening in the Hall. She and Daniel would play, Nancy would sing and she'd speak about the projects the estate was planning over the coming months: the renovations to the house, the season of art exhibitions she was putting together for the spring and the lecture series that Daniel was arranging.

Looking suitably bohemian in a long paisley dress and her fox fur, she'd met their guests at the gatehouse and walked them through the gardens. Robert had accompanied her, answering questions, and enjoying the compliments he received. Mrs Fitzgerald had asked him if he'd give a talk about the gardens later in the evening, reflecting on the work completed so far, and outlining the plans for the year ahead. As he'd made notes, he was conscious that they hadn't yet had a conversation about renewing his contract, but everything Mrs Fitzgerald said implied she wanted him to stay. Might he trust that would be the case?

The fire had been lit in the great hall, music stands were ready on the dais, and rows of chairs were laid out. Robert's

designs for the remodelling of the parterre garden had been
mounted on card and hung on the wall at the back of the room.
Mrs Fitzgerald had framed some of the plans from the archive,
the original design for the topiary garden and eighteenth-
century perspectives of the approach to the house. Some of
Daniel's photographs and Iris's morning sketchbooks were also
on display, showing the evolution of the work over the past year.
Iris had squeezed Robert's arm as they'd looked over this collection together and told him he must feel proud and confident
when he spoke tonight.

A number of Mrs Fitzgerald's county friends had come
along, a few people from town had bought tickets and there
were a handful of new faces who were keen to tell everyone
they'd soon be moving onto the housing estate. A Mr and
Mrs Danbury (now retired, but he formerly in fitted carpets)
sounded proud that their names had been the first on the
waiting list. There was a Miss Birtle, a pharmacist's assistant
from the town, who was buying her first home with a family
inheritance, and a Mr Chilcott, a dealer in horticultural chemicals, who tried to sell Robert a product for eliminating weeds
in gravel. A Mr Pemberton turned out to be a piano teacher,
and an admirer of Daniel's compositions, while a Mr and Mrs
Graham had three young children and were eager to speak
with Faye about the school. They all clearly felt an excitement
at the prospect of living at Anderby and a keenness to contribute to the community. Smiles were exchanged between the
Greenfielders as it became apparent that the arrival of the new
people might not be the disaster that some had once feared.

Mrs Fitzgerald opened the recital with Satie, playing slowly
and tenderly, then Daniel joined her with a selection of Edward

Elgar, Vaughan Williams and finally one of his own pieces based on old Gloucestershire folk songs. The melody of the Elgar Cello Concerto took Robert back to hearing Daniel playing in the orchard. Calculating on his fingers, he worked out that was eleven months ago. It seemed longer. So much had changed since then, and he felt sad to recall the apple trees around them as the cello had played. Robert had worried about Daniel during the summer; he'd looked anxious and occasionally he'd struggled to control a stammer in his voice, but he seemed to have re-found his composure over recent weeks.

With the performance concluded, Daniel spoke of how Jewish people were no longer allowed to be members of orchestras in Germany, how the music of Mendelssohn, Mahler and Brahms was now banned, and how even statues of Wagner had been defaced because his second wife was Jewish. There was both sadness and anger in his voice and Robert sensed that if there'd been any apathy at Greenfields, any loss of sense of direction, it had now gone. Daniel turned to Mrs Fitzgerald as he finished speaking and she nodded to him.

Robert went to get himself a whisky. He'd never been required to address a room before and felt a little apprehensive at the prospect of doing so. He met Faye by the drinks table. She'd been asked to speak about the school after he'd given his talk on the garden. He wondered if she perhaps needed some Dutch courage too.

'How do you think it's going?' he asked. He poured her a drink.

'Good. I've got three new pupils for the school. A couple of months ago, I feared we might have to close, but it's looking as if we might double our numbers next term.'

'I'm glad to hear that.' He touched his glass to hers. Her marcasite earrings caught the candlelight and, standing at her side, Robert could smell the violet scent she was wearing. Daniel had been taking photographs of the room earlier and it had occurred to Robert that he wished he had a photograph of Faye. When he was with her, he was always conscious that he mustn't stare at her.

'People seem to be interested in the garden plans.' She gestured to the group at the back of the room. Mrs Fitzgerald was pointing a finger at the designs and nodding and smiling in response to questions. Turning to look around the room, she caught Robert's eye and beckoned him over.

'Will you excuse me?' he said.

'Of course. Enjoy your moment, Capability Brown.'

He heard the front door bell clanging as he picked his way between the chairs. He noticed Daniel leaving to answer it.

Mrs Fitzgerald took his arm as she introduced him to a Mr Lovett-Smith, who was planning to remodel the garden of the former rectory he'd just purchased. Robert was shaking the man's hand as he heard shouting in the corridor. He turned to see Daniel in the doorway trying to stop someone entering the room.

'I want to speak to my wife!' Teddy's voice demanded.

There'd been a scuffle in the passageway. Teddy was drunk, Daniel said, he could smell whisky on his breath, but he'd insisted on speaking with Gwendoline and the two of them were now together behind the closed door of the sitting room. Daniel stood in the corridor by the door, clearly anxious. Leaving the others to face the questions of their guests, Robert and Trudie went to join him.

Gwendoline had gone very pale, and for a moment Robert had thought she might faint, but she'd put on a dignified expression as she'd left the room. Her mouth had been set, her eyes were giving nothing away, but what thoughts raced behind that resolute exterior? Had she been expecting that Teddy might come back one day?

Robert could hear their voices inside the room now, and while he couldn't make every word out, the tone was clear enough. He also heard Trudie's deep intake of breath at his side and put his hand to her shoulder. She widened her eyes at him, the look conveying alarm.

'Why is he back?' she whispered.

'Burned through the money already?' Robert shrugged.

'If that's the case, he's got a bloody cheek.'

Daniel creased his brow, clearly trying to listen to the conversation on the other side of the door. Robert could hear Teddy speaking in a pleading voice and Gwendoline sounding distressed and angry. He might still be her husband, but Robert didn't like her being alone in the room with Teddy, and Daniel clearly felt the same.

'Is he apologizing?' Trudie asked. 'Does he expect her to take him back?'

'He's had a skinful,' Daniel said. 'He's drunk enough to have persuaded himself that she might.'

'Would she?' Robert asked.

His eyes met Daniel's and he saw concern there. 'I sincerely hope not.'

Teddy was shouting suddenly, there was a noise like a piece of furniture being dragged across the floor, and then the sound of glass breaking. Daniel's hand went to the door handle.

'And, of course, dear, loyal, noble Daniel is here to rescue you!' Teddy flourished his arm at the door.

Daniel was right: Teddy looked full of whisky, wild-eyed and reckless with it. There was broken glass on the floor around him, a chair had been turned over and Gwendoline was standing behind the settee. She was holding her hand to her mouth.

'Can a husband and wife not have five minutes of privacy? Do you people have no manners?'

'I'm not sure Gwendoline wishes to talk to you,' Daniel said.

'I'm sorry?' Teddy turned to him. 'Do you decide who Gwen talks to now, Molyneux? I'll speak with my wife if I damn well want to. Oh, but you've probably made a move, haven't you, Danny Boy?' He grinned nastily and wiped his mouth with the back of his hand. 'I should have known you'd be in there as soon as I was gone. You've always had designs on Gwen, haven't you? Yes, I was aware of that. You never hid it very well. But the problem is she's out of your league, old boy. Gwen might have a few miles on the clock now, but she'd never notice the likes of you. I mean, look at yourself in the mirror!' Teddy laughed, but then stopped and turned to his wife. His expression changed. 'Dear God, you haven't, have you, Gwen? You wouldn't lower yourself to *that*, would you? Was it out of pity?'

Gwendoline flew across the room and slapped her husband. 'How dare you? Daniel's worth ten of you.'

Teddy reeled back with shock and blinked hard. He stared at Gwendoline, he looked as if he might hit her for a moment, but then took her wrists in his hands instead. Robert and Daniel rushed forwards at the same moment. As they did, Teddy dropped his wife's arms and dipped to lift the neck of the broken bottle from the floor. He held it towards them.

'I'll bet you've all been rallying around her, haven't you? "Poor Gwen. Wasn't he a rotter? We'll take care of you now."' His tone was mocking, but then it hardened: 'You're all a set of leeches. You've been bleeding her dry for years. You know you have. Do you really believe she can afford to keep the rents so low? And let you treat this place as your own? Don't judge me, because you're just as bad.'

'Put the bottle down,' said Daniel.

'He's right,' Trudie said. 'You need to leave now, Teddy. Think about what you're doing.'

'Oh, go to hell, Trudie. Mind your own fucking business.'

'Please, darling, put the bottle down.' Gwendoline took a step towards him. Robert could hear her trying to control her voice. 'If you want to discuss it, we can.' She put a hand to his arm. 'But do let's calm down.'

'Darling is it now, eh?' He waved the glass and laughed. 'That's a gear shift! Wasn't I a shit five minutes ago?'

Daniel lurched forwards and tried to grab Teddy by the wrist. They struggled together. Teddy looked like he didn't care about the consequences and Robert didn't know which way this was going to go. But Daniel managed to swing Teddy's arm back and the bottle smashed against the fireplace. Robert stepped in and, together with Daniel, they bundled Teddy to the door.

He swore and kicked as they manhandled him down the passageway. They were all bastards and bitches and everyone had done him wrong. Teddy spat as he cursed them, struggled and bellowed like a bull, but Trudie had the front door open and they threw him down the steps. They bolted the door before he could get to his feet, and Robert and Daniel stood with their backs to it, both of them shocked and short of breath. Within seconds, Teddy was pounding his fists on the door. Robert felt the physical force of his anger. Teddy kicked at the door and pulled the chain of the bell violently. It clanged manically over their heads.

When the bell finally stilled, they waited in silence. Robert could hear Daniel breathing heavily at his side. He fully expected something to be launched through a window next. He was readied for the sound of it. Teddy was wild enough tonight. He could hear his footsteps circling on the gravel outside, but then finally retreating.

'He'll come back,' said Trudie.

'We need to call the police,' Daniel said.

When Gwendoline appeared in the hallway she was as pale as a ghost. She pressed her palms over her eyes. Daniel went to her and put his arms around her.

'It's over now,' he said. He stroked the back of her head.

She pulled away and looked at him. 'Over? It's barely begun. He's taken everything from me, manipulated me and deserted me, and he's still not satisfied. Now he wants a divorce and half the value of the house.'

Chapter Forty-Nine

Faye saw the last of the guests out. Many of them had questions she couldn't answer – and, as they departed into the night, she wondered what they might encounter. Was Teddy still out there? They'd heard his motor revving and the tyres spinning on the gravel, but could he still be somewhere on the estate? Robert had waited by the door with her and she'd felt some relief when it was finally bolted.

'We can't leave her on her own tonight, can we?'

'I agree,' Robert said. 'He was unhinged enough that he might do anything. He was like a wild animal when we tried to get him out.'

'Could he genuinely force her to sell Anderby? On what grounds might he divorce her?'

'Daniel doesn't believe he'd have any case. He thinks he's probably just spoken to some solicitor in a pub and heard the words he wanted to hear.'

'He doesn't know when to stop,' she said. 'It's outright cruel. He's really showing his true colours now, isn't he?'

'Gwendoline looked devastated. I think her last scrap of faith in him was destroyed tonight.'

'Is your face alright?' He'd taken a blow during the scuffle and a bruise was starting to show on his cheekbone. She winced in sympathy. 'Does it hurt?'

'It does when I smile. Please don't make me smile.' He did anyway.

They'd moved into the sitting room. Trudie had swept the glass away and they were pulling armchairs towards the fire. Nancy and Phyllis had been down to the kitchen and came back with mugs of cocoa on a tray. Daniel's hand had been cut in the tussle with the bottle and he was talking quietly with Gwendoline now as she cleaned and dressed the wound.

'He's trying to persuade her to call the police,' Faye said. She sat down between Trudie and Robert on the settee.

'She must do,' Trudie said. 'She should have done it last time. I hope she's listening to him.'

'Gwendoline doesn't think he'll come back. She says he'd be too ashamed.'

'He might be sleeping the drink off somewhere now, but I don't believe embarrassment will bar him from coming back,' Robert said. 'Does Teddy "do" shame?'

'I suspect he doesn't know the meaning of the word. If he's talking about divorce, it needs to be on record that he's been violent and stolen from her.'

'And deserted and manipulated her,' Trudie added. 'She said that, didn't she? From what we know now, it's pretty obvious that he coerced her into the land sale.'

'There have been years of manipulation and lies,' Robert said. Faye heard a halt in his voice, as if he was reconsidering his words, but then he went on. 'Mr Kelly told me that he knew Teddy back in Dublin. All his background is a fiction. He's lied to her all along. I haven't mentioned it to anyone previously because it would be awful for her to know just how much he's deceived her. But I guess it's all going to come out now, isn't it?'

Faye stared at him. 'Mr Kelly knew him before?'

'So he set out to deceive from the start?' Trudie asked.

'Mr Kelly doesn't have a good word to say about him. Speak to him yourselves. He knows all about Teddy.'

'If all of that is true, surely he'd have no claim at all on the house? He's played a cunning game so far, but turning up here full of drink and threats wasn't very clever, was it?'

'I guess he's running out of options? He stank of whisky,' Robert said. 'He'll probably regret it when he dries out.'

'Ye gods, the brass neck of the man!' Trudie was nursing her cup and sitting forwards in her chair. She still looked a little shaken up. 'You know, I thought about Guy tonight. He could be wild like that. Quite out of control sometimes. There was a period of my life when I spent a lot of time sweeping up broken glass and wondering whether I ought to call the police. I should have done sooner. Gwen must.'

Faye turned to her. 'You did what you felt was right for Guy. I can't imagine how I would have coped.'

Faye understood that Guy Colville had come back from the war with an addiction to opiates. He and Trudie had had a riotous time around London together, all parties and nightclubs and endless streams of champagne, but there had also been periods of violence and him being locked behind the doors of secure clinics. Gwendoline had once confided that Trudie had been all bones and bruises when she'd first arrived at Greenfields.

'I miss him sometimes, but I don't miss the scenes,' Trudie went on. 'I've been considering that I might finally get around to scattering his ashes this coming spring. He's been sitting on my mantelpiece for almost a decade. I can't keep him there forever. He's a magnet for dust.'

'You should.' Faye took her hand. 'I think that would be a healthy thing for you to do.'

'I said I'd cast him on the waves at St Tropez – that was where we first met – though he'd probably be more at home trodden into the beery puddles on the floor of some London boozer. He could be a frightful shit, an absolute swine, but I did love him,' she said.

'I know you did.' Faye leaned across and kissed her.

As the clocks struck eleven, Gwendoline suggested they all ought to go home. She said she'd bolt the doors and would be perfectly safe behind them. But they were all in agreement that they didn't want to leave her tonight.

'I won't be on my own, though. I have Hubert with me, Iris and the children are here, and I can call on Mr Kelly if I need him.'

'And we don't want them to be murdered in their beds either,' Trudie said.

'Murdered? Don't be silly! Teddy wouldn't do anything like that.'

'Are you sure?'

When they refused to relent, she and Iris went upstairs for blankets and pillows.

'She's agreed to call the police in the morning,' Daniel said, when Gwendoline had left the room. 'What he's done needs to be on record and she can't be expecting he might come back at any time and behave like that again.'

'Absolutely.' Faye had seen the alarm on Gwendoline's face when she'd heard Teddy's voice. Daniel was right: she couldn't live in fear that he might do this again.

By the time the clocks struck midnight, Phyllis and Trudie were sleeping. Nancy had fetched Kitty and they'd gone upstairs with Iris and the children. Gwendoline and Daniel were still speaking in hushed, serious tones. Robert remained next to Faye on the settee and she could sense he was alert to every sound outside. The light from the candles trembled on the walls and seemed to make the darkness beyond deeper.

'I felt sorry for Trudie earlier,' she whispered. 'She hardly ever talks about Guy. She must have had a very difficult time with him.'

'How did he die?' Robert asked.

'He was found dead in an alleyway at the back of a nightclub.'

'Suspicious circumstances?'

'No. He was full of booze and God knows what else and had choked on his own vomit. He used her pretty abysmally, by all accounts, but she made excuses for him – it was the war, it was his nerves, it was his parents' fault – and she blamed herself at the end.'

'Poor Trudie. No wonder you renounced men. There are some pretty shoddy examples around, aren't there?'

'And people ask me why!' She looked at him and thought he was a rather nice example. 'Perhaps it wasn't entirely his fault, though – I shouldn't be glib. The war ruined so many men's minds, didn't it?'

The thought occurred to her: might Robert be obliged to go to war at some point in the future? Could it happen again in their lifetime? She had a fleeting image of him standing in a doorway in a uniform, then turning and walking away from her. She felt a sudden protectiveness for him and wanted to grasp his hand.

'One day I'll tell you about my father,' he said.

'Yes?' she replied, bringing herself back to the moment. But then she could see he was reluctant to say more.

'It's for another time, but suffice to say he'd seen a lot of violence during the war and he brought it home with him. My brother suffered the worst of it. We didn't have the happiest family home.'

She could tell from his face that it was difficult for him to talk about this. She wanted to ask him questions, but told herself that she must hold back. 'How horrible for you.'

'My grandmother was always adamant that it was the fault of the war; she said he hadn't been that person before he went away. I don't know how I'd cope in the same circumstances.'

'I hope you'll never have to find out.' Faye sincerely hoped that. 'It can't have been easy for your mother either.'

'She died when I was a baby. I never really knew her. Perhaps it was for the best that she didn't get to see the man my father became.'

'I'm so sorry.' How fortunate she'd been, she realised, to grow up in a house full of love and laughter, to be part of a family where she'd always felt safe. 'If ever you want to talk, if you ever feel it might help, I'm here to listen.'

'Thank you.' He looked down, his face solemn, but then he gave her a smile of such simplicity and sincerity that she felt an urge to put her arms around him. 'You should get some sleep,' he said softly.

'I'm not tired.' Her nerves were on edge still and she was

conscious that he was listening to every owl call and fox yowl outside. 'You got out of making your speech anyway.'

'I'd forgotten all about that. I wasn't looking forward to it, but I'd rather have faced questions about herbaceous borders than Teddy's fists.'

'I could tell you were nervous about speaking. You made a sprint for the drinks table!'

'I've never had to make a speech before. I don't know how to speak in public. I've spent all week making and revising notes and trying to predict what questions they might ask.'

Faye looked at him. She'd once thought him too sure of himself, but had that been a front masking insecurity? 'You're not who I first supposed you were,' she said.

'That's cryptic.' He narrowed his eyes at her. 'Dare I ask who you thought I was?'

'I thought you were rather an arrogant young man.'

He laughed quietly. 'Yes, I seem to recall you told me that. Wasn't I selfish and complacent too?'

'Horribly!'

He grinned and then frowned. 'We got off on the wrong foot, didn't we?'

'And stubbornly stayed there for some considerable time. I'm sorry. I probably didn't make much effort to get to know you.'

'Likewise.' He leaned his head back, seeming to be in thought, and then turned to her. 'I regret that. We said some pretty horrid things to one another that day in the orchard. I'd take those words back if I could.'

'Can we begin again?' she asked.

*

Robert hadn't really slept. He seemed to have heard the clocks striking each hour of the night. He'd been conscious of every owl screech, the unfamiliar creaks of this old house and of Faye's presence at his side. He must have drifted off to sleep some time towards dawn, though, and now woke up with her head on his shoulder. He inhaled the scent of her hair and listened to the soft rhythm of her breathing. She was so peaceful and he didn't want to wake her. He didn't want her to move away.

He sat thinking of how they'd begun again last night, the understanding they'd found in their whispered words. He hadn't dreamed her smiles and her empathy, had he? Faye sighed in her sleep and he thought that he didn't ever want them to misunderstand one another again.

He looked around the room. The candles had burned down, but in the grey dawn light he could see the sleeping faces around him. Only Daniel was awake. He was hunched by the fire, rekindling the flames, and looked haggard with sleeplessness. What thoughts were going through his head? His feelings for Gwendoline had been made apparent to all last night – not just with Teddy's vicious words, but through his own selfless actions – and Robert found himself hoping she cared for him too. Daniel was a good man and he would always stand by her. If one positive thing came out of last night's crisis, he hoped it might be that.

Daniel turned and Robert lifted his hand in acknowledge-ment. Daniel mouthed that he would go and make some tea for them and Robert smiled his assent.

He shut his eyes as he listened to Faye's steady breathing. He heard the birds beginning to sing outside. There was a blackbird's fluting notes, the distant caw of a crow and then the doorbell was clanging again.

They all awoke with a start. Robert saw alarm on Gwendoline's face and Faye's hand gripped his. Trudie went to the window and peered around the edge of the curtain.

'There's a police car outside,' she said.

Daniel had made it to the door before Gwendoline. As Robert came into the hallway, he saw the police inspector taking off his hat and asking if he might speak privately with Mrs Fitzgerald. Before they departed, he caught the words 'accident' and 'fatality' and heard Teddy's name.

Faye couldn't stop shivering. It was sleeplessness, she supposed, and the shock. Phyllis had brought in a tray of tea, which they'd drunk in silence, and then by mute mutual consent they'd left Daniel and Gwendoline to conclude their business with the police.

'The motor spun off the road?' Phyllis asked when they were outside. 'That was what the constable said, wasn't it?'

The morning air was sharply cold and Faye was glad to stand with her arm linked through Robert's. She was too tired and shaken by the news to consider what anyone might think.

'On the bends near the quarry,' he replied. 'He must have lost control of the wheel.'

'How awful,' Nancy said. 'I hated him last night, he frightened me, but I would never have wished that on him.'

'Poor Gwen. What can we do?'

'I imagine she'll need some time to take it in,' Robert said. 'Daniel will stay with her today.'

They went their separate ways and Faye walked back towards the cottages with Robert.

'I know it's probably inappropriate in the circumstances, but I need a brandy. Do you want one?' She also didn't want to be alone.

They sat together on her settee and didn't speak much. There didn't seem to be much left to say. Faye's head reeled when she thought how Gwendoline must be feeling and she wanted to close her eyes. He put his arm around her and she lay with her head on his chest. She was glad of his understanding silence. Explanations would wait for another day.

Chapter Fifty

In recent days, as Faye had regularly appeared at the door of his cottage, Robert had become conscious of his living space, how bare and poor it was. With her eyes in the room, he saw the wear on the rugs, the damp on the walls and the cracks in the plaster. Though she'd never suggested it, she made him want to paint the walls a sunny yellow, to hang paintings that would please her eyes and to unroll soft Turkish carpets at her feet. But last night he hadn't given a thought to the room around them. Last night he had finally kissed her.

They had talked past midnight again – there suddenly seemed to be so much they urgently needed to say to one another – and then it had happened as she'd left. Robert had wanted to kiss her for a long time, he'd imagined it repeatedly, but couldn't be certain she felt the same way. There'd been no doubts last night, though. As Faye had looked up at him in the doorway, unspoken words had passed between their eyes. He'd felt a certainty then, a rightness and a need, and the touch of her lips had told him that he hadn't been mistaken.

After a restless night, he'd got up at first light and had spent the morning pruning the glasshouse grapevines, but he went about his work in an automatic way, every sound and play of the light, every texture and scent seeming to take him back to thoughts of her. Now seeing Daniel walking towards him in a black suit, and remembering that Gwendoline had attended a funeral today, Robert felt guilt at his own distracted happiness.

'How is she?' he asked.

Iris had tentatively enquired as to whether Gwendoline would like them to attend the funeral. They would all have been there, if she'd wanted their support, but she'd said she'd rather it be private. Given the circumstances, it hadn't felt appropriate to have a lot of ceremony and overblown sentiment. Daniel had helped her with the arrangements and had accompanied her today.

'She's taken a sleeping tablet,' he replied now. 'She needs some quiet and some calm. It will take her a while to come to terms with everything, I expect.'

Daniel looked exhausted too, Robert thought. He'd been spending a lot of time with Gwendoline, they'd clearly talked a great deal, and it couldn't be easy for him to watch her trying to reconcile her feelings for Teddy. At one moment she'd be fiercely angry, Daniel had said, the next disbelieving and a minute later she'd collapse in tears for the loss of the man who she'd lived with for twelve years. As Trudie had said, human brains and hearts don't always communicate terrifically well and sometimes we can't help loving the people we shouldn't.

'It all went as planned?'

Daniel loosened his black tie and nodded. 'As much as these things ever can. I have to say, it was hard to believe he was in that box. I kept thinking about how wild he was that night and expecting the lid to spring open and him to come roaring out.

God knows what was going through Gwendoline's head as we stood at the graveside.'

She'd wanted greenery from Anderby to make the wreath for Teddy's coffin. Robert couldn't help asking himself if Teddy would care, but he'd cut winter honeysuckle, hamamelis and branches of mahonia. It was important to Gwendoline and that was what mattered.

'Did anyone else attend?'

'A handful of his racecourse friends were there, a cousin from Dublin and an old army pal. I spoke with him afterwards and, between you and me, it was rather enlightening.'

'In what way?' Robert asked.

'The story about Teddy having known Gwendoline's brother looks ever more suspect, and he was certainly never a captain. He was a private in the artillery with a long disciplinary record. Apparently, his military career was all absences without leave, petty thefts and reprimands for insolence. The friend laughed as he told me. Teddy seems to have taken insubordination to extravagant lengths. I suppose he may have crossed paths with Hugh at some stage during the war, it's not beyond possibility that they met, but they were never brother officers.'

'So Teddy was a fake in every aspect? Do you suppose he deliberately sought Gwendoline out?'

'Quite possibly. He may have seen a newspaper article about her buying the Hall and got a sniff of money, but he stayed for twelve years, didn't he? That's no quick swindle. Personally, I feel inclined to curse him as a cad and a confidence trickster – but, whatever his initial motives, maybe he cared for her to some degree?'

'Or cared for her money? You still haven't told her any of this?'

Daniel shook his head. 'Can you imagine how awful it would be for her, to work back over their history and cast it all in a different light? How it might hurt her pride? No, I think it would be kinder to let her continue to believe they had known happiness, but that it just went wrong at the end. She's been dispossessed of sufficient consoling lies. Can we keep it to ourselves?'

'Of course.' Robert looked at Daniel and thought what a thoroughly decent man he was. 'I told Faye and Trudie, but they've promised not to say anything.'

'How was Trudie?'

'Putting on a brave face.'

It was a week of two funerals. Trudie had left for Dorset that morning. Given her inclination for bold prints and violent colour combinations, it had been striking to see her in a plain black woollen coat. She'd looked very pale as she set off and was hiding her red eyes behind dark glasses.

'I'm glad for her that they were reconciled before the end,' Daniel said.

'She's always portrayed her mother as a terrible old tyrant, but I suspect they may have had some personality traits in common – not that I'd dare suggest that to Trudie.'

She'd admitted to Robert that she and her mother had fought again when she'd gone home for the final time, calling one another every vile name they could bring to mind, but then they'd cried and embraced.

'I know they've been at war for years, but I wouldn't be surprised if this loss hits her hard,' Daniel speculated. 'I hope she'll choose to come back here after the funeral. Anderby does have a capacity to heal – but then Trudie already understands that.'

Robert hadn't considered that Trudie might not return. Was that a possibility? 'Anderby wouldn't be the same without her.'

'It would be rather more sober and tranquil – but, no, it would be a great loss.'

Chapter Fifty-One

Faye had copied Hardy's 'The Darkling Thrush' onto the blackboard and had tasked the children with writing their own poem about snow. She'd reminded them of a walk they'd taken through the wood last December and asked them to recall its sensations – the cold they felt, the winter light, the scents and sounds and textures of that snowy day. She remembered their footprints circling back towards the Hall, the low sun illuminating the front elevation, and thinking that it looked like an illustration from a children's book. The snow-blanketed ground was violet in that light and the sky was the colour of old gold. Then, as she'd stood there, she'd spotted Gwendoline walking across towards the cottages in her sable coat and a man following behind her. He was wearing a dark overcoat and carrying a suitcase and Faye hadn't wanted him to be there. 'This is a mistake,' she'd said to Daniel that day. If the vote had gone her way, Robert would never have come here.

She wiped the chalk from her hands, sat down behind her desk, and tried once again to focus on the essays she was meant to be marking. She seemed to have been re-reading the same page for the past half hour. It slightly frustrated her that she found her thoughts returning to Robert so frequently – she should be more sensible, she reprimanded herself – but she'd also caught her own reflection smiling this morning. After a year of conflicted feelings for him, being with Robert was now surprisingly uncomplicated. She only wished she could rewind twelve months, begin again on better terms, and not have lost so much time.

'Miss?' Kitty had her hand in the air. 'Please, Miss?'

'I'm sorry, Kitty. Yes?'

'Do we have to make it rhyme?'

'That's entirely up to you. It doesn't have to rhyme.'

'Nancy says poems that don't rhyme aren't proper.'

Faye smiled. 'It can be what you want it to be.'

Could she say that of this relationship with Robert too? He'd reminded her last night that she'd renounced men. She'd replied that she was prepared to make one exception. This was just a trial, though – she'd raised a teasing eyebrow at him as she made the caveat – and if she wasn't convinced by the experiment, she might go back to abstention. He'd promised to make a supreme effort to convince her.

'Miss Faulkner?' Erin had her hand in the air now. 'I can't think of anything that rhymes with frost, Miss.'

'Can anyone help Erin? Can we suggest a word that rhymes with frost?'

Eight faces frowned in concentration. Eventually Maudie thrust a hand in the air.

'Yes, Maudie?'

'Lost, Miss. Lost rhymes with frost.'

'Quite right, Maudie. Can you think of anything that might be lost in the snow, Erin?'

The child pondered. 'A glove?'

'Anything else?'

'A scarf?'

It wasn't the stuff of epic poetry, but ... 'Very good, Erin. See if you can work that into your poem.'

Faye didn't have a great record with men and it made her reluctant to give much of herself away at this stage. After walking out with Mark for six months, she'd discovered that he'd never quite finished his relationship with his former fiancée; it had come to light that Callum had a slightly too intimate connection with his flatmate, Alex; and latterly Richard had chosen his career over her. She'd gone about with a self-consciously intellectual crowd in Hampstead – everyone had to be a writer or an artist of some kind – and when she'd coupled up with those men, she'd always felt she needed to live up to a particular image. As pairs, they had to be seen to be mutually enhancing and, as such, there was something of a transaction in these relationships, a measuring and a reckoning of relative worth. She didn't have to try hard with Robert, though. She could be relaxed, be frank, be foolish with him and couldn't remember when she'd laughed more. There was nothing she must hide from him, no part of her history or personality that she didn't want him to see, and he clearly felt the same. There was something simple and natural about being with him, and he made her like herself more.

'Are you alright there, Ewan?' He was wriggling in his seat. Oh no, it wasn't worms again, was it?

'It makes me feel cold to think about the snow, Miss.'

'That's good. That's the power of your imagination, Ewan.'

The child nodded gravely. 'Can we imagine going to the seaside next, Miss? And eating an ice-cream?'

'Won't that make you feel cold too?'

Ewan gave this some thought. Faye noticed he'd written a few words down on his paper, but had mostly been drawing a picture. He was his father's child. 'Yes, but that would be nice cold, Miss.'

Ewan and Erin didn't seem to be missing their father. Faye had been concerned they might be unsettled by their experience, but they appeared to have slipped back into their lives here seamlessly. She'd noticed a difference in Iris since she'd been back, though: she held her shoulders in a new way and smiled more; she dressed differently and had begun painting again. She felt as if she was at the driving seat in her life once more, she'd said to Faye. She'd taken off her wedding ring and found herself again.

Faye considered, if she committed to Robert, would she lose something of herself? She'd had to compromise and sacrifice in relationships before, but Robert wasn't like those other men. Dare she hope it might work out differently this time? Could this yet be called a relationship? Could she risk wishing it might be?

'Miss, are you smiling because you're thinking about ice-cream?'

'Yes, that's right, Ewan.'

Chapter Fifty-Two

Daniel found Gwen in one of the rooms she was preparing to let out. She was wearing paint-splattered overalls and had a green scarf wound around her head. She'd worn black for a week, been introspective and inclined to shut herself away, but then had seemed to make a decision and for the past fortnight had thrown herself into this work. At Teddy's graveside, the priest had talked of how in death there is a reminder of the fleetingness of life, how it should recall us to be kind and courageous and live fully. Those words had struck Daniel. The priest might as well have prodded a finger at his chest. They hadn't spoken of it, but did those sentiments have a resonance for Gwen too?

As Daniel entered the room, she was standing at the window looking out towards the roofs of the new housing estate. She turned as she heard him and smiled over her shoulder.

'You know, I've trained my eye not to see the houses,' she said. 'It's curious how the brain works, isn't it? I don't do it consciously, but when I look out I now always direct my gaze towards the west.'

Daniel went to stand at her side. The leaves of the oak and beech trees were red and gold below. When they fell, as they soon would, the housing estate would be all the more visible. 'The roof tiles will weather with time,' he said. 'The years will pass, the colours will mellow and the trees will grow.'

'I feel I've weathered rather a lot over the past year.'

'You don't look it.'

'I'll take the compliment, but I'm not sure I believe you.' Her smile didn't last as long as he wished it would. 'Time might mellow it, but it will never be beautiful and it will always be on my conscience. Maurice wasn't wrong about that. Teddy introduced me to Mr Houghton, you know. He set it up and made it sound such an intelligent idea. It was going to be the answer to all our financial worries. It was the only way we could raise the money that we needed for the roof. Part of my brain would like to blame him, to lay all of the responsibility at his door, but I signed the papers. You've never asked me about that – you're too considerate to ask – but I do regret it.'

'Did he pressure you to sign?'

It took a moment for her to reply. 'Yes,' she finally conceded. 'We argued bitterly about it. He told me we'd be ruined, we'd be finished, if I didn't do it. Greenfields would be over. We'd have to sell the house. But he didn't forcibly put the pen in my hand.'

Daniel could imagine Teddy dialling up the pressure, cajoling, coaxing and then coercing. He doubted that he'd ever intended the money to be used for the roof. Gwen must have had that thought too, mustn't she?

'You shouldn't devote too much time and energy to regret,' he said. 'In some ways, all of this has given Anderby a new lease of life.'

'Do you sincerely think that?' She turned towards him.

'Just look around. Iris is taking on the workshop, we've got joiners and plasterers moving into the house in January, and we'll have fifteen pupils in the school after Christmas. There's a new vitality here, a new enthusiasm. All the upheaval over the houses has made us take a fresh look at what we're doing here and we're moving forward with new focus. Don't you feel that?'

'You make it sound like a health tonic. The patient has been reinvigorated! Oh, forgive me for laughing. You're always so resolutely upbeat, Daniel. You dear man! I do like the way you look at things.'

He felt embarrassed, but in a pleasurable way – and more so then when she linked her arm through his and leaned her head against his shoulder. 'All will be well,' he said. 'You'll see.'

'When you say it with such conviction, I can almost be-lieve you.'

'I've got something for you – an early Christmas gift. It's outside. Put a coat on and come and see.'

Gwen peered into the back of the van and gave him a quizzical look. 'Fruit trees?'

'They're apple saplings. I do appreciate that chocolates or perfume might be a more conventional Christmas present, but I thought we could plant a new orchard, that we could do it together. Yes, it will be years before we get the cider press working again, but it's an investment for the future, isn't it? Something to plan for, something to look forward to.'

'Oh, Daniel!' She put her hands to her face and looked as if she didn't know whether to laugh or cry.

'I bought thirteen trees. One for each year we've been here. We could perhaps add a new tree every year. That way we can keep the orchard healthy. A lot of the trees in the old orchard were past their best, but we can begin again with a sense of purpose. I've spoken with Robert about it and there's a good site to the south of the walled garden.'

'Are you trying to make me feel better?' She took her hands away from her face and Daniel was relieved to see she was smiling, not crying.

'Is it that obvious? Is it working? Besides, I miss the cider. There's self-interest in it too, of course.'

'You really are the most thoughtful man.'

'Am I? I'm not sure that's true. Did I do the right thing?' He had to ask it. 'I mean, when Teddy came back – maybe I had no right to intervene? I keep thinking about it and asking myself if things might have worked out differently. I keep running back through the events of that night and questioning whether my actions made it all go in the wrong direction. Did it need to end up with his car spinning off the road?'

'You mustn't think like that. *Please*, don't!' She stepped towards him and took his hand. 'You did the right thing. You always do. I'm grateful to you.' The turret clock struck midday as she said it. She looked startled by the noise, but then her expression softened. 'Did you wind it?'

'Do you object?' He wasn't certain he ought to have done this either.

She shook her head. 'I'm glad to hear it again. Could you keep it wound for me?'

'Of course.'

They'd come to sit on the bench in the white garden. The roses had finished and the first frost had blackened the dahlias, but the seed heads of the alliums and sea holly made pleasing architectural shapes. Gwen's hair glowed with the winter sunlight behind her, like the gold leaf around the heads of saints in old paintings.

'I've been thinking about him a lot recently,' she said.

'Hugh?'

She nodded. 'I got the box of his letters out recently. Do you recall that I'd thought of publishing a volume of his poems years ago? I might begin that project again in the New Year.'

'I'm sure you'd find some consolation in it.'

It had always seemed like a door that had been left half open and Daniel felt it would be good for her to complete it. There would be heartache in the task, he knew, but it would also help her to move forwards, he sensed. He'd returned to working on his *Passchendaele Requiem* recently, feeling that he needed to finally finish that too.

'I wish Hugh could have been sent here the first time he was wounded. It might have made a difference.'

'For his state of mind?'

She turned on the bench and smiled at him, but it was a complicated smile. 'There are some of his poems and letters that I probably wouldn't choose to publish.' She took a breath and looked to be considering her next words. 'I've never been entirely honest with people about Hugh's death. When we received the telegram it said "Died of Wounds".' She framed the phrase with her fingers. 'It wasn't until later that I found out those wounds were self-inflicted.'

'Suicide?' Daniel said the word cautiously.

'Hugh was always of a nervous disposition, he was like that from being a boy, but he began to struggle to control it. He was in a dark place psychologically, a confused place, and couldn't find a way out. He put his pistol to his own head. One of his fellow officers told me, but they were kind enough to cover it up. My parents never knew and I'm glad they didn't. But afterwards, when I went back through his letters, I could see the signs of it coming. I read them again now and it's glaringly obvious. How did I not see the signs at the time?'

Daniel looked at her and pitied her. He'd known that dark place too. In the late summer of 1918 he'd been drawn to clifftops and rooftops and had hesitated with a razor blade in his hand. Perhaps he'd be able to talk to Gwen about that one day? 'I'm so sorry. I had no idea.'

'I've never shared that with anyone before. Teddy didn't know. He told me stories about Hugh being brave and well respected and making the men laugh. He meant to comfort me with that, and I appreciated it, but I knew my brother was never really that man.' She pulled her sleeves down over her hands and crossed her arms over her chest. 'Some people would say I ought to feel ashamed because other men gave their lives fighting courageously, they might call Hugh's choice cowardice, but I don't feel shame. I just feel profoundly sad for him – and that sadness became a momentum, an urgency, when I came here. I needed to balance it out by doing something meaningful and positive.'

'I understand,' he said. 'And you have.'

'Have I? Sometimes I look back and wonder if we've merely been amusing ourselves here. Have we really achieved anything, Daniel?'

She was ethereally pale with shining eyes. He couldn't help

staring at her. He'd loved her since the day he first met her, but more so at this moment than ever. 'Can you seriously question that? You've created a community where people feel safe and supported and care for one another. You've made it possible for dozens of people to pursue their creative ambitions, hundreds of students have passed through the summer schools over the years, you've attracted important speakers here and you've brought Russian ballet and Balinese theatre to deepest rural Gloucestershire! You established a school which turns out happy, confident, inquisitive children, without you the Hall might very well have fallen to the ground, and you've been a champion for fairness and kindness. Can you really doubt that you've achieved anything, Gwen? You've done so much here and we'll do more yet.'

'If we've achieved anything, Daniel, it's been when we've pulled together as a group. Can we still do that?'

'Of course we can.'

'You know, I was reading about German Jewish refugees arriving in London this week. They've been forced to flee their homes and they've lost everything. I've been thinking that I'd like to get in touch with some of the refugee organizations and find out if we could do anything. We could possibly offer some accommodation here. What do you think? We could try to help them find employment and give them the opportunity to speak out about what they've experienced. I feel like we have a responsibility to do something. Do you agree?'

'I wholeheartedly agree. This morning I read that Mussolini is now threatening to withdraw from the League of Nations – had you heard? First Japan and Germany, and now Italy? It feels like everything is running in the wrong direction, doesn't it? Like every country is turning in on itself.'

'All the more reason for us to maintain our sense of direction. Can we do this together?'

He took her hand. 'I've no desire to be anywhere else.'

Chapter Fifty-Three

Faye locked the door of the classroom. She ought to have tidied up before she left, there was glitter and cake crumbs all over the floor, but she just wanted to get home and turn the key in her own door. Perhaps then she might finally let herself cry.

Normally, she loved doing the Christmas stories with the children, making cards and decorations, and talking about all the traditions. It was something she looked forward to each year, but she'd been short-tempered and distracted all day. Her mind kept going back to what she'd seen that morning, alternately making excuses for them and finding new ways in which she felt humiliated. Every image of mistletoe made her feel foolish and she could have cried over a hundred small irritations today.

It was Trudie's way, Faye had told herself several times that afternoon, that was just how she was with men; she was a casual tease, an innate flirt, and she was emotional at the moment . . . but could there be more to it than that? She'd always made no disguise of the fact she found Robert attractive. Faye had noticed how she always stood a fraction too close to him and found any excuse to link her arm through his. He generally looked slightly embarrassed by her comically coquettish comments and had never given any sign that he felt anything more than friendship for her. But could Faye have misinterpreted? Had something been going on between them all of this time?

He'd gone out to cut holly, ivy and yew branches to decorate the Hall. He said he'd also spotted a clump of mistletoe in one of the poplar trees and had taken a ladder to cut some down. Concerned for him climbing the tall ladder, Faye had gone out to watch, and that was when she'd seen him with Trudie.

As Faye had walked towards them, Robert laughingly held up a piece of mistletoe and Trudie had stepped towards him and kissed him on the mouth. She'd seen that Trudie had initiated the kiss, but he hadn't pushed her away, and when they'd parted he'd simply looked amused. At that moment, as Faye took in what she'd witnessed, her instinct had been to turn on her heels. But then Robert had seen her and was raising his hand.

'Look, darling, Robert's found mistletoe,' Trudie said. 'We've just been trying it out.'

Trudie wasn't in the least embarrassed, but Faye had found herself looking between her face and his. She'd felt uncomfortable and confused and suddenly angry. Was it acceptable that he should kiss Trudie and seemingly think nothing of it? There was a print of Trudie's scarlet lipstick on his mouth – so glaring, so callous it had seemed. Faye had felt an urge to step forwards and to scrub it from his face, but she'd backed away instead.

She'd left them, finding an excuse to go. Walking away, she heard them continuing to talk lightly, indifferently, and there was the sound of his laughter again. Faye didn't require Robert to write her poetry, or put a ring on her finger, but he should respect her, shouldn't he? It was natural that she felt hurt and disappointed, wasn't it?

Her thoughts had returned to the girl called Esther today and the accusations that her parents had made. Robert had recently told her the story of how he'd come to be dismissed from his previous employment and Faye had accepted his version of events. But had it all been as innocent as he claimed? Should she have asked more questions? Robert was intimate with Iris and Gwendoline too, was tactile with all of them and seemed to be everyone's confidante. Faye had liked that he was comfortable in female company, she'd supposed it showed a sensitivity of spirit, but could it actually be the case that he had a rather casual attitude to women? Had a lot of them passed through his bed? Hadn't her instinct been that he was a little too overtly charming when they first met? Faye had thought she knew Robert, that they had an understanding, but could she have misunderstood? Did he, after all, not feel the same way as her? Had she been an idiot again?

It began to rain as she made her way back towards the cottages, softly at first, but then coming on heavily. There was a strange, unnatural tint to the light and then the trees were rocking. Within minutes her clothes and shoes were saturated. The rain felt like needles on her face as she titled her chin back, but it ran her tears away.

Chapter Fifty-Four

Faye had fallen into the habit of knocking on his door around seven o'clock every evening and he'd begun to watch the clock. As the minutes ticked around, and passed the hour now, Robert wondered what might have delayed her tonight. He wanted to talk with her, to hear her voice, to tell her about his day. She wanted it to be like this too, didn't she? Just for a moment he questioned himself – could it be that he needed this more than she did?

The rain was still coming down in torrents as he stepped out. Water was pouring from the Hall's downspouts, gargoyles spat and gutters spumed. He wondered if Gwendoline might be rushing around with buckets and hesitated, considering if he ought to go over and help her. But Mr Kelly's van was parked up, so she'd have assistance if she needed it.

He ran along to Faye's cottage with his coat over his head. The rain was streaming down the windows, but there she was, sitting on the settee in her lamp-lit room with a blanket around her shoulders and a book on her knee. The cover of the book was closed and she looked lost in thought. When he knocked, it took her a moment to come to the door.

'It's a filthy night,' he said. 'Is your hair wet? Aren't you cold? Do you need me to bring some more logs in for the fire?'

'I got caught in it as I was on my way back from school.'

'I missed you,' he said, still leaning in the doorway. She hadn't yet invited him in. 'I've been waiting for your knock on the door.'

'Have we fallen into a routine so soon?'

She seemed cool, brittle, cautious suddenly – was something wrong? 'I like our routine. You do too, don't you? Are you alright? Can I come in?'

Faye stepped away from the door and went back to her place on the settee. She looked tense, but as if she was making an effort not to show it. 'I supposed you might have got bored with it,' she said.

'Me? Bored?' How could she imagine that? He came to sit down at her side. 'Of course not. Absolutely the opposite.'

'It can get dull having the same dish every night, though, can't it? Variety is the spice of life and all that.'

There was an archness in her tone. He didn't like to hear that. He didn't want to go back to them misunderstanding each other. 'Faye, please tell me if I've done something to upset you.' He reached for her hand.

'I think it's perhaps me that's been a little silly.' She took her hand away. 'I've been reflecting on it; what with all the upset over Teddy's death, I perhaps let my heart get the better of my head.'

'I'm sorry? What do you mean by that?' The idea that she might be having second thoughts alarmed him. 'Faye, I don't understand.'

'It's been very nice, but I think I've let myself get rather carried away.'

'"Very nice"?' he repeated. 'I feel as if I'm having my home-work marked. Very nice, but could do better?'

'Perhaps.'

'It's been more than "very nice" for me.'

'Has it?' She suddenly looked as if she might cry, but then seemed to find her resolve once more. She pulled her bare feet up onto the settee and hugged her knees. 'I refuse to let you upset me, Robert.'

He put his hand to her shoulder. 'I never want to upset you. Not ever!'

'Well, you've got a peculiar way of going about it.'

'Faye, please talk to me,' he implored. 'Tell me what I've done.'

He heard her take a breath. 'The fact you don't even seem to realize says a lot about your attitude. I saw you kissing Trudie.'

'What? When? Oh God!' He couldn't help but laugh – it was the relief as much as anything. 'The mistletoe, you mean? But that was absolutely nothing! I haven't given it a second thought. *She* kissed me and there was no meaning to it.'

'You didn't exactly recoil from it.'

'Should I have looked horrified? That wouldn't have been kind, would it?'

'But you didn't look at all surprised. Does she kiss you often?'

'You know what Trudie's like! It's just her manner – just how she is with men. She's an indiscriminate flirt. She blows kisses and wolf-whistles at all the builders!'

'Blowing kisses is one thing, but . . .'

'Yes, I'm extremely fond of her, she's a dear friend, but I have no romantic feelings for her. I can't recall she's ever kissed me before.'

'Don't recall?' Faye laughed mirthlessly. Her fingers began to pick the wax from the candlestick. He found himself wanting to reach out and make her stop. 'You mean you might have forgotten? Do you kiss lots of women and think nothing of it?'

'Faye! What am I meant to say? I care about Trudie, and I'm concerned for her at the moment, but I don't have *those* sorts of feelings for her. There was no meaning to that kiss. Nothing at all. I'm sure she hasn't given it a second thought either.'

She looked at him as if she was trying to measure him up. Her unfaltering blue gaze scrutinized his face. Did she believe him? He had to make her believe him.

'I didn't know what to think when I saw you,' she said. 'I'm not a possessive person, but I felt confused and upset. Of course, I did.' She snatched a tear away quickly with the back of her fingers. 'What was I meant to think?'

'I wouldn't mind if you were to feel possessive. I feel a little possessive of you, to be honest,' he admitted. 'I don't know what I'd do if I saw you kissing another man.' The thought of it made something like panic flood his chest. 'I understand and I apologize. It will never happen again. The truth is I can't stop thinking about you. I think about you all day long. I've never felt like this about anyone before. Faye, please, can you forgive me?'

Time seemed to move forwards terribly slowly until she nodded her head.

Chapter Fifty-Five

It was the last market before Christmas. As well as their baskets of brassicas and pumpkins, leeks and parsnips, Phyllis had made Christmas puddings to sell, jars of mincemeat and bottles of sloe gin. They decorated their produce with sprigs of holly, and there were displays of glazed hams and dressed turkeys and piles of tangerines on the stalls around them. Everywhere there were the spice, citrus and roasting meat scents of the season and the shop windows tempted with boxed chocolates, game pies and iced gingerbread. Robert could hear a brass band playing somewhere, the passing shoppers exchanged Christmas greetings and there was an irresistible feeling of goodwill.

Faye had said she'd forgiven him, but Robert still felt he needed to earn her trust back. He'd hated the feeling he might have lost her confidence again, and he wanted to show her he was worthy of her trust. He was newly conscious of how his conversations with other women might look, had cooked Faye supper, and had planted her window boxes with winter pansies. He meant to steal away to the bookshop to buy her a gift this morning, and had asked Iris to paint a card for her, which all the children in the school could sign.

He would gladly have spent all his savings on Faye this

Christmas, but he'd also confided to her that he was worried about the imminent expiry of his employment contract. Mrs Fitzgerald had taken him on for a year and that would be over at the end of this month. He couldn't help wondering what might happen if he found himself unemployed in January. Was there a way he might stay on at Anderby, even if Gwendoline could no longer afford to pay his wages? Faye said there was no danger of his contract not being renewed and he ought to put his mind at rest by simply asking Gwendoline. He didn't like to force the question on her, to embarrass her by obliging her to talk about money, but hoped there was meaning in her talk of trimming the Virginia creeper in January and sowing sweet peas in the glasshouse in February.

'She might be intending to put it to a vote at the next meeting,' Faye said now. He'd just bought them both measures of hot spiced cider and she was warming her hands around her cup.

'Hell, will you veto me again?'

She smiled impishly. 'I'll have to give it some consideration. I still don't like the idea that we're charging people to enter the gardens.'

'I am looking at alternative ideas. You know I agree with you that they ought to be open to everyone.'

'Even if they walk on your lawns?'

'Perhaps I can put up some signs,' he said, seeing she was determined to tease him.

Faye stood to serve Laura Bradley and once again refused to take the young woman's money. 'I didn't come to your stall expecting charity,' she protested.

'I know that,' Faye said, 'but please let us help.'

There'd been a carol concert in the great hall the previous

evening and the proceeds from the ticket sales had been donated to the town's fund for the unemployed. Robert hadn't seen the signs of it when he'd first come here, everything had appeared prosperous and comfortable, but perhaps he hadn't looked for it very closely? Now he noticed the women who counted the money out from their purses carefully, the children who were just a little too thin, and how many men there were walking the roads. He'd read in the newspapers that there was to be a hunger march on London early in the New Year and Faye had told him about another suicide on a local farm. They'd put a collecting box on the stall this morning and thanked their customers when change clattered into it.

'Are you giving me a look?' Faye asked as Laura departed.

'I'm not,' Robert replied. 'We shouldn't take anything back with us today. If you can give it to people who need it, we must.'

'You've changed your tune. I recall you saying, "But what will Mrs Fitzgerald think?"'

'It's taken me a while to get used to your ways of doing things. As an outsider, it's really quite a challenge to figure out the Greenfields rules! But Mrs Fitzgerald would applaud what you just did, I'm certain of that.'

'You always were Gwen's pet!' Faye laughed as she linked her arm through his.

'I admire her. I respect her. I'm grateful for what she's done for me.'

'That much is clear. I suspect she's rather fond of you too.'

'Do you honestly think she will keep me on? I feel I've barely even begun. There's still so much I want to do.'

'You're a through-and-through Greenfielder now, aren't you, Robert Bardsley?'

'At some stages over the past year I've doubted what that means, but I am now devoted to the cause.'

Faye slid her arms around him under his overcoat. 'I do admire conviction in a man.'

Chapter Fifty-Six

Trudie had offered to make her special punch to give the last residents' meeting of the year some feel of festivity. But there was some relief amongst the group when Nancy and Phyllis had insisted they'd make mulled wine instead.

Gwendoline had been planting apple saplings with Daniel all day and the cold air had brought a glow to her cheeks. Robert had volunteered to assist with the task, but they seemed content to go about it together. He'd intuited it was possibly best not to be insistent with his services. Faye had suggested the activity was probably therapeutic, that they might derive some reconciliation and resolution from going about it together. Trudie said she could think of another word for what they might get out of it, but it wasn't quite polite. Daniel was sitting to Gwendoline's right at the head of the table this evening and, with this arrangement, there seemed to be a new stability in the room. Robert wouldn't go so far as to say that Daniel looked like the cat who'd got the cream, but he now seemed to be in the place where he always ought to have been and there was a serenity to his face tonight.

Gwendoline began the evening's business with an update on the art season planned for the spring. She'd worked studiously through her book of contacts and had managed to secure some well-known names. As well as lending artwork for the exhibitions, several of them had also agreed to donate pieces to the charity auction which would conclude the season. The money raised was to be donated to the German Refugees Assistance Fund. Mr Kelly's work on the roof was progressing well, she informed them, and there were currently no buckets collecting drips. The power lines put in to service the housing estate would be extended to the Hall in the spring and several of the apprentices who'd be joining the scheme for carpenters and plasterers would be moving into rooms in January. Finally, she told them that Mr Houghton was negotiating terms with two recently graduated art students who were interested in renting Maurice's old studio.

Phyllis reported that the café's takings were up, with a noticeable amount of new business from the bungalow people ('We must stop calling them the bungalow people!'), and there was also an increase in local trade. Faye confirmed that fifteen pupils would be attending the school after the Christmas holiday and Daniel would return to do a few hours' music teaching every week. Iris said she'd decided to take on less illustration work and had recently sold three paintings to a dealer in London. She'd privately told Robert that he was keen to buy more of her work and she now smiled at him across the table. Trudie had two new contracts to supply boutiques and Queenie had had a successful encounter with a prize-winning Sealyham called Rupert and was expecting puppies in January. Nancy would be on dog-minding duties in March while she was travelling. She had considered having Guy's ashes interred alongside her mother in the family vault – just for devilment – she informed them, but in the end had decided she would finally take him down to the south of France.

'The renovation of the gardens progresses, of course,' Gwendoline continued. 'I hope we'll be able to open for a longer season next year and I've been thinking that I'd like to drop the entrance fee. We could perhaps have a donation box by the gatehouse instead and people can make a contribution if they're able. What do you think? We could get more feet through the door that way and it would probably bring additional trade to the café.'

'I'm thrilled to hear you say that, obviously, but can we afford it?' Faye had raised her hand. 'Would the likely revenue cover the cost of employing Robert?' Her eyes met his.

'The gardens have made an overall profit since we opened to visitors. I hope we'll get more people through the gate next year; I've been speaking with a journalist friend who thinks she might be able to drum up some publicity, so it's a risk I feel we could take. Plus, we could subtly apply pressure to visitors who have particularly deep pockets!' Gwendoline smiled at Faye. 'It goes without saying that I'd like to renew Robert's contract,' she went on. Her attention turned back to the room. 'He's worked indefatigably over the past year, made a welcome contribution to the community and I felt proud of the gardens this summer. The shadow of Lady Margaret's disapproval might actually be lifting! I assume there'd be no dissent to the work on the gardens continuing?'

Robert felt a surge of relief, but then a moment of anxiety as he waited to hear if anyone would object. He didn't dare look at the faces around the table, but glancing quickly at Faye to his side, he saw her arching an eyebrow at him. She took his hand under the table.

'Good, that's all agreed, then,' Gwendoline concluded. 'Robert, was there anything you wanted to say?'

'I'd only add that I've been working on ideas to make the gardens more of a valuable asset for the community,' he began. 'It's early days, I'm still researching possibilities, but I'm looking into whether we could set up a horticultural training programme, along the same lines as the apprenticeship scheme that's being rolled out in the Hall. I'm exploring ways to bring in young people and also those who are currently out of work and might like to acquire new skills. I want to investigate how we might establish links with horticultural colleges, and charities, and perhaps we could make connections with older local people, those who have knowledge that's in danger of being lost. I've lots of ideas,' he said, suddenly realizing he was going on. 'Essentially, I want the gardens to work for us, helping us make connections and sharing their benefits, rather than them merely being a luxury for the sole use of the Anderby community.'

'I think that all sounds most promising,' Gwendoline said.

'Well, I never,' whispered Faye. 'I wholeheartedly retract the accusation of complacency.'

'I wanted to say a word about the housing estate too.' Gwendoline pushed her papers away and sat back in her chair. 'I've met several of the people from the new houses over the past week, as I'm sure you have as well, and they've all been friendly. One or two of them might actually have been a touch overfriendly . . .' She frowned and seemed to be reconsidering her words. 'A chap pounced upon me yesterday, asking if I was the "lady of the manor". When I admitted to something of the sort, he launched into a lengthy interrogation, wanting to know how he might get his son into the grammar school. "Could you pull any strings? Do you know any of the governors?"' She widened her eyes, then looked to Faye and smiled. 'I informed him that he needn't worry because we have an excellent school here at Anderby.'

Motorcars and furniture vans had been coming and going all week. Robert had watched settees being negotiated through front doors, curtains hung at windows and new lawns being rolled. It still saddened him to recall the orchard, but the newcomers smiled as they walked through the grounds, expressed appreciation for the vistas and weed-free gravel, and he'd already had offers of assistance with pruning hedges and mowing the grass. Anderby suddenly felt to be more inhabited, more animate, and he sensed a collective will to make it thrive. This wouldn't be the disaster that people had feared, would it?

'This is a new chapter for us,' Gwendoline went on, 'and we must begin it with generosity, I feel. To that end, I had considered whether we ought to invite the new residents to participate in these meetings, to make them open to all. It would be a way of extending a hand of friendship, and I'd value their input and support. But, of course, it's up to you ...' She looked around, clearly trying to gauge the mood of the room. 'I would like them to feel that they're part of our community and it would be in keeping with the original spirit of this venture, don't you think? Should we invite them in? Would you be willing to agree to that?'

'It's time to open our doors,' Faye said.

They all applauded the motion.

Chapter Fifty-Seven

It was Gwen who had suggested she should take on Cecil's old studio. She'd said Iris ought to have a dedicated place to work. She would never have asked for it, but as Gwen had insisted, she'd gratefully accepted.

Gwen wanted to stage an exhibition of her work as part of the season she was arranging for the spring. She'd talked of how she'd like to show both some of her old collage pieces from Venice and Paris, and her new paintings of the garden. The timing seemed a little premature, Iris felt under some pressure, but as she laid out her brushes now, she thrilled at the idea this might be possible.

Some of her equipment had been boxed up for years and unpacking it here had brought back memories. Iris had thought of the version of Cecil she'd met at college, the most beautiful young man back then, with his bright dark eyes and liquorice-coloured hair, and how she'd sought his company and approval. Iris felt regret that things had soured between them, but she also remembered the ambition she'd had back then and how she'd had to put that aside for the sake of her marriage.

In the process of clearing out the studio, she'd unearthed relics of Cecil's time there. Years of discarded cigarette ends had been trodden into the floor, she'd found a half-drunk bottle of whisky in a niche in the wall, and there was an old jumper hung on a nail that was almost stiff with plaster. Bringing it to her face, Iris recognized the scent of her husband's body, but she felt no pang of longing.

Teddy's return had made her think about how she'd feel if Cecil came back and hammered on her door, but, realistically, she knew it wouldn't happen. Having spent the past five years at odds, they'd been remarkably accommodating in negotiating the arrangements for the children. He was paying her a generous allowance and had agreed that Ewan and Erin would come to him during some of the school holidays. With four county boundaries between them, Iris found she liked her husband more than she had done for many years.

She and the children had remained in the rooms they'd tumbled into on the night of their flight. Gwen said she enjoyed the noise and the energy of the children being in the house, that they gave it life, and they loved being allowed to explore all the cellars and attics. Ewan spent hours watching Mr Kelly working, and he kindly tolerated the boy's never-ending questions, while Erin and Kitty thundered up and down the stairs with Hubert all day long. Ailsa was walking now, albeit unsteadily, and her elder siblings hefted her about like a large doll, delighting in the new skills and words she was learning each day. Gwen showed remarkable patience as the girls raided her wardrobes and tried all her lipsticks. People had ceased to remark upon it when they appeared at mealtimes with fox furs around their shoulders, with heavily rouged cheeks, lavender-blue eyelids and reeking of Shalimar and Chanel No. 5. Life was chaotic and unconventional in many ways, but Iris felt a new lightness and freedom.

She'd swept the walls and the floor of the studio, cleaned the windows and scrubbed the plaster from the workbench. She'd whitewash the walls in the spring, she'd decided, and meant to ask Robert if he could build some shelves, but for now, with the paraffin heater going, it was a warm, bright and perfectly quiet space of her own. She'd been sketching the winter shapes of the trees this week and, in her mind, she could visualize precisely the painting she was about to begin. She felt calmer, more settled, more focussed than she had done for a long time, and this morning she had a sense there was much to look forward to. She poured herself another coffee and began priming the canvas.

Chapter Fifty-Eight

It might have been warmer to sit around the kitchen table, but there were thirty of them for lunch today and, as Gwendoline said, they so rarely had opportunities to use the formal rooms. Robert breathed a smell of wood smoke as he entered the great hall, and a spice and citrus scent from the piles of oranges that Gwendoline had studded with cloves. The children had assisted with the decorations. They'd fixed great armfuls of holly over the fireplace and all the antlers on the walls had been draped with curling tendrils of ivy. With a yule log smouldering in the grate, the room looked set for an Elizabethan feast.

'Come in, darlings,' Gwendoline said. 'You're just in time. Have a glass of sherry, won't you? Major Turnbull has kindly brought a whole crate.'

She was wearing an emerald green tussore dress and her hair, piled high, looked particularly fiery today. Sparks might leap from it at any moment. With a string of grey pearls around her white throat and her lips painted red, she had that Gloriana grandeur about her once again, and it was impossible not to notice the admiration on Daniel's face as he looked at her.

'You've met our new neighbours, haven't you?'

She'd invited all the residents of the new housing estate to join them for lunch today. A Mrs White had brought an enormous trifle, Mr Danbury had handed over a potted stilton, and Major Turnbull (ret'd), who dealt in fortified wines, had contributed port as well as sherry. Trudie was presently sitting next to him and they were merrily maligning customs officials and import regulations together.

Christmas wreaths had appeared on some of the doors of the housing estate this week, and there were perambulators in porches and lights in the windows at nights. People spoke of 'The Close' now, milkmen and postmen had added it to their routes, and neighbours were shaking hands and establishing acquaintances over garden fences. As promised, Mr Houghton's men had been around and had planted a young apple tree in the front garden of every house. The attached white labels fluttered in the breeze and the infant stems looked unpromisingly flimsy, but thirty-three new apple trees now grew at Anderby and their roots would anchor down in time. As Robert looked around the room he reflected he'd been the newcomer here a year ago, unsure of his place, unsure of the rules, feeling very much the outsider, but over the past twelve months he'd become rooted to Anderby too. He felt an excitement at the prospect of another year in the garden, a year of restoration and rekindled purposefulness at Anderby, and while they would all miss the serenity of the old orchard, new shoots would grow. The proportions of the great hall could sometimes feel too lofty, on occasions it seemed to diminish and subdue gatherings, but lively conversation echoed up to the Elizabethan roof timbers today and the carved angels looked down with expressions on their faces that suggested they'd seen it all before.

*

Faye and Robert took glasses from the tray and went and warmed themselves by the fire.

'You look beautiful,' Robert whispered into her ear. 'I've never seen that dress before.'

Faye had put on her best dove grey dress and a length of Venetian glass beads that she'd bought from Trudie. 'I don't often have occasion to dress up.'

'That's a shame,' he said. 'Perhaps we should find occasions? Should we make that a resolution for the New Year?'

The last time she'd worn this dress, Teddy had given her a slow up-and-down look and his tongue had flicked across his teeth. Faye hadn't liked that look. It had made her want to rush back to her cottage and change into her most unflattering tweed suit. But Robert looked her directly in the eye now and smiled his handsome, steady, uncomplicated smile.

'Pity Maurice isn't here, eh?' Trudie said as she approached them. She twiddled a piece of holly between her fingers. 'All this pagan greenery would have him frothing at the mouth. It's just his thing. He'd be holding forth on Yule and Mummers' plays and the Lord of Misrule.'

Robert had promised not to linger in the vicinity of Trudie and mistletoe today, but Faye had realized that she'd never really had any grounds to doubt him.

'The presence of our new neighbours might have made him froth all the more,' Robert suggested.

'I've heard he's taken on a studio in the Brecon Beacons and is living with a woman called Morgana who calls herself a white witch.' Trudie's eyes widened with amusement.

'Is that true?' Faye could picture them circling moss-grown stones together, slightly bedraggled in the rain, but so intense in their emotions that they gave off steam. 'He must be in his element.'

'It's a shame the couple who are taking on his studio couldn't be here today. Did I tell you I met them? She's a sweet young thing and he's a dashed good-looker. He has shoulders like a stevedore and great big baby-blue eyes. I suggested to him that we might be able to work on some designs for ceramic beads together . . .'

Faye linked her hand through Robert's arm and pressed her lips together, suppressing the urge to smile. Trudie would be ever thus.

Major Turnbull appeared with the sherry bottle and insisted on refilling their glasses. 'I've been telling this good lady how thoroughly at home I feel here already,' he said, putting a hand to Trudie's shoulder. 'There's space to breathe here, a sense of history and a better class of people – people like us, cultivated people, who appreciate the finer things in life.' He raised his glass to the group and gave them a self-satisfied smile. 'They were building a council-house estate on the field behind my pre- vious property, you know. A shocking business! A real bad show. Of course, we protested against it, but we were accused of being snobbish and uncharitable. I ask you! It comes to something when an Englishman can't defend his home any longer, what?'

'Accused of snobbishness? Outrageous!' Trudie winked at Robert.

Faye coughed as the sherry hit the back of her throat.

Robert left Faye and Trudie gently sparring with Major Turnbull and went to see if Nancy needed any help with the food.

'Can I carry anything up from the kitchen?'

'That's sweet of you, duck. I'll not refuse your offer of help, but we'll perhaps give it another ten minutes yet. I say, have you seen?' She nodded over her shoulder to Gwendoline, who was linking Daniel's arm. 'Is there something ...' She let her question tail away.

'Perhaps the start of something.'

'I'd be glad for her, glad for both of them, actually. They both deserve some kindness.'

'They do.' He watched as Daniel gave Gwendoline a smile that was as warm as a three-bar electric fire. 'I heard the piano earlier. I think he might have been playing his new piece for her.' The music had been compelling and moving, and Robert had found himself standing in the passageway, unable to walk away.

'I saw her afterwards. She looked as if she'd been crying, but she said it was very beautiful.'

Robert nodded. He knew Daniel had been working on the piece for ten years, on and off. It seemed significant that he'd completed it now.

'I must say, Kitty's looking very grown up today.'

Kitty's hair had been set into sausage curls and she kept nodding her head to make them bob. She and Erin swung their black-stockinged legs under the table and repeatedly tried to steal sips from Iris's glass of sherry.

'She's pleased with herself now, but I had to put it up in rags overnight and you should have seen the faces she pulled. You'd think I was murdering her! I'm surprised you didn't hear the screams.'

'I can imagine,' Robert smiled.

'She'll be thirteen in January. I dread to think what that's going to be like. If she has anything of her father in her, there's trouble ahead.'

'I hope you don't mind me asking, but I've never known – is Kitty your daughter or Phyllis's? Sorry, can I ask that?'

Nancy's face seemed to harden momentarily, but then softened once again. 'Don't worry. I don't mind you asking, sweetheart. Kitty is *our* daughter, we agreed on that long ago, but I carried her. Her father was a sailor who didn't wait for an invitation. Kitty doesn't know her dad's name and, to be honest, I have no idea whether he's alive or dead now. I could have tried to contact him, and let him know I was expecting, but I didn't feel especially inclined to. He didn't give me a choice and I didn't see that he deserved one either. Do you think that was awful of me?'

'No, not at all. I think Kitty's very lucky to have the two of you.'

Robert carried the roast beef up from the kitchen – everyone applauded as he entered the room with it – but it seemed appropriate to defer to Daniel to carve. He took his jacket off and rolled up his shirt sleeves, looking as if he'd been waiting all of his life for this task. Robert began to help Nancy and Phyllis to serve, but Gwendoline insisted they put the dishes down the middle of the table and that everyone could pass them around.

Iris reached out to steal a roast potato with her fingers. As Robert caught her eye, she smiled. She was letting her hair grow, wearing gold hoop earrings today and looked every inch the artist in her peacock-print blouse. Sitting with her children to either side, Robert thought he'd never seen her look more contented.

'There's something I've wanted to say,' Trudie spoke up then, 'and this seems as good a time as any.' Conversations were broken off and they all looked towards her. Robert wondered if she was going to announce that she'd be leaving Anderby. She was winding her ebony beads around her fingers and looking uncharacteristically apprehensive. She took a mouthful of wine and cleared her throat. 'As most of you know, the old gorgon and I made our peace at the end and it seems she revised her will again in the days before she expired. I'm legally obliged to keep three Dachshunds in chopped liver for the remainder of their lives, and there's a mysterious bequest to a young man I'd never heard of who she'd taken to calling her "special nephew", but she left me the family pile. The place is verminous; it's riddled with woodworm, overrun with mice and the settees are all hopping with fleas, but the agent chappie positively salivated over the ceiling paintings. Damn good job he was looking up!' She blinked her eyes wide and took another swig from her glass. 'Anyway, I've put the sale in his hands. There'll be a whacking great lump of death duties to pay, but I've decided that I'd like to give the sum that remains to the trust here.'

'But that's your family home!' Gwendoline protested. The serving spoon clattered from her hand. 'Haven't your people been there since the Domesday Book? Aren't there generations of your family in the mausoleum? And haven't you just interred your mother in there? It's a tremendously generous thought, darling, but please don't make an impetuous decision that you'll live to regret. You're mourning at the moment. You need to reflect and give it some time.'

'It's not a spur-of-the-moment decision. Really it's not. I've given it a lot of thought.' Trudie's voice was more decisive now. 'It's a damp, dark, grim old house and I was always thoroughly miserable there. Quite frankly, this place is the first real home and family I've ever had. I want to stay on here and it would please me to help you. Anderby put me back together; I'd very possibly be pushing up daisies now if it wasn't for you and this place, Gwen, and I'd like to make sure that it will be here for other people in the future. Would you allow me to assist? Please?'

Gwendoline stared at her and finally nodded. 'If you're absolutely certain it's what you want.'

'It is. Sincerely. Most definitely.'

'I've been wondering,' Robert put in, 'do we have to call you Lady Gertrude now?'

Trudie had been looking as if she might cry again and it rescued the mood. 'If you do, I'll scratch your eyes out, Robert Bardsley.'

'We should have a toast before we eat, shouldn't we?' Gwendoline proposed. 'As has been our tradition, I'd like to suggest we drink to community, creativity, equality and education. We can still do that, can't we?' She looked around the table, some uncertainty showing on her face.

'Of course!' They all raised their glasses.

The motto sounded a little odd, after the events of the past year. Robert found himself measuring each word in his mind, but there did feel to be a reinvigorated sense of community around the table today. He'd noticed how their new neighbours joined them in their toast with particular enthusiasm.

'And I think we should also drink to friendship this

afternoon,' Gwendoline went on. She looked towards Trudie and smiled. 'It's been a year of upheaval, of departures and arrivals, testing for us all at times, but let us look forward with resolve and optimism.'

Her voice faltered momentarily. Robert knew she was thinking of Teddy, that violent departure, but then she reached for Daniel's hand.

'And we should raise a glass to Gwendoline,' Daniel said. 'For sharing this Christmas meal with us, for letting us call Anderby our home, and for being the embodiment of everything that is best about this venture.'

'To Gwendoline and Greenfields!'

Planning his work for the spring, Robert had spent the morning in the archive. He'd thought of how the garden had evolved over the past year, how it had spent four centuries continually evolving, as it expressed the various passions of the generations resident at Anderby, the conjunctions and chances of their lives and the fashions of each era, and how it would move into the future adapting to the needs of those who would come after. There would always be change, but also continuity, and as he'd looked through his designs that morning he'd felt a satisfying sense of the two being reconciled.

He stepped away from the dining table and went outside to smoke his cigarette. The garden had retreated into its subdued winter colours now, and dusk was creeping in from the woods around, but his eyes painted in the forms and bright hues of the summer to come. In his mind it unfolded like a Persian carpet and he felt gratitude that he would be here to see it.

He walked around to check on the climbing roses and took

in the view of the front elevation. The roses had put on a valiant
but not entirely impressive show that summer. He'd fed them
with blood and bone meal this week, would prune them again
in February, and give them a dressing of compost in the spring.
Five days ago, when he'd last looked at them, there'd been no
signs of life returning, but today there were new green shoots
showing all along the stems.

'So this is how it is,' Faye said, appearing at his side. 'I've
committed myself to a man who sneaks away from the table to
check on his roses. You know, I could become jealous of this
garden and how much time and care you lavish upon it. Please
tell me you weren't having thoughts about compost?'

'I might have been.' He couldn't help smiling. 'But these
aren't just roses – they're like the ravens at the Tower. I feel that
if they die, Anderby will be done for – and I most certainly
would be.'

'Golly. Must we pray for the roses?' Faye touched her fingers
to the stems. 'Will they survive another year?'

'They're showing all the right signs.' He put his arm
around her.

'It feels as if we're beginning again, doesn't it?' Faye suggested. 'There's a sense of optimism in the room today – and
Trudie has effectively just secured our future. It's exciting, don't
you think?'

'Only slightly marred by Major Turnbull going on about
litter louts, hoodlums and riffraff? It struck me that I might be
the closest Anderby gets to riffraff.'

'Oh God!' She turned to him with her eyes wide. 'He needs
some working on, doesn't he? Some of the things he said to
Trudie and I! Still, we'll mould him to our ways in time.'

'Mould him to our ways?' Robert repeated. 'Have I uncon-
sciously been moulded to your ways? Is that what you do to
people here?'

'I did have initial misgivings, but really you've been a great
success.' Faye grinned up at him. 'You've worked out remarkably well.'

'Hang on, Greenfields isn't actually a cult, is it?'

'Don't worry, darling. Nothing sinister.' She pulled his face
down to hers and kissed him tenderly. 'Just don't ever think of
trying to escape, eh?'

He stood with her in his arms and looked at the Hall. The
refrain of music he'd heard Daniel playing earlier returned to
him – so melancholy, so fragile somehow – and he contemplated how this place had known profound sadness at points in
its history. He'd watched Daniel and Gwen exchanging smiles
and making plans today, though, and Faye was right – there'd
been a sense of hopefulness in the room. In the last of the
low evening light, the Hall looked like a rose gold casket, all
enamelled with greens and greys and stuck with moonstones.
Standing here, Robert knew with strange certainty that this
image and the feeling of this moment would remain forever
in his memory.

Afterword

This novel was inspired by the utopian communities that emerged in the wake of the First World War. The people who founded these social experiments believed it was time to re-think fundamental values and felt compelled to do everything in their power to ensure that future generations would never know the ravages and sorrow of a world war. They didn't just want to attribute blame for the conflict, but to find practical solutions that would stimulate positive change. They chose to see this as a moment of opportunity.

Learning about these communities, which emerged all over the world in the 1920s, I became particularly fascinated by Dartington Hall. In 1925 Dorothy and Leonard Elmhirst acquired an 800-acre estate in Devon, looped around by the River Dart, with a ruined medieval manor house at its centre. A member of the wealthy and influential Whitney family of New York, Dorothy was troubled by a sense that her inherited fortune hadn't been earned by ethical means. Wanting her money to now do some good, she'd spent her twenties devoting her energies to various philanthropic causes. Leonard, her second husband, was an agricultural economist, originally from Yorkshire, who'd worked on community projects in India with the poet and social reformer Rabindranath Tagore. Leonard had lost two brothers during the First World War, at Gallipoli and on the Somme, and Dorothy's first husband, Willard, had died of influenza while in Paris for the Peace Conference.

Arriving in Devon, Dorothy and Leonard aspired to create a model community that offered participants a co-operative, fulfilling way of living. They wanted to experiment with new farming methods, explore how they might integrate the arts into everyday life, provide progressive schooling for children and ongoing educational opportunities for adults, with all members of the community having a say in decision making. 'We believed that not only should we provide for the material well-being of our people here, but for their cultural and social needs as well,' Dorothy said. 'And in our dream of the good life, we counted on the human values of kindliness and friendship to bind the community together.'

By the 1930s, Dartington employed several hundred people and was attracting artists, writers, philosophers, economists, social scientists and politicians from around the world. It also welcomed refugees fleeing totalitarian regimes in Europe, many of whom were important cultural figures, further enhancing Dartington's reputation. As the estate's disparate projects grew, so it became difficult to maintain unity and a sense of focus, and several of its businesses haemorrhaged money, but many column inches were written about the community and influence extended out from it. 'In regard to almost everything we do for Dartington we feel that we are not doing it for ourselves nor for our generation only, but for those who will succeed us twenty, fifty, and a hundred years hence,' Dorothy said. 'We are only a link in a long chain, but I think it's worth forging that link as well as we know how.' Anderby Hall and its residents are entirely fictional, and their project is on a much more modest scale than Dartington, but I wanted to infuse my imagined community with some of its spirit.

Many of the utopian communities that were founded in the interwar period no longer exist – and those that survive have changed their focus over the years. All too often groups struggled to hold fast to their founding values, while endeavouring to be financially self-sufficient. Since the COVID-19 pandemic there's been a resurgence of interest in alternative ways of living, as people once again re-evaluate their priorities, look to the future and are drawn to the idea of being part of a community. Today's social experiments focus on addressing the challenges posed by climate change, globalisation, consumer culture and hyper-individualism, but they all still aspire to create models for living that will influence the wider world. The core belief of the interwar utopians – that change for the better is possible – continues to inspire hope.

In November 1918, just days after the Armistice, Prime Minister David Lloyd George promised to make Britain 'a fit country for heroes to live in'. The legislation that followed, the Housing and Town Planning Act of 1919, was a landmark in that for the first time central government provided financial support for local authorities to undertake mass house-building schemes. Within three years, half a million 'homes fit for heroes' would be built, it was pledged, but delivery fell far short of that target. By the end of the 1920s Britain was suffering an acute housing shortage. It was estimated that one million new homes were needed.

Despite the impact of the worldwide Depression, the 1930s would be a period of unprecedented house building in Britain. By 1933 the country was experiencing a building boom and over the decade almost three million houses were constructed, mostly by small, private companies.* Building materials were cheap, labour was plentiful, and banks and building societies offered favourable lending terms to both the construction trade and would-be home buyers. With agricultural prices depressed, land was affordable and widely available, and there was an almost complete absence of planning restrictions. Similarly, with their owners struggling to afford the upkeep, many country estates were sold to property developers. It's estimated that 400 historic houses were demolished between 1920 and 1950.†

House builders of this era didn't always employ architects and they used construction techniques that didn't require high skill levels. Designs that sold well were replicated – and mock-Tudor detailing, which so enraged self-proclaimed 'men of taste', sold particularly well. Soon suburbs were spreading out from cities and 'ribbon developments' stretched out of towns along arterial

---

* In 2024, the UK government committed to a target of building a million and a half new homes over the next five years – comparable to the peak house-building levels of the mid-1930s.
† In 1936 the National Trust established a Country Houses Committee to help save endangered estates. The Trust's Christian Socialist founders had wanted to preserve landscapes for the people ('to provide open-air living rooms for the poor', as Octavia Hill put it), not to save aristocratic piles, but with so many properties in peril, the organisation's focus would shift. In 1937 it persuaded the government to pass the National Trust Act. This allowed residents to remain in their homes, but to transfer ownership to the Trust with a tax-free endowment.

roads. Only around 10 per cent of families owned property in 1914, but by the start of the Second World War almost a third of the population were home owners, many of them enjoying the suburban dream.

Not everyone was happy, though. Soon there would be protests about design standards and lack of planning, and uproar that the countryside was being irreparably despoiled. The Council for the Preservation of Rural England (founded in 1926) tried to rally public opinion, published design guides and lobbied for planning legislation. This would eventually come. The Metropolitan Green Belt around London was first proposed in 1935, the same year that the Restriction of Ribbon Development Act was passed. In 1944, the Town and Country Planning Act empowered the government to create a national list of buildings of special architectural or historic interest for the first time, and the 1947 Planning Act brought all kinds of development under planning control.

In the meantime, Britain grappled with the dilemma: which should take priority – homes for the people or protecting the countryside? J. B. Priestley said this issue was becoming a 'battlefield'. Most Britons believed their fellow man had a right to a comfortable home, he reflected, 'yet we know too that if the country were thus absolutely shut off from beauty, in the long run nobody would be really happy, for some part of the good life would be lost forever.'

A century on, that dilemma is still with us.

Acknowledgements

In my experience, writing doesn't necessarily get easier with practice (alas!) and I owe a debt of gratitude to the team at Simon & Schuster for giving me time to work on this novel and helping me wrestle it into shape. In particular, I must thank my wonderful editors, Clare Hey and Louise Davies. I feel very fortunate to have your expertise on my side, your care for getting the details right, and your patient, good-humoured support. I'm grateful to my agent, Teresa Chris, for giving me these opportunities, for championing this story at the start and always being there as my wise, well-informed and encouraging guide. Thank you to the sales and marketing teams who work tremendously hard to get my books onto shelves, to all the reviewers and bloggers who've been so generous over the past five years, and to you for reading. I hope you've enjoyed your stay at Anderby.

Good Taste

CAROLINE SCOTT

Good taste is in the eye of the beholder ...

England, 1932, and the country is in the grip of the Great
Depression. To lift the spirits of the nation, Stella Douglas is tasked
with writing a history of food in England. It's to be quintessentially
English and will remind English housewives of the old ways,
and English men of the glory of their country. The only problem
is – much of English food is really from, well, elsewhere ...

So, Stella sets about unearthing recipes from all corners of the
country, in the hope of finding a hidden culinary gem. But what
she discovers is rissoles, gravy, stewed prunes and lots of oatcakes.

Longing for something more thrilling, she heads off to
speak to the nation's housewives. But when her car breaks
down and the dashing and charismatic Freddie springs to
her rescue, she is led in a very different direction ...

**Full of wit and vim, *Good Taste* is a story of discovery, of
English nostalgia, change and challenge, and one woman's
desire to make her own way as a modern woman.**

Available now in Paperback, Ebook & Audio

SIMON &
SCHUSTER